SILVER CREEK
BODYGUARD

LINDSAY
McKENNA

ZEBRA BOOKS
KENSINGTON PUBLISHING CORP.
www.kensingtonbooks.com

To all my loyal readers who have stuck with me
for forty (!) years so far! Amazing!
Thank you for your readership.
I'll keep writing . . . you keep on reading ;-)

Chapter One

April 2

Alone. What had changed? *Nothing*.

Wes Paxton had always been alone from the day his unknown mother had placed him on the doorstep of a fire station in Fort Worth, Texas, and abandoned him to a heartless world. No one wanted him, passing him from one foster family to another. In his teens, he was always in trouble, rebelling, angry because he got the message, every day, that he was seen as worthless. No one wanted a dark-haired, gray-eyed lanky kid. His only claim to fame was that he was damned good on the football field, a high school quarterback, his team taking the state championship, with him at the helm in his senior year. Not even that win could fill the hole in his heart that had been there for as long as he could remember.

The stars twinkled and danced above Wes. Standing momentarily outside his Fort Worth, Texas, apartment where he'd stayed and lived during a year-long rehab from a wound, he looked up at the sky, which had always been a comfort to him. Maybe because there were so many stars, all crowded and packed together like one big, happy family that got along with one another, was the reason.

Remembering many times when it became intolerable in the next foster family he'd been passed on to, he would go outside and lie down on the grass, hands behind his head, and get lost in his star family, as he silently thought of the Milky Way, which covered the sky. There, he felt a kinship. Stars did not kick you out of their family. Nor did they care if he was an orphan no one wanted.

Outdoors, it was quiet compared to inside the next foster home. He needed the quiet. Craved it, because it settled his roiling inner life and shut up that yapping voice inside his head that reminded him that no one had ever really wanted him. He was seen by the family he lived with as nothing more than a check every month from the state. He'd been nine years old when he realized he was a body that was worth so much money, and that was all. He also knew there were good foster families around. It was just his bad luck, was all, not to get one.

Lifting his tan Stetson, moving his fingers through his short dark brown hair, he settled it back on his head. Despite being a perennial problem child growing up, he'd managed to graduate with a high school degree. He'd made friends with a police officer, Tom Harvey, who had spent ten years as a US Navy SEAL, got out of the military and then went into law enforcement. Wes had been a rebellious fourteen-year-old, and he had given him something he'd secretly craved: care and attention. Tom was like a father to him, although Wes never said those words to him. He had always daydreamed of what a real, loving father would be like.

Tom, who was in his forties and had a family of his own, took him under his wing when he was a freshman in high school. For the first time in his life, Wes felt wanted and he lost his angry, rebelling disposition. He became a member of a city-wide project called Tom's Boys in Fort Worth. For once in his life, he knew that someone cared about him. At times, it felt like he was a drug addict, high on the praise and sincere attention. A smile or a pat on the shoulder from the policeman made his heart burst with joy. And how he looked forward to when he would wrap his arm around his shoulders and give him a bear hug. Tom introduced him to football, where Wes not only bloomed, but fiercely excelled beneath his tutelage, attention, and genuine care.

He was responsible for teaching him to be a quarterback. The police officer had been one himself as a teen in high school, and told Wes that he had the smarts to do the job and do it well. How much Wes looked forward to the thrice weekly workout times with him! It fed his starving, thirsty soul, and salved his shattered heart, and for the first time in his life, he felt like he wasn't worthless, after all. He likened himself to a potted plant that was slowly dying due to no water being given to him; and that three times a week, Tom watered him emotionally, giving him hope, his care and attention, feeding his deeply scarred soul. For the first time, Wes had hope, his life steadying out beneath Tom's quiet, gentle nature, watering him symbolically, and he began to grow into a strong, thriving man, his confidence and self-esteem soaring.

How lucky he'd been those last four years of his young life. Turning, Wes looked at the darkened building one last time. His mind moved back to after graduation when Tom suggested he go into the Navy and become a SEAL; that he was a good fit for it.

He'd managed to survive BUD/S, the first step in

becoming a SEAL. Tom and his wife proudly looking on in the audience at Coronado, clapping for him as he graduated. The SEALs became his new family, one that embraced him, fed his hungry soul, and once more, he excelled. At twenty-nine, he was shot in a battle. The upper part of his right lung was damaged and had to be removed; and he was forced to leave the community.

Mouth tightening, Wes turned, walking toward his black Ford pickup in the parking area. In the truck was the next chapter in his life, and all his possessions were in the back. He was moving to Wyoming, employed by a global security company, hired by his old friend Steve Carter, from his SEAL days, who had offered it to him after Wes completed a year of medical therapy and transition. He was still adjusting to the loss of one-third of his right lung, but improving every day to the point that he could work once more and earn a hefty paycheck.

As he slid into his truck, the black and silver cab on the back of it holding his life's belongings, he slowly drove through Fort Worth, where he'd been born thirty years earlier, looking for an exit that would take him west, and later on north, to Wyoming. His mind wandered back to that fateful day when he lay in the hospital, recuperating from the lung surgery.

While in the San Diego naval hospital, his cell phone had rung one day, and it was from Steve Carter, owner of Guardian Security, whose headquarters was in Silver Creek, Wyoming. The phone call was like a lifeline to him.

Carter had spent ten years in the Navy, and been the Chief of his SEAL team. He had left the military at twenty-eight, and created the world-renowned security company. Guardian Security seemed like a good name. But Steve was born and bred in Wyoming cattle country, grew up on a ranch, was a wrangler, and he wanted to hire women and men with that kind of background. The term "guardian," Steve told him, referred to a special group of cowboys who rode around a cattle herd at night, keeping them safe from predators. And his business was hiring security contractors who kept their clients safe from another form of predator.

As a teen, Tom used to take him and a group of "at risk" boys out to a nearby cattle ranch outside of Fort Worth every summer during school break. They lived, slept, and worked as a team, and learned the rudiments of becoming a wrangler. Riding horses, branding, vaccinating, and herding cattle was something Wes grew to love. Being out in Nature, out of the suffocating city, gave him a new appreciation of ranching, which was big in Texas. And with that background, Carter had met him shortly after he got out of the naval hospital and had separated permanently from the Navy.

Steve had filled him in on his popular security company. Wes liked the fact that they shared not only a wrangling background, but were part of the brotherhood of SEALs. And SEALs took care of their own, which is why Steve flew into San Diego to talk to him about a future job with his company, urging him to join it. Wes decided to throw his lot in with Steve and the other military vet men and women whom Steve employed at Guardian Security. Wes had had a year of rehab to undergo in order to get back to full strength. Steve had been willing to wait to hire him after he'd successfully completed them at a VA Hospital in Dallas, Texas.

Now? Steve had called him as soon as he'd successfully finished the strenuous challenge. He'd said, "An interesting first assignment has just come up, and I think you're a perfect fit for it. Let's talk."

The light from the dash reflected into his thought-filled gray eyes as he continued to drive west. It was April and where he was going, it was going to be damned snowy and cold. And icy. Or both. Wes had gotten used to warmer climates, most of his SEAL assignments having been in jungle and warmer climes where Spanish was spoken and it was a second language to him. Rubbing his jaw, he knew that when Steve used "interesting," it was probably going to be an offbeat assignment. The SEAL Chief only used that word sparingly when his team was under his command. Wes found out quickly when Steve said it, it was going to be a mission that was really outside the normal boundaries their black ops unit operated within.

Steve reminded him that a wrangler was someone who could do anything with nothing. They were hardwired MacGyvers who could figure out what was broken and how to fix it; or if trapped, how to get out of the situation, alive. Baling wire and chewing gum, Carter drilled into them. Two really good items to have in one's arsenal, that was for sure. One corner of his mouth hooked upward. What SEAL didn't have black humor as part of their stock-in-trade. Well, pretty soon, he'd find out about this "interesting" first assignment that Steve thought he was the "right fit" to take on by the horns.

April 4

"Welcome home," Steve told Wes as he came in several days later to Silver Creek, Wyoming. Wes shook his hand and sat down in the man's cramped, super-neat office. "And welcome to Guardian Security. I just got a call from Amy, our Human Resources gal, that all your papers are in order and you're ready to go."

Wes said, "Good to hear." He looked around the spare room painted a light blue. On one wall was evidence of Carter's many accomplishments. As a SEAL, Steve had taken college courses, coming out with a master's in business administration. There was no question his former chief was one of the best in the SEAL community; a stickler for organization, discipline, and creative thinking outside the box. "It's damned cold up here, Steve. We're jungle rats, not cut out for this kind of thing."

"Yeah, I know." The ex-SEAL chuckled darkly, pouring them each a hot mug of black coffee. "I was born here in Silver Creek, Wyoming, so I grew up with this snow, ice and cold. After going into the Navy and joining the SEALs, my next ten years was spent in the jungles and highlands of Central and South America. Go figure." He grinned and sat down. "But let's talk about you. About this 'interesting' assignment. I needed someone with a variety type of background on this one."

Sipping the hot brew, Wes liked that every time he saw Steve, he was wearing cowboy clothes, a black leather vest over the long-sleeved red shirt, and his black Stetson was always hanging nearby off a wall peg. "You used 'interesting' and that got my attention."

"Why did it?"

Lifting a brow, Wes said wryly, "You never used them lightly with our team when we were preparing to go on an op. It was the kind of mission that required the baling wire and bubblegum. Every time."

"Yeah, I'm a wordsmith at heart," he agreed, giving him an evil grin. "I see you as a Jack-of-all-trades, Wes. Able to take on a more offbeat kind of assignment than most. Generally speaking, SEALs are really good at that type of mission situation. I know you probably thought you'd have bodyguard jobs involving businessmen going overseas and protecting their arses."

"Right."

"How do you feel taking on a female client right here in Silver Creek for a first assignment?"

Shrugging, he said, "Is that why you used the word 'interesting'? It involves a woman instead of a man? Or, you want to ease me into the security business due to my lung issue and see if I can cut it?"

Chuckling, Steve passed a file to Wes. "Wounds like yours take time to heal, and it doesn't hurt to ease into contracting. Silver Creek has a top-rated hospital. Should you need anything, it's nearby. And to be honest, the first man I assigned to our client, they did not get along. He was an ass-kicking ex–Delta Force type, and he couldn't fit into the job that the client demanded of him. About a third of our clients are women. And forty percent of my employees are female, as well. We do a lot of business with both genders."

"No one can say you're patriarchal," Wes deadpanned. That always got Steve going. He was part Eastern Cherokee, raised in the old ways of his mother's people, whose reservation was in North Carolina. His mother had married a very rich rancher, Robert Carter, in Silver Creek, Wyoming, and she had raised and trained him in a matriarchal culture. That meant that Steve viewed both sexes as equals, as well as giving them respect. Males raised in a patriarchal society mostly demeaned women, disrespected them, and never treated them the same. Wes didn't even know the word until Steve told him what it meant when in the SEALs. He'd gone through so many foster homes that he really hadn't been imprinted, or maybe brainwashed, into a patriarchal male mold.

Wes felt that his own raising was neither, which pleased

him immensely. Maybe by being left to his own means, his own genetic matriarchal inner knowledge pushed him in that direction without him ever realizing it. He'd had DNA testing done and it showed he was fifty percent Native American. Maybe that's why he and Steve had such a tight working relationship when in the SEALs. Steve recognized his own kind. Wes saw his friend's light blue eyes sparkle over his dryly asked questions.

"No, never patriarchal, that's for sure," Steve replied with a short laugh. Becoming serious, he pinned Wes with a stare. "But we know at least one of your parents was Native American. We'd talked about this before a number of times when you were a SEAL. There were ops where I needed someone who didn't leave a footprint in the earth. I often gave you those types of assignments that involved having to gain trust from those who distrusted us. Plus, your skin color is brown, which fit into the Central and South American missions our team were given. And you delivered every time." Steve slid him a file across the desk. "Open the file. Let's sit with it and I'll fill you in on what's going on with my unhappy client."

Opening it, there was a color photo of her. His heart leaped, which caught him off guard. There was a young woman, maybe in her late twenties, braided black hair and an oval face with high cheekbones, staring back at him. "Is she Native American, Steve?"

He rocked back in his chair, giving Wes a pleased look. "Sure is. Not only that? She's part Eastern Cherokee, like me. So, we share something in common. And"—he sighed—"when things went south with the first bodyguard, she trusted me enough to try and find a special someone who she could relate to the second time around."

"That's pretty synchronistic that she shares the same nation's blood as you do, Steve."

"Well, I come from the Wolf Clan," he said. "She's from the Paint Clan."

"What's the difference?"

"Paint Clan produces the healers, medicine women and men. The Wolf Clan produces the leaders and the various chiefs for the nation."

"And here you are, in another career, leading," Wes noted. The woman was very attractive, but Wes kept that comment to himself. "What do you want me to know about her?"

Putting his booted feet up on his desk, fingers laced together across his waist, Steve said, "She's not the normal client a security firm would see walking through their front door. She's interesting for many reasons. Her name is Sara Woya Romano."

"What does 'woya' mean? That's certainly not Italian like her last name."

"Very astute," Steve praised. "It's an Eastern Cherokee word and it means 'dove.'"

"She looks very much at peace," Wes agreed. "Does she live on the reservation in North Carolina?"

Shaking his head, Steve said, "Her mother is Tsula Romano, and she is a full-blood Eastern Cherokee. Tsula is a very rich and a super successful business woman. She created an organic soapmaking company seven years ago in Dallas and it's gone global. Her ex-husband, Leo Romano, is a piece of work. He's sitting in a US prison right now for fraud and money laundering for the Cosa Nostra in Sicily. Tsula divorced him years earlier when she found out he was involved in illegal and criminal activities. She married him thinking he was the owner of a software company. He lied to her, of course."

Wes nodded, and Steve continued speaking, reading from the file. "Tsula didn't want to bring up her daughter, Sara, in a household like that and she divorced him, but stayed in the same city, and Sara lived full-time with her mother, but her father had visitation rights. Sara would spend her summers, when school let out, with her grandmother Adsila, a healer and herbalist in Cherokee, North Carolina. She was out daily with her grandmother, in the Smoky Mountains and hills of their huge reservation, learning about herbal medicine. That long lineage of family knowledge had been passed on to Adsila, who passed it on to Sara. Later, she went to the University of North Carolina in Asheville, getting a degree in botany and a minor as a paramedic. In her spare time, she served her local volunteer fire department on the reservation, taking classes by day, volunteering her medical services on weekends when on summer breaks."

Steve broke from reading, and gave Wes a pleased look. "Sara is the epitome of a Paint Clan healer; she's gentle, kind, and compassionate. She's also armed with a medical background, plus all her years of being schooled in herbs by her grandmother Adsila. Sara helped out at the health clinic on the reservation, as well."

Steve smiled and continued. "Some background intel you need to know about Sara and her family. Leo Romano had a lot of women on the side. Shortly after Tsula found out about Leo's illegal operations, she sent her daughter to live on the reservation on summer break, and her divorce was finalized. In a matter of a month after that, Leo married another woman, Victoria Lucinda, and she had a son by him, Manny Romano. This monster boy grew up under daddy's wing, learning the illegal trade.

"In the meantime? Sara was twenty-five and started

being stalked by Romano's soldiers. She moved back to Dallas and lived with her mother. She didn't want to be involved in her mother's soap company, but instead, worked in the city, offering her services to Latino families who grew up on herbal medicine. In her spare time, Sara worked with various fire departments and their paramedics. In the Latin quarter, she held clinics with their permission. That went well until there were attacks on Sara's life.

"Tsula called me and wanted her daughter to 'disappear' and get out of Texas, and go somewhere in backwater, USA, to protect her from Leo's henchmen. She felt Manny Romano, Sara's half brother, was ordering the attacks on Sara. In the original prenup that Tsula had with Leo, their firstborn child would get the money and estate after they both died. So you can see why Tsula figured out that Manny, who is a sociopath like his father, and who is running the criminal elements now in his father's software business, wants Sara dead and out of the picture. And if that happens? I'm pretty sure Manny will go after Tsula next. He'll kill both of them sooner or later."

Scowling, Wes muttered, "Her mother is the one who asked for a bodyguard for Sara?" Frankly, in his private opinion, Sara Romano looked like the last person to be the daughter of a Sicilian Mafia father. She had golden-colored skin, and he thought it was due partly to her Native American blood. It was the kindness in her face, the tenderness emanating from her green eyes, large and framed with thick black lashes, that spoke of her being a healer. Her mouth was softly shaped, the corners naturally lifting upward. He tore himself from drowning further into her photo.

"Sara didn't want a bodyguard, to be honest with you,"

Steve said. "But her mother insisted." He gave Wes a wry look. "The first one, the ex–Delta Force operator Zane Werner, was, in Sara's words, 'like a Mack truck plowing through my office.'"

"Not something I'd want on my résumé," Wes said, his frown deepening.

"I agree. We work hard to pair up a client with a body-guard around here"—he sighed—"but sometimes? The nature of the job just isn't a fit for either the contractor, in this case, or the client."

"What was Werner's problem?" Wes wanted to know.

"Well, she lives in a turn-of-the-century Victorian three-story house here in Silver Creek. It's on the National Heritage register of Historic Places and is beautiful. Right behind it is a single-story horse barn and carriage house. Sara hired a woman master carpenter and her team to renovate it into the twenty-first century. It was just completed and my employee, whose more patriarchal than I like, didn't think he should be used to carry boxes of quart jars filled with herbs and set them where Sara needed them in her clinic or the retail area of the building. He was thoroughly briefed by me that even though he was hired as a bodyguard, he was to go undercover as her assistant."

"Oh?" Wes wondered what that entailed.

"Are you at all up on herbs and herbalism?"

"Not at all."

Steve made an unhappy noise. "Well, that was the only way Sara would agree to have a full-time bodyguard around: He or she would have to help her. She'd teach the person as time went on. And," he said, shaking his head, "when Werner found out what she was asking of him, he thought it was beneath him to be, what he termed, nothing more than 'a grocer dude.'"

"I'll bet that didn't land well," Wes said, liking Sara's pluck and the fact she was the owner of her own business; Werner was not. "He was supposed to fit in, not stand out like a sore thumb and cause friction with the client."

"Yeah, well, you're right. Sara told him to leave, picked up the phone and called me and told me what had happened. She said the guy's bullying energy was wearing on her, and she just didn't have time to deal with him. She's busy setting up her retail, lab, and clinic, as well as dealing with moving in."

"She's under a lot of stress," Wes said.

"Yes. The fact that she knows that Manny Romano is probably trying to find her whereabouts right now—that's a big stress. Plus, she moved away from her family, now is setting up a new business and all, both of which are enough to make anyone feel under thumbscrews. She never struck me as someone who had a short fuse, but she was angry about Werner's antics and how he treated her."

"I don't blame her at all, then," Wes said.

"So, you're not giving me that horrified look like you're going to find an arrow through your heart if you take this job?"

A croak of laughter filled Wes's throat. "I think Sara was right to ask for someone new. Now, I don't know if I'm the one for this job in regards to her herbal background. Maybe a woman contractor filling those shoes would be better."

"The woman I know who would be perfect is on assignment right now in Belarus and not available," Steve muttered unhappily. "I know you to be a good listener, Wes. You're a thoughtful person, thinking before you speak. You don't blurt the first thing that comes to mind. And I know your patience and know it well serving under my command as a SEAL. You were the guy who contacted American charities for donations to small villages where kids didn't have shoes. You worked with the Red Cross and other organizations to bring in US volunteer medical doctors, optometrists, and dentists, to serve these out-of-the-way villages, and get kids and elders the health help they needed. I know you had a really rough landing when you were born, but your character and personality make you a team person, a supporter, and you like to help people who have less than you ever did."

Nodding, Wes said, "So? Where is this going, Steve?"

"Instead of just assigning you this detail? I'd like you to go over and meet Sara, let her explain what she does, the kind of work an assistant would do, and get a 'feel' for the role, first. Then, I'll contact her and get her evaluation of you, and see if she's confident that you could work for her as well as guard her. What do you think about that?"

"I think it's a wise move. Normally, as I understand it, most security firms try to do a personality matchup that makes the client feel like we're a team, and not at odds with one another."

"You're right about that," Steve said, pulling his feet off his desk and sitting up. "How do you feel about this so far?"

Shrugging, he said, "Well, I don't think my health is an issue on something like this. From what you've laid out, it's more a personality get-together, or clash."

"You know? SEALs, the really good ones, ran on their psychic intuition." He jabbed his finger at the photo in front of Wes. "What's your gut feel when you look at her photo?"

"Highly intelligent, doesn't suffer fools, very caring and compassionate, but she's no pushover, either. I can feel the warrior in her."

"Good assessment. She doesn't suffer fools at all."
Steve gave him a wolfish grin.

Chuckling, Wes added, "I prefer people who speak up
about what their needs are. I don't care if they aren't necessarily PC, and I'd like a down-home kind of chat with
one another to keep communication open between us."

"Oh," Steve said, "she's all of that."

"Is her mother like that, too?" he wondered.

"Same-o, same-o."

"Good. I don't like political speak or gaslighting types
or passive-aggressive kinds who always say they're the
victim."

"Sara will never be anyone's victim." Steve chortled,
pointing at the file. "If you take this assignment, you'll be
living in her home. You know that. Right?"

"I figured I would be."

"You'll have to defer to her on everything. It's her home.
You're a guest."

"Got it."

"The level of threat to her right now is low," Steve said.
"She just moved here three months ago. I'm in touch with
the county sheriff, Dan Seabert, who, by the way, is an
ex-SEAL, too. We're working together on finding out
more about Manny Romano, the half brother of Sara, and
finding out just how far his reach really is. I've got a line
into the FBI, and I'm awaiting a thick PDF document on
the kid, who's playing Mafia kingpin while daddy is in
prison. Once I get that, I'll know more and I'll draw you
into that intel. I don't want to scare Sara. I want her to go
on and live her life, not be stressed out every day that
someone will walk through her clinic door and shoot her.
Every incident involving her—and, we think, the Romano

family—is in that file. You can see what kind of skullduggery they've tried on Sara earlier. Every hit on her has been more brazen and more dangerous. Given that Manny is a snot-nosed twenty-five-year-old, a braggart, arrogant and know-it-all, he may well up the ante on taking out Sara. He knows she's gone into hiding. Another security firm out of Dallas has sent a bodyguard to Tsula, her mother. So, they are both being guarded, but that doesn't mean they're safe. We need to know that, they don't."

Picking up the file, Wes said, "Right. I'd like to meet with Sheriff Seabert myself."

"Well, let's get past Sara liking you enough to trust you to be her bodyguard, okay? Once we have a signed contract with her, I agree with you on this."

Rising, Wes put the file in his briefcase. "Roger on that one."

Standing, Steve walked around his large desk, opening the door to his office. "I'll call Sara now, and let her know you're coming over." He looked at his watch. "It's 1000 hours."

"Ten a.m. to civilians," Wes said, picking up his brief-case.

"Yeah, damned if I can get Zulu time out of my head." He laughed, standing aside, holding out his hand to Wes.

"Go look around Silver Creek for about an hour? Get some breakfast. I want time to call Sara, answer any of her questions, and you drop in at 1100 hours to the office around the back of her home. Her address, cell phone number are in your file."

"Sounds good. I haven't had breakfast yet, so I think I'll find a café."

"Olive Oyl's on Main Street is the ticket," Steve assured him. "Best full breakfast in town. It will spoil you."

Nodding, Wes shook his boss's hand. "I'll wait for you to text me."

"Roger that."

Wes walked down the hall toward the reception area. It was a quiet place, a rather large, two-story redbrick building, nothing hinting at the fact that probably one of the finest retired SEALs in the country was heading up a powerful, but little known, global security agency. He settled his tan Stetson on his head.

He handed in the security badge he'd been given earlier, signed out on the roster, and left the building, heading for his black truck in the parking lot. The sun felt warm and welcoming on the shoulders of his sheepskin coat. The sky was a marine blue, and it almost hurt his eyes to look at the intensity of the color. The town was small, around ten thousand people, the main highway historically interesting. The people of Silver Creek loved color. They had painted one- or two-story Victorian and nineteenth-century homes that were now turned into businesses, into what looked like a basketful of brightly colored Easter eggs on the main street. There were false fronts above each one, reminding Wes of Amsterdam in the Netherlands. Each three-story, narrow building had fancy woodwork that was painted on the edges with either silver or gold paint. Some were a bright pink, others a summer green, or sun gold, or pale blue. It made the place look historic and yet pretty to the eye. There was obviously a lot of pride in how the town looked, everyone working together, and he felt that was a good sign. Maybe, either by chance or not, Sara had chosen a town that suited herself, from Steve's cursory description of her.

Climbing into the truck, he set the briefcase on the floorboard, out of sight. He looked the part of a wrangler with a Stetson in place, well-worn cowboy boots, jeans, and a blue chambray, long-sleeved shirt. It was nothing fancy, but then, as he punched in the address for Olive Oyl's Restaurant on his smart phone, he drove out of the parking lot, heading to Main Street, bodyguards didn't stand out. They melted into the fabric of what was surrounding them. Shadows of a different kind.

Wes couldn't shake that photo of Sara Romano. He knew all the details, tons of them, were in that file, plus the thumb drive Steve had given to him. She was beautiful in his eyes, but he didn't dare confide that to Steve. One of the regulations of his security company was that the bodyguard not become personally entangled with the client. Ever. It had been a long time since he'd been so powerfully drawn to a woman. And it was just a photo! Wes was having all kinds of bells and whistles going off deep inside himself. That shook him, because he'd *never* had that kind of reaction toward one. And this was far more than just a sexual response. Wes had learned the hard way with women when he was a SEAL. He'd had plenty of women who chased him, not the other way around. These ladies had a desire for SEALs, calling them heroes. But in his world, he didn't see himself being a hero. Instead, a patriot who served the greater good of his country.

Wes found himself hoping that she was not engaged or entangled with a partner. Why? He didn't want to look too closely at the question or the answer. He'd never been a ladies' man. He wasn't the cock of the walk or a rooster strutting around his strength, power, or anything else. Maybe it was his upbringing, all those years in that blur of foster homes. He'd learned young to be a shadow, and not garner attention, which never ended well for him. His SEAL team friends liked to go out and drink, dance, flirt, take a woman to bed. That had never been for him and would never be. They referred to him, teasingly, as the "quiet one" of their tight group. Wes wasn't sure he should be grateful for not carousing with his team. Most of his friends eventually got married, but within five to seven years, they were divorced. That wasn't what he wanted.

Tom had instilled in him that there was such a thing as "forever love." He had met his wife when he was a twenty-two-year-old SEAL. And in some ways, Tom was more like him: quiet, unaggressive, and certainly not a strutting ego-busting braggart like some of his friends had been. Tom remained married to his wife up to this very day. Wes dreamed of the very same thing his mentor had. It had been his time with his family as a teen, that he realized just how neglected and abandoned he'd been. The happiness and teamwork of their family was so different from the way he'd been raised. He wanted the same kind of happy marriage; never believing it would happen to him, however. Still, deep in his wounded heart, he yearned for exactly that, but he wasn't about to admit it to anyone, much less himself.

The other thing confusing him was *why* had he experienced such a heart-rending reaction to Sara's photo? She was a stranger. And it could well remain that way, too, if she didn't think they could get along well enough for him to be her bodyguard. If that were the case, he was out of the picture. Well, one thing for sure, in another couple of days, he would know from Steve if he had the job.

Again, his heart swelled with such yearning just thinking about Sara, that it completely flummoxed him. *What* was this reaction all about?

Chapter Two

April 5

Sara clicked off her cell phone after talking at length, and rather heatedly, to Steve Carter. Her mother had egged her on to hire a bodyguard because of what they both thought were Manny Romano's blundering attempts to get rid of her one way or another. Each attack had been clumsy, poorly executed, and she'd either recognized the Mafia soldier coming her way or sensed it with her super-refined intuition, avoiding the trap that had been set to take her life. Her mother had always said she was psychic, but then, members of her family from the Paint Clan of the Eastern Cherokee, had always had what they termed "the Sight."

Pursing her lips, she slid her cell phone into the pocket of the crested apron she wore. Sitting at her desk, which faced the door of her clinic and public area where people could buy her tinctures, salves, lotions, and other organic health and cosmetic offerings, she'd learned early on to have an escape plan. This large, roomy one-story building was built in 1900 to house carriages, stables, and horses; and in 1908, the owner had expanded it to include the new

Model T cars. The space had been constructed of Canadian cedar, brought in by train by the very rich Dr. Elias Henry.

After three months of serious renovation to the five-thousand-square-foot barn, she'd had it transformed into a modern-day storefront. When a person came to buy herbs, they would walk in a door framed with colorful stained-glass flowers. That way, Sara could see *who* was approaching her business. Although the two large display windows were necessary because they brought in good light, she'd also had four large skylights built so that her lab area and shipping area would be in the back and labels easily read, as well provide strong lighting for her supplies, and her clinic. She preferred sunlight, seeing blue sky, even if she had to be inside a building for hours daily.

Well, now what? She'd allowed Steve to gently urge her to agree to see this potential bodyguard replacement. Sara decided on a different tack with this man, whose name was Wes Paxton. When the first security operator was assigned, he dismissed his need to know what she did. But wasn't that part of the agreement? That whoever was assigned would become her assistant? It would be excellent cover, in her opinion. And then, of course, Zane Werner had told her he wasn't going to be her lackey.

Blowing a black tendril away from her eyes, she quickly slid her long, slender fingers through her loose black hair, taming it across her shoulder, the heavy strands hanging halfway down her back. Werner was a jerk, pure and simple. She'd gritted her teeth for a month, and then she'd had enough. These security types were getting a minimum of a hundred thousand dollars a year to protect her! His arrogance rubbed her raw. *What a sexist jerk.*

Well, Werner was finally out of her life. If she hadn't liked Steve Carter so much, she'd have called her mother and told her to find another security company with a better contractor who she could work with. Sara wasn't all that keen on a bodyguard, anyway. By leaving Dallas, Texas, where her mother's business and life were centered, she felt that disappearing into the woodwork, so to speak, would hide her from blundering, stupid Manny, her half brother by her father's second marriage.

It was almost eleven a.m. She looked up and studied the concrete sidewalk that went around the side of the beautiful Victorian home, thanks to her mother purchasing it. The man coming around her home was tall, at least six feet, wearing a tan cowboy hat, a sheepskin jacket, jeans, plus a set of warm gloves. He was still too far away for her to make out his features, but she could see he was alert, studying the eight-foot-tall lilac walls that followed the wrought-iron fence around the property. He walked easily. The way he moved made her think of the hunters on the Eastern Cherokee reservation. They were taught to walk that left no sound when the heel and the rest of the foot met the earth. Hmmm. Was he Native American? she wondered. But then she quickly reminded herself that Steve had said Mr. Paxton was an ex–Navy SEAL, so of course, those black ops types would know the secret of silent walking; no one, not even an animal, would hear their approach.

He wasn't overly muscled like Werner, who worked out religiously two hours a day at the local gym. She couldn't stand these hulk types of males, anyway. No, he reminded her of the hunters among her people: on the lean side, tightly muscled from hours of walking. But his gait was easygoing, fluid and unhurried. Werner always marched along like the arrogant fool he was. She hated even being around him after the second week, barely able to tolerate his behavior, treating her like she was some petulant child and not a woman who knew herself, owned her own business, and was capable as well as fully independent. *Patriarchal know-it-all! Baked-in sexism against women.*

Pressing her lips together, she watched the man's movement down the sidewalk. As he drew closer, the eastern sun highlighting his oval face and high cheekbones, her first impression was he looked calm. That was good. His eyes were widely spaced apart, large and intelligent-looking. She watched with interest as he unobtrusively checked out the area around him, but it wasn't obvious at all; he behaved more like a tourist looking here and there, was all. She wondered what color his eyes were. His nose had been broken at some point in his life. Often, she could look at a person and receive an overall impression. She'd been able to read energy around a person since she was a young child. Unlike Werner's smug face, this contractor looked kind and sensitive. Relief began to trickle through her. Did she dare hope this man would be a good match for her needs? She stood up, moving around her U-shaped desk that she'd put together with three different pieces of antique furniture. A U-shape reminded her of a woman's womb, of creativity, and in her trade as an herbalist, she always felt like an herbal midwife of sorts, birthing herbs, formulas, and such, and helping interested people learn how they could improve their health.

Smiling to herself, she smoothed down her apron, which fell to just above her knees. It was April, very cold compared to Texas where she was born and raised. Wearing a pale pink angora sweater with a cowl neck beneath the apron, and a pair of loose-fitting jeans and comfortable leather oxfords along with thick socks to keep her feet warm, she moved toward the door to meet him.

Their eyes met as she opened the door. She liked that they were a gray color, reminding her of a turbulent, stormy sky. He halted a respectful distance away from her, his briefcase in his left hand, and he removed his Stetson.

"Ms. Romano?"

His voice was low, the timbre riffling through her, making her heart stutter in response. His hat hair made him look endearing. "Yes. You must be Mr. Paxton?"

"I am." He held out some identification from his company, which had his photo on it. She took it, looking at it and studying him. Her lips had been pursed but as the seconds ticked by, they softened and he saw her wariness begin to dissolve.

"May I enter?"

She handed the ID to him and pulled the door open. "Come on in . . ." Sounding a bit breathless, she could feel the quietly reined power, the energy, that surrounded him. There was nothing obvious about him, but to her, she was supersensitive to people in general. In fact, he seemed more a shadow than real to her. Shadows hid things. What was *he* hiding from her? Shutting the door, she turned to him. His gaze once more met hers. Heat flooded her lower body and then moved upward to her heart and lungs, making her feel somewhat stunned by his presence. He didn't scare her. He impressed her. "Why don't we talk at my desk?" She gestured toward a chair she'd placed in front of it, opposite where she would sit behind it.

Nodding, he moved toward it, casually observing the retail part of the store.

She liked that he seemed to be absorbing the area, the many shelves, the colorful products placed upon them.

"I like how it smells in here," he said, giving her a slight smile.

"Welcome to my world of herbs," she said. "I love the natural fragrances, too. It's different on every day, depending upon what I'm formulating in my lab."

"Some of them I can ID, but most of them, I can't," he admitted, moving the chair to the corner so he would sit facing the display windows. He set his briefcase on the oak floor next to the chair. Sitting down, he placed his hat to his left in a clear spot on the wide polished desk.

"What can you identify?" she wondered, moving into the U and sitting down in her chair.

"Cloves, ginger, cinnamon . . . I was lucky enough to spend a few nights every week over at my friend's family home. Frannie, Tom's wife, would always make an apple pie when she knew I was coming over because it was my favorite. She used those spices in it. Brings back really happy memories to me."

A part of her began to sigh in relief. He seemed so easy-going compared to Werner. Understanding that a contractor was not a personal buddy, she tried to choose her questions carefully. "That's a lovely memory. Do you cook?"

His mouth quirked. "No . . . never got into it."

"Nowadays, most boys growing up have mothers who get them into the kitchen to learn how to cook and clean and take care of themselves. I think that's a good idea." She saw a brief glint of sadness cross his eyes as he leaned down and took a yellow legal pad out of his briefcase along with a pen.

"I just didn't get the chance," was all he said.

"So? Where do we begin?" she asked, feeling a blanket of deep sadness enveloping him. She sensed he was being evasive, but she didn't know why. What bothered her was the deep sadness she felt. It was depressing to her. "To be honest with you, Mr. Paxton, I've had my fill of the other contractor, Zane Werner, and I didn't want a replacement. That's no afront to you, but I'm fried from the experience I just disentangled myself from a couple weeks ago."

"Steve told me there was a mismatch personality-wise between you and Mr. Werner."

He was diplomatic. Another worry began to dissolve. "Are you always like this?"

"Like what?"

"Well"—she stumbled, trying not to be coarse about her opinions on Werner and superimposing them on him—"you just seem more a shadow, very quiet, and you feel like a deep, deep lake where you cannot see what is below the water surface."

His eyes gleamed with thoughtfulness, but his face didn't alter in expression. "Did Steve share with you any of my SEAL background?" he asked.

"No . . . he didn't. I just assumed you were all alike." Again, that glint in his eyes that did not transfer to his expression. He felt off-limits to her. Women were open and men were closed up tighter than Fort Knox. That was her experience. It was a pity that Mr. Paxton wasn't more forthcoming. He seemed, well . . . nice . . . even approachable. So far . . .

"A SEAL team usually has ten members," he offered, "and they're as different as ten people you might meet walking down any street."

"Oh . . . well, I just thought . . ." She grimaced. "You killed for a living." The words came flying out of her mouth and she instantly regretted it. It came out sounding like he was little more than a murderer of human beings.

He sat a little straighter. Nodding, he said, "That's true."

"I'm sorry, I shouldn't have framed it like that." Pushing her hair across her shoulder, she said, "I'm overreacting to Mr. Werner, the other contractor. He was positively brutish, bragging about how many people he'd killed." She shivered, her shoulders rising and falling momentarily. "Lives are precious. All lives, Mr. Paxton. I know in your line of work, from what Steve shared with me, that you're more than just a hired killer, but that's what Mr. Werner called himself."

Giving her a sympathetic look, Wes said, "I was the medic for our SEAL team, Ms. Romano. I guess you could say that I was half and half: half taking lives when necessary, and the other half trying to save lives on my team, or those of the children and adults who lived in the villages, working with the civilian populace and helping them where we could."

Her fingers touched her lips and she stared at him. "Steve didn't say you were a medic."

"You seem shocked by it."

"I-I just didn't think about SEALs in those terms, I guess. You saved lives."

He sighed and shook his head. "Not always. I wanted to, but sometimes, the wound was beyond my skills in the field."

"I'm a licensed paramedic."

"Yes, Steve told me that."

"Where did you receive your medical training?"

"I was one of the SEALs to go through A school with the Army Special Forces medical training center," he told her. "It was far more extensive training than what a paramedic receives. I was trained for field surgery, if it was needed."

Her lips parted. "You're right, paramedics don't do that type of medical work at all. I'm not a big fan of war, you must know that. I think there's a lot of other ways to stop aggression."

Giving her an understanding look, he said, "But not always. Black ops like us are the tip of the spear when every other type of diplomacy has failed and there's still naked aggression aimed at the US, or at innocent villages that evil men want to overrun, rape the women, kidnap the children for sex trafficking purposes to sell them to the highest bidder, and then kill their fathers and husbands. We always stand in the breech between diplomacy and action in our trade."

Sara quivered inwardly over his raw, unvarnished description, but it didn't make it any less awful for her to see the verbal pictures he painted for her. "Yes . . . I'm aware that sometimes, we need people such as yourself." Giving him a frustrated look, she muttered, "Look at me in my circumstance, for example. I have a half brother, Manny Romano. I believe my father, who is in prison now, is orchestrating everything from behind bars. Manny wants me out of the picture permanently. He wants my father's estate once he dies. The issue he's confronting is that legally, it goes to the eldest child: me."

"My info says Manny is the second child by a second wife, Victoria?"

Nodding, she said, "My mother signed an ironclad prenup with my father before she'd consent to marry him. I'm to receive the entire estate, although Great Spirit knows, I don't want anything to do with it. Or him. Or Manny. My mother and I are nothing like them."

"I can see that," he said, looking around the quiet interior of the building. "Maybe the exact opposite?"

"I took after my mother and her people, thank goodness," she admitted, opening her hands. "My life has always revolved around life, not death. My focus is helping other people with herbs, trying to give them relief from their symptoms."

"That's a worthy life to live," he agreed quietly, jotting down some notes. "My mentor, Tom, who is part Eastern Cherokee, taught me as a teen about the Native American way of seeing things: that we're stewards of the Earth, and of our children's children."

Her eyes widened enormously. "Why, yes!" she said, her voice enthused. "How wonderful you had him in your life. Is that why you walk silently? Did he teach you how to do that?" She saw one corner of his mouth lift a bit.

"Yes, among my education about how Native Americans work as one with Mother Earth and all her relations, Tom taught me his philosophy of life. He had been a Navy SEAL, too. When I met him, he had transitioned to civilian law enforcement after retirement."

"Oh," she gasped, her hand flying to her heart, "you have *no* idea how wonderful it is to hear that coming from you!"

He gave her a humored look. "Tell me more?"

"Well," she said, speaking rapidly, "Mr. Werner is patriarchal, didn't respect me, treated me like a brainless twit, and he felt I needed to hear all his bragging about his life as a Delta Force operator. He'd tell me how many men he'd killed, thinking that it would impress me. Every time he talked about the death of others, I wanted to cry. All of life is sacred. It hurt me to hear him speak of those things." She tapped the area of her heart. "Literally, I would cringe inwardly."

"I'm sorry," Wes said, meaning it. "That's not the job of a contractor to interrupt your life on any level. We're to be shadows, seen but not heard from—unless you ask me a question, of course. My job is to keep you safe, not tell you about my life or make judgments about yours."

Wrinkling her nose, she muttered, "Believe me, you're a breath of fresh air, Mr. Paxton."

"So far, so good," he said lightly. "I'm very interested in this assignment, but I want to understand why you want someone who can double as your assistant and go under-cover as your employee."

"Because I need an assistant," she said. "And if I hire someone else to do that, then what are you going to do? Sit around and watch me all day? That would drive me nuts."

Chuckling, he nodded. "Yeah, I don't like being watched like a bug under a microscope, either. No privacy."

"Exactly," she said, becoming excited. "This way, if I teach you what an herbal assistant does in a situation like mine, where part of my day is spent as a clinician, and the other part is making up the formularies or herbal prepara-tions, you can still be around me, but busy. You won't be bored, believe me. And if you don't want to do that? Then I will be forced to hire someone, train them, and you'll sit around a lot. Mr. Werner refused to become my assistant."

"I like your idea. It actually makes my job easier. I can move around with you and no one is going to think any-thing other than I work for you. That's great cover."

Relief sheeted through her. "Seriously?"

"Sure." He pointed to the rear of the building. "I'm seeing a lot of jars, large and small, and I'm already interested in what's in them."

"That's your medical side coming out, no doubt?"

"Most likely," Wes agreed. "I'd like to get more into your personal background and family issues. That's important for me to know. If your half brother shows up here? I have to be able to ID him, for example."

"Yes, that makes sense. May I make you a cup of herbal tea first, Mr. Paxton?" She pointed to a tea and coffee table near the door where patrons could pour it for themselves. "We could go sit in the alcove. See? It's over there. Two nice, comfy, overstuffed chairs with tables next to each one."

He twisted around and saw them in the corner near the picture window. "Sure, better than a straight-backed chair," he joked.

She suddenly smiled, feeling the weight of the world sliding off her shoulders. "Oh, good! Come on, follow me!" and she hurried out from behind the desk.

Wes unfolded himself and looked beyond Sara, to the concrete walk and surrounding grassy lawn on either side of the building, looking for a human or out-of-place movement. The crested apron she wore was made of sturdy canvas material. She was walking so quickly, the corner flaps were raising and lowering with each of her steps.

"I have several types of wonderful herbal tea. I make them fresh, every morning," she offered, pleasure in her husky tone as she gestured to the table that had a flowery oilcloth across it. She liked that Paxton stood at one end of the table, facing the window, giving her space. With Werner? She felt as if he were sexually stalking her, wanting her. It was an icky sensation she picked up around him.

"If you're feeling down and you need a lift? I have rose petal tea here." She held up a clear glass pint jar with pink, red, and white dried rose petals in it. "If you're feeling stressed, and a lot of people are nowadays, I have the lovely lemon balm tea." She picked it up, the dark green leaves dried along with some of the flowers. "Or, if you're tired and jet-lagged? I have gingerroot tea that's guaranteed to perk you right up."

She held up the jar that had thin, yellowish bits of the dried rhizome within it.

"I could use that energy lift," he admitted wryly. "I drove here from Texas in my truck. I arrived this morning."

Opening the jar, Sara poured some of the tiny cut rhizome into a tea ball, poured the hot water into a delicate bone china hand-painted flowery cup, setting it on the saucer. "You would be tired. That's a long drive. Let the tea steep for ten minutes. Over here is local honey, which I love. But if you want white sugar or perhaps some food-grade vegetable glycerin for sweetness, instead, they are available. And some almond milk if you like milk or cream in your tea."

He took the handle of the tea ball, moving it slowly, seeing an amber color trailing out of it and infusing the steaming hot, clear water. "I like it straight. Which tea are you choosing?"

"Lemon balm. I've been drinking it daily," she said wryly, fixing her own tea ball and pouring a second cup. "I opened up the store just last week and I'm pretty scattered without someone to help me. Right now, I'm open Tuesday through Saturday. If things pick up and people find out about me, I'd love to do some beginning herbal classes for those who are interested."

"Did you do that back at your other store in Texas?"

"Yes. I also did five-hour workshops, and I had a huge clientele. I want to start out slow and stay under the radar here in Silver Creek. I'm going to be busy enough with Dr. Cooper's prescriptions that she wants me to create, plus run the retail portion and so much more."

"Sounds like a lot," he agreed, giving her a thoughtful glance. "So Werner was really stressful?" He saw her black brows bunch.

"Every day? I'm surprised I lasted thirty days with the likes of him."

He looked around. "I saw on the entrance a sign for clinic hours. What is that about?"

She gestured to the open door that led to the other half of the building. "As a paramedic and a master herbalist, when I moved here three months ago, I contacted the local naturopath. They are schooled in herbalism, homeopathy, and other alternative health treatments, and they are licensed by the state medical board. Dr. Blaine Cooper, a naturopath and a wonderful woman in her forties, was happy to see me coming into town. She's in need of herbal preparations for her patients and I can make them here, in my lab. She can, also, but she's swamped with patients and wants to outsource the formularies to me. I took clinical herbal schooling for four years in Texas, and with my paramedic license, she sees me as someone she can trust with the individualized formularies she prescribes for her patients. And, she sends patients to me who have acute ailments like a cold, sinus infection, or flu, which herbs can treat naturally and without traditional medical drugs."

"Isn't that the slot herbs fill in the health and medical world?"

"It is. Most herbalists are not at the clinical level. In fact, most people want to just use herbs for their family. I have a lot of beginner books on herbalism if you'd like to learn more?"

"Very much so. Maybe you can pick out one or two that you feel would be a good starting point."

"I'll do that," she promised.

"How are the people of this valley responding to you coming in an and setting up your business?"

She smiled and moved her tea ball around in her cup, the liquid turning a light brown color. "To my surprise, Silver Creek people are really oriented, first, to natural and alternative medicine. In the months I've been here, I've gotten quite a few folks who want to treat their health concerns with herbs instead of traditional medicine. Mary Bishop, mother of Chase Bishop, who owns the Three Bars Ranch here in the valley, is the force behind organic, non-GMO food here in the valley. I had a long two-hour talk with her at her store, the only grocery store in town, about how I could fit into Silver Creek."

"I hear Mary is the queen of the valley," he said.

"Sort of. She's beloved by everyone. Mary helped me not only to figure out where I'd fit in, but we had tea with Dr. Blaine Cooper a few Saturdays ago, and that's how I became acquainted with her. Plus, Mary said her son is growing medicinal herbs on his ranch with direction from Dana Gallagher, who bought the Wildflower Ranch just outside of town. Dana came here last year and she connected with Mary because she wanted to cultivate herbs and other fruits and vegetables, all organic, and I got to meet with her, too. She and Mary worked with Blaine on what kinds of medicinal herbs to grow in this valley. This year will be the first year that they can be harvested, and Dana has asked me to come to her ranch and get whatever I need for my clinic. I was very excited about that because

I like to forage and find herbs that grow in a given area. Most of the time, I have to buy from trusted herb suppliers, but I'd much rather go out in the field and forage for them myself, bring them here"—she gestured toward the back of the building—"and go through the process to make salves, lotions, liniments, or other formularies."

"Good connections," he murmured. "Do you find that not all health conditions respond to herbs?" he asked, taking the tea ball out of his cup and placing it in another container.

"Not always," Sara agreed. "That's when I turn the client who comes to me, over to Dr. Cooper. Or, if they need surgery or other specific medical intervention, we have a small but wonderful hospital here. Blaine is going to introduce me to the medical doctors she works with, and wants me to cultivate a relationship with them. As a clinical herbalist, I have a fairly good medical training, but that's in addition to me being a paramedic. The hospital ER department has already signed me up and I'm on call with the hospital as a paramedic when they need an extra set of hands and eyes, or when they're shorthanded. I won't be dispensing herbs there, but I'll be doing all I can to help out."

"Sounds like you've made a nest for yourself here," Wes said, taking half a spoon of honey and stirring it into his tea as a trial. Coffee was his thing, which he drank black. But this tea looked like it could use something.

"Coming here was like entering Shangri-la for me. I had very heavy demands at my clinic and I employed ten people to help run it, when I lived in Dallas. My name got around and the large Hispanic population came to me because most of them were raised on herbs by their parents. They trust the herbs. They know they work. Come on, let's go sit in the alcove and we can chat some more."

Wes took the chair that faced the window. She took the other one. "I'm surprised Werner didn't say something to you about having this alcove at the front of the store."

"Why?"

"We keep our clients away from big display windows like this," he said, sipping the tea.

"Because someone could shoot me through the window?"

"Yes. Or at least, see where you were and then look for another entrance to this building to slip into and reach you."

Mouth quirking, she sipped the fragrant lemon balm tea, hands beneath the saucer in her lap. "He said nothing about such things."

"Is there another exit to this building?"

"Yes, the rear door is actually a place where a truck can back up to a dock and unload supplies I've ordered."

"Any others?"

"There's a door next to the dock. I had a large metal garage door installed that anyone inside it could press a button and it would open up."

"Who has a set of keys to this place?"

"Just me."

"Didn't Werner?"

"No." She saw him scowl and look away from her for a moment. When he turned, his face was arranged in that same look she couldn't interpret. "You look upset."

"A little," he admitted hesitantly. "Did Werner go over anything with you, as the client, and himself as the contractor? What he expected of you?"

She shook her head. Again, there was censure in his darkening gray eyes. Perhaps she could figure out what he was really feeling even if he wasn't showing or acting upon it. Eyes were the mirror to a person's soul as far as she was concerned.

For the next ten minutes, he went over the rules between the client and contractor. When he finished, he asked, "Do you have any questions?"

"I like that we have a secret code word that tells me there's danger," she admitted.

"And if I tell you to drop to the floor, run or whatever? You do it without question. Right?"

"Right," she answered. "Do you wear a gun?"

He seemed taken aback by her question. "Yes."

"Werner wore his where everyone could see it. I thought that's what contractors did. My customers were *very* upset seeing a weapon around. I didn't like it, either."

Biting back a groan, Wes said, "If we're undercover or protecting a client in everyday situations, we never let anyone know who we are, much less what we're carrying."

"Thanks for letting me know. Steve said something about setting up an appointment for you to talk with the sheriff if I approved of you. He said that you needed a lot of confidential law enforcement information on my father and Manny, and their Mafia soldiers who work for both of them."

Nodding, he said, "That's right. What I'd like to do, now that I've gotten protocols out of the way from my end, could you show me the rest of the building, as well as what my duties as your employee would be?" Wes hesitated. "Unless you don't find me acceptable. If you don't, then we'll have tea together and I'll leave and let Steve know."

She sat up straighter. "Why . . . I'd hadn't even thought of you leaving . . . You're very different from Werner." She looked toward the door midway in the wall that would take them to the other two-thirds of the building. "I'm excited to show you my lab and the supplies. You have a medical background and I really love that. Plus," she said, her voice dropping to a throaty whisper, "you act like a medic, not a contractor. I could see you were genuinely interested in the teas in the jars, and what they were used for."

"You could see that?" The corners of his mouth barely moved upward.

"In your eyes. You know? They give you away."

"Only with you. I'm not guarded with you, Ms. Romano. I won't ever be. I need a healthy line of communication with you at all times and there may come a time when voice commands won't do. I need you to read my eyes, my expression. With you? I'll be open and available so we're both on the same page should things go south."

Finishing her tea, she placed it on the table, which held a doily that had been crocheted by her grandmother Adsila. "That makes me feel even safer. You're not very readable, you know?"

He chuckled. "I guess that comes from being in the black ops community for a long time."

"Come with me," she urged, standing. "You have to like this undercover job you're going to take, Mr. Paxton. Because if you don't? Then you let me know and I'll look to hire someone else and you can be my shadow."

His grin increased as he finished off the ginger tea and set it down on a doily that had been hand-painted, the flowers colorful in that circle of crochet. Rising, he said, "My medical side, my pharmacy side, is always interested in chemistry."

"Oh," she said, humor in her husky voice, gesturing for him to follow her, "you're going to get a crash course in pharmacology, believe me."

The door to the rear of the store was solid and that

suited Wes. He followed her through it and then closed it behind him.

"What if someone comes in the front of the store?" he asked her, looking around at the well-lit area. Beneath him was a solid oak floor, blond in color. To his left was a glass-enclosed area that had a horizontal laminar flow hood.

"There's a buzzer that automatically sounds in my lab area as well as the supply area," she said. Halting, she smiled up at him. "You seem really interested in the hood over there. Have you used one before?"

"Yes, I trained on them. That's a really nice one. Expensive, too."

She grimaced. "You're staring at ten thousand dollars to buy that piece of equipment. My mother wanted me to have the best of everything," she said, walking toward the fully glass-enclosed lab. "Most herbalists don't have one, but since Dr. Cooper wants me to act as an herbal pharmacist for her, making up formulas for her patients, I have to have one."

"I'm impressed," he murmured. The horizontal laminar hood was at least twenty feet long. There was a stool where a person could sit at the long, sterile white table, plenty of room to put herbs, glasses, quart jars or whatever she used. The reverse air flow would come from inside the building, be sucked up under the glass shield that was across the top half of it, protecting the person sitting or standing there from breathing in anything that was being worked with. HEPA filters, he knew, would take care of any bacteria or virus that were 0.3 microns or larger. That took care of most infectious stuff floating around in the air.

Placing her hand on the dull-looking steel surface of the table beneath the hood, she said, "I'll teach you how to use it when it comes to working with herbal formularies."

Sara tried to tamp down her excitement over this quiet, sharply observing man. For whatever reason, she felt deeply drawn to him because of his sincerity and the way he conducted himself.

"So? Am I hired or fired?" he teased, barely smiling, holding her widening gold-brown eyes.

Laughing over his teasing, she said, "You're hired, Mr. Paxton. Are you ready to be immersed in my world of herbs and healing?" She saw he was pleased. Almost holding her breath, Sara found she wanted nothing so much as Wes Paxton to be her partner while her life was in danger. Somehow, she knew he'd take a bullet meant for her. It wasn't a pleasant thought because there was so much more to him and Sara quietly admitted that she wanted to know the man beneath the stoic expression he wore.

Dipping his head, he murmured, "I'd like nothing better. This fits hand-in-glove with my training and my interests."

Relief flowed through her. "Oh, good. Thank you . . ." It came out breathless, her heart swelling with not only relief, but a sense that he was like a treasure chest to be explored. And now? Sara knew they'd have the time to do just that. Well, at least she would! She wasn't able to pick up on whether he felt a kinship with her or not. Time would tell.

Chapter Three

April 6

"This is your half brother," Sheriff Dan Seabert told Sara and Wes, handing them photos from a thick file in front of him. They were in his office.

Wes passed the photo to Sara, who, he swore, was growing pale. Her gold skin looked washed out as she stared down at Manny. She dropped it on Dan's desk, rubbing her hands against her dark brown slacks, frowning, not making eye contact with it. He, on the other hand, burned the twenty-five-year-old's face into his memory. "Looks like a hippie out of the nineteen sixties," he told Dan.

"Yeah, this kid—according to your boss, who gave me this file—doesn't brush his teeth, comb his hair, hates taking a shower, and wears his clothes for as long as his mother will let him get away with it."

"He's always hated being clean," Sara muttered, "ever since he was born. According to my father, Leo, he would scream his head off as a baby when his mother, Victoria, would wash him daily."

"Weird," Dan agreed, giving her a sympathetic look.

There was a knock on the door and it opened. It was Steve Carter.

"Sorry I'm late," he told them, pulling up a third chair next to Wes and nodding to Sara.

"We just started," Dan said. "Get yourself a cup of coffee and we'll get going on this briefing."

Steve set his computer laptop bag aside, got up and poured himself a mug of black coffee and sat down. "Let's do this."

Dan handed him the photos. "These are yours, but this is where we're at in our briefing."

"Roger that." He opened his laptop, typing quickly, and putting it on share with Wes and Dan's laptops. "Sara," he said, giving her a look, "what can you tell us about your half brother? I know you covered all of this with me months ago, but I think your assessment, which is critical, will help Wes and Dan understand your half brother a lot better. Are you up to this?"

She clasped her hands in her lap. "Yes . . ." she began, her attention more on Wes, who didn't know her half brother at all except what Steve had typed in, making a bio on him for law enforcement and her bodyguard. "I wasn't a constant in Manny's life. The older he got, the more he 'teased' me, but it was done on purpose and his aim was to hurt me."

"Like what?" Wes asked her quietly. "Could you give me examples?"

Quirking her mouth, she said, "As a baby . . . one year old, it was as if he knew I was his competition and enemy even then. He would pinch me, over and over again, leaving black and blue marks on my arm or neck." She touched her face. "When he was two years old, he'd scratch my face, neck and arms."

"He saw you instinctively as a competitor for your

father's attention?" Wes surmised, feeling bad for Sara because he could hear the pain in her husky whisper and in her eyes.

"Yes . . . it seemed, from the time he was born. I've never seen another child do that to someone."

Steve cleared his throat. "I have a staff psychiatrist, Sara. If you need some help on understanding people like Manny, we can set up an appointment for you to talk with Dr. Judy Gallagher. You'll like her. She was in the Marine Corps as an officer, saw combat via black ops units, got PTSD, and is the right person to talk with. She's an extraordinary human being and I think she can open the lens on your half brother. Matter of fact? It wouldn't hurt if Wes goes with you or separately, whatever you want. He needs to get the underpinnings of Manny, too."

"Yes," Sara murmured, "I'd like that." She gave Wes a glance. "And I'm fine if we do it together."

"Great," Steve said, typing it into his laptop and sending off a secure, encrypted email message back to his office staff. "Done. You'll get a call from one of my schedulers later today as to time and date."

"Was Manny a troublemaker in school?" Wes asked Sara.

"I never went to school with him, but I do know, via my mother, that he was *always* in trouble with anyone who was 'in charge' at the school. He ran with a white nationalist boy gang. They kept their name and what they were, pretty much hidden. It was the first 'gang' that he ended up running. And getting into more trouble."

"Some people," Steve said, "are just plain born mean."

"Evil," Sara corrected him. "My father never laid a hand on me or Manny. Whatever is wrong with my half brother, looks to be genetic."

"And your father's ties to the Cosa Nostra go back four generations over in Sicily," Steve said. "We call people like that 'bad seeds,' and it's like a miasma, a disease that runs through the DNA of the family."

"Well," she sighed, "it missed me. I'm so much like my mother's side of the family and so unlike my father's side. One side is of the light, the heart. The other side, dark, evil, and heartless."

"We're glad," Dan said, "you're on our side," and he gave her a kind look.

"Makes two of us," Sara said passionately. "I can't stand to be anywhere near Manny. I'm very sensitive to people and their energy," she said, opening her hands, "and when I'd been forced to be around him earlier in my life, I always felt like someone had poured garbage all over me. It was an awful feeling."

"Your mother knew," Steve said. "She got you and her out of the marriage and family ASAP."

"My mother is very astute. The divorce occurred because when my father was arrested by the FBI, years ago, it was the first time she knew of his 'other' life as a godfather in the Cosa Nostra. He lied to her. She thought he was the owner of a software company that was successful. He never told her about his 'other' illegal business."

"It had to be a terrible shock to her," Wes said, seeing pain once more in her gaze. He wanted to put his arm around her, protect her, and try to remove the anxiety he saw. The stress of this meeting was clearly etched in the way the corners of her soft mouth pursed inward.

"More for my mother than me," she offered. "But as I grew up, and I had to legally fulfill visitation rights with my father, I began to slowly see what she saw. Manny was always aggressive and antagonistic when my mother dropped me off for the visitation. She kept her worry to herself, but I could feel how much she didn't want me to go to the estate."

"This went on until you were eighteen?" Dan guessed.

Nodding, Sara said, "Frankly, I learned when I had to visit, to go to my old bedroom, lock the door, and only open it when the maid brought me lunch. Manny used to throw a basketball against the door just to scare me. I never knew when he might do it. I kept a pair of earphones on, watched my laptop and tried not to be so frightened. I always feared, as he grew older, taller, and stronger, that he'd break the door down and kill me. It was just a sense or a feeling. He never threatened me vocally, but I could see the murder in his eyes toward me. I was fine hiding for eight hours in my bedroom. As I grew older, I brought homework with me, or projects for the day. I wasn't bored and it was the safest place I knew of in the house."

"Did your father ever see you?" Wes wondered.

"No. He was always at his office. By the time the weekly visitation hour, four p.m., rolled around, my mother picked me up and I was free of Manny."

Dan gave Wes and Steve a dark look. "Terrible way to have to grow up."

Both men nodded, saying nothing, but it was written clearly in their expressions, a mixture of disgust for the half brother and sympathy for Sara.

"I survived," Sara said firmly. "My mother runs her organic soap company business, and I love what I do. I want to alleviate people's suffering, not add to it like Manny and my father do."

"Well spoken," Steve praised. For the next hour, they went over every bit of intel on Sara's father and her half brother. At the end of it, Steve said to all of them, "Sara has agreed to work with Wes. I'm going to trigger other necessary contract documents starting when I get back to the office." He reached into his briefcase and took out some papers, handing one to Wes and Sara. "This is the contract, Sara, between us and you. You've made it clear that Wes is someone you can work with and we're all happy about that."

She smiled tentatively. "I think Mr. Paxton and I will get along well," she affirmed. "I'll read through this contract and get it back to you tomorrow."

"Sounds good," Steve said, pleased.

Wes stuck his copy of the contract into his briefcase sitting against the chair leg.

"On my part," Dan said, "I'm going to have a photo of your half brother given to every law enforcement agency in my county. I'm involving other agencies outside my county, too, just in case."

"That's good to know," Sara said, standing and smoothing down her slacks. "Now I can get on with my life."

Wes stood and picked up his briefcase after sliding his laptop back into it. He nodded to Steve, who was doing the same, and shook hands across Dan's desk. Sara also extended her hand to Dan, thanking him for his help.

Outside, the sun was shining, nearly ten a.m. Wes looked around, scanning, as he always did out of habit. Sara walked at his side, a few feet between them. It was chilly, and she wore a gray, black, and white wool cape over her shoulders, the ends of it around her knees. Today her hair was in one long braid that hung between her shoulder blades. He opened the door to his truck for her and stepped aside.

"You're *such* a throwback," she said, grinning and climbing in.

"Sometimes, things from another era are still in vogue," he informed her, meeting her grin with one of his own, closing the door for her.

Once in the cab, he drove toward the center of town, toward her beautiful and colorful Victorian three-story house. Glad that her home was off Main Street, a block away, made him breathe a little easier. The town was awake and there was plenty of morning traffic.

"Do you like your bedroom in the house?" she wondered.

"Sure," he said. "What I like most are all the antiques in it. Makes me feel like I've time-warped back to 1900."

"I love that house," she murmured, looking out the window at the colorful buildings that reminded her of Easter eggs. "I love antiques, too."

"Hmmm, something we have in common."

"I'd like something else in common with you," she began. "Are you okay with calling me Sara and I can call you Wes? Are bodyguards okay with that?"

Sliding a glance in her direction, he slowed mid-town and turned into a side street. "Sure. I'd like that. No sense on standed on protocols. We're going to be working together and living in the same house. Makes sense to me." Actually, he was relieved that another wall she'd silently placed between them was now being removed. After hearing how Manny tortured her emotionally, mentally, and physically? He now understood why she was gun-shy of men in general, that her world was one of hiding and not being seen. Now he could appreciate her more, and also it helped him to understand the way she lived her life.

"Good," she murmured.

They turned into the concrete driveway. He always

drove down to the end of it where the wall of lilac bushes began.

"Why do you do that?" she wondered, climbing out.

"What?"

"Park so far away from the street. That's a long way to back out."

He shut his door and came around after routinely checking out the area, to where she stood near the passenger door. Already, he'd trained her to wait for him and not take off without him. They both had a set of keys for the front door. "Because it's safer," he said, walking with her on the redbrick sidewalk that led up to the huge wraparound porch. There was a porch swing in bad need of a good sanding and repainting. Maybe he could fix that for her. Wes didn't ask himself why he wanted to do helpful little things for Sara. The more he knew about her personal growing-up years with her father and brother, the more he felt deeply for her. He'd never had a family, and she had. But in some ways, hers was worse than his was, in his opinion. Somewhere along the line, he always thought having a family was a wonderful, loving experience. He knew better, of course, as he matured. Now, Wes was quietly reassessing how he saw having a family versus not having one. He could have been unlucky like her: born into a rat's nest of lies, intrigue, confusion, with a half brother who wanted to kill her.

Unlocking the door, he went inside first, stopped in the foyer and looked around, his sight, hearing, and sense of smell online. Finding nothing out of place, he stepped aside, allowing her to come in. The red and gold carpet runner in the foyer, along with a beautiful mahogany sideboard, plus the overhead light, made him once more think he was in another world.

Sara waited patiently for him to close and lock the door. He then turned and led the way down the long hallway paneled in part with mahogany and the rest in a flowery wallpaper. He'd investigated every nook and cranny in the old Victorian home, found a hidden room and escape route in the library, where one wall opened up to reveal its whereabouts.

"Where to now?" he asked.

"I want to get into my comfy shoes, my apron, and go out to the office and work. Are you ready to start Herbs 101 today?" She smiled up at him.

That was the first real, warm smile she'd shared with him, and it felt fortifying and damned good as it flowed through him like bright sunlight. The way her eyes sparkled split through the dark, intense world he lived within. "Okay, let's get to it. I'm all ears and eyes."

It felt as if another barrier, a serious one, had suddenly dissolved between them. Wes walked ahead of her to her second-floor bedroom, and then opened and searched behind each door and examined the rest of the room. This was how it was going to be, and if she was frustrated by it, there was no sign of it. "I'm going to go through the rest of the house," he told her. "Lock the door behind you. I'll knock once and let you know I'm back. You open it up so I can see you're in there and okay." He pointed to the door. "We need to get a two-way peephole so you can look through it and see who is outside of the room."

"It's on my to-do list," she promised, following him up the curve of mahogany stairs. "And getting in touch with the alarm company Steve had asked me to contact."

"A lot of safety has to be built into this home," he agreed, cresting the stairs and looking down the hallway. There were two bedrooms and his was across the way from hers. Not wanting to ruin the uplifting mood Sara was in, he held back on a lot of other questions he had for her that had not been discussed at the sheriff's office. Right now, Wes wanted her to be happy because as he read her expression, it was lighter, her skin color had returned to normal, and he felt girlish energy around her, like a child having fun on a playground. His heart hungrily absorbed it, like the starved beggar he was discovering within him.

With the PTSD, he hadn't been interested in relationships at all. He was hiding, he realized, just like Sara had hidden in her bedroom from Manny for more than a decade. Both were wounded. Both were trying to appear normal when there was no such thing. He didn't know about Sara. Did she have nightmares like he did? Wishing he had a more intimate friendship with her, that would have to wait and he'd see if it developed or not. His heart, however, wanted to dive right in, which surprised the hell out of him. Was it possible that he wanted to actually start living again? Not be cooped up in an apartment when not working? Having no friends, no outside activities? It was shocking to him to think that it was happening. Patience, which was a key player in his life, had taught him that time would reveal what he wanted to know—and not on his schedule, but hers.

As they approached the herb facility behind the Victorian home, he took the lead, now on full scan. If Sara was upset with this new procedure to her life, she didn't show it. Opening the door, he went inside while she waited in the retail area. It took ten minutes to clear the large building. There were plenty of places for a killer to hide, and he made damn sure no one was anywhere in the vicinity. He'd given her a fob that had a red, green, and yellow light on it. Red meant someone was in the building. Yellow meant something wasn't right and he was going to investigate further. Green meant no one was around and to go ahead with whatever was on her agenda today. He pressed the green button after double-checking the door and hangar latch.

As he ambled up toward the front, he saw a woman carrying a baby, her expression strained, walking swiftly toward the door. The store opened at ten a.m. and he didn't see Sara anywhere, figuring she was probably donning her daily uniform of either a white lab coat over her civilian attire or that canvas apron of hers. There was a dressing room in back and he skirted her desk, opening the door.

"Hi," the woman said, "who are you? Where's Sara? I really need to see her about my baby."

"I'm Wes Paxton, her employee. Come on in. I think she's in back. I'll go get her." He gestured to the alcove where the upholstered chairs and small table were set. "Have a seat," he invited.

"Thanks," she whispered, moving toward the alcove.

Wes almost ran into Sara on his way to the dressing room. She had her apron on, her long hair tied up into a thick knot at the back of her neck. He told her about the woman and baby.

"Okay. Why don't you sit behind my desk in the meantime? You can hear our conversation and eavesdrop."

"Sure," he murmured, moving aside.

Wes made his way around her U-shaped desk and sat down. He wanted to look like he was doing something instead of staring at the stressed woman and crying baby.

Grabbing a notebook and pen, he opened it, beginning to take notes and also keeping an eye on the sidewalk outside the store, as well.

"Oh, Sara! Jody has been crying nonstop!"

Sara sat down and eased the six-month-old Jody from her arms. "Is she eating?" she asked, kissing the baby's red, wrinkled brow, setting her across her lap and opening up the blanket, gently moving her hands across the pink onesie.

"She's got a good appetite, but she just screams after eating the last three days. I can't get any sleep. No matter what I do, she's wailing. I'm so afraid . . . I can't figure out what's wrong with her . . ."

Giving Elizabeth, the mother, a sympathetic look, she hoisted Jody across her shoulder, patting her gently but firmly in the small of the back. "Let's see if this works?"

Abruptly, Jody let out the biggest, noisiest burp, and her mother's eyes widened enormously as another burp followed, a little less explosive than the first. Sara began to gently run her palm up and down the baby's back. Jody stopped crying.

"Looks like it might be colic," she told the mother. "Do you burp her after eating?"

"Always . . . but watching you? I don't think I was doing it right."

Turning Jody over, she handed her back to her mother. "Something else might be going on here. Are you on a store-bought formula?"

"Yes," she muttered, shaking her head. "I should have breast fed her, but I work . . ."

"I understand," Sara whispered. "It could be that the formula is causing a lot of gas in Jody's digestive system."

"What do I do, then?" she pleaded, holding her daughter,

who was now very sleepy and happy to be held and rocked in her arms.

"We have to experiment," Sara said. "Mama's Store has fresh goat's milk for moms just like you. Some babies are allergic or have an upset digestive reaction to cow's milk and/or formula like she's on right now. The only way to be sure is to switch to goat's milk and see. The goat's milk, which is wonderful, is far more compatible with a baby."

"But does it cost a lot?"

"Mary, who runs the store, will give you a huge break in price based upon your monthly salary. She wants moms to use goat's milk."

"I know she works with Tracy and Tom, who own a huge goat farm outside of Silver Creek."

"Yes, and they provide Mary daily with fresh goat's milk for moms who want to use it instead of cow's milk."

Elizabeth's face softened, her daughter asleep. "Oh, this is so good, Sara. She's quiet."

"There was a lot of gas in her tummy and that's what was causing the discomfort," she said, reaching out, squeezing Elizabeth's arm.

"I'm going to drive over right now and get some goat's milk."

Sara stood up and reached for a tincture. "I want you to give her a drop on her tongue if she starts crying again like that. This is chamomile and it's in a food-grade glycerin, and will taste yummy to Jody. It will start getting rid of that gas in her digestive system."

Elizabeth gave her a sorrowful look. "I'm plumb out of cash. Can I—"

Slipping the small amber eye-dropper bottle into her hand, Sara whispered, "Just take it. You're sleep deprived. Go get the goat's milk and be sure to see Mary first, in the back, in her office, and she'll make sure you pay very little for the goat's milk. Okay?" Sara smiled gently down at the twenty-two-year-old mother.

"But . . . I can reimburse you when I get paid next week, Sara. I don't expect you to give us handouts."

"No worries. Consider it a gift from me to you, okay? You and Jody need a couple of good nights' sleep. Will you let me know if the goat's milk is more to Jody's liking?"

Standing and pulling the blanket across her daughter, snug in the crook of her right arm, Elizabeth said, "I promise, I will." She leaned forward, giving Sara a quick, hard hug. "Thank you," she whispered, her voice wobbly. "I didn't know who to go to, Sara. I can't afford a doctor." She blinked several times, trying to stop the tears watering in her eyes.

Sara placed her arm around Elizabeth's waist. "I understand," she whispered. "Did you know that Dr. Blaine Cooper, the naturopath, is taking on new patients? She has a sliding scale, so you won't have to pay much because she wants her services to be affordable for everyone."

Elizabeth brightened. "I've only been here six months, since having Jody, so I don't know everyone here in town."

"Let me help you, then." She released her and went to her desk. Wes handed her a white business card. Turning, she slipped the card into the pocket of Elizabeth's hoodie. "That's Dr. Cooper's phone number. She's got a nice practice of pediatrics, too, so I think you and Jody will fit right in. Do see her when you can?"

"I will," Elizabeth promised, giving Sara another hug.

Opening the door, Sara said, "Stay in touch . . ."

After Elizabeth left, Sara turned, feeling Wes's intense

stare on her back. "It's going to be like this every day," she warned him.

"There's a lot of people without enough money to last more than a month," he said, sadness in his tone. "You really helped her in a lot more ways than maybe she realizes."

Sara sat down in the chair against the wall behind her desk. Wes turned in his and met her gaze. "My mother's company makes a whole line of baby lotions, salves, and glycerin tinctures like chamomile for colic."

"You don't make them yourself, here?"

"No, I'm way too busy to do that kind of work. I have to keep up with Dr. Cooper's prescriptions and formularies, plus my time in the lab, dealing with retail customers, and the three days when I do examinations on people who want an herbal remedy instead of something stronger, like pharmaceutical and prescription medicine."

"And because of all your medical training, you know when an herb might be the right call versus something stronger?"

"So far," she murmured. "I'm glad to have Dr. Cooper here. We have a really great working relationship. Her major was in herbology, so when we get together, we talk 'herbalese' with one another."

"And leave poor uneducated people like me not knowing what you're saying."

Her eyes sparkled. "Well, toward that end? Providing we don't get anyone for about half an hour, let's go to the library section. There's some books you need to read. It will help you immensely when I drop into herbalese."

He smiled a little. "I'm open to whatever you think I need to read and in what order."

"Are you always so easy?" she teased, laughing a little.

"No, but I'd like to think I know when I'm in the presence of a master and figure I need to listen and not talk."

"Well, I don't know about a master, Wes. I learn something new every single day. Herbs are just as complex as traditional pharmacy and their medicines."

"When I was in Afghanistan, where we were stationed in the Sandbox, there was an old Afghan grandmother, Farzaneh, which means 'a wise woman,' that I got along with really well. She was the 'doctor' of her village of a hundred and fifty men, women, and children. I know enough Dari, one of the main languages spoken in that country, and I spent a lot of my time in the village helping her out, but also learning a *lot* about the herbs and formulas she mixed up for her people." He gave her a wry glance. "She was a virtual encyclopedia on the herbs in her valley. I used to go with her in the spring and summer when she needed to gather particular herbs for her medicines. I liked going because she pooh-poohed the Taliban, and felt she was safe out in the wilds, but I didn't want her out there alone. I always carried my rifle and was in constant radio contact with my base if anything happened."

"She was a very brave woman," Sara said, giving him a tilted-head look. "Did you write down any of what her medicines were for, or how they helped a human being?"

"Naw . . . now I wish I had, because I saw her every year. She used to tell me what they were, what they were good for, and stories about her village people trusting her and using them. I guess that's why I was a little excited about being given this mission with you. In some ways, just watching you a few minutes ago, you behaved just like that elder did. Just going into her hut, you immediately felt her love and care. It was real and it was palpable to everyone. She was always babysitting babies and younger children, and she constantly had a bunch of them around her, in her lap, laughing and playing."

"She must have been a breath of fresh air to you? The job you held in black ops was taking out bad guys."

"Yeah," he murmured, sitting back in the chair, holding her gaze, "I liked going over there, visiting her, bringing her special things that she always gave away to mothers, children, and babies. She wanted nothing for herself, content with the way she lived."

"What did you bring her?" Sara wondered, drawn into his story.

Shrugging, he said, "Well, I got her medical supplies, at first because the villagers didn't have gauze, tape, antibiotics, needles, syringes or dressings. She needed them, too. I kept her supplied while I was stationed there."

"Did you help her as a SEAL medical person?"

"Yes, we'd hold clinics two times a month. I could usually get another SEAL to work with me, or sometimes we had a civilian dentist or eye doctor in the area, and he would come over and help, too."

"Farzaneh must have been very grateful to you, Wes."

"She was, but she reminded me of a grandmother I never had, and she was the perfect person in my life to be that for me. I spent five years in that area and she was a gift to me because I got to see how much she loved, kissed, cuddled, and held the children."

Frowning, she said, "You didn't have grandparents?"

Wes hesitated and then said to hell with it and told her briefly that he was abandoned at birth. Instantly, Sara's face fell and he felt the full warmth of her compassion embracing him. He wasn't sure what to do because he was fairly sure she wasn't even aware of that tsunami of caring sympathy she exuded toward him. Already, he'd seen it with Elizabeth and her baby, Jody. The moment Jody was in Sara's arms, she stopped screaming, her tiny voice falling to whimpers; as if realizing this incredible, almost magical being of a woman would take care of her, keep her safe and take away her suffering and pain. The gold in her eyes emphasized that as she stared in shock at him and his admission. Never had a woman affected him so deeply and intensely as Sara did. Giving himself an internal shake, Wes muttered, "Look, this is a world of suffering as far as I'm concerned. There aren't many happy endings. From my perspective, there is nothing but pain down here. The key is living with it, but not letting it run your life."

She sat back, fingers lacing in her lap. "And yet, look at you. I admit I know very little about you, really, but you've come through a lot of challenges and you seem the better for it. You don't lack compassion or empathy for others from what I can see."

Grimacing, Wes wanted the spotlight off him, unable to deal with the depth of care he felt coming from her to him. "Well, I'd like to swing this conversation to some notes I wrote."

"Sure."

"What is food-grade glycerin?"

"In herbology, we use it because 'food grade' means that humans can eat it without it harming them. There's a number of other levels of glycerin that are not."

"Good to know." He checked it off, lifting his head, a quick scan through the windows and sidewalk, and back to his other question. "I was impressed with your conversation with Elizabeth, giving her good intel, guidance, and instructions."

She smiled a little. "Anyone who's been to a medical doctor gets ten or fifteen minutes with him or her. That's not always enough time. When I have my clinic"—she pointed toward the lab area where she had her office—"they get thirty minutes. Sometimes, forty-five. Or, I'll set up a second appointment on another day, to finish what was started. I have my client take a very detailed account of their symptoms—or of the person or child who needs help. That information is given back to me a week ahead of their actual appointment."

"That way you have the time to read up on the intel and be ready for them at their appointed time."

"You're good," she teased, grinning. "Yes, exactly. Based upon their past and present symptoms and issues, I've already sketched out possible primary herbs and secondary ones to resolve their issue or symptoms, for best results."

"Don't you need a real office assistant?" he asked.

"You're it, Wes."

"I'll be making appointments and stuff?"

"Don't whine. It doesn't become you."

His lips twitched. "You'd be a good instructor for the SEAL team training center."

It was her turn to grin. "Somehow? I don't think this is beyond your scope to do. I don't know you that well, yet, but from what I can see? I silently refer to you as Superman." She beamed at him.

Chapter Four

April 10

Manny hated these Monday missives from his father, who sat in Rikers Island in New York state. Just because his father was in prison didn't mean he was helpless. Far from it. For the last five years, Leo Romano had built a "team" of criminals inside the prison to do his bidding. Literally, he was the "boss" inside Rikers.

He was kingpin now, and so Manny had to take his marching orders. His father was in for fifteen years. At twenty-five years old, Manny liked the freedom to indulge his whims because the network with his father's soldiers was still intact. He was the CEO and ran their software company, and it was worth a billion dollars. He hated being in an office, even though it was in a skyscraper in downtown Dallas, Texas. He'd much rather be out in the wilds of the land in his ATVs with his rich friends of his own age.

Sullenly, he opened the handwritten note as he leaned back in the black leather chair behind his desk. He hated Mondays. He hated Sara and her mother, Tsula. It rubbed him raw to know her mother had a super-successful soap and cosmetic business that continued to expand here in Dallas. He'd like to order his soldiers to blow the whole damn building up and her, along with it. But his father said no. Manny didn't understand his decision. Tsula had divorced him, and that is what made him grit his teeth. The prenup gave everything, once Leo died, to her daughter, Sara, and nothing for him. Nothing. There was no way to change this and no court would go along with the change. It was a done deal. How he hated those two women.

There was another problem Manny was grappling with, and not having the success he wanted in overcoming it. His father's nemesis was a Russian Mafia kingpin, Ivan Bobrov, who was constantly challenging the territory his father had created. Little by little, Bobrov and his goons were doing more than encroaching. They were boldly taking over neighborhoods that gave his father's empire monthly money. And there had been plenty of battles between the soldiers, and loss of life. Leo was constantly barking at him on their cell phone calls, to meet Bobrov head-on and start taking back the neighborhoods he'd stolen from Leo. He wanted a war.

Grudgingly reading the note, it said, *Give me an update on the soldiers sent to find Sara. I know she's hiding somewhere and I'm hoping it's in Texas. She and Tsula are tighter than fleas on a dog's back. Find out what's going on. If we can't find Sara? Get some hackers on it, break into Tsula's company, find any evidence that she's using some kind of device talking with her daughter. That way, we'll find her. If you don't? You don't get anything after I'm gone.*

Anger sizzled within him and he clenched his right fist momentarily and then relaxed it. *Dammit!*

Pushing his shoulder-length black hair off one shoulder, dressed in ATV riding gear, including some very cool-looking Italian handmade black leather boots that came to just below his knees, he shook his head. His father, for whatever his reasons, wanted Sara kidnapped, taken overseas and put into a permanent exile. Why didn't he just put a bullet through her head, instead? That's what Manny wanted to do. And put a second bullet in her mother's head. Get rid of both of them. But Leo didn't want them killed. He just wanted them permanently out of the way, and he did not want his daughter to die.

Looking down at the note, it was his father's usual laundry list for the software company, which was doing well and remained on the legal side of federal and state laws. He knew some good hackers, outside his company, black hats, who he'd pay well to sneak inside Tsula's company hardware and find out where the hell Sara was at. His company had always been a front for their drug and money-laundering business. He'd put out the orders and they would get it done.

Sitting up, he jammed the note into his tight leather pocket. Somewhere out beyond Dallas, at one of his favorite spots to race his juiced-up ATVs, he'd burn it so no trace was left for the Feds. Victoria, his mother, wanted him home for dinner tonight. That might or might not happen. He'd much rather spend his time with his friends. Besides, he hated her whining. It drove him crazy. She played the victim, spending thousands of dollars every week at posh fashion stores on gowns for parties at their home. He'd rather spend it on the fastest ATVs his mechanics could create.

There were several new and exciting ATV racing events he wanted to attend. There was one in Colorado, another in Montana, and the last one, in Wyoming. He spent most of his time touring with his ATV crew, his mechanics and team members. On one wall of shelves, he had ample proof that his ATVs were the fastest, the most tested, and had taken the brutal punishment from the wild lands they raced upon, and come out champions, time and again. Winning never got boring.

These three new events he'd earmarked because all of them were wildland tracks and he wanted to test his ATVs against unique and unknown challenges. That excited him. The winter snow had to melt and release its grip on these states, all of the events taking place in June and July. He liked the mountains and was looking forward to the time away from his boring software business. Anything to get away from this stuffy skyscraper and out into clear, pure air.

Pulling the door to his office open, the staff of three women all raised their heads from their desks simultaneously. All blondes. He liked blond-haired women. "I'm leaving for the day," he told Mandy, the one nearest to the office, the head assistant. "Get Jason if something comes up." He smiled to himself. Jason was forty years old and the CFO, Chief Financial Officer. He was the guy who was the glue of their company. He was reliable and had made this company what it was today.

As he went down the elevator to the garage, where his limo and driver waited for him, he wanted to think about how to find Sara. Tsula was easy: She was here, in Dallas, running her company daily. Maybe he should put a detective on the mother. He'd get black hats to hack her system and try to find out through emails, Zoom, or some other internet communications, if she was talking with Sara.

Tsula was always flying in and out of the airport for business meetings to other states, and even to Mexico and

Canada, where she was increasing her presence in those countries with her company's products. Had Tsula sent Sara to one of these countries as her emissary?

As he stepped out of the elevator, his bag in hand, which contained his helmet, gloves, and electronic gear, he decided to change up how things were being done. Find Sara and his worries were half over. Then, he'd have Tsula killed in what would look like an accident of some sort. Free from them, Leo could rewrite his will because with both of them dead, the prenup had no hold on Manny's getting the billion dollars, finally.

April 11

It was clinic day for Sara. Over the past few days, Wes was getting into the rhythm of her life, all the while continuing to stay alert for any warnings that she was in danger. He sat at her U-shaped desk, the appointments on the computer screen. She spent half an hour with every patient. Any orders for prescribed herbs, or a tincture, salve, ointment, or lotion, were sent to Wes and he had to locate and package them, and take the person's insurance information afterward. He was learning to be an office pogue. Some clients were sent for an appointment with Dr. Cooper, the naturopathic doctor. Others, who were medically beyond the ND's licensing expertise, he handed them business cards and they would contact the doctors themselves.

Glancing at his watch, it was four p.m. The day had gone smoothly, but there was always an intensity to people who were not well. They all looked to Sara for help to relieve their symptoms or pain.

Her last patient of the day arrived, an older man, Harry

Carr. He was in his eighties, flyaway white hair, and he sat in the alcove, sipping hot rose hip tea and reading a magazine, waiting his turn. At five p.m., the clinic closed. Wes found himself hungry to have some personal time with Sara. She was constantly fielding phone calls from other patients before and after the clinic, as well as every other day. He was amazed at how she handled the demands, the urgency, or panic of her patients with a low, quiet voice, never telling them to make an appointment, unless absolutely necessary. The soothing tone of her voice tamed him, too. He didn't know how she did it. A lot of women were ace multitaskers and that was something Wes had to learn as an operator; doing many things simultaneously, and not missing a beat. His skills were trained in. Her juggling capabilities were genetic.

She liked her job, but Wes wouldn't necessarily frame it as that specific word. Sara loved helping people, relieving their suffering, and seeing them get better. The big surprise was how herbs filled an empty space between wellness and getting so sick that they had to be seen by a doctor. When he wasn't busy scheduling appointments, answering the phone, and chatting with the patients coming and going, he continued to focus on boning up on herbology. He had his latest book at his elbow, along with notes and questions that he'd ask Sara later, once they were closed for the day.

April 12

"It looks like you're getting into the swing of things," Sara complimented Wes as he locked the door and set the alarm system for the building's premises. The afternoon was chilly and it had rained half a day. She had hung up her white clinic coat back in the office and wore a bright green wool shawl around her shoulders, to ward off the high humidity and chill.

"Getting the hang of it," he agreed, walking on her right side, slightly ahead of her as they went to the back door of the Victorian home. In a minute, they were inside where it was warm, leaving the chill of the spring weather behind.

"Everyone seems to like you," she said, loosening the shawl as she followed him down the hall. "They asked me why you never smile."

He glanced at her sideways, keeping his attention on the first floor of the home. "Did it bother them?"

"No . . . a couple of them, all women, wondered why you looked so sad. I told them I didn't know." She halted at the end of the passageway, allowing him to do his thing. She didn't expect an answer from him because there was a feeling of focused intensity settling around him as he moved silently away from her and disappeared. It would take him about seven minutes to "clear" her home. Sara would be glad when this was over. When could she go home to visit her mother? Not soon, Steve had warned her.

In this first week, she'd become attached to having Wes around. It was easy to relax in his presence. He was a good listener, didn't interrupt her when she was speaking, and always had some wise or practical answer to her questions. She ached to talk with her mother, and they'd agreed that once a week, they would buy burner phones and speak to one another. There were times when she just wanted to pick up the phone and talk with her, but she couldn't. Missing Tsula was real, and she lightly touched the area of her heart, feeling the ache and loss of connection with her. Damn her father and his son, Manny.

"All clear," Wes said, poking his head around the corner of the banister after coming down from the second and third floors.

"Good, because I'm starving!" she said, moving toward her bedroom down another hall on the first floor. Over her shoulder, she said, "Are you going vegan tonight with me, Wes?"

"I'll try it," he said warily, walking behind her. Their bedrooms were opposite one another.

"It won't kill you," she teased, slipping into her room. "See you in a little bit . . ."

Wes knew she would take a quick, very warm shower, change clothes, get into a pair of comfy slacks, her tennis shoes, and a warm sweater. April in Wyoming was still cold, and freezing was normal at night, even here in Silver Creek, which had what everyone called a micro climate. He was glad they didn't get hammered with outrageous temperatures or alien-like snowfalls that occurred elsewhere.

There wasn't much for him to do, so he went to the kitchen and set the rectangular mahogany table for them. By the time he was done, she was in the kitchen, beginning to make their dinner. He knew she liked a light herb tea, such as red hibiscus flower petals, and made her a pot of it. Actually, it tasted pretty good and he found himself drinking it through dinner instead of his normal cup of coffee.

"Can you handle vegetarian chili?" she called over to him as she entered the kitchen later, grinning mischievously in his direction as he finished setting the table.

"Absolutely. It sounds good, Sara." He liked the way her name rolled off his tongue; it was musical and it held such warmth and promise. He tried not to absorb how pretty she was to him. The soft, fleecy pink trousers along with a red turtleneck sweater complemented her gold skin and black hair. "What else can I do?"

"Make us a small salad?" she said, pointing toward the refrigerator.

Wes nodded. "Anything in particular?"

"No, I trust you."

"Good to know." He smiled a little, opening the door and picking out several veggies from the crisper. He set them on the counter near where she was working over the stove. "I'm sure your patients trust you."

"Absolutely, they do." Her smile broadened. "They also like and trust you, too."

"They don't know me."

"I don't believe you have to know every tiny detail about a person to know whether or not they can be trusted or liked. It's a nice compliment," she said, stirring in pinto beans. The scent of onion, a bit of garlic, and cumin mingled in the kitchen and she inhaled it, her stomach growling.

Getting all the salad fixings laid out on the kitchen counter in an orderly row, he said, "You had quite an interesting group of people come in today."

"Young, old, and in-between," she agreed.

He pulled down two bowls, shredding the red lettuce into them. "I didn't know what to expect. I guess I didn't realize how many people believe in herbs."

"You don't have to 'believe' in herbs to let them work on your behalf," she said drolly, stirring the diced tomatoes into the skillet. Reaching over, she put a second iron skillet on the gas stove and pulled out a package of pre-made tortillas from the fridge.

"That's kind of hopeful to me," he said, chopping up carrots next. "There isn't a complete reliance on prescription drugs like I thought."

"My mother and I wrote a book on how herbs are rightfully thought of first, before those drugs. It was a bestseller. She writes a weekly blog on our website about how a particular herb can be helpful to people."

He sliced some radishes into the salad. "I like what you do. So many people can't afford drugs in the US anymore. If I go to Europe? They're cheap. But here, it's highway robbery."

"Exactly," she said, putting the lid on the chili to let it simmer for a while after putting chunks of tofu in it, stirring it into the tangy, spicy mixture. Taking the tortillas, she put one in the skillet, warmed it, and then set it on an awaiting plate with a white linen napkin over it.

Finishing up the salads, he took the bowls to the table. "Do I look sad to you?"

She smiled a little, stirring the chili. "That's because I know a little of your past. Maybe if you try to smile a little bit, they won't see you as sad." She finished warming the tortillas and handed him the plate to take to the table.

"I need to work on that. I don't want them feeling sorry for me."

"Just remember, a smile from you makes *them* feel better and they are usually not feeling too perky when they come in to see us."

"That's a good point," he agreed. Pulling back the chairs, Wes placed a trivet in the center of the table for the large black skillet she was cooking with. She had said "us" and not "me." For whatever reason, that made Wes feel good. "I'll work on it."

Twenty minutes later, she called, "Dinner's on," and placed the pot of chili on the trivet in the center of the kitchen table. "Let's eat! I'm hungry!"

Wes pulled out her chair for her and she thanked him, sitting down. He brought over the warm plate of tortillas. They sat opposite one another at the table, the chili between them, the air filled with mouthwatering herbs and spice scents. "I shouldn't be this hungry. All I did was sit at a desk today."

Laughing, she opened the dark green linen napkin and settled it across her lap. "Oh, you did a *lot*! I'm sure this kind of job is rather tame for you? Becoming a sous chef?"

He took her bowl and spooned some of the steaming chili into it. "If you compare my time as a SEAL, when we were always in backcountry, yes, it seems rather tame in comparison."

"Do you miss that kind of work, Wes?"

"Not really. I was getting to the end of my abilities physically. I called it quits at the right time." He filled his bowl with the chili.

She passed him the tortillas. "These go great with the chili. Texas style."

He took two. "Smells great. Good and spicy, the way I like it. Thanks for making it."

"Oh," she said, spooning into her bowl, "you're going to get your turn at cooking around here, too. I won't be at the stove every night."

"I'm weak on vegan recipes."

"You can read. I can choose what I'd like to eat and you can basically make two different meals for us the nights you cook if you don't want vegan."

"You live dangerously, Ms. Sara."

Laughing heartily, Sara said, "Remember? Everything is equal between us. I'm going to hire a very nice woman, Daphne, who has a little girl, Lily. The tyke is one year old, and her mother is going to become our housekeeper. I hate housework, and this way, she'll make enough monthly to leave the women's shelter and have an apartment and life once more."

"Not going to hire a cook, then?" He gave her a hopeful look.

"Not a chance. Our housekeeper will be here for a few hours a day and then leave."

"We'll need to run her name through law enforcement," he said.

"Yes, that's fine. You can always let her in and she can tell us when she leaves and you can lock the house up afterward."

"Now you're thinking in security terms," he praised.

"I don't like to," she said, "but I'm grateful for it right now." Her brows moved down and she stared at Wes. "Do you really think they'll find me?"

"I don't know," he said. "All we can do is prepare for it and stay alert. I worry about your mother, too, because she's in your half brother's backyard. You said she had security protection."

"My mother isn't going to let anyone push her around. She's got her company in Dallas, and she's not leaving. I wish"—she sighed—"that this was just a bad dream I'm having. Never did I think a half sibling would turn on, and want to kill, another member of the same family."

"History shows this has happened many times before," he said, giving her a sad look.

"I know, I know." She spooned another bite of chili. "I

try to forget it, but I can't. Manny stalked me in earnest anytime I had to be over at my father's home to fulfill visitation rights. He thought it was funny to be hiding somewhere and scare the wits out of me, or jumping me from behind, or hiding in my closet in my bedroom. All sorts of horrible, ongoing stuff."

"I know his kind," was all Wes would say. "They have a mean streak in them, but really? It's about power over someone else. Controlling them."

"Exactly." She hesitated and then admitted, "I would really love to do more than just go from my herb store to the house."

"What else would you like to do?"

"The herbs won't even start growing until probably late May around here, but I'd love to go visit Dana Gallagher's Wildflower Ranch. She and her husband, Colin, are raising a lot of medicinal herbs that are compatible with this area, for Mary's grocery store in town. She's invited me to come out and I'd love to do that and see her list of herbs. Can we?"

"Sure, not a problem. I think it's good you get fresh air, sunshine, and some exercise."

"I sit a lot," she griped, smiling wryly, finishing off her chili. "I'd also like to visit Lea Anderson. She's the wife of Logan Anderson, who owns the largest ranch here in the valley. He's been moving his cattle ranch into a more environmental footing, and he also has acreage for growing medicinal herbs, too. I'd like to get to know them better and see if they'll give me the list of herbs they're harvesting."

"You might as well know what's available and growing locally," he agreed.

"And I do love to forage for herbs, by the way." She

smiled wistfully. "Living in Dallas, my mother and I had to rely on herb suppliers for the most part, but here, because of the climate and altitude, there's lots of herbs that might be available to forage, which we can check out if we get permission from the owners."

"Dana and Lea may well know of the wildcrafting herbs growing here. You're after them, too?"

"Yes. I much prefer to gather locally, if possible. I'm crossing my fingers." She put the dinnerware aside, folding her hands on the placemat. "Do you mind doing these types of things?"

"No. I like learning."

"I really got lucky with you," she teased, grinning.

"I was talking with Steve yesterday and he was concerned about how we were getting along. I assured him we are compatible, and that made him very happy."

"He was very apologetic about sending Werner. For me, having you here is like a blessing of sorts. You have a good background in medicine and an understanding of pharmacy."

"Up to a point," he said, finishing off his bowl of chili and wiping his mouth with the linen napkin. "But I'm learning more every day. I lay in bed at night reading the next book you recommended."

"You're a voracious reader, Wes."

"Picked it up as a SEAL. We were *always* reading something."

"And I bet you had to memorize a lot of things?"

"Yes, just like you do when you're reading monographs on herbs. Same thing. Only this time, these plants can support good health."

"I hope you don't think I'm being too personal, but

could you tell me more about your growing-up years?" She saw him look away for a moment, his jaw clench, and then relax, as his gaze moved back to hers.

"It's not something I usually talk about, Sara, but with you, I guess I find it easier to do."

"We have a nice trust building between us, Wes."

Nodding, he said, "No question." He launched into his sordid family tale, making it as brief and emotionally sterile as possible. It was Sara's expression that gave him the courage to open up a little more. He knew how compassionate a person she was, watching her with her clients and those who came in the retail side of the store. Liking that she would reach out and touch a person's arm or shoulder, he'd seen the person's face relax, knowing that help of some kind was on the way. He spent more time telling her the whole story than he'd anticipated.

"And yet," Sara said quietly, holding his sad gaze, "you've turned out so well. I don't know what I'd do if I didn't know where I came from, who my parents are. It must drive a deep hole into your soul?"

His mouth quirked. "Good way of putting it. I literally feel like I have a hole in my heart and it's bottomless. But I've had that since I could remember."

"Didn't Tom and his family, who took you in, help heal you a little?"

Nodding, he said, "I consider Tom my father, if you want the truth. We're close, to this day. When I can, I spend the holidays with them, either Thanksgiving or Christmas. It means a lot to me . . ."

"And Tom was a SEAL, too, and he urged you to go into the Navy?"

"Yes, but he also said it was important for me to find a secondary career in something that interested me, while I was in the military. That's why I applied for Army Special Forces medical training. I've always been interested in that kind of thing."

"Why did you do that?" she wondered, resting her chin on her folded hands.

Shrugging, he managed a sour smile. "I don't know. Sometimes I wonder about that myself: Was one of my parents a doctor? A nurse? Somehow tied to the medical field? I have questions that I know I'll never get the answers to. That's the hard part, but I'm glad I took the training. It's useful no matter what I do with my life. I can possibly save a life, and that makes me feel good."

"I understand that," she murmured. "I feel good every time I can alleviate someone's suffering or pain."

"There's plenty of that to go around down here on this earth," he muttered, shaking his head. "A planet at war, where violence is everywhere."

"Is that how you see the world?"

"Yes. And no, I'm not depressed." He saw her look bemused. "My experiences growing up, until Tom and his family entered my life, justified that, Sara. Not all people are good people. There's evil out there."

"And yet, to counterbalance that? There's goodness, kindness, sympathy, and support from others, too. Don't you think it's a glass half full instead of half empty?"

"In my line of work? No. But in your life, with the exception of what's happening with Manny, who is evil, you've been on the good side, the positive one."

"Do you always want to be a contractor?"

"It's what I know and what I'm good at."

"Have you ever thought of becoming a nurse practitioner, a physician's assistant or, hey, going to medical school to become a doctor?"

"I've thought about it. But I'm thirty years old. I don't want to spend eight or ten years to become an MD. With my background in medicine the way it is, I know I could work at a hospital, but that's not where my heart is."

"Where is your heart?" she whispered.

He hesitated, giving her a grin. "Now I see why your clients love you so much: You have this unerring focus on who they really are and you put them in touch with it."

"Excellent analysis," she praised. "It comes naturally. If someone is sick there's a reason for it, and usually it's emotional or mental in nature. I learned through my grandmother and mother that finding that locked-up part of a person is the key to helping them, and it also frees the person of whatever burdens they are carrying. By doing that? The sickness that has appeared, begins to dissolve over time. Healing takes many forms."

"You're a key, all right," he said, looking away, allowing her deep wisdom to sink into him.

Silence settled between them.

"Well?" Sara prodded.

He rubbed his chin and then folded his hands. "I guess . . . I haven't really asked that question of myself." And then he added, "Maybe I was afraid of the answer."

"What about as a child? What did you dream of being or becoming? What did you love to do?"

"Oh . . . well, that was easy. I would climb a tree and be happy sitting on a limb, with my back against the trunk, watching the leaves dance and move."

"What else?"

"Being alone, letting my imagination take me to happy places. I guess I always looked for a way to get out of the foster house I was at, escape into the backyard, or go someplace where I was alone and out in nature. Climbing trees, lying with my back on the ground, watching the clouds go by . . . birds flying . . . anything that took me out of the hell of being forced to live with a family where all I was seen as was a monthly check coming in."

Nodding, Sara asked, "Nature was healing to you?"

"I guess you could say that. It was quiet, there was no screaming, shouting, getting hit or bullied. When Tom took me in, it was as if he understood I needed to be out in Nature because I always found a peace I couldn't find anywhere else."

"And with him having Native American blood in him? Did he take you out of the city and on the land?"

"All the time. He made it a habit that he and I would go on a hike at least once a week. Being in a large city, he knew where there were what he called nature spots, and that's where we'd go."

"And did it help you?"

"Yeah, I slowly got rid of that chip on my shoulder, my anger really reduced, plus he helped me see how to use anger constructively, not as a weapon to hurt myself or others."

"Tom is your guardian angel," Sara said, her voice low with feeling. "What a wonderful person he is. I would love to meet him someday."

"I feel the same way about him, Sara. He saved my soul and I know it. He gave me love for the first time in my life and I felt starved for it." And a secret part of him wanted her to meet Tom. He saw a lot of her attributes were also in Tom. He withheld what he thought, but the feelings were palpable within him.

"Love really is the answer for all of us."

"Tom is . . . well . . . even to this day, I will call him up, tell him what's eating at me and he'll always have some wise experience to share with me, and I'll digest it. Tom never forced any of his ideas or opinions on me. He always told me a story and out of it, I found it easy to make my decision."

"That's the way of our people," Sara said. "Our stories are handed down from so long ago, but they are just as important today as they were back then. My mother always told me stories growing up. She would read to me every night before bedtime. I always looked forward to those times with her because there were no interruptions, it was just the two of us."

"Tom became like that for me in the same way, although he never read to me at bedtime. I always had to go back to the foster family, but it was easy to do it since I went to school, hung around with him, ate with his family, studied at night in a spare room he had, and then, around dark, I'd bike back to my foster home."

"He gave you a safe place. What a wonderful, caring person he is. He used analogies, stories, as examples that you could understand and absorb into yourself. He left it up to you what to do with your new discoveries about yourself." She sighed, giving him a soft look. "What a wonderful role model he is to other men in families, on how to help lost children like yourself."

"I was lost all right. He found me. Much of what he showed me was from time as a SEAL, and he mixed in his Native American knowledge and training, too. That's why I went into the SEALs. I figured it would help make me a little like him, and I wanted to be that person." For a moment, he saw tears in Sara's eyes, but she blinked them away, giving him a watery smile that made his heart yearn for more times just like this one with her. "In a way," he admitted hesitantly, "you are helping me, too, whether you know it or not."

"Humans learn from one another, Wes. I'm learning from you, too. I come from another universe compared to the one you live in." She laughed a little.

"In a way," he said, nodding, "that's true. But learning and picking up good habits from other people is what I've always tried to do because I knew, in my early twenties, just how badly damaged I was emotionally. Tom taught me, like you do, that goodness abounds out there in the world right along with the evil. Before meeting him, I saw the world in pretty dark colors. I trusted no one. I always thought everyone had an angle and wanted to use me, not love me. I didn't know what love was until Tom and his family embraced me."

"But his family showed you the flip side of that darkness: light, love, and caring."

"Yes, they did," he said. Putting his plate aside, he added, "With you? I feel like I've evolved up another step in my learning and healing process, and you're in my life to teach me more of what I need to know so I can replace the coal in my sock, with light, instead." He was shocked how much he wanted to reveal to her about himself. It seemed natural, good, and it made him feel warm and safe. She was only the second person in his life besides Tom, to make him feel like that. Wes decided Sara had magic. And a huge, huge, wonderful, caring heart that she was able to effortlessly share with others. He almost said she was like sunlight to the darkness still living within him, intuitively understanding that the more he was around her, the more she would disperse that darkness and allow the light—perhaps even happiness, if he dared think that—to filter into his life.

She studied him and whispered, "I love that you want to learn. You see where your wounds are and I feel like you're always hunting for ways to heal them up instead of letting them bleed you dry."

"Spoken like a medic," he teased, lightening their conversation. "Stop the bleeding."

Chapter Five

April 15

Wes could see the excitement in Sara's face as they climbed out of his truck at the Wildflower Ranch parking area. Dana Gallagher stood on the sundeck of their double-wide mobile home, waving hello to them. Her husband, Colin, stood beside her, a friendly, welcoming smile on his face.

Wes had not met either of them before, but had gotten a thorough briefing about them from Steve. Liking the fact that Dana's husband of six months was an ex–Army Ranger, Wes felt an immediate connection with the tall, lean man with black hair, blue eyes, and wearing a black Stetson. It was chilly but sunny on the mid-April day as he automatically cased the place and then walked near Sara, through the gravel to the redbrick sidewalk that led up to the stairs to the sundeck.

Dana had long red hair, and it was loose and shining in the ten a.m. Sunday morning sunlight. Her eyes were large and green, her smile sincere as she walked with her husband to meet them. Wes slowed and allowed Sara to move in front of him as introductions were made. Eventually, he shook

Colin's calloused hand, and he pointed to the super-cab truck parked in the gravel driveway.

"Let's go climb in," Colin invited. "We're going to take you to the fifty acres we planted last year, and Dana can hardly wait to see all the plants start to peek above ground." He gave his wife a teasing look.

Dana handed each of them a spiral-ringed notebook with a pen. "You'll need these, and inside each one Colin drew a really nice map of what herbs have been planted and where they're at and how many rows there are for each of them."

"Plus," Colin told them as he led them to the super cab, "Dana has made a list of all the herbs by their well-known names as well as their Latin names."

"That's great!" Sara said, holding the notebook as if she'd been handed a bar of eighteen-carat gold.

"Climb in," Colin offered.

"Us girls are going to sit in back," Dana suggested. "The boys will probably want to talk about football, and I can really zero in and give you the information I think you're looking for, Sara."

The men traded glances, grinned sheepishly, and opened the doors for the women.

Once underway, Sara gazed hungrily through the statistics and information that Dana had meticulously compiled. "Oh, my," she said to her, "there's enough foraging of herbs here for more than just Mary's grocery store."

"Right," Dana said with a nod. "Mary has helped another family here in Silver Creek Valley set up a manufacturing plant where the herbs can be dehydrated, kept in a darkened and enclosed area, and then powdered and put into capsules. From there, they are bottled and labeled with Mary's store name, Mama's Store, and sold in her health food department. Eventually, she plans to have distribution to the larger cities in Wyoming, and then continue to branch out regionally."

"Mary is amazing," Sara agreed. "I've had tea with her and Cari at her home on her son's ranch, the Wild Goose, and she's just an incredible person who has magic."

"Well, she certainly helped me." Dana pointed to her husband who was driving slowly down a long, graveled road toward the hills in the distance. "Chase and Mary had Colin come over and help me get this place fixed up. That's how I met him."

Colin grinned and winked at her.

Dana smiled widely and patted his shoulder. "Without his help, the Wildflower Ranch I'd bought would not look as wonderful as it is becoming."

"You're a well matched pair," Wes said. "I noticed you're building a pretty large log cabin home on the other side of the road, opposite where you have the mobile home?"

"Yes," Dana said eagerly. "It's going to be one story, two thousand square feet, four bedrooms, and two full baths. Mary is working with a local logging company that is hand selecting, with the help of the Forest Service, certain trees. No clear cutting here!"

"That's good," Wes said.

"When will you be ready to move in?" Sara asked.

Colin laughed. "Well, with the April rains, and the place turned muddy, it's slowed down our time line. We figure that mid-June, it will be ready, the weather gods being nice to us and all."

"We're so excited!" Dana said.

Sara smiled with her. "We're all so lucky to live in this valley."

"Truly," Dana said, becoming somber. She pointed out

the front window of the truck. "There, on the left, about half a mile up, are the herb fields."

"Have any of them sprouted yet?" Sara asked.

Shaking her head, Dana said, "No, but in early May, as the soil starts to get warmer, they will pop. It's killing me. I'm so anxious to see how what we planted in the fall will grow this year."

"They will all grow," Colin reassured her. "Such a worry-wart."

Sara grinned over at Dana. "Wes said I'm a worrier, too, so you have good company."

The women gave one another buddy looks.

Pulling off the road, Colin parked the super cab and they climbed out.

Wes remained with Sara near his shoulder and he looked around the bowl-like area where the hills rose quickly and steeply to the north side of the ranchland. Below those hills were fifty acres of rich, dark soil that had been given a cover crop that would keep the heat of the earth around the seeds, protecting them from the cold winter. It would become, over time, a cover mulch and it contained nutrition for the herbs that would grow out of it in two or three weeks. Colin had unrolled a large schematic across the hood of the vehicle, which laid out the planted rows.

For the next hour, Sara was trained on the fields. Wes divided his time between looking casually around from time to time, and paying attention to Dana and Colin's information on the herbs.

By eleven a.m., they were done. Dana invited them to stay, have lunch with them, and Wes looked to Sara, who eagerly nodded yes to the invite. Over lunch, Colin filled Wes in on a white nationalist group that had been living across the highway from the ranch. He recounted what had happened. Although Wes had been filled in by the sheriff, Colin's details were important. Lunch was served, Sara and Dana both vegan, and he and Colin, meat eaters.

"Are they still out and about in this area?" Wes asked, wiping his mouth with a paper napkin.

"Not anymore. It got pretty much broken up last year. Since then, no one's seen any groups of men living up in that area." Colin finished off his roast beef sandwich and dove into the bowl of potato chips.

"The Forest Service is hosting a huge ATV championship race in that same area this summer," Dana added. "They've made a course and kept it environmentally safe for the surrounding forest and mountains. There's also a huge parking lot and other accommodations, as well. It's nothing like it was when I'd been kidnapped by those racist jerks last year."

Colin frowned. "That was a scary time," he told them.

"It was, but you rescued me," Dana said, giving him a loving look of admiration. She finished her peanut butter and lettuce sandwich, choosing some chips from the bowl.

"Well, you kinda rescued yourself and I found you later, by accident."

"Out here," Dana told Sara, "you had better have a pioneer can-do spirit to survive."

"I have it," Sara said seriously. She drank her warm red hibiscus tea that somehow, Dana had found out about. That endeared her to Sara. She was a person who cared about others and it spoke well of her in every way.

"Well, being Native American," Dana said admiringly, "and raised part-time by your family on the Eastern Cherokee reservation, has probably given you a lot of knowledge and know-how that even we could use now."

"I'd be happy to share when we can both find some time to do it," Sara said, smiling.

After lunch, they moved to the living room where there was a U-shaped davenport system along with three large coffee tables. Sara got out a list of herbs she needed for her clinic and store, handing them to Dana, who sat next to her.

"We have all of these," Dana assured her.

"Do you mind if Wes and I come over and forage and pick our own? I'd like to take them back to my office where we can make oil decoctions, tinctures, and lotions with them."

"No, not at all," Dana said, thrilled. "I hope I can come over and pick up some tips on how to do this myself?"

"Sure, you're more than welcome. I'm hoping to start beginning classes on herbs by late summer."

Eyes wide with happiness, Dana said, "Where do I sign up?"

"I'll put your name down. There's two other people, both women, who want to learn, also. There may be more who will want to sign up."

Rubbing her hands together, Dana said, "That's wonderful! You come out here anytime you want to forage. We have so much of each herb that whatever you buy from us, isn't going to cut into what Mary needs for her grocery store or her manufacturing facility."

"That's good to know. I'd also like to start fanning out and walking the land, and find out what is growing wild around here, too. Have you done any of that research, yet?"

"I did some of that last fall," Dana told her. She dug into her folder and gave her another handout. "I'm compiling a list of the herbs I found as I make these hikes with Colin.

I also take photos of each herb and where I find them. I have GPS coordinates on all of them."

"What I don't want to do," Sara said, "is over forage an area. I'd like to do a long-term kind of grid study of a specific area, see how much of a particular herb is there, and whether it can be foraged or should just be left to continue to spread and create more plants through natural means."

"We're in agreement," Dana said eagerly.

"There's a lot to do," Sara said, "but for me? I love to do this. I can get out of my clinic and store, and into the fresh air and sunshine."

"I think that applies to all of us," Wes said, remembering to smile a little. It wouldn't hurt him to try Sara's suggestion. Tom would sometimes remind him that a frown was a smile turned upside down. She was putting him more in touch with the depth of himself, a place he'd not wanted to go very often; but the way she saw the world, lived her life, inspired a part of him to give it another go. Wes saw Sara brighten instantly because he'd smiled. That made him feel good.

May 24

A thrill went through Manny as he leaned back in his black leather chair at the software office. His hackers, after a lot of sleuthing, had finally broken into Tsula's company. The report gave him exactly what he wanted, background on Sara's pursuits. Sara was in Silver Creek, Wyoming, of all places. His booted feet up on his desk, he smiled a little, rapidly reading the rest of the report. She had bought a house, thanks to her mother. Lived in town. Had a clinic converted out of a horse-and-buggy barn. She was doing the same things she'd done here in Dallas with the help of her mother's money: a clinic and an herb retail store.

Rubbing his bristly jaw, he looked up at the ceiling, the eastern morning sunlight streaming in a set of windows behind him. There were decisions to be made. What now? And who?

If his father got wind of his stealth in tracking down his nemesis, and his mission to kill her, Manny was sure he'd want to stop it. A part of him, the aggressor, wanted to see her in person, capture her, confront her, and then murder her. But his father wouldn't stand for that. And Manny didn't want Leo coming down on him, removing him from his software company and possibly getting rid of him. His father was a cold-blooded murderer who gave orders to his soldiers to take out, very carefully, anyone who didn't play by his rules. In the old days, a mob boss could get away with killings. But not now. Leo was smart enough to use other levers of his power to get an individual to either pay up, support his aims, or else. Dead bodies were not Leo's main menu item any more.

Well, it was on Manny's menu, that was for sure. First, out of curiosity, he wanted to see Sara for himself. He'd hire a detective and security agency who could easily send someone who was trained in such things, to Silver Creek, to suss out details on Sara. But he wanted to do it himself. He hated her. He wanted to see her suffer. Every time she had come over for visitation for a weekend, she was nothing but trouble. And he was on a short leash because Leo did not want his son to be hauled before some judge and get in trouble because he'd assaulted Sara. As badly as Manny wanted to do that as a boy growing up, he withheld his fist and rage at the strong, in-your-face Sara, because he wanted to be in his father's good graces. And in his own way, Leo had made time for Sara. Leo and Sara had nothing in common, and as Sara grew older and realized to her horror that Leo was a mob boss, she wanted absolutely nothing to do with him. But Leo forced Tsula to bring her daughter over, and even spend some holidays.

How Manny had hated Christmas or Thanksgiving! Every year, it was the same: Sara sullen, not talking, forcing herself to eat a meal at the family table. Leo went out of his way to try and engage her, but Sara refused to have any conversations with him. And he was happy she was acting like the sullen bitch that she was. At age eighteen, Sara's being forced to have visitation with her father, was finished. Not to ever see her again in his father's home had made Manny very happy. From then on, he could wage a silent war for his father's attention, and try to find a legal way to get out of that prenup Leo had signed with Tsula. To no avail.

He crossed his ankles, the report in his lap as he stared off into space. That was why both women had to go. Manny was fine with killing them. It left him all of Leo's holdings and money. Frankly, he didn't want to be a mob boss, or even learn how to be one. This software company was so popular, making a billion dollars a year, he had no need to put a toe into the illegal activities Leo had grown up with and led all his life.

His mind ranged over possibilities. Both women were herbalists. Why couldn't he put a deadly drug in the tea they drank? Or in one of those tincture bottles they always had on hand. But it had to be a poison that could not be detected by today's science. That would take some footwork to acquire. Manny knew such a drug was out there, but he hadn't made a serious effort to nail it down. Or? Capture Sara and take her to Timbuktu, never able to again step foot in the country of her birth? She would become "lost" to the world who knew about her, but that didn't bother him at all. The website she had, would be taken down. Her name would be erased as best his hackers could do, to make her disappear permanently off the web.

Tsula was another matter. He'd have to be very careful how he got rid of her. And Manny was thinking along the lines of killing her and disposing of her body so that she'd never be found. He didn't care what happened to her booming, very rich and successful company. Sara should be the first to disappear. That would drive Tsula mad with anxiety and fear for her daughter. No one would ever find her. She'd have no way to get back to the USA. And then he could deal with Tsula once and for all.

Or? Should he hire some of his father's men to find her and kill her in the mountains surrounding that valley where she lived? That might be even a better idea. Rubbing his jaw, he stared up at the ceiling. Which plan should he choose? Which one was most convenient? Bury her body somewhere in the mountains, never to be found? Or, kidnap her, send her over to a third-world country and ensure she could never return stateside?

June 15

"Look at this flower meadow!" Sara said, awed by the oval shape of it, the fir and pine trees surrounding it. There was blue lupine, green and white blossoms of the green gentian, fuchsia-colored sticky geranium, yellow heartleaf arnica, and dainty pink shooting stars. It made the meadow look like a rainbow! She saw Wes smile, and yes, he was sincerely trying to not look so stern and dour. Her clients loved the change in him and reacted in kind. She was seeing him open up like a shy flower, one petal at a time, but all good.

He was carrying a backpack, like she did, and Sara didn't ask what was in it, but suspected medical emergency supplies, a pistol and extra ammo. He always carried two quarts of water on the outside pockets. The backpack she wore contained four sandwiches, chips, cookies she'd baked yesterday, as well as two quarts of water. Plus, she always brought along a small Canon camera that she would use to take photos of anything she foraged or located today and would put them into her massive computer files on such herbs when they got home.

He halted beside her, checking out the surrounding tree line for anything that looked out of place. It was a warm June day, in the high sixties, the sky a dark, almost blinding blue. He took off his sunglasses, appreciating the myriad flowers waving among the different grasses in the meadow. "Looks really beautiful."

She breathed in the five-thousand-foot elevation air, smiling and closing her eyes as she lifted her face to the warmth of the sun. "I'm so glad Dana gave us coordinates for this meadow. I'd have never found it." She opened her eyes, smiling up at him. "And of course, I knew you would since you're the GPS wizard."

Chuckling, he slid the sunglasses above the bill of his baseball cap. "It was pretty easy. Rough road to follow, one that the Forest Service hasn't kept up for a long time." Half the time there was barely a road, obviously rarely used by anyone, except the Forest Service when necessary. "I get the feeling this is a fire road more than anything else. This isn't a tourist area and it never showed up on any trail maps."

"But your truck has high clearance, four-wheel drive, so you made it look easy."

Glancing at his watch, he said, "Took us an hour of climbing to get up to it from the main highway. Do you think it was worth it?"

She moved the strap of her canvas foraging bag to one shoulder so it fit diagonally across her body. "I think it will be. Dana gave me what herbs she could find here last fall. Of course, different herbs come up and bloom anywhere from early spring to late fall." She pulled a spiral notebook and pen from the bag. "That's why I brought this along. I want to write everything down, take photos, and then scour the whole meadow to see how much of a known herb is here. And we should make it a routine this year of coming up here every month, because different flowers and bushes will be in bloom until late fall."

"That makes sense. What if there's not enough of an herb that you ID in this meadow?"

"We note it, give an approximate number, and leave it to continue to seed and propagate," she said. "The Native Americans never devastated an area of an herb. They picked only so much and left the rest to continue to grow and reseed. That way, they always had a continuous supply."

"I like that you don't take any if there's not enough left to seed the next generation."

"Yes. Most herbalists are very sensitive to this, and what they'll do instead is order from an herb supplier who deals with eco-friendly farmers who grow and sell them." She pulled on a pair of gardening gloves. "Why don't you follow me around and I'll show you what I do and then I'll cut you loose and assign you a part of the meadow to research?"

"Wouldn't have it any other way," he replied, pulling out

a notebook from the pocket of his dark brown canvas shirt, along with a pen.

"What I'd like to do is just survey this meadow. I would ask myself: How many of each color flower do I see after I've identified them? Are any of them herbs that we use? Then, I'll go after the most plentiful one. For example"— she raised her hand, pointing at a nearby yellow flowered plant—"this meadow is filled with heartleaf arnica. That is a very important herb for us."

"In what way?" he asked.

"Arnica is made into a salve after being picked and put in an oil for at least a month to draw out its medical nutrients. Once the flowers are strained off, the infused oil is left. We never use this herb on broken skin, or on people who have rashes or skin abrasions, because it can cause irritation. Arnica oil has been around for centuries. For example, during World War One, the soldiers who cared for the mules and horses who pulled their heavy equipment and cannons, would routinely rub arnica oil into the pasterns and knee joints of the animals at night. This herb has a wonderful ability to pull out swelling in an area of the body, no matter whether human or animal, and it allows a much better blood flow into the spot, so it can heal. If you reduce swelling in an area? You automatically lower the pain and increase the healing."

"One of my brothers on our SEAL team was a horseman. He always had arnica oil in an unbreakable thermos that he carried with him."

Her eyes widened. "Oh . . . tell me more?"

"Funny coincidence," Wes said, seeing the excitement in her eyes. "I spent five years with him out in the field with our SEAL team, and his arnica oil was used by everyone. We'd always get our knees beat up, as well as our ankles. They'd ache and burn. He'd pass the arnica thermos around and we'd rub the oil into whatever hurt. In about fifteen minutes, everything felt better, looser, and there was a whole lot less pain."

"That's amazing! He was a SEAL using an herb! What did your boss think of it?"

"Not much. He didn't care what we put on our joints so long as it didn't smell and the enemy could catch a scent of it and target us as a result."

She leaned down, one knee on the earth, cupping the delicate yellow flower. "In my notebook I'll put it down as *Arnica cordifolia*. But most people, they'll either call this arnica or heartleaf arnica." She looked around. "I think we can safely forage it here in this huge, mile-long meadow. There looks to be enough, but we have to grid out the meadow and count the plants in each section to be really sure."

"Show me how you do that," Wes urged. "I've never picked an herb before."

Grinning, she produced a pair of garden snips from her forage bag. "I gave you a pair of gloves before we left. The oil of arnica, if it gets into any little cut around your fingernail or finger, can make it burn like fire. It can also infect you, because arnica carries a bacteria that we don't need inside our body. That's why it can only be used on unbroken skin, never used as a tincture or decoction, except as an oil. We'll collect enough to make about a half a gallon of arnica by collecting just the flower heads. I utilize it as an oil, and as a cream and ointment, also. Arnica is good, as you saw, for knee pain or aches, ankle pain, but also muscle aches of any kind, sprains, strains, bruises, swelling."

"And I want the gloves on why?"

"The juice, when you snip off the head of the flower,

below the receptacle or the flower itself, will leak out into your skin. Before snipping, I look the flower over, to make sure it's in full, glorious bloom, healthy looking, and that there are no bugs or other things on it."

"And if there is?"

"Shake them off," she said, laughing. "I always look carefully at the flower before I touch it. Some caterpillars are poisonous, or there might be an ant that will bite you, or a honeybee nearby who might want to take her pollen. When you do snip off the flower? I always tell the plant thank you. You can say it in your head to the plant, or out loud."

"I can just imagine a stranger walking by and hearing us talking to them," Wes said drolly, one corner of his mouth lifting in a smile.

"I grew up that way, Wes. I spent summer vacations at my grandmother Adsila's home on the reservation in Cherokee, North Carolina. I loved it. My mom would drop in about every three or four weeks for a couple of days for a visit. Those days were the most wonderful time in my life."

He watched as she knelt into the grass, closely examining at least thirty or forty arnica plants around her. The meadow looked like multicolored jewels, the colors of the flowers stunning to him. The sun felt good on his back as he slowly ranged his gaze around the entire oval area. He wanted to devote personal attention to Sara, who was busily snipping off the heads and dropping them into her forage bag.

He knelt down nearby, watching her gloved hands fly with almost ballerina grace as she collected the flowers. "Tell me why being with your grandmother was the best?"

"Well, she lived deep in a valley, the Smoky Mountains

surrounding her old log cabin. That cabin had been in her family for generations, and is at least a hundred years old. Her husband, my grandfather, died at forty-five in an auto accident off the reservation. She loved him so much that she never remarried. I love her deeply to this day, and she lived off the land and is a vegetarian. She said it hurt her heart if she would ever kill any animal in order to eat it. I loved staying with her throughout the summer because she taught me how to live off the land." She smiled fondly, pointing to another plant nearby. "You see this one, Wes? This is chickweed. People consider it a weed, but to Grandma, it was one of the most nutritious, edible plants we have. She would put it into her soups, stews, and made a wonderful salad with it."

"Where did she get protein?" he wondered, thinking that he'd have no energy without eating meat.

"Nuts have fat and protein. Where she lives, she has a huge grove of black walnut trees. One of my favorite times was to fly back there with my mom in the fall, and we'd pick up the black walnuts that fell from the trees. Grandma would have at least a fifty-gallon can where they were stored in a nearby shed until the outer skin dried up. We'd fly back for Thanksgiving and we'd hull all of them." She laughed and held up her gloved hands. "The juice of the black walnut hulls will stain your skin yellow for a long time to come, so we always used gloves to dig the meat out of the shells."

"Sounds like a Garden of Eden," Wes admitted, touching the low-lying chickweed, studying it with a frown. "This was a salad?"

"It truly is. I really miss not seeing my mom this year, with what's going on. My whole life has suddenly upended and I feel like I'm on the run, in a way. I can't go home, be with my mother or help her with her company. I had to close up my clinic, and that tore me up because I don't see the people who came for help as patients. They became friends." She sat up, giving him a sad look. "And I can't visit my grandmother because I don't want to involve her if Manny is sending out a Mafia soldier to kill me. They'd kill her, too."

His heart swelled with powerful emotion as he saw tears come to her wide, guileless eyes. "Is it possible Manny is full of hot air? The real leader of the Cosa Nostra is your father and he's in prison."

"No, Manny is that bad. I never thought," she whispered, resting her hands on her thighs, "that a baby was born evil. But I've changed my mind about that. My mother calls it a miasm, a dark stain of a disease, like alcoholism, heart problems or diabetes, or a murderous nature, or someone unable to control their anger, that winds its way through a family, generation after generation. Manny was born and he was always hurting others, whether it was an insect, the dog, or other kids, growing up. My father seemed pleased with his behavior. I hated it. Later, when I got older, I realized my father was 'grooming' him to take over the mob after he died. It's such a cruel world they live in."

Nodding, he reached out, briefly touching her slumped shoulder, bothered by how sad she'd become. "Maybe I should stop thinking I was so unlucky not to have parents."

She lifted her chin, meeting his gaze. "It's a 'be careful what you wish for' kind of thing, I've come to realize."

"Was your father like Manny?" he asked, wanting to keep his hand on her shoulder but knowing it was trespassing. Still, her eyes had softened when he'd briefly touched her. Wes was beginning to wish he wasn't her bodyguard for a lot of selfish, personal reasons.

She continued to pick the arnica blossoms. "He has a hair-trigger temper. It always scared me, and I can remember when I was very young, how frightened and threatened I felt. He wasn't angry at me, but my mother and he would get into hellacious arguments. She is a strong woman, matriarchal, and she refuses to back down to someone like him, or any man who disrespects women in general."

"When did your mother divorce him?"

"I was very young. But to be honest, I was glad to leave him and that house."

"But you still had to fulfill visitation rights and be with him, and later, Manny?"

"Yes, through age eighteen." She sighed, pushing her gloves against her jeans. "As I got older, more mature, I knew how to avoid Manny. Luckily, that old Victorian house had hidey-holes he still doesn't know about, so I could give him the slip, count the hours, and then meet my mom out front when it was time to leave."

"That wasn't a fun childhood," he agreed quietly, shaking his head.

"I survived it," she said, giving him a slight smile, moving her hand around in the foraging bag, seeing how many more blossoms she needed.

Wes stood up, making a sweep of the area as he held out his hand to her. She took it, and he savored the contact, however brief it was. "Where to now?"

She shrugged out of her backpack and brought out a fairly large paper bag. "I want to collect some of the chickweed."

"Why wouldn't you use a plastic bag for it?"

"Because it doesn't breathe." She held up the paper sack and said, "This bag will breathe and help the plants stay fresher until I can get them home."

He followed her, watching how she carefully collected the low-growing chickweed and placed it in the sack. "Where to next?"

"See that Oregon grape along the edge of the meadow over there?" She straightened and pointed across it to near the tree line.

"Yes."

"I need to replenish my supply of Oregon grape roots. Won't take long, and I don't need much."

It was a good half mile walk across the expanse to the bushy, shiny leaves and yellow flowers amongst them. Wes wished they weren't out in the open, and being unfamiliar with the area made him even more on guard than usual. "Okay, let's go," he said. Sara was a fast walker, but she would stop, lean down, peer through the many types of grass, looking for other herbs. He curbed his impatience.

Something caught his immediate attention: The birds that had been singing had suddenly grown quiet. It was a sign that a predator was in the area. And in his business, that could mean a two-legged human, instead of a hawk or eagle or four-legged animal.

There was a crawling sensation up his spine. Instantly, Wes went on full guard. What the hell! His mind whirled with possibilities. Rubbing the back of his neck, he slowly turned around, peering intently at the edges of the meadow.

Nothing. There *was* something, and he knew it. Danger was screaming at him. He trotted up toward Sara, who had walked far ahead of him at her fast gait. The grove of Oregon grape was at least ten to fifteen feet high and strung out with bright yellow flowers that resembled small gold candles in the dark green, shiny leaves. Looking like an eight-hundred-foot-long wall, it hid the thick woods not far from it.

Catching up to her, he gripped her left arm at the elbow. "I want you to walk faster. Don't stop. We need to make it to that grove ahead."

She looked up at him, shaken. "What . . . what is it?"

Mouth thinning, he felt himself going on full internal alert, the kind of alert a SEAL had that could save their lives. "I don't know, Sara. Just do as I ask?"

She gave a jerky nod, stretching her stride to keep up with him.

Wes saw the confusion and then the fear come to her large, widening eyes. He wished he didn't have to scare her like this, but it was important to reach that grove. It could give them cover.

Cover from what, he didn't know. Someone, more than one person, was following them. He could taste it now, the urgency drumming through him like a thunderstorm letting loose. His gut tightened. His eyes narrowed. They were being stalked. The sudden bitterness coating his mouth was the taste of dying.

Chapter Six

Wes tightened his grip on Sara's arm as they closed the distance to the grove. He felt her fear rising, saw it in the set of her mouth, the stiffening of her spine as she pushed through the knee-high grass.

His mind spun with scenarios. Was this her half brother's assassins after her? Sending his father's Mafia soldiers to do his bidding? Or maybe some other tourists?

Their truck was a mile away, parked on a barely discernible rutted road, most of it washed away by winter rains. This was not an area that people routinely hiked. Dana and Colin had given him directions to the road, and he'd gone to the Forest Service and gotten a map of this little-used or -known area of the mountains. It had been a fire road, to be used only if a forest fire was in the area. There were no trails built by the USFS around here. It was completely wild and left to Nature, not to humans. They were out in the middle of nowhere.

He'd already checked his cell phone and there was no coverage. Twenty miles away from this spot was the main highway. He was keenly aware of the lack of communication and help. They were dependent upon their own knowledge of survival.

He had to protect Sara. He'd been able, so far, to separate business from anything intimate or personal with Sara.

Until now.

He heard a *THUNK* from the left. Shock slammed into him.

Cursing, he jerked his head in the same direction as the foreign noise. There was a rocket-propelled grenade coming their way!

Stunned by the military weapon being fired at them, he yanked Sara to a halt.

"*DOWN!*" he yelled, shoving her headlong into the grass.

Would it hit them? He knew the explosive power of such a shoulder-held device. As Sara hit the ground with an *oomph*, he threw himself on top of her, his larger body flattening and fully covering hers. Within less than a second, a massive explosion occurred behind them. The earth convulsed. It moved upward. Fire and smoke belched outward. Rocks and dirt vomited toward the sky, then rained down upon them. Wes tried to shield Sara completely from the blast. But the worst of it was the violent, disruptive pressure wave, which could literally tear a man apart if he was standing too close to where the grenade had landed.

Hot air, flames, and dirt rolled over them. Wes buried his face next to Sara's, breathing through his mouth, praying that she too, had her mouth open. As the pressure wave hit them with stunning force, he grunted, feeling like a thousand fists were beating up his head, back, and legs. Pain was instantaneous. Eyes tightly shut, breathing harshly, he held on to Sara, who sobbed out of fear. Holding her down, because he had no idea of what was to come next, he kept her protected.

Another *THUNK!*

Wes couldn't believe it. They were firing one of these monsters at them again? The first landed behind them.

The second one hit somewhere out in the middle of the meadow, the earthquake tossing them into the air and hurling them feet from where they had been. The roar was ear splitting.

THUNK!

Sweat ran off him, mixing with dirt. "Keep your mouth open!" he yelled above the roar and near her ear. If a person didn't, the pressure wave would hit them and destroy their lung tissue, turning the lobes into Jell-O, instantly killing the person.

How many more to come? His mind spun with disbelief. Who the hell would fire three RPGs at them? Whoever it was, wanted them dead, no question.

The third RPG landed to his left, farther away, but still too close. The meadow was green and therefore, would not catch on fire. That was the only thing that had gone right for them. How many men were shooting at them? His mind clicked off possibilities. The pressure wave rolled over them and he held Sara tightly, taking the brunt of the invisible force once more. Once it had passed, he rolled off Sara. She lifted her head, her eyes dazed looking, blood running out of her nostrils, scratches on her face where he'd forced her into the earth to save her life.

Without a word, Wes looked around, grabbed her by her left upper arm and hauled her to her feet. They were surrounded by heavy dust hanging in the air along with black and gray smoke hovering malevolently across half the meadow where they stood. Right now, they were hidden inside that triangle of smoke from fired RPGs. There was no way they could be seen by their enemy. At least, not yet.

"Come on!" he yelled, hauling her forward.

Sara stumbled, caught herself and began to run brokenly next to him.

Wes kept his hand tight around her upper arm in case she fell. The grass was thick, and it curled and swirled around their boots and ankles. Heading for the Oregon grape grove, he moved parallel to it, making sure they were still hidden from their enemy by the smoke, dust, and debris hanging like a thick, dark cloud in half of the meadow. Rounding the end of the grove, he hauled her into the darkening woods on the other side of it.

"Okay, we've got to hide in that grove, Sara. They're going to start looking for us," he choked out, coughing violently as more smoke rolled slowly around them, continuing to hide them. "If they find out we're alive? They'll run us to ground and kill us."

Sara nodded jerkily. "Where?" she stammered, automatically coming into his arms, tears making tracks down her taut features.

Looking around, Wes saw an opening low to the ground and into the thick, tangled bramble smothered in prickly, shiny leaves that could hide them. "There! Come on, get down on your hands and knees and dive into it! Crawl toward the center of it as fast as you can. I'll be right behind you."

She grimaced, and did as he asked. Her backpack stopped her progress. Wes helped her wriggle out of it. She dove again, the loop of a shoulder harness around her arm, dragging the backpack along with her. This time, shutting her eyes, keeping her head down to protect herself from the many needlelike thorns on each leaf, she forged ahead on her belly, weaving in and around thick, sturdy trunks of the massive grove. Her ears were ringing and she could barely hear anything.

Wes shrugged out of his backpack, throwing it into the bramble, digging in, hurling himself forward. Once in, he turned, grabbing at dead, loose material, covering up their entrance point tracks. Once more, it looked natural and undisturbed, so Wes turned and continued to follow Sara. She was heading for the thickest, lowest, and darkest part of the grove, about two hundred feet ahead. Silently praising her sense of how to hide well, he shook his head, his ears ringing so badly that he couldn't hear a damned thing. He wouldn't be able to hear male voices or footsteps of their enemy coming their direction, he was sure.

The Oregon grape grove was a mass of sharp needles on every last, single leaf. The wood was hard, immovable and rough. Continuing to push the backpack ahead of him, he kept glancing out of the shadowy, thick foliage, trying to see if their enemy was coming for them in the direction of the meadow.

Gasping, Sara stopped and turned, their heads close to one another. "Farther?"

"No," he whispered. "Lie down. Don't move. Are your ears ringing?"

She grimaced and nodded, wiping the blood away from her nose.

"Mine, too. We're sitting ducks if we can't hear. I'll lie next to you, but we can't talk. We don't dare. If they hear us, they'll hone in on the voices and kill us." He saw her eyes grow huge with terror. Reaching out, he touched her mud streaked, bloody cheek. "Hang in there. Stay close to me. I'll use hand signals you can see, if necessary."

Wes didn't have long to wait. He saw five men, all dressed like deer hunters, two with military M1s under their arms, the other three with emptied RPG tubes on their shoulders. They were slowly walking around a half mile area, the entire grass area gone, nothing but disturbed soil blown up and destroyed by their weapons. As he lay with Sara at his left shoulder, he'd taken out his pistol and snapped off the safety and put a bullet into the chamber. He could feel her still breathing hard, mouth open, arms crossed, her chin resting on her hands as she, too, watched the men slowly, carefully, combing the area, all five of them strung out in a single line, looking right and then left.

Slowly, Sara's hearing was returning to her in incremental units, the men a long way from where they were hiding. Her heart wouldn't stop pounding and she was thirsty, her mouth dry. Observing the focused intensity of Wes, his attention wholly on the five men, she realized she was seeing the man who went to war routinely every day. She could feel the tension in him, the fierce focus on their enemy. War wasn't something she knew, but Sara realized with an awful sinking feeling in her stomach, that they were in one. And there could only be one outcome and one set of survivors. Terrified of dying, unsure how to get out of this, her life was literally in his capable hands. Did they stand a chance? She didn't know.

For another hour, Wes watched them carefully comb the area for their bodies. They found nothing. The leader, a swarthy little man with dark brown, longish hair and ferret-like eyes that missed nothing, kept glancing toward the grove.

"There's no fuckin' way they didn't get killed. We zeroed in on 'em. There's no way they survived this!" the Ferret said.

"Maybe," a black-haired man carrying an empty RPG launcher, spoke up. "We hit them square and blew them into little pieces . . . nothin' left of 'em. That's why there's no bodies for us to find. No one could have survived that attack."

"Well," the Ferret snapped, "you'd better hope that's true. Manny will have all of us killed if we let them escape. We have to bring home *proof* we killed them. He'll never believe us otherwise, and we won't get paid. He told us: no video of her dead body, no money."

Wes heard the last exchange, the breeze across the meadow bringing their voices into his range. His ears were still ringing, but at least he had some semblance of hearing returning.

Glancing to his right, he met Sara's scared gaze. She was frightened and he didn't blame her. Reaching out, he placed his left arm across her shoulders, squeezed her gently to reassure her, and then forced himself to break contact. He wanted to do so much more for her, but he couldn't. Not right now. Maybe never. These five goons were hit men sent by Manny Romano to kill Sara and get her out of the way.

Sara's heart froze as all five of them headed toward the grove where they lay undercover. Wanting to cry, wanting to run, she forced herself to follow Wes and his calm demeanor. He lay utterly still, one hand across and in front of his chest, his right hand holding the Sig Sauer P226 pistol that could be fired in a heartbeat. She didn't want to die! Not this way! Her mother would never know what happened to her! They would never find her body. A coldness slithered through her and she trembled inwardly, feeling boneless, unable to protect herself.

But Wes was protecting her. She couldn't believe how calm he was! Her stomach knotted and it was hard to breathe as the men drew closer and closer. Now, it was easy to hear their rough, guttural voices. She knew her father hired all kinds of men, killers, to do his bidding. Had he set this up? Or had her half brother, Manny? If nothing else, Sara wanted to survive this to find out.

For the next thirty minutes, the five men walked up and down the woodland line. Wes remained on guard, noting that the enemy wore sidearms, mostly Glock 17s, two had M1 rifles, military grade, the kind he used to carry as a SEAL. These hired guns, from everything he could see, were ex-military and knew how to use the weapons they carried. There was a sack with each RPG carrier, indicating there were other rounds they could use if they were discovered. The Ferret was the leader and there were indicators he was an ex-operator. In what branch, Wes didn't know, but he was thorough, and that is what made him such a lethal adversary.

Moving his gaze to the right, he saw that Sara had lain down, facing him, her right cheek in a slight depression, hiding her completely from anyone outside the grove. He admired her strength. She had not cried or shown any weakness in the wake of these hunters of humans. And despite their situation, Sara remained calm, clearheaded, and listened fully to any instruction he gave her. That could, in the end, save their lives. He was used to this, used to stalking an enemy and getting within striking distance. His heartbeat was a normal rhythm, not heightened as he was sure Sara's was, but she was an unarmed, untrained civilian thrown into this hell. He wondered briefly about her backbone; if it came from the warriors genetically in her bone and blood. There was a set to her lips, a glint in her eyes—although showing her fear, there was also something else . . . a remarkable resilience under life-and-death circumstances. There was no question in his mind that her DNA was of warriors on the front lines, regardless that she was an herbalist.

Circumstances outside a person's normal experience would always show Wes what they were made of, how they would react under terrifying stress, and the possibility of dying. It was in such crisis situations, the true depth of a person would be revealed fully. Times of danger always tore off the veneer of civilization, tossing it in the trash, and the naked truth about a person would shine through, for better or worse. He liked Sara's stubborn demeanor, that flex of her lips, corners pulling in, that told him she was ready to fight, not run. The fierceness to survive this experience was mirrored in her face, the tension hovering in her expression, the courage he saw in her eyes regardless of how scared she was. She was thinking through it, fully present, and that was an amazing discovery to him. He had a fighter, like himself, in this debacle. The ache in his heart grew. This was the kind of woman who he had hoped to meet at some point in his life, but never for a moment thought it could ever happen. Now, it had. And there was no guarantee they'd get out of this alive.

Sara wanted desperately to move. Dusk was falling in the area and Wes had remained silent long after the five men left the meadow after circling the grove and then ranging farther into the woods, searching for them. She had to pee! Glancing over at his shadowed face, she made a sign asking if they could talk to one another. He gave a brief nod.

"I have to pee so bad it hurts," she whispered.

"They're gone, for now."

"Can we get out of here?"

"Yes. But let's do this as quietly as we can. I'll turn around and go out first. If all seems safe, I'll raise my hand, and then you come out."

Anything to pee! "Hurry," was all she said. Wes moved silently and she was amazed because the stickery dry leaves were thick. Maybe it was his SEAL training? She wasn't sure, but wanted desperately to get off her belly and onto her hands and knees to follow him out of this claustrophobic underbrush. Still, she waited.

Once he emerged—slowly, like a dark, lean shadow against the dusky woods behind him—she saw him looking around and finally lift his hand in her direction.

Once she was out, he pointed to a tree with a thick trunk. "Go over there, hide behind it," he coaxed, giving her a sympathetic look.

"Don't you have to go?" she demanded in a low tone.

"Yes. I'll be next."

Sara didn't need another reason to head to that tree, watching where she put her feet, barely able to see any branches or pine cones that might be on the slippery brown-needled surface. Stepping on them could make a noise in the stillness, so she moved slowly. In no time, she was finished and pulled up her pants, slipping out from behind the trunk. Wes was nearby, always on guard. It made her feel safe.

"Your turn."

Nodding, he moved around her, disappearing behind the tree. Looking around, she could hear crickets singing here and there. Deeper into the woods, she heard the soft, soothing call of an owl.

Wes rejoined her, helping her get her backpack in place on her back. He then pulled on his own. Moving to her side, he said, "We're going to have to move into the woods. My gut tells me this isn't over with these goons. We need to figure out how to get to our truck. I'm sure they saw the truck from whatever they drove up in."

"Okay, but how do we get back to it?"

"I don't know. I have a map of the area. Right now, I need us to find shelter and a place to hide from them overnight."

"Why would they come back here now?"

"Because the leader is black ops and he didn't look at all convinced we'd been blown up in that RPG attack. Operators run on instinct and gut survival knowledge. He senses we're in this area, alive. And I believe he and his men may camp overnight, and come back here in the morning to really begin a grid search for us. There's at least five of them. He may have one or two other men staying with the vehicles. I just don't know how many are in this group, and that makes it important for us to get out of this general vicinity. I want to keep to the pine needle floor here because it's very tough to track or to even find a human boot track in that type of surface. It rained up here a day or two ago, so soft imprints of our heels will be covered by the drying pine needles springing back into place."

"I'm hungry," she said.

"Yeah, we both are." He held out a protein bar to her. "One for you and one for me. Let's eat as we walk. I've brought a pair of night vision goggles with me." He produced them and hung them around his neck. "This will make it easy for us to get into the forest and not be stepping on fallen tree branches that could snap under our weight and give our position away."

"What else do you have in that backpack?" she demanded, shaking her head.

"Anything that can help us survive," he assured her. "Ready?"

She nodded. "We have to get out of this alive, Wes."

He moved toward her, reaching out, gripping her dust-coated hand. "You're doing great," he rasped. "I'm proud of you, Sara. I wouldn't want anyone else at my side in this kind of situation."

She squeezed his long, large-knuckled fingers. "Thanks," she began, a catch in her tone, suddenly feeling emotional and frightened by the enormity of their circumstance.

"We'll get out of this sooner or later," he assured her quietly, holding her faltering gaze, tears glimmering in her eyes. "You're a very brave person. Ready?"

"As I'll ever be . . ." Her voice wobbled.

"How's your hearing? Has it returned to normal yet?"

"Yes . . . how could you know?"

He grimaced. "I've been shot at by RPGs when I was over in Afghanistan. I know the drill. So long as your eardrums aren't blown, we're in good shape to hear the night sounds."

"Right now? I'm so glad you've had those experiences. I had no idea what that sound was."

"If I hadn't shoved you to the ground? You'd be badly injured." *Or dead*, but he didn't say it. She was shaken enough.

Sara frowned and nodded. "Thank you for saving my life . . ."

His mouth moved and softened. "You're doing fine. Grab hold of my belt with one hand and follow me." He pulled on the NVGs, turning them on. "If you need something? Give my belt a sharp tug. We don't talk from here on out. If I suddenly stop, don't say anything. Just freeze in place, because I heard or saw something."

"Okay," she said, feeling the warmth of his low, gritty voice. He squeezed her shoulder and it made her feel better. Safer. And then they were off, heading into the black maw of woods that she knew were all around them, but that she could not see. Only her fingers wrapped around his belt, and munching on the protein bar became her world.

According to her watch, it was ten p.m. when Wes finally called a halt. Her legs ached from hiking the hilly forest, up and down and around them. He would stop every half hour, listen, rest for ten minutes, sip some of their water, eat another protein bar, and then keep heading in an unknown direction. She trusted that he knew where they were. When they rested, he would pull out a compass, rechecking the direction he wanted them to go. As she stood at his side, hand wrapped around his belt, she squinted, thinking there was a much larger hill that they were standing at the bottom of. Knowing better than to speak, she waited, the coolness of the June night turning very cold. Luckily, they both had coats that they'd brought along, knit caps and gloves. One didn't go into mountainous areas like this unprepared. More than ever, Sara was glad they were both hiking-savvy and knew what survival goods to bring with them. This time, it could literally save their lives.

Wes turned, pushed up the goggles, his mouth near her ear. "This is a huge hill. On top of it are a lot of dead trees and I think we can make a good nest of sorts out of it. Being on top of the hill gives me an advantage of seeing anything coming our way, including those goons. The hill is about five hundred feet high and there's a lot of tangled brush on it. How are you feeling?"

"Tired, my feet ache, I'm cold, but I'm okay." Sara could swear she saw him smile, but the darkness was complete around them.

"In about fifteen minutes, we'll be at the top and I can find us a place to get into and get out of some of this cold air. It's close to freezing right now."

"No argument. Lead on . . ."

He pulled the NVGs down across his eyes, turned, and they began the trek up the hill through thick underbrush.

Sara was breathing hard by the time they crested the uneven top of the hill. Wes stopped and handed her the NVGs.

"I want you to see where we are. Put them on and look around. This reminds me of when I was a kid and we'd make forts out of sheets and cardboard boxes."

She settled them in place, seeing the grainy green, amazed at the amount of trees, very old ones, that had died over time, then fallen. The top of the hill looked like a place where six or seven matchsticks had been thrown. The huge girth of these giant old trees made part of the hill look like two walls of a house that remained unfinished. "Wow," she whispered.

"Yeah, it's a good, strategic place," he said, satisfaction in his lowered tone. "I think I see a good place to stay tonight."

She handed the NVGs back to him. In no time, he'd carefully led her through the logs and they dropped into a recessed area. Stopping, he gave her the NVGs once again and she looked around at the place where they'd stay overnight. There were two logs across one another and where they met, there was a large depression.

"What made that hole?" she asked him.

"More than likely a black bear or something. They have favorite places they like to sleep," he told her, taking the NVGs from her hand.

"Where's the bear now?" she muttered, frowning, looking around even though the pitch-blackness revealed nothing.

"I don't know. It's not around now, and that's all I care about. Come on," he urged her quietly, "let's get into that hidey-hole . . ."

In a matter of minutes, Wes had taken her backpack and he'd pulled out the space blanket that she carried. "You'll use the backpack as a pillow and wrap yourself in this," he said, handing it to her.

Sara relished the lean, strong warmth of his hands as he transferred the blanket to her. "What about you?"

"I'll be right beside you with the same gear. I'll go into the hole first and then I want you to come in and curl yourself up into my arms and against my body. That way, we can keep one another warm through the night."

Sara gulped a little. She was exhausted, her mind so much mush, and all she wanted was to rest and sleep. "Okay," she whispered.

In a manner of minutes they were tucked within the depression that was at least four and a half feet deep. Within it were soil and pine needles. She couldn't see anything in the darkness, the blanket wrapped around her. She felt Wes place his arm around her shoulders, situating them so that they leaned against one side of the hidey-hole, and he brought her against him. She smelled the sweat of his body, but she knew she must smell as bad. His whiskered jaw met her hair, some of the strands pulled as she allowed him to cradle her body into his, her head resting against his broad, solid shoulder. So many emotions rose in her as she trusted him fully, his other arm coming around her, cocooning her against himself. A ripple of need moved through her as she felt him position her so she truly could relax. His breath was warm and moist across her cheek. It felt as if he were giving her a featherlight graze with his calloused fingers. But he wasn't, it was just her fatigued emotions, strewn across the expanse of herself, that imagined it.

"Okay?" he asked her gruffly. "Are you comfortable?"

"Oh," she sighed, burrowing her brow against the column of his neck, "this feels wonderful, Wes . . . thank you for being my pillow and mattress . . ." She heard a low chuckle in his throat.

"What's so funny?" she asked sleepily, closing her eyes, so glad to be pressed against his curved body.

"I've been called a lot of things in my life, but never a pillow or a mattress."

A tired smile pulled at her lips as she sank further and

further into exhaustion that was now claiming her. "You out do a five-star hotel bed and linen, believe me."

He gave another low chuckle. "Sure of that? My smell is enough to scare off a grizzly right now."

"I smell just as much as you do. Don't worry about it." She felt his hand graze her shoulder, making sure her blanket was in place to keep the cold out. Touched, she felt hot tears rush to her closed eyes. She'd never had a man be so tender and thoughtful toward her. Yet, he was a SEAL. He had killed for a living. Sara couldn't put the two together.

"Depending upon dawn tomorrow," he said against her hair, "there's a river about a quarter of a mile from here. If we get lucky, if that vermin isn't still nosing around? We'll go there and wash up. I have a towel, washcloth, and soap in my gear."

"Ohhhh," she whispered, nuzzling her face against his exposed neck, "that sounds like heaven, Wes . . ."

"SEALs have a saying," he said, "one is none and two is one."

"So you brought the kitchen sink with you in that heavy pack of yours?"

"Yes . . . and right now, it's going to pay off for both of us. Between what you brought in your pack, and mine, I'm hoping to outmaneuver those killers and get back to the truck."

"Will they be hunting us tonight?" she asked wearily.

"Doubtful. They'll make more noise and give away their position than if they waited until daylight."

"I have six protein bars in my backpack."

"And ten in mine. That should keep us fueled. We'll have water, too. We should be okay."

"I'm so scared, Wes."

He squeezed her gently. "Anyone would be. We just had three RPGs thrown at us and survived it. You've got to be shaken by it."

A tear slipped down her cheek and she awkwardly tried to wipe it away. "I-I'm trying to be like you, Wes. You seem so stable and unfazed by all of it. Just the opposite of me."

He sighed and cupped her cheek, feeling the trail of tears. "It's okay to cry," he rasped, lips against her brow. "I've cried plenty of times, by myself, on some of the missions we went on. Life and death are something to shed tears over, so go ahead and cry. I'll just hold you . . ."

A sob burst out of her and she buried the sound of it against his neck, face pressed into his flesh, his large hand, his fingers, curving lightly around her head, holding her tightly as she shook and trembled. The whole day had been an unfolding nightmare. It was surreal to Sara, but very, very raw and real when those men hunted the perimeter, trying to peer into the thick, prickly bushes within the grove, trying to find them. Her other hand reached up, against the wall of his chest and the blanket around him. When he began to rock her a little, she cried even harder, smothering the sound, choking it back.

"No one can hear you, sweetheart, just let it rip . . ."

And she did. Sara lost track of time, utterly spent after that thunderstorm of tears and terror coming out of her. Wes cradled her as if she were some beautiful but fragile human being and despite her own anxiety and fear, she could feel care radiating from him to her like a thousand blinding suns. How could this be? It had to be her imagination. The slight rocking motion soothed her and he said nothing more, just his moist breath flowing across her cheek now and then.

Tears drying against her face, eyes tightly shut, she fell into a deep, deep healing sleep, safe in the arms of a man whose heart was incredibly gentle with her. Somewhere in her half-awake, half-asleep mind, she felt her heart blossoming wildly with need of Wes. She really didn't know this man at all. And if she survived this, she wanted, more than anything else, to know his heart, which had touched hers with such tenderness on this dangerous night.

Chapter Seven

June 16

Wes couldn't sleep, as fatigued as he was. Despite losing a part of one lung, he was still in top physical shape, unlike Sara, and having been a SEAL who would mercilessly push his body beyond anyone's endurance, was the reason why. Between the tops of the thick evergreen forest, he could see stars twinkling and slowly moving across the ebony sky. They were like small diamonds sewn into the fabric of the dark velvet. Sara was warm and soft in his arms.

How many times had he wished that it could be so? Despite fighting his attraction to her, he knew he was losing the battle, and probably the war, to do just that . . . stay at arm's length from her. She had no idea how drawn he was to her. After all, he'd been trained to never broadcast anything that he didn't want others to see. Moving his hand gently from her blanketed shoulder to her elbow, resting it across her rounded hip, a broken sigh whispered from his lips.

Closing his eyes, jaw resting lightly against her thick hair, his nostrils flared and he inhaled her scent. There was an underlying fragrance that was only Sara and sometimes, when they worked close to one another in the lab, he caught a delicious whiff of her essence, sending him spinning into that hungry desire for her.

Opening his eyes, he forced himself to do a 360-degree check on the night sounds around them. This was early summer, so there were crickets out and about and he could hear them off and on. If anyone was near, particularly anything threatening, they'd stop "singing." This forest was no different than any other, whether in Afghanistan, Iraq, or South America, where he'd had missions over his span of being with the SEALs.

The fragrance wafted into his flared nostrils and, feeling guilty, he deeply inhaled her scent, sending him once more into that inner euphoric world he kept tightly chambered against his outer life as a bodyguard. The closest he could come to her essence was the frankincense he had smelled at a spice market in Kabul one time. The pitch from a particular tree was the resinous source for that heady, rapturous perfume.

Yes, he felt like a thief, no question. No woman had ever felt as good as she felt in his embrace. The trust she'd given him made him feel even more guilty. Sara had come to him with fear and anxiety, stressed out beyond anything she'd ever encountered in her life. He'd eagerly opened his arms to her, thrilled as she nestled her head against the crook of his shoulder, her soft, strong dark hair against his neck; cheek warm, firm, and reminding him of a fuzzy peach on a sunny day.

Would she have come to him, otherwise?

How he wanted to say yes, because there was some kind of invisible magic growing subtly, yet with the strength of eiderdown, between them. Sometimes, when he was near her, he'd catch her looking at him, her eyes softened, and his heart would instantly pick up a beat, as if recognizing that look and what it meant. He parried that with his conscious mind, telling himself she felt sorry for him because he was an aimless, adopted waif, with no parentage, no nothing.

Sara was empathetic and he'd come to recognize that quality in the Afghan women who were the midwives, the doctors of the villages. They had to treat everyone who came to their hut. The midwives were no less affected by the sick or ailing person in pain who was begging them for help, to stop the agony. Stop the suffering. But he also saw what it took out of these great-hearted women healers from the villages. They grew old long before their time, the wisdom of their experiences shining in their eyes, but their bodies beaten down from taking the blows, absorbing them for their crying and hurting patients, time and time again.

That was what he recognized in Sara. She might be a master herbalist, but above and beyond that career, she was a master empath. Sometimes, she would laugh and hold up her long, slender hands, showing them to him. They had many cuts, scratches and callouses where she'd used her blade to forage herbs, as well as always being in soap and water. She washed her hands so many times a day they were dry and the skin was cracked from such constant abuse.

How many times had he wanted to fold her beautiful, artistic-looking fingers into his large-knuckled, deeply calloused hands and hold them, warm them and care for them, care for her. Wes had long ago tamped down on that wish to do just that. He was sure Sara would think he'd overstepped his bounds, going from distant bodyguard to a man with honest and serious intentions toward her.

Tonight, he'd been able to slide his trembling fingers

against her wet cheek, in an almost caressing motion over and over again, wiping away the tears of terror she was shedding, getting that poisonous toxin out of her system, releasing it through her emotions. Those stolen moments meant more to him than anything ever had when it came to making a physical connection with Sara. She had no idea how much gratification and gratitude he felt toward her as he held her close and safe, softly catching those large, warm tears and removing them from her cheek. So many times as a lonely, frightened little boy, he had so badly wanted to run into the arms of an adult who would protect and hold him safe. That had never happened for him. Because of what he ached for and was never given, he knew how important it was to give Sara what he'd been denied. He could hold her safe. He could give her protection. And in some convoluted way, it salved his own soul.

Wes took a slow, deep breath, seeing it was one a.m. The constellations had changed above him, shifted in a particular direction, new stars twinkling upon them now. The breeze was slight, though cold, but always carrying the delicious aroma of the woods around them. Sometimes, the breeze changed direction and he could smell the sharp, crisp heavier scent of the clean water of the river, which wasn't far away. The heavy, moist scent of the Earth herself rose up and he felt like he was in a revolving perfume bottle, getting to inhale each distinct, natural scent. To him, all were healing as he slowly breathed in deeply, taking the richness of each one into himself. He felt it was a gift, one that money could never buy, just as no amount could have placed Sara in his arms, fully and solidly against his body on this starry night that whirled silently above them.

Sara moaned, the sound muted against his neck.

Automatically, Wes tightened his arms just a little to let her sleeping mind know that she was being kept safe; that all was well and she could release her fear. Her breath changed and he frowned, feeling her breasts against his body, respirations coming more quickly. Frowning, he grimaced. He would bet anything that she was reliving the RPG attack. Her one hand that lay against his chest began to curl against his flesh. *Nightmare.* He knew them too well. He had to do something or he knew the scene she was reliving was going to awaken her and she might scream.

Another whimper came from her and he pulled her fully against him, hand against the back of her head, face pressed into his chest, should she cry out. Her breathing became harsh and she started to fight him, her hand raising into a fist, her other hand pushing hard against him. Damn! She was strong! A lot stronger than he'd given her credit for.

"*Sara!*" he hissed against her ear. "*Wake up!*" His voice was low, gritty, and hard.

Instantly, she stopped fighting. Breath coming in sobs, her eyes flew open, confusion in them.

Wes saw the terror mirrored as the starlight shone in her huge eyes as she stared up into his, unseeing. "Shhhhh," he rasped, holding her tightly so she couldn't get away and make a lot of sound. "You're safe, Sara. *Safe*. It's okay. It's Wes . . ."

Choking, she managed, "Oh . . . Wes!" and a wrenching sob followed.

Groaning to himself, he saw tears sparkling in her eyes, then trailing down her tense cheeks, falling rapidly off her jaw, soaked into her clothing or sliding down the space blanket. He reached out, releasing her, smoothing her uncombed hair. "It's all right, sweetheart, it's all right. You're here with me. You're safe . . . safe . . ." How much that word had come back to haunt him! Now he was uttering it for another frightened human being. He'd remembered his own terror, hiding in a closet, trying to outsmart the man who wanted him to call him 'daddy,' and then whip him with a belt because he'd awakened him by screaming, trapped in a nightmare.

"Shhhh," he whispered, touching her cheek, brushing the tears aside. He knew how good crying was. For him, as a child, and even as an adult, it was a blessed release of that caged terror that was eating him from the inside out. "Safe . . ." he repeated near her ear. Her struggling had stopped and she blinked owlishly up at him, her expression bewildered.

Wes saw she was starting to come out of the nightmare, starting to recognize him. That was good. He kept up his ministrations, each time smoothing her hair or wiping the tears from her cheek, until finally, she calmed. He stopped when he saw she was back with him, released from the trauma.

He loosened his arms from around her so she could sit up. "Okay?" he asked. He saw her give a jerky nod of her head, her fingers trembling as she awkwardly tried to wipe away the rest of her falling tears.

Wes retained his arm around her waist, giving her space, but in no way would he take his touch away from her, understanding how important contact was right now. He'd learned the hard way how much touch was a major healing unguent for every human being, including himself.

She sniffed and he dug for a tissue in his side pocket,

pressing it into her opening hand. Her sobs had stopped and that was good. Looking around, he keyed his hearing to the night sounds that had continued around them. Relaxing, he devoted all of his attention to her.

"You were having a nightmare," he explained in a low tone. "I was afraid you were going to shout or cry out. It could give our hiding place away . . ."

"Ohhh," she moaned, her voice muffled against the tissue, wiping her eyes, hands falling away, staring at him. "I-I'm so sorry, Wes . . . I didn't mean—"

"It's okay," he soothed, reaching up, drying her cheek. "You couldn't know."

"B-but . . . you did . . ."

He gave her a mirthful look. "Yeah, in my black ops business, nightmares and reliving a trauma are kind of the norm. You know?"

Shaking her head, she felt how messy her hair was and tried to tame some of it back into place, giving him a look of abject apology. "I-I didn't know. I must have woke you up?"

"No, I'm on duty. I was already awake."

"When are you going to sleep?"

"When I can." As he removed his fingers from her cheek, she caught his hand, folding it between her own in her lap, holding on to it like a scared child. Shocked by her gesture, he sat very still, watching her. Her large black lashes were beaded with tears, her expression one of silent pain, her soft lips tightened, the corners drawn in, telling him of the anguish she was experiencing. "I'll be okay. This is old hat to me. When I was a SEAL, we would go forty-eight hours without sleep on some missions." His assurance seemed to stun her, but at the same time, mollify her worry. He felt her soft fingers moving across the hand she held and the sensation was one of a drowning person grabbing hold of a life preserver. He liked the idea she saw him as a safe harbor in this storm that was mounting around them. As she threaded her fingers between his, he gently closed them around hers. Instantly, the stress in her face disappeared. She shuddered, closed her eyes, bowing her head until her chin nearly touched her chest.

"We're safe here," he said, hoping that it would further ameliorate the anxiety that he still saw deep in her haunted eyes. "You aren't used to being bombed and then chased down to be killed. Anyone would have the same reactions you're having now, Sara."

"You seem like a mighty sequoia tree, so stable and strong, and I'm this tiny, thin baby pine tree growing next to you. It's as if you can take the winds of trauma and walk through the storm without bending or flinching." Her voice was hoarse. "And me? I'm feeling like the weakest link, the one who is like a clam without a shell in this storm that is raging around us. Oh, I know this isn't over. I have no idea what will happen next. Or"—she teared up—"if we'll be murdered by those men my father and half brother have sent to kill us."

"Let *me* worry about that," he told her gruffly, meaning it, holding her shattered gaze. "You're the innocent in all of this, sweetheart. But you have me, and I'll be damned if we won't get out of this alive. I want you to have your life back, Sara. You're a healer—"

"And you are the warrior."

He gave her a one-sided, terse grin. "That's all I know, Sara. I'm *your* warrior. I would die to keep you alive and you've got to know that. Your life is a helluva lot more important than mine. I've seen you with the people who come to your clinic: babies, children, adults, and the elderly. You have magic with them and I've seen it up front and close. I have nothing to give anyone."

"Except your life," she uttered darkly, frowning at him, holding his hand even more tightly. "And don't you *dare* for a nanosecond think your life isn't worthy of saving just like mine. All humans have capabilities and skills, Wes. We have different abilities, but you can't put a price on one that is higher than another. That's not how this works."

His grin tightened. "Yeah, I can and do put a price on my skills versus yours. That's my job. I assess risk and danger. That's all I know. I'm good at it, too. And by the grace of God, you listened to me and did exactly as I told you when we hid in those brambles. And we got out of that trap and escaped because you listened to me."

She wrinkled her nose, pulling her fingers from his, but soothing the hardened flesh over the back of his hand. "Because I *trusted* you, Wes. I trusted you with my life, but I wanted to save your life, too. That's why I listened and did exactly as you instructed." She sniffed. "That's why I did it. You're so special to me. I lay there in terror, thinking that whatever is between us was going to be destroyed in a second by those men. I couldn't stand the thought of losing you now that I've come to know you." She loosened his hand, wiping the tears from her cheeks but never allowing her intense gaze to leave his. "Ever since I met you, I felt some kind of soft, warm heart connection with you. I couldn't explain it. That had never happened to me before and Great Spirit knows, I would never lie about this to anyone, especially you."

He sat there, disbelieving what he was hearing, speechless, honed in on the warmth of her fingers caressing his in her lap as she continued to wipe away the trailing tears from her cheeks with the other one.

"I was afraid to tell you how I felt . . . I mean, I wasn't sure what was happening to me . . . so fearful that whatever it is that I'm feeling, it's one-sided, that I'm no more than a body to protect."

He gulped and closed his eyes, his whole heart focused on how tenderly she stroked his hand. It felt so damn good. It felt wonderful. Sara's touch was unlike any other woman he'd ever met. What courage she had in telling him how she felt, but at the same time, Wes knew how trauma could break loose the truth within a person toward another person. This was her moment of truth and it involved him. The realization was stunning to him. His voice was low and choked sounding. "I didn't know . . . I mean, I thought sometimes, Sara, that when you looked at me, it made me feel good . . . but at the same time? I also thought that look was one of pity because I'd slipped up and told you I was an orphan and had bounced from one foster family to another. I thought you were feeling sorry for me."

Her hand stilled over his as she absorbed his barely rasped words. "No, my look to you wasn't filled with pity, Wes. Not ever. I was just trying to figure out what you were thinking. How did you feel toward me? Was what I felt one-sided? Was it just me and my flights of imagination? Because whatever brought us together was serious. Oh, I know you are my bodyguard. But"—she smoothed her wet fingers against his in her lap—"there is something very real and wonderful strung between our hearts. And I've felt it from the first time I met you. Over time? It's only grown and I don't know what to do with it. I was afraid to tell you . . ."

"You're far braver than I am, Sara," he admitted, holding

her unsure gaze. He curved his fingers around hers. "I felt something similar when I met you. I liked you the more I got to know you, watch you daily with others, and I found myself floundering between remaining a professional and trying to stop what my heart was feeling for you, instead." He gave her an ironic look. "If I gave in to my heart, my dreams . . . well, that would be a distraction of the worst kind. I would lose my edge and put you in jeopardy, or worse."

"You're so hard to read, Wes . . ."

"That's intentional because my job is to remain alert, above any human wish or desire."

"And yet . . . we have this other thing going on invisibly and silently between us." She caressed his fingers and gave him a sad look. "My life is worthless. My father won't give up on killing me, and neither will Manny. They want me dead and out of the way." She sighed and glanced around, then up at the scintillating swath that resembled starry diamonds strewn across the dark sky. Looking over at him, she said, "I'm a liability of the worst kind."

Nodding, he growled, "Someday, it will end, Sara. Things will come to a head."

"But where does that leave us? Our desire to be with one another and have a connection?"

"It can't be, Sara." Those were the hardest words he knew he'd ever speak. Her eyes widened with surprise, and then reality came to her, and it was heartbreaking for her and him, but he wouldn't admit that to her. "If you aren't alive, then we can't explore what might have been. For me to keep you alive? I can't be distracted. I have to have a hundred percent focus or nothing."

She sat there, head hung, her lower lip quivering. "And

I put your life in jeopardy plus my own. I-I wish I could just disappear, Wes. Where they would never find me . . ."

He squeezed her hand. "That's not reality, either. We're just going to have to play out the hand we've been dealt. It won't be easy. It's probably the hardest thing either of us have ever been challenged with."

"Got that right," she muttered darkly, frowning, meeting his gaze. "Well, since this is *my* fight? I'm a hundred percent in it, just like you. I'll give you everything I've got, Wes. I'm not as physical as you, but I have eyes, ears, and a brain. I can be a help to you."

"Two sets of eyes on this gang seeking to locate us is a good thing," he agreed. "And I want you invested in this body and soul. It's the only way we're going to survive it." He would not go into details on what might or could happen. Right now, Wes wanted her exactly where she was: defiant, righteous, and a warrior like himself, because it was going to take all those abilities, that warrior recipe, to survive this and other future attacks. "We'll do this together."

"Good, because I never want you thinking of me as a useless partner."

"Oh," he said, leaning back and releasing her hand, "I'd never say that about you. Your Native American heritage tells me that. I've seen you give looks that were definitely a warrior in hiding, but the warrior blood was there."

"I'll do everything I can to assist you, I promise." She pulled the blanket up to cover her head. "Can I rest against you again? Is that all right?"

He opened his arm. "Come on. We're a team, a partnership. We'll keep each other warm while you sleep through the night."

She went to him, a stubborn look on her face, her lips

set. In no time, she sidled up beside him. "It's as if we are two long-lost puzzle pieces," she whispered, snuggling into him, her head resting against his shoulder and neck. "And we've found one another . . . finally . . ."

He tucked her in and rasped, "I like that idea: two lost puzzle pieces finally finding and fitting together with one another."

"Good night . . ." she whispered, closing her eyes.

"Sleep," he rasped against her hair, relaxing and feeling how good she felt against him once more.

"I'm going to dream of us," she said softly, nuzzling. "You can't stop me from doing that . . ."

His mouth softened. "Dream for both of us, then."

"I will . . ." Shortly she dropped back into a deep sleep, her hand resting innocently against his chest.

Wes lay there replaying their conversation, wishing with his heart that he did not have to turn off and destroy whatever had been budding and growing between them. To do anything less would be to put Sara in real jeopardy. Still, his silly heart yearned with hope . . . that maybe someday or in some way, they could have the time and safety to explore what lay so softly and alive, between them.

A pink dawn slowly crawled upward, sending the darkness scattering and replacing it with color as he watched through the canopy of trees. The world was silent. As the temperature had fallen throughout the night, the night sounds had quieted. Now, he heard the birds perched in the trees beginning to awaken.

The sounds of the forest were calming to him as he lay on his back, Sara tucked in beside him. They had kept one another a lot warmer because they'd rested close together.

And she'd slept deeply this second time around, the trauma released through tears and sharing words that had meant so much to him.

Drawing in a slow, deep breath, he watched the tips of the trees, the breeze gone, the sky lightening slowly, that fragile pink color slowly being replaced. He'd had the rest of the night to feel his way through the amazing and surprising talk they'd had with one another. Wes knew that trauma often tore the reality away and truth came with that removal. He'd heard what he'd hoped for, and then hadn't dared believe Sara's admittance at first, stunned by it. Now, he knew she was as serious toward him as he was toward her. And it was the most tragic honesty he'd heard in his lifetime. It was coming at the wrong time and place. There was no way around it and it hurt like a gnawing ache in his chest, his heart clamoring that he should be able to have both, but he knew better. And how he wanted it different.

Grimly, he knew the path of his life: seeing the dessert, but never being able to partake of it for himself. The only time he'd been given a reprieve was when he met Tom, and he became a part of his family, even though never adopted by him. Tom had shown him humanity, care, the human touch that he'd never had like that before. And now, Sara was like that dessert to him . . . but she was out of reach. And because he was a warrior who dealt only in reality, this couldn't end well for him. He wondered if he would ever deal with this kind of terrible tease from the cosmos, something he wanted so badly, but never able to get there to grab hold of it and make it his own. His heart yearned for a dream that would never be.

Giving Sara a squeeze to start awakening her, the deep darkness of the forest was still with them and it was time to move to the river. They needed water; they'd consumed all they had in their packs. He had purification tablets to make it safe to drink. For just a moment, he wanted this one, last moment with her, lightly resting his jaw against her silky hair. Inhaling her scent was like inhaling life and all the good things that it carried with it. Knowing his ending was different than that, he rasped, "Sara, it's time to wake up . . ."

She stirred, mumbled something, and then as Wes opened his arm, she groggily sat up, rubbing her eyes.

"It's still pretty dark," she said, beginning to look around.

"We have to move in it," he said. "The river is only a quarter of a mile away. I want to get down to it and see what's there, where we can maybe hide from them if they're looking for us."

"Okay . . ." she said, sitting up, pushing her hair away from her face, the space blanket falling around her hips. "Pee time . . ."

He pointed to another part of the top of the hill. "Go over there. You'll have privacy." He handed her some tissues. "I've got some toilet paper in my backpack."

She slowly got to her feet, barely able to see beyond the toothpick piles of tree trunks that surrounded them. "No, this will do . . . thank you."

Wes got busy while she was gone, packing everything, pulling out two protein bars which would be their breakfast. In no time, Sara was back. He helped her shrug on her backpack.

"Ready?" he asked, handing her the protein bar.

"Yes."

He liked the strength in her low tone, the glimmer of the warrior in her eyes. She reached out, gripping his hand for a moment.

"Look, I know this isn't the right time to talk about us on a personal level, Wes, but last night's talk was a game changer, I think, for both of us." Her fingers tightened around his as she looked up into his deeply shadowed face. "I'm tabling it. I'm not willing to throw what we have away. Neither of us deserve that."

In that moment, he wanted to sweep her into his arms and kiss her until they were both breathless. Instead, he said, "Okay, let's table it. We need to leave. Follow me." He released her hand. This time, she could walk without holding on to his belt, the light enough to make up the difference.

For the next fifteen minutes, Wes moved silently through the forest. The birds were waking up in earnest now, flitting through the boughs and tops of the trees. It was near freezing because he could see his breath. The smell of the river was stronger. It smelled clean and unsullied by pollution as it flowed down from the Continental Divide to the west of them, no marks of humans along its winding path. On his map it was called the Blue River. Slowing down as he heard the water, there were huge fifteen-foot stands of willows, so thick that it was like a wall between their approach and the unseen river on the other side. On his map, it showed it was a small river, with no indicator of how broad its expanse.

Sara had learned to remain close to him when they stopped. He looked around the dark forest that was awakening, heard the natural sounds, assuring him no human predators were in the same vicinity. He noticed she was looking around a lot more, trying to become a second set of eyes and ears.

"We're going through this wall of willows," he told her. "Follow me."

The long, narrow leaves swatted against them, thick and heavy. He pushed through the wall, which was easily ten feet thick. Halting on the other side, he saw that both sides of the clear, clean blue water had a wall of willows. Heaving an inner sigh of relief momentarily, he saw the green grass beneath his feet, about fifty feet from the bank of the slow-moving river that looked placid, almost like a mirror. Still waters ran deep. He wondered about that. Sara came and joined him, looking around.

"This is beautiful," she said, awe in her tone.

"Yes . . . clear blue, like the name. I'll bet there's trout in there."

She smiled. "It's partly fed by a glacier, from what you showed me on the map. It's going to be plenty cold."

Studying the area, the river ran from the west to the east. His truck was west of the position they were at right now. "It looks like that wall of willows goes on forever," he said, pointing.

"Mary said that this area was heavy with moose, whose favorite food is willows."

"Then we might run into some."

"Do you know what kind of temperament they have?"

"Steve, my boss, told me they're twitchy, which means they are unreliable and could charge you. They stand seven foot at their shoulder, and a bull moose can weigh fifteen hundred pounds."

Mouth quirking, she muttered, "That's like having a freight train around."

"Yeah, not good."

"I don't see any up or down the river, Wes."

"Well, we have another issue with stands of willow," he told her. "It's June and the elk have had their babies in May and June. The mothers hide their babies in these," he said, motioning to the willow wall. "The only problem is that this is grizzly and black bear country. Grizzlies actively forage and hunt willow stands to sniff and find the elk babies."

Making a sad sound, Sara whispered, "Oh, no . . ."

"Grizzlies are a threat to us, too," he said, glancing over at her. "Normally, the way to alert one that you're in the area is to make a sound."

"But if we make sound, Wes, if those guys are still hunting for us, they could hear us."

"Exactly. We're caught in between. If we surprise a grizzly in this stand? He or she could charge and kill us, too."

Groaning, Sara's eyes rounded. "This is getting worse, Wes, not better . . ."

Hearing the terror in her tone, he nodded. "Not the best of circumstances," he agreed.

"You're the master of complete understatement."

Grinning sourly, he reached out, squeezing her shoulder to give her some kind of sense of safety when there really wasn't any. "You do the best you can. We need to head west, because I'm estimating about two miles to where the truck is parked."

"But those men could still be around."

"Yeah. It's going to be dicey because we don't know if they left or not." He pulled out the map, opened it and studied it. "This river goes northwest at a certain point. That's where we leave it and move back into the forest, heading in the direction of where the truck is located."

Sara wrapped her arms around herself for a moment. "I feel we're like that Light Brigade that Lord Alfred Tennyson wrote about: *The Charge of the Light Brigade.*"

"Oh," he deadpanned, "you mean the six hundred British

who rode into the 'valley of death' and all of them were killed?"

"Exactly."

He stood there and smiled down at her. "But we aren't the Brits. And we're not arrogant, and we aren't going to ride into a valley, which was a major strategic blunder."

Sara gave him a googly-eyed look but said nothing.

"We have guns. They had sabers."

"And our enemy has RPGs," she reminded him tartly.

"Don't go all pessimistic on me," he teased, grinning. "We'll take this a step at a time. First, we need to find a way to get back to the truck. And we should be able to tell when we parallel that road we were on, whether or not that gang is still parked there or not."

"I'm not usually pessimistic."

"Well," he said, looking behind them, seeing all was quiet and no animals thus far, "we have to be on top of our game and we will be. Come on . . ."

Chapter Eight

June 16

They moved down the row of willows, the river on the other side, with a twenty-foot width between them. Sara wasn't so sure about it, but followed Wes dutifully, trying to tame her own fear that a big, hulking grizzly was somewhere in there, unseen and unheard, waiting to jump out and get them. Her imagination was scattered and going wild once more. This wasn't anything like the beautiful Smoky Mountains where her grandmother lived. They felt safe, nurturing and caring, compared to these rugged mountains. These willows were none of those things. But she couldn't blame the poor plants. Wes had given her vital and important information, to be on the lookout because they were high in the mountains where wild animals and predators ruled, not humans. He hadn't told her to scare her to death. Still, her gaze kept moving along the wall of willows because it could mean exactly that: life or death.

When they stopped about half a mile down, Wes turned to her. "How are you doing?"

Grimacing, Sara said, "I feel like a four-year-old with an out-of-control imagination."

"Oh," he said, nodding, his gaze ranging down the line of willows that they'd just come from, "a grizzly leaping out and getting us?" He gave her a sympathetic look.

"You're good," she muttered. "I'm not very proud of myself. I was thinking as we were walking that my grandmother's home is in a beautiful valley in the Smoky Mountains of North Carolina, and how safe they felt compared to here."

"They don't have grizzlies," he reminded her gently. "Black bears, yes, which have nothing like the power and aggressiveness of a grizzly. You can scare off a black bear by just yelling at it. With a grizzly, it's a whole other thing. You yell at it and it's coming to make you his dinner."

"Wouldn't we hear one if it was in the willows?"

"Maybe. Maybe not. For their size, and the males can reach eight hundred pounds, they're completely silent. They've learned how to be that way as they search for food in these willow stands."

"Did Steve Carter teach you about them?"

"Yes. He was born here in the Silver Creek Valley and he knows these mountains like the back of his hand. His family has a small ranch here. He's done a lot of hiking in and around this area, which is why he told me of his experience before we left to come up here to this meadow."

"Have you ever seen a grizzly?"

"No," he said, smiling a little, "and I don't want to, either." He patted the holster. "A pistol is not going to stop a charging grizzly unless I get really lucky and put a bullet in his skull. Steve said they can hit twenty-five miles an hour in seconds. They're on you before you know it. They're the A predator around here." He looked upriver, studying the wall of willows. "I wouldn't mind seeing a moose. Steve said if you don't look them in the eye, and back off, you're usually safe and the moose won't feel threatened and charge you."

"I'm liking moose already," she said, managing a half smile. Up above them the sky was light, the sun above the horizon. "How far do you think this wall of bushes goes?"

"Don't know. But it's more a positive than a detriment."

"Because it hides us from those men, if they're still around trying to locate us?"

"Bingo. My gut tells me they're still around. I heard them say that they needed photos of our dead bodies in order to go home and collect their reward."

Shivering, she rubbed her upper arms, frowning. "Sometimes, Wes, everything seems surreal. I feel like I'm reading a comic book or something where the baddies are chasing the hero and heroine."

Giving her an understanding look, he offered, "It can feel surreal, that's for sure. But what we shared with one another last night? That was real. And genuine." *And good*, but he didn't add it.

Her heart swelled with need of him. Her voice was low with feeling. "That was as real as it gets, Wes."

"I wish," he muttered, "that we weren't in this situation right now. I'd rather focus on us than this." He gestured toward the willows.

"Makes two of us." She peered up at his somber expression. "Listen, what's the possibility that we can learn to be good friends? My grandmother taught me a long time ago that friendship was the best basis for a lasting relationship."

He pondered her suggestion. "I like that idea, although I've never had a woman who was just a friend."

"Well you've lost out."

"That's true," he said, digesting the idea. "And once we

get out of this mire, we'll still be working together if your mother still wants you to have a bodyguard. My cover is as your assistant, which is a good one, and I like what I'm learning about your world of herbs."

"I'm sure my mother will want you with me. As long as my father and half brother are plotting to get me out of the way, she knows I need extra protection."

"That's the hard nut to crack," Wes agreed grimly, meeting her worried gaze. "But I'm going nowhere, and I like that we appreciate one another."

"That's another tenet of friendship—the appreciation of the other person."

"Hmmm, maybe we're moving in that direction and didn't even know it?"

She smiled a little, wishing she could be back in his arms, feeling how he fed her emotionally as he held her warm and safe through the cold night hours. "Maybe we already were on that path, but it took this event to see it?"

He rubbed his bristly chin. "That's a good observation. That's a start. I like it. Do you?"

She saw the teasing in his eyes, and felt as if he were trying to lift her spirits and ease her worry and anxiety. "Yes," she answered softly, "I do . . ."

"An hour at a time," he counseled, pulling out his map and studying it for a moment along with their position on his pocket compass.

"I just wish I had that inner toughness or shield, or whatever you want to call it, when things are threatening."

"It's something that got trained into me," he said, tucking the map away. "You're handling this really well for a civilian, Sara. I'm proud of you."

"I don't feel as confident as you do."

"You have other skills we need on our journey." He

pointed beyond the willows. "About another mile and we'll leave the river and head another direction. Would you like to stay here for a bit and get washed up? I've got soap and a washcloth you can use."

Sara rolled her eyes. "I'd give anything for a hot shower and getting clean."

His lips lifted away from his teeth. "Thought so." He shrugged out of his pack and pulled out the items, including the small towel, handing them to her. "I can't give you a hot shower, but soap and water can work their own special miracle."

"What about you, Wes?"

"I'll wash up a bit after you're done. I'm going to do a little reconnoitering around the area while you get cleaned up."

There was a slope from the bank to the edge of the river, easy enough to walk down and then kneel in the damp, sandy soil. It was all that she needed, leaving her pack where he stood. She saw how Wes studied the entire area, always impressed with his abilities. He seemed to absorb the atmosphere, the environment, and take it inside himself to check it out. Getting down on her hands and knees after finding a shallow, curved area in the bank, the idea of getting somewhat clean felt like a small miracle itself. In minutes, she'd shed her coat and shirt and slimmed down to a sleeveless cream-colored tank top.

The chill of the early morning made her hurry up and wet the cloth and apply the soap. In no time, she had washed her face, neck, arms, and hands. Taking the small towel, she'd dried off. Standing up, she shrugged back into the layers, slipping into the warm down nylon coat. As she turned, out of the corner of her eye she saw something brown dart out of the willows toward her. Gasping, she leaped on the bank.

Wes, who was down the line, heard her gasp, whirling around, his hand going for his holster.

It was a rabbit!

Hand against her neck, her heart pounding in her chest, she saw it scamper past her and then dart back into the willows, disappearing.

Wes came up, frowning. "It was a rabbit. You all right?" and he drilled a look in her widened eyes.

"Y-yes," she gulped, pressing her hand to her heart. "I thought . . . I thought it was a grizzly bear at first . . ."

He slid his arm around her, bringing her against him, giving her a squeeze and then hesitantly releasing her. "It's okay. There's lots of critters that live in the willow stands."

Pressing her hand to her forehead, she muttered, "I was so scared, Wes."

He frowned, watching the area where the rabbit had leaped out of the stand and had run down it, finding another place to dodge back into it. "Stay here? I'm going to check out the stand where it came shooting out. I think something was chasing it . . ."

Staring upriver, Sara's voice quavered. "Be careful . . ."

Wes moved away, drawing his pistol, keeping it at the ready, a bullet in the chamber. The smell of the river was clean, the air cold and crisp. He kept as much distance between himself and the willows as possible. What had scared the rabbit out of its hiding? Standing near the bank, honing intently in on the stand, his hearing acute, he could hear rustling inside it, but couldn't make out an animal. A bear would sure as hell be something big and he'd see the difference between the green of the leaves, the yellow bark on the supple willows compared to a brown hulk hidden in it. Standing still, he waited. Soon enough, a badger appeared. At first, the animal with the wedge-shaped head and black, glinting eyes, studied him, freezing.

They stared at one another for a long minute. The badger decided to turn and disappear back into the willows.

Sliding his pistol back into the holster, Wes turned and walked down to where Sara stood, fear in her expression.

"It was a badger. They eat anything, even a rabbit. He's not a threat, so relax."

Heaving a sigh, she whispered, "Thank goodness . . ."

"I'm going to wash up," he said, pointing at the cloth and soap sitting on the bank. "Do you feel better?"

"Just getting partly clean was good," she agreed, her gaze never off the stand of willows. What else was in there? Was a grizzly hiding in there, too? She hated when her imagination took over.

"My turn," he said.

"How come there's no scent to the soap?" she asked.

"In my business as a SEAL, we used soap with no odor to it. The enemy could pick up the smell of it and locate us."

Lamely, she looked up at him. "Oh . . . yes . . . that makes sense . . ."

"It will take me a few minutes. You just watch the area in general. We should be okay. Give me a call if you spot anything?"

"Oh," she said, finally feeling her heart settling down in her chest, "I will . . ."

Wes went to the place where she had washed up earlier. Shedding his coat and several layers, his top half was feeling how cold the air was as he knelt down, scooping up the washcloth and soap.

Sara tried to ignore his blatant maleness. He had a large,

powerful chest, his shoulders always drawn back, proud looking or maybe it was the military in him. Dark hair dusted his chest, the ropy power of his muscles in his arms attested to his being in top shape. She saw a number of pink, shiny scars here and there and one large one on his upper right chest, plus several smaller ones on his arms and back. The woman in her, dizzied by his male scent, felt her lower body heat up, ache, and want him on a far different level. It had been a long time since she was drawn to a man. Most of them did not interest her in the least. Wes was different. She didn't know why, but he was. And his moving from one foster family to another, never knowing his parentage, he somehow didn't see women as sex objects, per se. She was sure with his intense, roughened looks, that he was a magnet to other women. It would be foolish of her not to think that he hadn't had affairs, or perhaps some long-term relationships in the past.

As she kept an eye on the willow stands up above and below them, she saw nothing more, much to her relief. Her body and heart moved gently back to Wes despite the looming danger. He had to be free of a relationship to have told her how he was feeling toward her. Some men lied about such things, but she couldn't believe that Wes would do that. He had such honor and integrity about him. His word *was* his honor, she thought, watching the play of muscles in his back as he washed up, rinsing the cloth in the cold waters of the river. He had more bravery than she did. He brought the water against his face, neck, and arms, washing away the soap. Where she was standing downwind of him, she had the urge to turn, walk up to him and ask if he wanted his back cleaned up as well, but hesitated. Did friends do that for one another? Or was this her strictly female side who yearned to share so much more with Wes? Was it a bridge too far? Too intimate? What then? No, it wasn't a good idea, Sara finally thought.

As Wes dried off with the towel, he got to his feet, turning toward her. He'd washed his hair, as well, rubbing it briskly to dry it. She should have thought about her hair but hadn't. Reminding herself that he was used to operating in the wilds, he was taking full advantage of this river water. It was a silent pleasure to watch him get dressed, running his long, calloused fingers through his hair, taming the short strands back into place. As he pulled on his coat, he lifted his chin, giving her an intense look. It felt as if he were sending charged particles to her, inspecting her, making sure she was all right. That was the feeling she got from that glance in her direction. And then he automatically pivoted, his gaze sweeping up and down the long stand of willows. Sara knew he missed little, seeing shadows or light, looking for color differences in them. He was the consummate hunter. That gave her a sense of safety.

Walking up to her, he said, "Ready to go?"

"Yes. Do you feel better? Cleaner?"

He grinned a little. "Felt damned good. Come on, follow me. Let's see if we can remain shadows. I need to ascertain whether those men are still around or not . . ."

Wes had seen the look, a woman's look of interest, in Sara's gaze as he'd turned, naked from the waist up. That made him feel good. Not that he could do anything about it right now. *Maybe never.* His lower body had responded to the yearning in her eyes. Friends? They had to learn how to be friends. *Not lovers.* His heart burned with need of her as he walked down the river bank, forcing his focus on his surroundings. She was a distraction of the worst kind, but he would never tell her that. Wes had no desire to hurt her feelings. Sara was not a trained black ops operator like he was.

As the sun rose, they moved another mile before the willow stands began to be less and less. He'd seen white-tail deer, does with fawns, on the other side of the river. He'd seen that Sara had also spotted them. Pulling up for a moment to enjoy the deer going to the water to drink, he absorbed her features, which glowed with excitement. The deer didn't seemed to be bothered that they stood a hundred feet away on the other bank, as they drank. There were four does and four fawns. Wes knew that bucks never were with the females and their fawns except at breeding time.

They took a time-out, ate their breakfast, which comprised one protein bar apiece. They had to conserve their food. He'd filled their water bottles and put purification tablets in each one earlier. Hopefully, soon they could find his truck and get the hell out of this predicament. But something told him they were still being hunted. He didn't think the leader, that ferret-like small man who reminded him strongly of an operator, was going to give up easily.

In another hour, they were out of the willows completely. Wes led them back into the thick stands of pine and fir, more on guard. The sun was up, slats of it shining through the thousands of trees on a slight slope. The knolls were plentiful, smaller lumps of ground covered with brown pine needles. In some spots, as they walked carefully, not wanting to snap a fallen tree branch, there were plenty of black rocks, indicating a volcanic birth to this particular area. In other places, the rocks were outcroppings and Wes was glad to have such a place to hide, if necessary. Sometimes he halted, Sara coming and standing close so that they couldn't be overheard talking in low tones with one another. They would drink water, sit down and rest, usually in a group of bushes that hid them from prying eyes.

"How close are we to the truck?" she asked him.

"Maybe forty minutes. We're about half a mile from the track that we took to drive up here."

She nodded, scanning just as he did. "We're a lot more vulnerable out here, aren't we?"

"Yes. I'm trying to pick trees that have a wide girth because they will hide us more than thin, spindly trees will."

"What if they haven't left?" she asked warily.

"Too many variables. I'll have to see it and then figure out a fix."

"Do you think they're in the area of the meadow?"

"No. Their leader is an operator. He's probably widening the search in the area where they fired those RPGs, Sara. He'll fan out in about a forty degree wedge with his other men and they're going to be looking for footprints, broken branches on bushes, or disturbed pine needles to try and track us."

She sighed, shaking her head. "There's so much to this . . ."

"Welcome to my world during the SEAL years," he teased, trying to lighten the worry he saw in her eyes and pursed lips. Lips that he found himself urgently wanting to feel against his own mouth. How would Sara taste? Her scent made him yearn for her in every possible way. Wes wasn't sure he could be a friend to her, such was how she stirred him up without even knowing it. Still, he had to try, no matter what.

"They taught you all these methods?"

"Yes."

"Wes? Did you ever get married?"

He met her gaze. "No. A lot of my team did, but the rate of divorce among operators was sky-high. I guess"— he sighed, giving her a wry look—"I wanted a forever marriage like Tom and his wife, Frannie. Maybe I'm old-fashioned; thinking that when the right woman comes along, we'll have forged a relationship that will really be forever. Seeing Tom and how happy he and Frannie are, how much they share similar interests, I wanted that, too." He held her gaze. "How about you? Did you ever get married or live with someone?"

"No," she said adamantly. "So many men are chauvinistic. I could never find one who wasn't." She smiled a little. "Until I met you."

Perking up, he said, "Tell me more?"

She picked up a brown pine needle, breaking it into small sections, watching it fall between her crossed legs. "My grandmother told me stories when I was growing up and stayed with her on summer vacation, of how braves behaved and treated their wives. The more she told me, the more I saw the distance between white men and the men on the Cherokee reservation."

"Give me an example?"

"My grandmother's husband, who had passed many years before her, always asked her for her ideas, her suggestions or ways that she could help him if he needed an extra hand. He treated her with respect and everything they did, they talked out together. It wasn't as if my grandfather had to have his way. Very often, it was my grandmother's wisdom and intelligence added to the mix of whatever they were dealing with, and he bowed to her knowledge. He didn't insist he was always right. Nor did he ever put her down."

"So, it really was an equal, respectful relationship," Wes murmured.

"Yes. It doesn't mean men are in charge or have to have their way. Women are seen as wise, and whatever they say carries extra weight because they are the ones who birth life. A man cannot. In our society, we work off one another's strengths, not our weaknesses."

"I like that," he said, nodding thoughtfully.

"Let the person who has the skill, knowledge, or ability, take the lead on whatever it is. Like now," she said. "You know land survival in a way I do not. I defer to you and your experience, and I'm learning, too. You're a good teacher, Wes. You explain things to me so I can understand why you're doing what you're doing."

"But you bring skills to our situation, too," he pointed out. "You're my second set of eyes and ears, Sara. I rely on you just as much as you do me."

Tilting her head she said, "The way you work with me, bringing me into your circle, relying on what I know, see, or hear, is teamwork. Do you think the SEALs are like that?"

"Well," he said, humor in his tone, "up to a point. You have to remember, that until recently, it was an all-male gig. In the SEALs you each have skills, and you rely on others with their skills if needed at that moment in a mission. We rely heavily upon one another in every way."

"But if you had women in your ranks? How would they be treated?"

Wes chuckled grimly. "Not well."

"That's too bad," she said. "We have women chiefs, women warriors among our people. All are judged on their skills and talents, not their gender."

"I don't know about the SEALs, but I can see changes taking place for women now," he said.

CRRAAAKKKK!

Wes pushed Sara to the ground, his whole attention on the sound of a limb being stepped on somewhere to the left of their position. He felt Sara freeze. Pulling his pistol free of the holster, he looked between the thick leaves of the bushes that they lay behind. Cursing silently, he saw the Ferret with two other men, slowly making their way through the forest. To his relief, they were headed away from them, going north, toward the river. They carried M1 rifles and he didn't see any RPGs among them. And more than likely, they had bullets that could explode inside a human and kill them instantly. He kept his hand on Sara's back, silently telling her not to move.

Looking in the other directions, Wes wondered if the other men were elsewhere. He saw nothing. The three enemy were not aware of them. Relief sagged through him. As soon as they disappeared, no longer in view, he gently helped her sit up next to him.

"Ferret and two more men, carrying rifles, not RPGs, are headed in the direction of the river. I didn't see the other two men."

Sara picked pine needles out of her hair. "What does this mean, Wes?"

Grim, he rasped, "That they're not giving up on finding us."

"If one of them hadn't stepped on that limb . . ." She halted, giving him a frightened look.

"Ferret might be black ops, but the other two men aren't," he said, watching the area. "One of them stepped on it and gave us the warning." He didn't want to tell her that the possibility that those three might have gotten a lot closer to them, possibly hearing them talk in low tones, could have started a firefight; and he knew his pistol, which was only good for fifty-five yards of accuracy, was no match for those M1s.

"What now?" she whispered, her gaze pinned on where the three men had disappeared.

"We've got to get to where the truck is at. It's our only way out of here."

Nodding, she said, "Can we go? Can we get out of here?"

Hearing the fright in her tone, he nodded. "Sit up and I'll help you on with your pack. I don't want to stand up. Not yet . . ."

Struggling, they sat and helped one another and then strapped them on, ready to move. Wes took a long, intense look around. He slowly got to his feet, holding out his hand to Sara, bringing her to her feet. Her fingers were icy cold. It hadn't warmed up that much yet and probably wouldn't until this afternoon. And by that time, he wanted to get the hell out of here. "Watch where you step," he urged her. "Follow me . . ."

"How far is it to your truck?"

"Not far . . . We're going to go slow and carefully, Sara. We can't rush this as much as I wish we could."

Nodding, she fell in behind him, turning, scanning the area. Where were those two other men? Out hunting them, like Ferret and his men? Once more, her stomach tightened, her heart rate taking off. Was there any end to this hunting of them? All she wanted was her life as an herbalist, helping people, relieving suffering and pain. And yet, right now, Sara held little possibility of getting out of this alive.

Wes broke into a trot, giving her a sharp gesture to do the same. What did he see? Or hear? Frantically, Sara looked around. The sharp stench of something burning, part metal, part rubber, stung her flared nostrils. What was it? Looking around, weaving in and out among the trees, forcing herself to avoid stepping on any branches lying on the pine needle floor, she felt terror and didn't know why.

Their pace picked up. She was running full tilt, trying to keep up with Wes and his long, ground-eating stride. It took everything to stay within a few feet of him. Luckily, she had long legs, too, and now they were running hard. Wes dodged behind a long, low rise covered with bushes, and she followed. He speeded up, heading for the other end of it. He had angled them to the left, closer to the track where the truck was parked. Anxious, she looked right and left, the smell becoming stronger. Her nostrils burning with whatever was in the air, unseen.

As they broke from the rise, Sara gasped.

Wes suddenly stopped.

She slammed into him, stumbling. Falling.

Wes twisted around, grabbing at her arm, preventing her from hitting the ground. He broke her fall, going down with her, shielding her.

Gasping, breath broken, Sara jerked a look up at him. His face was hard. Lifting her head, pushing up into a kneeling position beside him, a low moan broke from her.

"No . . ." she cried softly.

Wes kept her head down. Ahead of them were two gray trucks that had brought the five men to the nearby meadow. His truck was parked about a hundred feet behind; the hood was open and a fire was blazing within it. There wasn't a lot of smoke and he realized they had thrown a canister, something like a flash-bang, into the engine to destroy it.

Sonofabitch! He saw two men, both bearing M1s, smoking cigarettes, languidly looking around as the engine on his truck continued to be destroyed. He sat there, his arm around Sara's shoulders, her face pressed into his folded arms on the ground, trembling. Ferret had probably ordered the destruction of his truck; he wanted to find them, but not give them an escape route. Mind whirling, Wes considered his options. And none of them were good.

Chapter Nine

June 16

Gunfire suddenly erupted behind them. Sara ducked her head and gasped. Wes turned toward it. The echo and re-echo rolled past them. She saw the two men suddenly halt, and one was on a radio, talking to someone.

"Stay down," Wes ordered tightly, crowding her up against a tree to protect her with his own body.

Heart pounding, Sara whispered, "What is going on?" She could no longer see anything.

"The two men are getting into the two pickups. They're going north, toward the river area where we spotted the other three."

She peeked out and saw both gray trucks spinning tires, kicking mud up into the air, swerving, the back ends fish-tailing. The roar of the engines filled the area. In moments, they careened past them and disappeared up the track. She sat up now that they were gone. "I wonder what happened up there?"

Jaw tight, Wes nodded. "I don't know. But plans have to change for us."

She stared at him. "Can't we hurry down the road and get to the main highway?"

"That's twenty miles away, Sara. And if these men come back this way, which they'll have to, sooner or later, they could spot us in the woods paralleling it."

Giving him an anxious look, she said, "But . . . we're in the woods!"

"That doesn't mean we won't be easy to spot." Wes turned and gestured down the road they'd come up on. "See how well spaced these trees are?"

"Yes."

"Where we were in the meadow when they nailed us, the woods are very, very dense. It's harder to see us in a situation like that. But here, our movements would be easy to spot. We'd have to be at least half a mile into the forest and away from this road in order not to be seen."

"What are you thinking, then?"

Giving his truck a miserable look, he turned toward her. "We're going to take advantage of this situation. We'll head across the road and dive into the woods that parallel this long meadow where we were at originally."

"You could use your cell phone when we get back into a lower elevation where it picks up a signal. You could call for help."

He stood and holstered his pistol. "You're right. I'm intending on us moving as fast as we can to the end of the meadow, using the tree line to hide within. Once we get there, we can begin to angle down the mountain slope toward the highway. I don't know what the landscape is like in that area, but we'll find out." He held out his hand to her. "Come on . . ."

Instantly, Sara was on her feet. He helped her on with

her pack and then put his across his shoulders. Her heart wouldn't stop pounding. "Why did they destroy your truck?"

"Because they *think* we're in the area. They aren't sure we're alive or dead. They need photos of us to take back to their bosses to get paid. We can't let them know we're still alive." He squeezed her hand. "Ready?"

Giving a jerky nod, she whispered tautly, "Let's go!" Wes moved like a silent shadow and she, not so much. They crossed the road and he immediately dove into the tree line, avoiding the meadow itself. She watched where he stepped, avoiding creating footprints in the muddy area near the tire tracks, choosing to step on grass clumps instead. She did the same.

Feeling safer in the woods, which grew denser as they trotted through them, Sara began to understand Wes's reasoning for going this route. Moving closer to him, her breath coming fast, she asked, "When do you think they'll be back here?"

"I have no idea, but we're not sticking around to find out. How are you doing? Am I going too fast for you?"

"Not yet," she huffed.

"You're brave," he rasped, reaching out, touching her shoulder, giving her a warm look of encouragement.

How badly she needed his touch! And those words. The expression on his face, glistening with dampness as they jogged, had a look of pride for her toughness in this situation. It fed her and she maintained her brisk trot, sometimes dodging between trees, keeping up with the pace he'd set. Off to her right, she saw the meadow, but he was leading them farther away from it while continuing to parallel it. Sara knew he wanted the darkness of the thick growth of trees to hide their presence. Would they get out of this alive?

In another half hour, they'd come to the end of the long, oval meadow. Wes slowed and stopped.

"Let's take a breather," he said, taking off his pack.

Sara emulated him, sitting near his shoulder. "I'm so thirsty!"

"Keep hydrated," he urged, looking around the area. Above them, a hawk flew and circled the meadow, looking for breakfast on four legs.

Wiping her lips, she said, "Now we head down toward the highway?"

"Yes. But it's a good twenty miles away, Sara. We can't do ten-minute miles because you're not in shape for that kind of demanding run."

"How long will it take for us to reach it?"

"I figure twenty-minute miles at a fast walk and jog. And then we're going to have to rest for ten or fifteen minutes every now and again." He drank deeply from his bottle. "Sixty minutes means we'll cover roughly three miles, with probably a quick ten-minute rest stuck in there somewhere, depending upon how we're doing. That's roughly five to six hours from now when we should hit the highway itself. Even then? We'll have to be careful because we don't know what these men will do. Will they leave this area? What direction will they go if they do? Will they head for the town or not? We can't be seen walking on the highway or they'll fire on us."

Sara frowned. "I hadn't thought that far ahead, but you're right. Maybe there's brush or some kind of tree line to hide in?"

"Unknown," he said. "I'll have to evaluate it once we get there."

"That's a lot of hours to get out of here. I wonder at what point your cell phone would work? Calling for help?"

"That's something we don't know, either," he said, capping the bottle. "A lot of unknowns."

"At least those men can't follow us in their trucks through this kind of forest growth," she said. "You left information with Colin Gallagher before we left the Wildflower Ranch to come up here. Don't you think he'd wonder where we were by now? We had told him we'd drop by and see him and Dana on the way back, to let them know we found the meadow and got the herbs."

"I'm worried about that. He and Dana might try to come up here, looking for us. They are the only ones who know where this meadow is located and where we were going to be. I told Colin we'd be back by dusk last night."

"And since we didn't show up? What do you think he'll do?"

"He'll be concerned. He might think we had a flat tire or some kind of engine trouble with the truck, most likely."

"He wouldn't suspect armed men," she said, worried. "If he or Dana came up here? They could kill them, too!"

"Yes," he agreed, his voice low and grim. "Another reason to push hard to try and get into cell phone range. I wished to hell I knew where that edge of it was located on this mountain slope . . ."

She pushed her bottle back into her pack. "Would he call Dan at the sheriff's department?"

"I don't know. I wish I did."

"If anyone comes up that road, they could be killed by

those men." She shivered, rubbing her arms, giving him a desperate look.

"It bothers me, too. I weighed us coming here for better hiding versus paralleling that road in the woods and more than likely being seen sooner or later by them."

"This is an awful situation . . ."

He reached over, gripping her hand. "Look, we're still alive, that's what counts right now."

She held his hand, relishing the quiet strength of it, the calluses against her softer palm. "What were they shooting at, do you think?"

"I don't know." He reluctantly released her hand and uncoiled, hauling on his pack. "Maybe they ran into a grizzly if they began to follow that river with the willow stands?"

"Poor bear," she said, getting to her feet. Wes helped her on with her pack.

"Maybe the grizzly got them."

She managed a sour grin. "Let's hope so . . ."

"Ready?"

"Let's go, pardner . . ." She saw one corner of his mouth barely lift at her teasing.

"You're brave, a good partner to have," he reassured her. "Let's go at a slow trot. Once we leave the meadow area, neither of us know what the land is like. We have to be on top of things, Sara. If you see something? Tag me with your hand. Don't speak. We're back into mute mode. Let's go."

"Six miles," Wes said as they stopped to take a break. He saw the film of perspiration on Sara's wrinkled brow.

She was a trooper and he was amazed that she had kept up with his pace, which wasn't easy.

"Ugh," she muttered, looking at the tips of the trees bathed in rising sunlight, plopping down behind huge Oregon grape bushes that stretched for more than a quarter of a mile. "I need this rest."

Wes studied their location. The landscape had gone from thick woods, a soft, brown pine-needle floor, into a more rocky area, nobs of black lava stone rising here and there. More than once, they'd both tripped and fallen over rough, black rocks with sharpened edges, hidden by the pine needles. "Hydrate," he told her, holding up his cell phone, punching it on, hoping to see bars.

There were none. Turning it off, he pushed it down in his back pocket once more. "No bars," he told her, kneeling down, opening his pack and pulling out a third bottle of water. He had two more pints left.

"I'm wishing I'd brought my cell along," she muttered, sipping the water. "But it wouldn't get bars any sooner than yours will."

"That was on me. I told you we wouldn't need it, that I had mine. Big mistake on my part," he said grimly. Her black hair was frizzy along her temples, drawn back into a ponytail. He longed to cup her jaw and kiss her gently. Just to taste her. To let her know his feelings toward her. Friendship, he'd finally admitted, wasn't where he wanted to go with Sara. More than anything, Wes wanted a serious relationship with her. He knew what it was like to fall in love because it had happened to him once. Now, those feelings were alive and clamoring within his heart, throbbing in his soul, because there was no doubt she was the woman he'd dreamed about having in his life someday. What would Sara do if he admitted that to her? Walk away? Want friendship only? He didn't know and was afraid of her answer. Long term? If they were together? There was Sara's murderous family. At least her monster father was behind prison bars. But Manny? He was a wild card, young, immature, feeling his power and so very self-centered and selfish, not to mention, sending men out to murder Sara. What kind of life could they have? It all seemed so hopeless to Wes in the long run. Yet, never had he wanted anyone more than Sara. The last forty-eight hours had shown him that, for sure.

"The land disappears in front of us," she said.

Wes nodded. "A steep hill or a cliff, probably."

"With lots of sharp, nasty rocks to trip us up."

He slugged down the last of the water, capped the empty bottle, placing it back into his backpack. Glancing over at her, he saw Sara staring at him. He couldn't read what he saw in her eyes. "You okay?"

"I guess," she said, opening her hands, pushing them down the sides of her jeans.

"What's bothering you?" He thought she might be utterly exhausted and was worried that she'd slow them down, getting in cell phone range later, not sooner.

Brows raising, she managed a one-sided grimace. "Us. Well, I mean our talk about turning whatever we have between us and becoming friends?"

"Yes?" He cocked his head, holding his breath, afraid that she had come to some kind of inner decision about them and it was going to be bad news. Wes had gotten used to getting bad news a long time ago because his life was a crooked path at best, with sharp turns and continual disappointment.

"I . . . ummm . . . well, to be honest, Wes, I don't think I can do friendship with you."

He stilled, keeping his face immobile. "I see . . ."

"No, you don't. I just find myself wanting *more* than friendship with you. I think being friends is a good platform to work from for some people." Her voice fell and she avoided his sharpening gaze. "I just see you as a wonderful man that I'd like to have a lot more than friendship with." Lifting her chin, she stared at him. "How does that make you feel?"

Hell! He tried to squash his sudden, euphoric emotional reaction to her words. "Friendship is a good thing," he agreed, swallowing hard, holding her softening gaze. How beautiful were her forest-green eyes framed with long, black lashes. Eyes he could drown in for the rest of his life. But he didn't dare go there. Not now. Especially not now. "I want to share so much with you, Sara, but we're in a jam right now. I don't know how this is going to end . . ."

"Do you like me?" she demanded archly, frowning.

"Of course I do."

"How much, then?"

He hesitated, scowling. "Look, we're in a dangerous situation—"

"Darn you!" she huffed, getting to her knees, framing his face with her hands, giving him a fierce, frustrated look. "Stop mincing words with me, Wes! I don't want to die without knowing you feel just as powerfully for me as I do for you!"

He almost smiled, but thought better of it. Here was the fierce woman warrior taking what was hers. His heart thudded once to underscore that wonderful discovery. Her fingers felt warm and soft against his face. He reached up, gently removing her hands and taking them into his own. "I was hesitating, Sara, because we're in danger and could die. I wanted to wait until there was a time to sit down and talk fully and honestly with you."

"And if we get wounded? What then? And what if only one of us makes it out of this mess? We're sitting here and don't know how we honestly feel toward one another. I need to know how you feel about me. *Really* feel about me."

Holding her hands, he nodded. "Okay . . . while I feel friendship is a great base to grow from with you? I also have other dreams for a future with you, Sara."

"What kind of future?" she insisted, holding his stare.

Gulping, he rasped, "I'm so damned afraid to tell you how I really feel, Sara. I'd rather face M1 rifles and RPGs than share my dreams with you."

"Why?"

"Because I'm afraid my dreams aren't the same as yours." He saw her roll her eyes, the frustration evident. "I'm afraid of your rejection of me. That's what this discussion really comes down to."

"I understand, but if you were shot? Wouldn't you want to know my feelings for you before that? I have dreams, too."

Wes almost slipped and wanted to say that she was like a riled-up female cougar, but wisely refrained from uttering those words. Taking a deep breath, he rasped, "My dreams, ever since I saw your photo that Steve handed to me before I met you, haunted me. There was something about that fierce warrior look I saw burning in your eyes. I felt my heart tumbling, falling, wanting to know so much more about you on a personal basis, Sara. To me? You are an enigma, a woman of immense knowledge who has a huge, caring heart and is able to relieve other people's suffering. When I'm around you? A lot of my own, internal suffering, goes away. It's as if you are balm for my wounds I carry from when I was young. You give me a deep sense of peace, as well as calm. I feel centered and hopeful. It doesn't matter what you're doing, there's a happiness around me and I know it's because of you . . ."

"Oh," she whispered, suddenly emotional, "I didn't realize any of this, Wes . . ."

"There's more . . . You wanted to know my dreams. Right?"

"Oh, yes, I do. Tell me? Share them with me?"

Her husky pleading, that caring look in her gaze broke the barrier of fear within him. "I find myself dreaming that you think the same of me, which I know isn't possible. But I dream of having a serious relationship with you. I like spending time and place with you. You make me happy. A friend of mine, a fellow ex-SEAL, Cal Sinclair, works for Steve, and was born and grew up in the valley. He just finished building a huge two-story log cabin by hand in his time off between missions that Steve assigns him. Talk about dreams. He began building that cabin by hand because he fell in love with a woman named Sky Lambert, who was a Blackhawk medevac helicopter pilot in the Army. They were assigned to a top secret base in Afghanistan. She was wounded and he got her to Bagram for treatment, and that was the last he ever saw of her. Cal has been searching for her ever since, and he built this cabin for her. His dream, he'd told me at one time, was to marry Sky and present the cabin to her as a wedding present."

"How tragic," Sara whispered. "Will he ever find her?"

Shrugging, Wes said, "I don't know. Steve has a global search going on for her. If he locates her, he'll tell Cal and then he can go find out if the love they had for one another in Afghanistan is real or not."

"She ran?" Sara guessed. "From something? Him?"

"No, I don't think this had anything to do with him. Something else. Cal aims to find out if Steve can locate her whereabouts. I guess what I'm trying to say is that I worry how I feel toward you, Sara, and that it might make *you* run away from *me*. That maybe what I dream about, what I hope would happen over time, might not be what you expect or want."

"The only way to know is to talk this out," she said, urgency in her tone. "No one's a mind reader here, Wes. What am I to you?"

He hesitated fractionally, and then, in a low voice, he said, "You're the woman I want in my life, Sara." There, it was out. He saw her expression of surprise, and then her eyes became luminous with unshed tears.

"I have a tough time when I remind myself that you're here as a bodyguard. Instead, I want you as more than that. I want you to be free to fall in love with me . . ." she whispered unsteadily, as if steeling herself against his possible reaction to her low, husky admission. She saw his eyes widen and then narrow upon her.

"You . . . you're falling in love with me?"

The disbelief in his tone serrated her heart. "What's not to fall in love with?" she demanded. "I know you're an orphan, Wes. I haven't walked in your shoes, but I can guess how much of a hole is in your heart, being abandoned by your mother and father, and what it did to you. How you saw the world." She rubbed her wrinkled brow. "I would feel that I was unlovable, that there was something wrong with me, that I could be thrown away. I wasn't worth keeping." She saw him wince, but he didn't tear his gaze from hers, his mouth a hard line. It told Sara so much in that moment, that he didn't feel worthy of being loved even by her. The signal had been sent to him early in his life and scarred him permanently. At least, until now. Fingers tightening around his, she repeated, "I'm falling in love with you, Wes."

He closed his eyes, and she could feel as if a deep, inner earthquake of emotion was rumbling through him. Did he love her? She wasn't sure. He hadn't used that word. And that word meant everything to her. Were they on equal footing with one another or not? Breath suspended, she saw his eyes open, the turmoil, pain, and hope in them as he stared hard at her, the silence so deep and yet so fragile strung between them. Sara felt as if Mother Earth were holding her breath, waiting for him to speak. Waiting for him to decide what would happen to her life.

He reached out, barely grazing her cheek. "You're right on all accounts, Sara. I never did feel love until I met Tom and was sort of integrated into his family. I always shied away from that word, love. I had never felt it until they took me in and made me feel like a real member of their family."

"You were so lucky to have met Tom," she agreed quietly, moving her fingers across his strong hand holding hers.

"I'm falling in love with you, too, Sara."

His rasping words, filled with pain and hope, blanketed her, wrapped around her heart and fueled her dreams. Giving him a tremulous smile, she released his hand, got up on her knees, threw her arms around his shoulders and leaned forward, her lips molding hotly with his mouth.

For a moment, Wes froze. And then, as she moved her lips softly against the hard line of his mouth, feeling his response, his hunger for her dissolved all of the fears she couldn't possibly know. Breath warm and moist against her cheek, she closed her eyes, inhaling his scent as a man, glorying in the strength of his mouth sliding wetly against hers, a celebration for both of them overcoming their own personal fears.

Her arms tightened around his neck and she leaned against him, her breasts pressed to his chest, his arms enveloping her, holding her tightly to him, as if he was never going to release her, but it showed her the depth of his growing love for her.

As he lifted his hand, moving it gently across her hair, caressing her shoulder, following her supple spine, her skin riffled with heat and need of his masculine form of gentleness, memorizing everywhere he slid his hand. Breath becoming ragged, their kiss deepening, her breasts aching to be touched and brought to throbbing life, she felt Wes begin to ease away from her. Heart pounding, she groggily opened her eyes as their mouths parted. There was apology in his look, desire burning in the depths of his eyes, a hunger for her she felt all through her body. He wanted her, body and soul. But now? It wasn't the time.

Sitting back on her heels, she tried to tame her hair with her hands, giving him a slight smile. "We could get carried away . . ."

"I want to," he answered gruffly, staring hard at her, "but wrong time, wrong place."

"Ever the bodyguard," she agreed, nodding, feeling as if her heart were going to tear out of her chest, joy funneling through her as never before. Reaching out, she caressed his jaw, which was prickly and unshaven. "Can we table this until we get out of this?"

"We have to, Sara. I'd like to lie here and we could explore one another, touch one another . . ."

The wetness between her legs was testament she wanted the same thing as he did. "What a special hell," she said, giving him a wry look. "For both of us."

He managed a cutting half-smile. "Fact, for sure."

She looked around where they sat. "I don't know about you, but I want to get going. I want us to find that cell phone boundary. The sooner that happens, the sooner we can get to safety." *And in one another's arms*, but she didn't release that thought. The bulge in his pants told her everything, that he wanted her badly. Trying to push the need for him away, which was nearly impossible, she said, "Are we ready?"

Nodding, he stood up, pulling the backpack onto his back. Holding out his hand to her, he said, "I like seeing your fierce warrior side," and he slid his fingers into hers, bringing her slowly to her feet.

"You've seen my herbalist side up until now," she whispered, allowing him to help her on with the backpack. "You're right: I have another side."

"Oh," he said, holding her glistening gaze, "I've been very aware of it. You're like a tireless mustang, pulling that strength from deep within you, keeping up with me. I didn't think you could, but you've surprised me again." He leaned down, brushing her lips and straightening. "A backbone of titanium."

Snorting softly, she grinned, walking toward where the land dropped away. "Women are never called weak in a matriarchal society, Wes. Not ever."

"I believe it," he said. As they approached the edge, they halted.

Sara scowled. "Wow, what happened here?" The dropoff was exactly that. There was a huge cliff of blackish-gray basalt lava, staring at them. It was at least three hundred feet high and unscalable. Looking right and left, it appeared to be a black fence that grew less and less high as it moved along the crest for at least a half a mile in each direction. She looked up at Wes. "Go around it?"

"Yes." He pointed to the left. "This one gets negotiable about half a mile from us. Let's go."

They took the challenge and he broke into a slow, steady trot, Sara close to his heels. The pine needles were dry on the surface and as always, slippery. There were hidden lava rocks beneath, so she took her time in looking ahead to ensure she didn't step on one and end up falling. Wes, also, had slowed because of the threat of the unseen rocks beneath the pine needles.

Finally, they rounded the end of the lava formation. Below it was a steady downward slope, but it, too, had a lot of lava outcroppings, even some that reminded her of a fort being built, over six feet tall and curving.

"Just be really careful," he cautioned. "I'm going to do a diagonal across this slope and then we'll cut back and do it the same the other way, all the while, descending."

"Sounds like a good plan. It's more stability for us than trying to attack that slope straight down."

"That's an accident waiting for sure," he muttered, frowning and casing the area.

"Who knew this was here?" she muttered, coming and standing at his side, glad to have a breather.

"The forest is always a surprise. We had this same thing over in Afghanistan. We'd run into some hellacious geography that no one knew about because we didn't have infrared that could tell us about such things."

"I wonder how far this goes?"

Twisting around, looking up at the lava wall above them, he said, "This looks like a volcanic vent. Lava oozing out of the ground, building up and then creating this wall."

"Are SEALs taught geology?" she asked, impressed with his knowledge. She knew plants, not rocks.

He smiled a little. "Just a personal education of mine. I loved collecting pretty rocks as a kid. Always had my pockets full of them. I took a couple of college courses on geology after I got into the SEALs. Most guys were doing serious study into ammunition and different weapons while I wanted more knowledge of the land, the geography of it, and how it might help or impede a mission."

Giving him an admiring look, she said, "Maybe, if we get out of this? You can teach me what you know?"

"Be glad to," he said, smiling a little. "How are you doing?"

"Fine. Does your cell phone show bars?"

He turned it on and held it up above his head for a moment, then looked at it. "DOA. Let's keep going. Sooner or later, it has to hit a boundary where we can make that call."

Taking a final drink of water from the bottle, Sara tucked it into the outer pocket of her backpack. "For as far as I can see, we have lava rocks and pine needles."

"Yeah," he muttered. "Not good. It's going to slow down our progress." He took out his compass, making sure they were heading in the correct direction that would help them intersect the highway. Tucking it away, he said, "Let's go."

Chapter Ten

June 16

Later, Sara knew they'd traveled another six miles. The landscape hadn't changed much. Too many times they had slipped, almost twisted their ankles or worse, had tripped and fallen. Her knees smarted where she'd stubbed her toe on an unseen rock and she'd tumbled end over end. The look of terror in Wes's face told her a lot. He'd made her sit while he made sure her limbs weren't sprained or broken. Luckily, only bruises here and there and a slight twist to her ankle—this time. They took a break, hydrating, each of them having only one pint of water left in the two backpacks.

Wes cautioned her about their speed because the slope had become an even sharper decline for as far as they could see. The landscape was changing down below. She didn't see many black rocks poking up in the floor of the forest. Sara kept mute about her ankle, feeling some pull on it, knowing that if she wasn't careful, she'd really damage it. And then what? She'd become a terrible liability to them, slowing them down. Worrying that Colin or Dana

Gallagher might come up that road, looking for them, scared her badly, but she kept her worry to herself. Wes helped her up, gave her a tight, hard embrace, kissed her hair and then released her. Just having a little intimacy with him made her heart soar, despite their tense circumstances.

"The sun is on the tops of the trees," she said, pointing upward.

Wes glanced. "More light is better. It's so dark in here it makes trying to dodge these damned hidden rocks, even harder. The light is welcome." He held up his cell phone and then studied it with a frown. "No bars."

"But you had bars when we were on the highway," she said.

"We did. But how far does that stretch up the slope of this mountain from it?"

"I hope we don't have to go down to the highway to find out."

"Me too," he said, turning it off and pocketing it. "Ready?"

Nodding, she gestured for him to set the pace. Tightening the straps on her pack, she fell in behind him as he took a slow jog, weaving in around the trees, but also watching out for those hidden rocks beneath the forest floor. The slope became steeper and she would catch herself sliding on the needles beneath her hiking boots. Luckily, they had good, deep tread and it stopped her from falling on her butt. She'd slowed considerably and had her eyes more on the ground than looking too far ahead, not wanting to fall again. Even Wes had checked his speed.

The land grew even steeper than before after they hit their next mile. The trees had opened up far ahead of them and Sara found that strange. Frowning, she saw pieces of hand-hewn four-by-four posts scattered haphazardly about a wide area around them, here and there. Had there been a house here at one time?

Wes suddenly disappeared!

"*WES!*" she yelled, skidding to a halt. Gasping, Sara saw a huge hole in the ground, dust rising in the wake. "*WES!*" She scrambled awkwardly, being careful, the hole opening up even more. He'd fallen into it!

Gasping for breath, she saw several more of those long, huge pieces of lumber, mostly hidden by pine needles. Scrambling, she didn't dare get too close to the maw, the edges crumbling in, more dust rising. It was a sheer drop-off, the gravel loose, the clouds of dirt rising below her. Looking around, Sara realized that the slight hump in the ground was probably the rest of the opening. Neither of them had seen it, it was so slight, almost unnoticeable.

"Sara!"

She anchored. "Wes?" she called out, her voice hoarse with fear.

"It's an old mining entrance," he called.

She couldn't see him. "Hold on, I'm going down below it."

"Be careful," he yelled. "Go around!"

Heart pounding, she made it around to the opening, following an old lumber wall that was the partially hidden frame to the dark entrance. Skidding down one side, she landed on her butt, sliding the rest of the way down to the bottom.

Panting, scrambling to her feet, racing to what looked like a partial opening, she could see him. Up above, a good twelve feet above her head, was where Wes had fallen into the mine, and she saw heavy cobwebs and pine needles at the entrance. Clawing them away, the dust flying everywhere, her eyes widened.

"Wes!" He was sitting up, his hands on his right ankle.

"Be careful where you walk," he warned.

She heard the tightness in his voice, saw how pale he'd suddenly become. "A-are you hurt?" She knelt down opposite him, sliding out of her pack and dropping it beside herself. She moved close to his extended left leg.

"I didn't see this coming," he muttered unhappily, his long fingers searching over the leather-covered area of his ankle. "I think I've broken my ankle, dammit."

"Oh . . . no . . . What can I do? How can I help?"

He grimaced, slowly pressing his fingers into his right ankle covered by the leather boot. "I've broken it, for sure." He cursed softly.

"Blood!" she whispered off key, pointing to the red fluid oozing out the top of his boot. "What can I do, Wes?"

"Nothing," he growled. "The top of the boot is acting like a cast for the break. I can feel the bones grinding against one another every time I try to turn or twist it."

"Then, you have to leave that boot in place. You could have an open fracture, Wes."

Grunting, he said, "Figured as much. There's blood. This boot will stop me from bleeding out." He looked up. "This is an old mine, mostly hidden by time, debris, and pine needles. I didn't see coming at all."

"I didn't either," she said, getting up, coming to his left side, touching his shoulder. "You can't walk on that."

"No," he rasped, giving her an apologetic look. "Of all the bad luck . . ."

"Give me your cell phone," she said, extending her hand toward him.

He turned enough to pull it out of his back pocket and hand it to her. "See if we have a cell connection?"

Hands shaking, she turned it on and walked out of the mine shaft, looking for a connection. "No," she said, coming back in, frowning. "Wes, you need help. I'm going to take your phone and keep heading down the mountain. That highway is only two miles from here, at the most. I'm bound to run into the cell tower coverage between here and there so I can call Dan at the sheriff's office, and he can get an ambulance out here for you."

He nodded and drew in a deep, ragged breath, the pain coming in waves up his leg. "Call Steve first, then Dan. He's got some of his operators back from missions right now. He can get out here a helluva lot faster than Dan can. Tell Steve everything. We've got weapons in-house, so tell him about those five men stalking us. We don't know where they're at, and we may need that kind of fire power to not be killed."

"I need to call Colin and Dana, first. We have to make sure they aren't on their way out here."

"You're right. Do that and then speak to Steve, and tell him what's going on and give him our GPS locations. Ask him to call the sheriff's department, and fill him in on how dangerous this is."

She gave him a worried look, seeing more blood oozing out the top of his boot. "I will. I'll be back as soon as I can, Wes."

"Wait!" He grabbed her wrist. "You have to be careful, Sara. We don't know where those killers are at. You can't show yourself to anyone on the highway. Find a place to hide to make those calls, okay? Stay *away* from the highway at all costs." He released her wrist and pulled a notebook and pen out of his pocket with a shaky hand. "Give me the GPS for this place?" he asked her, his voice low with pain.

She quickly gave him the coordinates from the cell phone and he wrote it down, tearing the sheet of paper out and thrusting it into her hand. "When you find cell coverage? Tell Steve this GPS where I'm located. Tell him to send at least one or two of the operators at the office to my location after they find you first. Then, I can get down off this mountain and close to the highway after the ambulance arrives."

Rubbing her wrinkled brow, she nodded, stuffing the paper into her blouse pocket. "It can't be far away, Wes. Only two miles . . ."

He pulled his pistol out of the holster. "You have to take this, Sara, just in case." He held it out to her.

"No . . . no, I've never used a gun, Wes. I-I couldn't kill anything . . . anyone . . . Please don't make me take it. You keep it. How do we know they aren't hunting us? They might come upon you before we can get help. *You* have to keep that gun!"

He closed his eyes and his hand curled into a fist. "Get going. Be careful . . ."

She leaned over, kissing his sweaty brow. "I love you, Wes . . . hang on to that. I'll be back as fast as possible!" She rose, stuffing the cell phone in her other pocket. "You stay alive. You hear me?" Her voice cracked.

Wes saw tears come to her eyes and she battled them back. He nodded. "I'll be fine. We'll get through this, Sara . . . just be *careful* . . . I don't want to lose you now that I've found you . . ."

She gave him a wobbly smile. "Oh, don't worry . . ."

She stood up, shrugging into her backpack and trotting down the slope.

Cursing richly, Wes slowly dragged himself inside the mine enough so that he couldn't be seen by possible enemies. Never sure where these five men might be, he took no chances. His mind canted towards Sara. She wasn't trained for this, dammit! Frustration bubbled up with another powerful wave of pain, making him grit his teeth. He breathed raggedly, leaning back against the rock and dirt of the mine wall, a huge adit post between him and the entrance.

The pain passed and he sat up and got out of his backpack. He dug for a small first aid box. If nothing else, he was going to dull this gnawing, intense pain. In his days as a SEAL, they carried morphine on them. Steve gave all his men and women, when starting with his company, a SEAL first aid kit that contained that opioid. Now was the time to use it. The pain would be dulled, but the drug would not knock him out. He'd still be clearheaded, his senses going back on line, instead of the pain washing away his ability to remain alert.

In minutes, he'd taken the morphine and the pain almost instantly began to abate. His breath had been racing right along with his heart due to the injury. Now, as he leaned back, eyes closing in relief, he rested, knowing that he was going nowhere with this injury. Sure that he had an open fracture, the possibility that the sharded bone had cut into either a vein or artery in his leg, was very real. He could bleed out and he knew it. No way did he want Sara to find him dead by the time she returned.

IF she returned.

His mind went wild with scenarios and possible actions

with those enemies out looking for them. They'd shoot to kill her on sight. How badly he wanted to be there to protect her. His love overwhelmed him as the pain quickly receded. Looking around, he studied the ancient mine. Above where he sat, which was next to a huge timber keeping the top of the mine from falling in, he saw the axe marks all along the massive wooden posts. This was most likely built in the late 1800s, and he remembered Steve telling him that there was silver in these mountains, but there was even more farther west in another range. This was probably a silver mine. He even saw some rusty rails, mostly covered with debris, leading out of the opening, showing that they had mined and brought the rock out of a deeper area behind him.

His heart ached. He worried about Sara. She had more backbone than any woman he'd ever met. She didn't give up. Her strength was inspirational to him. She was incredibly gentle and so damned compassionate and caring with the sick. In a heartbeat, she'd figured out what to do and he was sure she was running like the wind right now, trying to find that sweet spot where the bars on the cell phone would appear. It had to be within a mile or maybe half a mile of that damned highway! And she'd been right that once she got the bars, she should waive any help from Colin and Dana, keeping them out of danger as this played out.

Wes knew the danger was very real. This was exactly like a SEAL mission, with unknown dangers lurking to take them down, never mind the enemy that would like to take them out, too. He looked around the maw. Colder air was flowing up and out of the mine. He couldn't see much of anything, the mine entrance having been hidden by years of neglect. There was no way he could have foreseen this, but it didn't stop his worry for Sara.

Sitting up, he checked the thick sock he bloused over the top of the boot. It was soaked with blood. Sure that he'd cut into an artery, lying still was the best thing he could do. His heart was always on Sara. Leaning back, he closed his eyes, sweat trickling down the sides of his face. The pain was masked by the morphine. He knew the drug would work for at least two hours and he'd have relief from the deep throbbing sensation. How was Sara doing? More than anything, he wanted to be with her. If one of them had to step off into this hole, he would rather it be him and not her. She'd told him she loved him. Why hadn't he told her he loved her? What the hell was the matter with him? Wes knew the gnawing pain that felt like a wolf tearing his flesh, tendons, and ligaments apart, was shorting out his ability to speak, much less think. Would he get a chance to tell her that he loved her? His fists curled and he lay in the semi-dark tunnel, the cold air making him shiver with dread.

Sara ran carefully, the land starting to level off a little from the steep slope that she'd just run down. The trees were farther apart, the wind tearing past her, the thud of her boots on the ground as she pumped her legs as fast as they could go. Glancing at her watch, she'd run for ten minutes. Breath coming in huge gulps, she skidded to a halt, finding a larger tree trunk that she could hide behind, scanning the area for any movement before she pulled the cell phone out of her pocket. Everything was quiet, but that meant nothing. Turning the phone on, she waited impatiently. Noting the battery was low, she knew she couldn't just keep turning it on and off.

No bars.

Wanting to cry, she pressed it off, jammed it into her blouse pocket and took off running once more. The trees were thinning and she could make out landscape miles away. Where was the road? Where? All she saw was undulating land, some green pastures far ahead where the trees were no more. Had Wes gone the *wrong* direction? Fear zigzagged through her, but she kept running as hard as she could, her footfalls sounding like thumps against a wood floor. For another ten minutes, she ran, her lungs were burning, her breath coming in sobs. Her knees felt sore and achy as she came to a halt.

Where was the highway?

Twenty minutes meant she'd run at least a mile. Shakily, she pulled the phone out of her pocket and turned it on.

BARS!

Gasping, she stared at it, blinking, not believing what she saw. Going to the address book, she found Steve Carter's private cell phone number, shakily hitting it.

"Steve here. Wes?"

"No . . . no, it's Sara. Steve, we need your help. I'm calling on Wes's phone. He's broken his ankle about a mile away from me, and he sent me to call you."

"I've got your location. You said Wes is injured a mile away from you?"

"Here's Wes's location." She sent the coordinates to him.

"Okay, got them. Thanks."

A sob broke from her and she cried out, "Steve, we're being hunted by five men that Manny or my father sent after us! They tried to kill us yesterday afternoon in the meadow where we were gathering herbs. They shot three RPGs at us!"

Carter exploded. "RPGs!?"

"Y-yes . . . we managed to escape. W-we've been on the run ever since. We couldn't get to Wes's truck because they burned up the engine. We had to get out of the area where they were staying. We've been working our way through the forest down to the highway. B-but I don't *see* the highway! I don't know where I am." She sobbed again, her hand against her mouth, breath coming in gulps.

"Hold, I'll check your GPS," Steve ordered. "Sara, you're half a mile from it. Is there a slope or hill in front of you?"

"Yes, it looks like a drop-off."

"Are you hidden within the tree line?"

"At the edge of it. I-I don't think I can be seen . . ."

"Don't go toward that highway. It's just below you on that drop-off where you're at, but from your position, you can't see it. I'm calling Sheriff Seabert. I've got two of my operators here and I'm coming your way in about two minutes. We're coming armed, and so will the sheriff and his people. Stay hidden!"

"Okay," she rattled, pressing her back up against the thick trunk of the pine. "We don't know where these men are, Steve. I'm so afraid for Wes. He can't walk. He says the break is a bad one. There's a lot of blood. He's at the entrance of an old mine, which is what he fell into when we were running."

"Okay, good intel. Stay put. Help is on its way."

Tears blurred her vision and she told him about Colin and Dana before she ended the call. Now, she had to connect with their friends. *Please, please let them be home*, she prayed, punching in the numbers. Dana answered. Sara knew she sounded frazzled and way beyond being upset. In so many words, she told them what had happened. Instantly, Dana called Colin over and put the phone on speaker. Sara repeated the information.

"Sara? It's Colin. Give me your coordinates and Wes's as well."

She gave him the numbers. "You have to stay home!" she cried out softly, looking around warily. Her skin was crawling. Was it her imagination? Or was someone who wanted to kill her, nearby? Panicking, she lowered her voice. "Colin! Someone's near. I can't talk anymore! Stay there! Don't get involved!"

Oh, no . . . Sara felt terror ripping through her. Off to her left, she recognized one of the men that had been guarding the two gray pickups. How did he get down here? Shocked, she froze, her mind paralyzed as to what to do.

Suddenly, up the slope, she heard a shot. It rang loudly and she felt as if it had gone straight through her, but it was the shock of the sound only.

More gunshots, only these were deep-throated and sounded like they were tearing the world apart.

Jerking her head to the left, she spotted the man who had halted; he swiveled around and then started running toward the sound of gunshots being exchanged, galloping up the hill, rifle at the ready. Sara looked right, then left. All clear! She quickly texted Steve Carter, that she heard gunfire coming from the area where she'd left Wes. Turning off the cell phone, torn, she didn't know what to do. She had no weapons. She didn't even know how to use one!

More gunshots riddled the area.

With a little cry, Sara whirled around, toes digging into the soft earth. She knew it had to be Wes who was under fire. The killers had found him! Tears burned out of the corners of her eyes as she raced up the slope. *No! No! I love him! He can't die!* And it was all because of her! Because of her murderous father and half brother. Wes had been willing to die for her but she loved him! He could *not* die! And she didn't know what she would do once she managed, if she wasn't shot first, to reach that mine where Wes was fighting for his life!

The slope was steep the last mile and she was sobbing for breath, her legs feeling rubbery, her lungs burning so deeply they hurt with every ragged inhalation.

Spates of gunfire were exchanged.

It seemed like an hour to Sara as she broke from a run to a trot, her legs so weak, she thought she'd fall and she still hadn't reached the top of the last slope where the mine was located. The gunfire continued to be sporadic. She could hear it coming from her left. Where had the man who she'd seen go? He had disappeared, running hard, the forest swallowing him up until she could no longer see or find him.

"SARA!"

Snapping her head around, she saw Steve Carter in full body armor, carrying an M1 rifle, helmet on his head, racing toward her, his face hard and expressionless. Right behind him, to his right, were two other men she did not know, dressed the very same way, carrying the very same kind of weapon. One of Steve's operators was carrying a sack at his side and she had no idea what was in it. They carried themselves like the operators they had been, without question. She halted, dizzied and weak from the physical demands, staring openmouthed at them.

"Stay down here. Hide. We'll take care of these bastards," Steve barked at her as he raced by.

With a little cry, Sara fell to her knees, shaking and weakened with physical fatigue. She watched the three men move up that steep slope like mountain goats, never breaking stride, never faltering as she had. Steve had Wes's location in that mine. That gave her some hope, but not much.

They disappeared over the slope and the last she saw was the three men splitting up, one going right, one going left, and Steve, straight ahead, rifle ready to fire.

Staggering to her feet, she trudged forward, wanting to get up that slope. *Wes! Please be alive! I love you! Don't die . . .*

Wes sucked air between his gritted teeth. He'd been resting, eyes closed, when he heard the loud crunch of gravel. Instantly, his lids flew open and he saw one of the men who had guarded the two gray trucks halt at the entrance to the mine. This time, the dude was holding an M1, peering warily into the dark maw of the tunnel. Lucky for Wes, he was sitting behind the huge adit post, unseen. Pulling his pistol from the holster, which already had a bullet in the chamber, Wes slowly lifted his hands, the pistol aimed at the man's head. Whoever he was? He wasn't military. Sloppy at best, he gave the tunnel a cursory look and didn't go any farther inside to check it out. If he had, Wes knew his life was gone. He could kill one, but the others? Were they carrying those RPGs with them today? All they had to do was yell, *Fire in the hole!* and they'd blast him and the front of this mine, bringing down tons of earth, and he'd be dead.

"Hey," the man called at the entrance, waving at his buddy.

Wes waited, his heartbeat slow. His mind whirled with questions. How the hell had they followed him *here*? *How?* Keeping a bead on the man, he saw another man he didn't recognize, carrying an M1, come over to the tunnel entrance.

"Find anything?"

"No." The man slid the strap of the rifle over his shoulder and pulled out an electronic device, showing it to the other man. "It says she's around here."

"Damn thing is a piece of shit! It's making a circle half a mile around us. She could be hiding in a dozen places."

The man shrugged his meaty shoulders. "Got me. I didn't buy this. The boss did."

"Coulda spent more and got a better device that would show her *exact* location, not a fucking general area."

"Yeah, well . . ." He sighed and shoved it back into his camo pocket. "At least we know she's in the area. That's a good thing."

"You think she's in this mine?"

"Nah, it's in real bad shape. I really don't wanna go in there. You see those overhead pieces of lumber? They're sagging and broken. The whole ceiling could fall in on us. I don't wanna die today." He turned, looking around. "Let's split up." He pointed outside the mine entrance in two different directions. "We'll check it out. That tracker we put on her backpack is working."

Snorting, the other man growled unhappily, "Yeah, with

a cheap piece of shit to show where she *might* be. Not her *exact* location."

"Well, she ain't in this mine that I can tell, so let's see if she's hiding behind one of the thousands of trees in the area of that tracker indicator."

Wes slowly lowered the pistol, his mind whirling. A tracker? A bug was placed on her backpack by one of them? When? Sara hadn't been out of his sight! How, then? That explained how they were up in the stands of willow by the river and almost ran into them. They'd used an electronic finder to locate the tracker. Had it been there *before* she'd moved to Silver Creek? Had someone placed the bug on it before she left Dallas? It would also explain how they knew Sara was up here in Wyoming. Damn! He'd gone through every piece of clothing she had, looking for any type of electronic device. The backpack was new to him. She must have had it in a box, maybe in a suitcase, and brought it out for use when she went foraging that morning. And he'd stupidly *not* checked it out. That was on him. *Sonofabitch!*

Moving a little, he grimaced at the pain lancing up his calf. The bleeding had stopped from what he could determine, which was good. Sara had been gone an hour and a half. Had she made cell contact with Steve Carter? The sheriff? Were Colin and Dana Gallagher told not to come up into this area? So many questions and no answers. He worried about Sara. Was she safe? Unharmed? How long before the cavalry arrived? He knew that the sheriff and his deputies had a two-fold job: find them, and then find their mutual enemy. Wes wasn't sure which they would be in contact with. More than anything, he hoped that if Dan had arrived, they'd taken Sara down to one of the cruisers and kept her safe inside it. He loved her. His heart ached worse than his ankle did.

A crunch of gravel alerted him. Who now? Lifting his pistol, both hands on the grip, he saw a third man with an M1, approach the opening. This one looked mean. His darkened face showed small, close-set eyes in a big, meaty head. A true hit man if Wes had ever seen one. He was looking slowly around the darkened adit, seemingly in no hurry to leave. Wes felt himself go into invisible mode. Many times on a night mission, they would freeze, should a sound be made, not wanting to alert the enemy. He held his pistol steady. He had a bead on the man's head. But he knew if he fired, he would bring the other four surviving enemies down on him, too. Mentally, Wes told him to back out of the tunnel, to leave it.

The man came forward a step into the tunnel, studying the roughened side of it. Then, his gaze went to the floor.

Wes froze. He hadn't covered his tracks! He'd dragged himself, unable to lift that wounded leg, down the adit to the area where there was some protection and safety. *Damn!* The man frowned, squatted down, his fingers reaching out, touching the drag line in the dust and gravel. He lifted his head, unable to see where the drag line went.

He stared into the maw.

Wes's finger tightened around the trigger. He was well hidden, but if he took another couple of steps, he'd find him. So much ran through his mind in those milliseconds. Sara's warm, promising kiss that held so much happiness and goodness to come for both of them. The flowery scent of her skin. The taste of her lips against his, feeling her womanly fierceness that was barely bridled, wanting to burst free, wanting him. All his dreams of her since that kiss flared wildly inside him. Undressing her, watching each article of clothing fall away to reveal the beauty of her body. Her arms around his neck, drawing him tight against her breasts, unafraid to let him know how much she desired him. The silky texture of the strands of her black hair between his fingers . . . all gone . . . just a dream that would never come true.

For the first time in his life, Wes put a price on his life. He did not want to die. Not when he'd finally found a woman who seemed to fit him as much as he fitted her. She was highly educated, intelligent, fearless, and proud of being a woman. Her appeal dizzied him, called to him, and he yearned for her, body and soul.

Most of all, Wes wanted to gently hold her. Tom had taught him that being gentle was welcomed by the other gender. He'd learned over time how Tom treated girls his own age, with respect, how he treated Frannie, who clearly loved him in a hundred small, everyday ways. Tom showed him how children should be loved. Yes, he'd learned love through Tom and his family. And he'd fallen in love with Sara, with her goodness, her honesty, kindness toward others, and treating everyone, regardless of gender, with respect and equality. She was a living role model, a fierce woman warrior who didn't back down from any kind of a challenge.

The man took another step forward, gaze on the ground, starting to follow that drag line in the semidarkness. Right to where he sat.

Wes fired.

The echo of the pistol was like a loud thunderclap echoing around his ringing ears.

The man made a croaking sound, the M1 falling out of

his listless hand, falling right in front of where Wes sat squeezed up against the wall. He collapsed, dead.

Stretching forward, grabbing the rifle, Wes hissed a curse as he dragged himself forward, his hand reaching out, clawing at the ammo belt around the man's waist. And he was going to need every bit of it if he was to survive what would be coming his way in a matter of moments . . .

Chapter Eleven

Steve Carter was in radio contact via his earpiece with Rob Bramwell and Chris Parish. Both men had been a part of his SEAL unit for nine years before they all left the Navy to start his global security company. These were men he trusted with his life. He dug the toes of his boots into the soft floor of the forest as they crested the steep slope.

Rob was to the right of him, Chris to the left, M1s up and ready to fire. Ahead, a quarter of a mile, he could see the maw of the old silver mine. Two men were at the entrance, firing M1s on automatic, into the tunnel. Sparks flew like fireflies within the massive adit as the bullets struck the rocks, careening off of them, ricocheting all over the place. Somewhere in there, was Wes.

"Fire at will," he ordered his men. If they hadn't been trained as SEALs, Steve would never have given such an order. These men were cold, calm professionals; and they knew one of their own, Wes, who had also been on their team, was taking intense fire right now.

The first bullet hit the man on the right, and the punch of an M1 rifle bullet slammed him three feet forward, the weapon flying out of his hands, the enemy landing flat on his face within the tunnel entrance, unmoving. The second bullet hit the man on the left, who had jerked his head up as he heard other gunfire coming from behind him. He'd made a pivot, lifting his M1 at them when a bullet struck him in the head.

The noise of gunfire suddenly ceased.

"Where's the other three men?" Steve radioed to his operators.

Both ex-SEALs slowed, looking around, on guard, weapons raised.

"Can't see anything," Rob reported. "No one else is around here."

Steve skidded to a halt at the entrance. "I'm going into the mine," he said. Was Wes alive? He didn't know but hoped like hell he was. First, he kicked the rifle away from each dead man, leaning down, fingertips on each one's neck, feeling for a pulse. They were gone. *Good.* Rob and Chris began to search their bodies for papers and identification. Then he saw another man, dead, in front of them, sprawled in the opening. That left two more men still on the loose and lethal to them.

"Wes? It's Steve. Are you in here?" His voice rang and echoed down the darkness. Steve turned on the bright LED light on the rifle, aiming it into the tunnel, lighting it up like the Fourth of July.

"Here! To your right, Steve! I'm behind the adit post."

"Coming in," Steve hollered, putting the rifle barrel down, the light flooding the dusty, gravely floor. "Two men are dead, plus one you must have shot. I'll have Bramwell and Parish out hunting the other two men in a minute. There's still a fourth and fifth one on the loose and we have to find them." He looked down at the meaty man who was facedown and dead nearby. "Looks like you got one of them yourself," he said, rounding the adit post.

Wes gave him a weary look. "Yeah, took him out. Where's Sara?"

"We ran into her down at the bottom of this slope. I told her to stay there, that we'd come back and pick her up once we cleared this hot zone."

"Was she all right?"

"Barely able to stand from all the running she did, but she's okay."

"You have to get to her, right away, Steve. There's a location-finder bug in her backpack. Whoever is still at large can find her. She's in danger right now."

"Damn. Okay." Steve turned and called out to Rob and Chris, sending them back down the slope to locate her by her GPS position and to be on the lookout for the last two enemy.

Setting his rifle aside, Steve leaned down, adjusting the light on it such that it lit up the whole area. Wes, in the meantime, kept his M1 up and ready, pointing it at the opening. That fourth and fifth man could come in and blow them away. Studying Wes's leg and ankle, Steve said, "They'll find her." He touched his lower leg. "Bad break?"

"Yeah," Wes huffed, sitting up more, laying the M1 across his lap. "Didn't see the opening to this mine shaft. It was covered with debris and pine needles."

"Give me some intel on the two other killers," Steve asked.

"One is the Ferret," Wes warned grimly. "He was the ring leader of this team and I'll bet everything he's been in black ops. They've got two gray trucks back on the road that we drove up yesterday morning. When all hell broke loose, Sara and I managed to follow the river east of their position. We then moved into the trees and were about a quarter of a mile from where they had originally parked their trucks. They destroyed my truck so we couldn't use it to escape. There was gunfire in the river area where we'd been earlier, and two of these goons hopped in the two trucks and took off toward the gunfire. That was the last we saw of them." He pointed to Sara's backpack. "I found out by listening to them earlier that someone had planted a bug into Sara's bag."

Scowling, Steve asked, "Did you check everything out when you went to live with her?"

"I did, but I didn't see the backpack until she pulled it out of a box just before we went to the meadow yesterday." Wes grimaced. "That was on me. I didn't thoroughly check it out before she put it on."

"We'll debrief on this at another time," Steve said roughly, pressing on his radio, connecting with the sheriff.

Wes listened to the back and forth communications. An ambulance was with the group speeding their way to the GPS location where Sara had been told to stay put. Steve gave them a heads-up that the two gray trucks were on that dirt road. Instead of stopping where Steve had along the highway, the sheriff was putting two deputies and their black Chevy Suburbans at the end of that road so no one could get in or out of it. The SWAT team was with them, and that made Wes feel better. Most SWAT members were ex-military and knew how to work in a group and shoot straight. In a matter of minutes, a plan was laid out and agreed upon. The sheriff had earlier deputized Steve, Rob, and Chris.

Wes wiped his sweaty brow, feeling the pain starting up more and more as the morphine wore off. Steve set his rifle aside, looking closely at the damage to his ankle.

"Have you got morphine?" he asked.

"Not anymore. I used my ampule earlier."

Steve pulled a small plastic box out of his side pocket. "You're looking pale and sweaty. Time for another one." He handed it to Wes. "I'm calling the hospital in Silver Creek. Dr. Kelly Ribas, orthopedic surgeon, is on standby and will check you out once the paramedics on that ambulance get you to their ER."

"Sara was telling me the other day that Logan Anderson, owner of the largest ranch in the valley, fell off a ladder in the barn and broke his ankle. That the doctor had to put screws in to hold it together. I met Logan about a week ago and he walks like it never happened. I'll be happy to have her check this ankle of mine out. I want to be a hundred percent when it's healed."

"She's really good," Steve assured him. "One of my female operators had a femur break on a mission, and I didn't think she'd make it back to duty, but Doc Ribas put her back together again."

"Is she still an operator?"

Steve grinned. "Yeah, out in the field again." He glanced down at the blood still leaking over the top of Wes's boot. "Good thing SEALs are really well taught with that EMT course they must take. Leaving this boot on has stopped you from hemorrhaging."

Nodding, Wes gave himself the ampule of morphine, tucking the box in his pocket. He glanced at his watch, worried for Sara. "Chris and Rob should reach Sara any moment now . . ."

Nodding, Steve stood and then took off as a call from Dan came in. "Just rest. Keep hydrated. As soon as I hear something, I'll come back in and let you know. The ambulance should arrive pretty soon. I'm going to go stand guard outside this entrance until we can account for those two men."

"Thanks," Wes said, leaning back, feeling weak and fatigued. All he needed was Sara. She was his world, his life and his future. All of Steve's employees were black ops people and all of them were in world class physical shape. It wouldn't take Chris long to reach the woman he loved.

Trudging one foot in front of the other, Sara no longer heard any gunfire. There was a sudden spate of it and then the forest grew silent once more. She couldn't see what had happened, or if Wes was safe or not, and was driven to disobey the order to stay where she was. That thought drove her on, as exhausted as she was. She needed to make sure Wes was alive.

Something caught her attention out of the corner of her eye. Instantly, she shrank against a huge tree trunk, her breath stuck in her throat, terror zigzagging down through her. Disbelief shocked her as she recognized the Ferret, that small, lean man with the black eyes, his face expressionless as he walked toward her, looking down at an instrument he held in his hand.

Looking for her!

For a second, she felt faint, seeing he had an M1 in his hands, dressed in camo gear, trying to find her and kill her. The terror subsided and turned into rage combined with the will to survive. He was coming in her direction. She looked down at her feet. There was a good six-foot limb that had fallen off the tree. That could make the difference. Sara didn't even think that she was outweighed by this murdering soldier, or out-trained, or physically not as strong as a man. None of that registered on her brain that was focused on him. If he came close enough? She could surprise him. Wes had told her that surprise always leveled the playing field with an enemy.

Mouth dry, her heart pounding so hard she could barely hear anything, she waited. Her fingers tightened around one end of the limb, the other held close to her body, hidden by the trunk of the tree. How badly she wanted to live, but she knew her odds of doing just that diminished with every step he took in her direction.

Now, it was a matter of waiting.

She could not risk peeking out from behind the trunk or he'd spot her. Would he be close enough for her to hit him and knock him out? That was her only possible avenue of escape. And if she missed? Or he was too far away to reach? Or she had to expose herself to hit him? So much could go wrong! Panic ate away in her chest, her breath growing shallow. Her fear was rising by the second.

The crunch of someone walking on a pine cone made her jump.

Close! He was so close to her position! Every hair on the back of her neck stood up.

She caught sight of his shoulder as he passed within two feet of the tree. Just as she saw his shoulder and back appear, she raised the limb.

Gritting her teeth, she swung the limb downward as hard as she could. The limb came down, striking him on the side of his head and neck. His black baseball cap flew off. He grunted.

Lunging forward, swinging the club again, Sara leaped from behind the tree, the second swing catching him off balance, the rifle in his hand dropping. This hit was solid, catching the Ferret in the face, and buckling his knees.

Sara gave a small cry as the man collapsed in front of her.

Hurry!

She dropped the limb, seeing that he was unconscious. In four steps, she picked up the M1, snatching it away. Blood was spurting from where the limb had glanced off the side of his head. He lay still.

"Sara! Sara!"

Giving a cry, she whirled around and saw two men in military gear, running up to her.

"We're with Steve," one of them said, skidding to a halt. "I'm Chris. Rob is coming. You're safe. Stand back, Sara . . ." He aimed his rifle at the unmoving Ferret.

Sara leaped aside, gasping for air. Her hands hurt and bled where she'd gripped the branch so tightly.

"Rob!" she whispered unsteadily, backing away as he approached her, a relieved look on his face. The operator was one of her clients; he came to her shop for an herb formula that helped him sleep. The other man, who she didn't know, leaned over, pushing Ferret on his back.

"Hey," Rob called, giving her a proud look, "you cold-cocked him."

"H-he isn't dead?" she whispered, tears brimming in her eyes. It was over! Rob and Chris would keep her safe.

Pushing the Ferret onto his belly, Rob set his rifle aside, pulled out a zip tie and tied the man's wrists behind him. "No, just unconscious. You did good, Sara. Are you all right?" He straightened and went over to her. Rob had placed his hand on her shoulder and it felt stabilizing.

"I-I'm okay, Rob . . . just scared to death. Where's Wes? Is Wes okay?" Her voice broke.

Rob patted her shoulder. "He's okay, Sara. The sheriff will be here anytime, there's an ambulance with them.

He's fine." And he gave her an intense look. "Any wounds on you?"

Managing a little laugh, she opened her bloody hands. "Just here . . . I'm so tired, my knees hurt, but I'm okay. I really am."

"You're a brave woman, Sara," he said, giving her a sound hug and then releasing her. Rob looked around the area, remaining on guard. Chris devoted his focus on the Ferret, who was groaning and starting to regain consciousness.

Rob said, "Sara, come with me. We have to go straight up this slope and we'll go left. Chris is going to keep this thug here until the sheriff arrives with his people. We still have one more enemy on the loose."

She gave him a startled look. "One more?"

"Yeah," he said, "we have three dead at the mine entrance, and then this guy. There's one more on the loose out there we have to find. I'll take you to Wes."

"We were the only two operators at HQ when your call came in to Steve." Rob walked over and took the pistol as well as a knife in a scabbard off the Ferret, who glared up at them. Chris jerked him into a sitting position. Picking up the weapons, he handed them to Sara. "Take these with you?"

Gripping the pistol and the scabbard, she gave a jerky nod.

Craning his neck, Chris looked down the slope. "Turn around, there's some deputies coming up to help us right now. The cavalry has arrived."

Sara was never so glad to see sheriff's deputies as right now. There were three of them, and she recognized Sergeant Pepper Warner in the lead, grim looking, her two men on her heels as they raced toward them in full gear, ready for a fight.

Sara saw Pepper give her a tight grin of acknowledgment. As the group came to a halt, she said, "Are you okay, Sara?" and pointed to the weapons in her hands.

"She is now," Rob said with a grin. He pointed to the Ferret. "And he's all yours. There's three dead up by the mine shaft, but we have one more on the loose and no one's seen him yet. Stay alert."

Pepper turned, pressing the radio on her shoulder, ordering the ambulance paramedics up from the highway and to bring a litter with them. She gave orders for one of her deputies to take Ferret to the cruiser below at the highway. The deputy hauled him to his feet and took him down the hill to where two cruisers were parked.

"I want to see Wes," Sara told Rob, handing off the weapons to another deputy.

"Go ahead," Pepper said, taking over the scene. "Rob? Will you escort her? Chris, come with me? We need to hunt down the last one."

Sara couldn't walk fast, and the pain in her knees disappeared because every step up that hill meant a step closer to Wes. That's all she wanted. All she needed was him. Rob showed her a shortcut and he took her hand to help her up and over a couple of small cliffs of rock and dirt. Finally on top, she saw the opening to the mine ahead of her. Steve was standing guard, on full alert. She broke into a wobbly trot, Rob at her side.

"Wes is doing good," Steve told her as he walked in with her, to show her where he was located. "Not really happy, but alive."

Sara couldn't hold back her tears any longer as Steve moved aside and she saw Wes for the first time since leaving him hours earlier. He gave her a wan smile and she saw how dark his eyes were. Steve had propped up his injured leg.

"Wes . . ." she whispered rawly, falling to her knees at his side, her hand reaching out, touching his cool, sweaty cheek.

"Hey . . ." he joked weakly, "I'm fine . . . really . . . How are you?" He looked up at her in the semidarkness.

Rob entered the mine. "You should have seen Sara in action. She took a two-by-four to the goon and put out his lights. You'd have been proud of her. I think we need to start calling her Wonder Woman."

Hand shaking, Sara touched Wes's hair, needing him, needing his touch in return. He slid his hand around her neck, drawing her gently downward until their lips touched. A low groan came from deep within him as her mouth hungrily took his, her hands framing his face.

Neither of them saw Rob quietly leave, giving them time alone.

Sara sank into the warm strength of Wes's mouth, glorying in his hand curved around her neck, holding her as close as they could get under the circumstances. Just being in contact with him, no matter how sweaty he was, how chilly the tunnel, her heart pounded with gratitude and joy. Finally, they eased apart, staring into one another's eyes, the silence filled with so much that needed to be said, but this wasn't the time or place for it.

"Your hands," Wes managed, his voice low and rasping as he turned them over, seeing all the cuts and blood across her palms.

"It's nothing," she assured him.

He kissed the back of her hand, releasing it. "I'm just sorry I wasn't there to protect you, Sara . . ."

She caressed his bearded jaw. "You kept us alive. You did everything you could." Hearing noise at the entrance, other people's voices, she looked up and craned her neck. "The paramedics are here. They have a stretcher for you, Wes."

"I'm ready," he said, releasing her hand that he'd held for a moment. "I want out of here."

As the two men showed up with the stretcher at the entrance, Sara got to her feet. "I want *you*."

Wes remembered very little, all his strength drained out of him by the brutal break on his ankle. The two male paramedics were as careful as they could be taking him down those slopes to the waiting ambulance below. Sara remained with him, giving him looks of worry and what he thought was love. Sometimes she'd reach out and touch his blanketed arm, strapped into the stretcher so he couldn't fall off. Steve and his team, plus Pepper's deputies, were still hunting for the fifth enemy soldier.

Once in the bus, as the boxy ambulance was referred to by law enforcement, they allowed Sara to sit up in the cab with the driver. She turned, keeping an eye on him as they turned around and headed back toward Silver Creek to the small hospital where Dr. Ribas was waiting to examine him and get X-rays.

On the way there, they found out that the fifth man was guarding the two gray trucks on the road near the meadow. They took him into custody.

At the hospital, Sara walked into the emergency room, where it felt so much warmer. Wes was whisked to the

X-ray area, Dr. Ribas with him. How badly she wanted to go and be with him, but it was impossible. Instead, Steve came and stayed with her out in the visitors' waiting room. He was on the phone most of the time, taking calls, but Sara appreciated his care and remaining with her under the circumstances.

A nurse came out and cleaned up her hands, bandaging them. Sara thanked the older nurse, who smiled and put soft dressings around each one of her palms.

"I'm putting on special waterproof dressings so you can go ahead and have a shower. Keep these on your right hand for at least three days, Sara. That's a deep, long cut you have across your right palm. I've stitched it up, but it needs time to seal up the wound."

"I will . . . thanks so much . . ."

Dr. Ribas came out of the ER doors.

"Sara?" she called, gesturing for her to come to the doors.

"Go," Steve said. "I'll be out here. Come and get me if you need me."

She touched his shoulder. "I will. I'll come and let you know whatever I hear." Because Steve had said he was sure Wes would have to have an operation on that ankle, and he was going to stay until the procedure was finished and he was assured Wes would be all right.

Sara hurried to the door, Dr. Ribas allowed her in, and the door shut behind them.

"Wes has an open fracture," she explained to Sara as they walked down the cubicles. "I'm prepping for surgery right now, but I want you to see him before we take him into the operation theater." She halted and pointed to cubical seven. "He's in there."

Moving through the curtains, Sara saw him lying in a

semi-upright position on his gurney, draped in white and blue blankets, wearing a light blue smock. Someone had cleaned him up; there was no more dust or mud streaks on his face, arms, or neck, and even his hair had been washed. He gave her a weak smile as she slid her bandaged right hand into his.

"Dr. Ribas said you need an operation. How are you doing?"

"You're here," he rasped. "That's all I really need. How are you doing?" He held up her bandaged hand, studying it.

"I got a few good cuts from wielding that branch. No big deal. I'm going to stay here with Steve. He's out in the visitors' area. Dr. Ribas said we could both wait in the surgery lounge while she fixes your ankle."

"That's nice of him to stay, but that's like Steve," he murmured, squeezing her hand very gently.

"Are you in pain?"

"No. They gave me morphine. I'm floating." He gave her a boyish grin.

She smiled, leaned over and kissed his damp brow. "I don't know how you can joke after all we've been through."

"Black humor, sweetheart. Operators live on it. We laugh instead of crying."

Nodding, she took in a deep breath and exhaled it. "Steve said that the sheriff is going to interview the Ferret. The paramedic fixed up his head wound, and now he's on his way to jail. Pepper and her group found the fifth man guarding their two trucks near the meadow. They took him into custody, and are taking him to the sheriff's office right now."

"Two out of the five have survived. I'll bet Dan wants to try and flip the two who are still alive, get him to spill the evidence, so he can go after your half brother and father."

"The Ferret doesn't look like someone whose going to flip. He's Mafia, Wes. They're loyal to the death. He'll never rat on Manny or my father. I don't know about the other guy."

"What this means," he said, giving her a sympathetic look, "is that with that tracker that was put on your back-pack?"

"What?"

Wes told her about it.

"Oh . . . no!" Sara moaned. "They know where I live here in Silver Creek Valley! I was wondering how they found me, Wes."

"Yeah, this isn't over, Sara, as much as we both wish it was. Talk to Steve. Tell him once I'm out of the hospital, we need a new house to stay at for now. Your clinic and Victorian home have been compromised." He saw her face fall with such crushing sadness. Squeezing her hand, he rasped, "Look, you're in shock. We need a few days of calm to sort this out with law enforcement and, I'm sure, the FBI. Ask Steve to find us a safe house here in the area? Only he will know where it's at. And we'll need protection. Ask him if Rob's available. He's the biggest, baddest guard dog around. I know Steve will assign him if he can."

Two pre-op nurses and an assistant entered the cubical. "Time for your operation, Wes," one of them called, smiling.

Sara leaned down, kissing him swiftly on the mouth. "I'll see you when this is over . . . I love you."

Wes gripped her arm. "I love you, Sara. Don't ever forget that . . ."

He was gone in a minute, wheeled out into the hall,

disappearing at the other end of it that led to the operation suites. Turning, Sara walked out of the ER. There, she saw Steve was standing with a nurse. He lifted his head as she drew near.

"This young woman is going to take us to the surgery lounge," he told Sara. "Ready to roll?"

Sara smiled a little. "Let's roll," she said softly, following them. Steve hung back, put his hand on her shoulder. "Wes is in the best of hands. Dr. Ribas came out earlier and said it would take maybe an hour or two at the most. They're going to keep him here at the hospital overnight."

Sara nodded, and they went down another hall in the busy hospital. "Wes said we need a safe house, Steve."

"Yeah," he said, nodding. "I've already got my staff on it, back at my office. In fact"—he winked at her—"they're already over at that pretty Victorian house you bought, packing up items and clothing you're going to need. And don't worry, it's all being taken care of for you. When we are in the surgical visitors' lounge, I'll tell you more."

Sara sat with Steve, the clock on the wall seeming to crawl by. They were the only ones in the room, and Steve chose a nice couch, brought out his Apple iPad and proceeded to fill her in on the safe house he'd chosen for them.

"Now, this isn't really one of my safe houses," he said, grinning, pulling up a photo of a white house with green trim, one story and with a white picket fence around it. "Logan Anderson has a number of homes for the wranglers on his ranch, and he was in the military, so I asked him for a favor. The home they're putting you and Wes in until we can untangle and resolve this mess, is near the center of his headquarters area. But it's hidden by a grove of trees and stands alone and away from the other homes where his wranglers and their families live. I'm assigning Rob and Chris to be your guard dogs. They will do twelve-hour shifts, around the clock. There's four bedrooms to this house. There's a mother-in-law house out back of it, and Rob and Chris will stay there. You two can have the privacy of the other house. Their job will be to stay close to you two. But they won't be a pain in the ass, and you will have plenty of private time together without even knowing they're nearby. My men will be in contact with my staff at all times. Sheriff Seabert will know where you're located, but other than Logan and his wife knowing your where-abouts? No one else will."

Sara drew in a painful breath. "Oh, Steve, this is so nice of you to do this for us. I feel like we've jumped out of the frying pan into the fire . . . I'm not safe anywhere, and neither is Wes."

He patted her hand. "A step at a time," he murmured, giving her a sympathetic and understanding look. "Have you talked to your mother yet?"

"Yes, I did. I told her what happened. She's unnerved by it, and so am I."

"For now," Steve counseled her gently, "you will be safe on Logan's ranch. It does mean you can't go back to your herb store and clinic. At least, for now. This thing will resolve sooner than later, I hope, so you can go back to having your life again."

Giving him a pained look, she whispered, "But I have so many clients, Steve. They rely on me . . . on the herbs they use and need."

"I said *for now*. You can always get Dr. Cooper to make them up for you at her office."

Relieved, Sara whispered, "That's such a great plan, Steve. And I know Blaine Cooper will be fine with taking care of my clients until I can again."

"I just got off a call with Dan. The FBI has sent in an agent and DOJ prosecutor to talk with the guy you call the Ferret. They'll also talk to that other soldier they have in custody. What they're hoping is that they can flip one or both of them. And if they do, that means one of them may give up evidence on who is behind this attack on you."

"For sure, it's my father and Manny," she muttered, scowling. "They want me dead."

"I know. I had a talk with the DOJ prosecutor earlier."

She stared at him. "Is there anyone you don't know?" she demanded, stunned.

He gave her a little grin. "I have my network," was all he said, lightly, giving her an amused look. "More importantly? This team coming in tomorrow will start seeing if the Ferret or the other guy will flip. So, don't give up yet."

Shaking her head, she whispered brokenly, "My father always gets his way. He's Sicilian Mafia. He has connections across the world."

"I'm not so concerned about him," Steve assured her. "It's your half brother."

"Manny? He's a punk. He hates me."

"Yes, but if the Ferret or the other dude flips and tells the FBI and this prosecutor who set this hit in motion, and it's Manny? Then Manny will go to prison for a long, long time."

"As long as I'm alive, Steve, whether he's in prison or not, he's going to send his soldiers after me to kill me. He can't get the family money if I'm alive."

"I understand," Steve said. "But let's just see how this plays out. Right now"—he gave her a kind look—"you and Wes need one another. You've been through hell. And it's going to take some time to unpack it all, emotionally speaking, for both of you. Let the law and the FBI do their thing. You can never tell what might happen."

"I wish I had your faith," she said bitterly. "But I don't. I'm always going to be hounded by the Mafia."

Chapter Twelve

Sara sat up as Dr. Ribas, dressed in her surgery green scrubs and cap, walked into the nearly empty visitors' lounge.

"Wes is doing fine," she assured them, halting before them. "I had to use some screws to put his bones back into place, but it's done and he should come out of this fine, along with some physical therapy afterward."

Relief washed through Sara. "And what about the bleeding, Doctor?"

"There was a tear in an artery, and I repaired that, also. Luckily—because he's a trained SEAL and I know from Steve that they all take an EMT course—Wes made all the right decisions. By leaving his high-topped boot on, it acted like a cast to keep those bones from moving around and doing a lot more tissue damage and potentially, worse artery hemorrhaging."

"And he's awake?"

"Yes, he is semiconscious right now. For the operation, I gave him a sedative and he went to sleep. There was no need to intubate him for this surgery. We have him in post op right now with the nurses, and within the next thirty minutes, we'll have him moved up to his room, where you can go and visit him. He's going to be tired, Sara, as I'm sure you are."

"I'm exhausted, but I want to stay with him, Dr. Ribas. I'm not leaving his side."

She smiled a little. "I figured as much. We're having a very nice and comfortable lounge chair brought in for you, along with a pillow and blankets, so you can remain nearby."

"Thank you," Sara whispered, feeling hot tears and blinking them away. "This has been so traumatic . . ."

Ribas nodded and said, "I know it has, for both of you. My office will set up a time after I see him tomorrow morning and release him back to you. They have your cell phone number."

Getting up, Sara hugged the doctor. "Thank you . . . so much . . ."

"He'll have a full recovery and in about three months, be good as new with some physical therapy."

Steve stood, shaking the doctor's hand. "You're a miracle maker, Dr. Ribas. Thank you."

She smiled and left.

Steve moved beside Sara. "I've asked Dan Seabert to keep Chris and Rob deputized because right now, you both need twenty-four-hour security. This way, Dan doesn't have to send two of his deputies to be guards, and I can use my own people who are between missions."

Giving him a grateful look, she said, "That sounds wonderful. But do you think there's more of that band of men who came in to kill me, around?"

Shrugging, he said, "We don't know yet, Sara. And I'm not willing to guess about it. Once we get you two moved onto Logan's ranch, hidden in the main headquarters area of his property, we'll assess it on a daily basis. Until those Mafia killers are questioned by the FBI and that DOJ prosecutor? And if they can flip them or not? We are on war footing."

Giving him a sad look, Sara murmured, "I understand." She reached out, touching Steve's arm briefly. "Thank you for everything you're doing."

Sara held her real thoughts to herself. She saw no end to the harassment she would suffer from Manny and her father. This was a skirmish. Something that would happen again, and her heart broke over it. Her life . . . and Wes's life, would never be safe. Giving Steve a nod, she said nothing more. Her focus right now was on Wes. He was the center of her life for every important reason. But the future looked murky and unstable. Right now, her heart, her world, was centered on Wes.

Sara could barely hold her emotions in check as the nurse led her onto the surgery recovery floor and took her to Wes's private room. Rob nodded hello to her, sitting in a chair outside the room. He carried a pistol on his hip and had changed into a clean set of civilian clothing. She touched Rob's shoulder, thanking him.

Opening the door, she saw Wes was sitting up, looking pale, but his eyes were clear and no longer dark looking. Sara turned, thanking the nurse who checked his IV, and closed the door as the nurse left his room. She saw a large lounge chair with pillows and blankets sitting on it, for her.

"How are you doing?" she asked, coming over and sitting on a chair next to his bed. He held out his hand to her and she took it, feeling some of her trepidation dissolving.

"I'm okay," he reassured her, his voice low and gravelly. "You look beautiful," he said, squeezing her hand, holding her gaze.

"And you have no idea how wonderful you look to me," she whispered, leaning up and kissing his cheek. Someone had shaved him. "Are you in pain?"

He looked at his leg that rested under blankets to keep him warm. A contraption held up the blankets so his ankle didn't have any weight upon it. "So far, no." He looked up at the IV suspended on the other side of the bed. "They've put some morphine in there to stop pain."

Just holding his hand, also clean and no longer dirty and dusty, made her feel better. She saw scratches on his face, and one of them on his left cheek had some tape across it. She guessed that it would hold the skin together so it could heal without a scar. "Why do you have so many scratches on your face and neck?"

"Blame the two of those goons that started firing down the tunnel after I took out their friend," he said. "There were ricochets all over the place and a number of those bullets grazed me."

Her stomach turned. "You could have been killed," she managed, her voice thin with terror.

"Yeah, for sure," he said, giving her a slight smile, reaching over and caressing her cheek. "But it's over, Sara. We've survived. That's all I care about."

"Steve said he was going to come up and visit you in a few hours. Right now? Sheriff Seabert is bringing a DOJ prosecutor and an FBI agent from the airport. They are coming to interrogate the Ferret and the other soldier."

Grimly, he nodded. "I hope they can flip one or both of them."

Shaking her head, she whispered sadly, "They are Mafia, Wes, loyal until death to my father and Manny."

"Fill me in? Tell me what I missed?"

She did, leaving some information out here and there. Wes drank from a glass of cold orange juice that was sitting on his tray. His voice was getting stronger and some color was coming back to his face. When she finished, she saw consternation in his expression.

"Logan Anderson is opening up his home and ranch to us?"

"Yes. Why?"

"He's putting everyone who lives there in jeopardy," Wes explained. "Manny will know sooner or later that his five-man assassination team is either dead or in custody. He'll tell his father. They'll cook up another plan to take you out. I don't like having anyone in this valley become targets."

"Sooner or later," she agreed, her voice low with emotion, "they will send another team in to find me, Wes."

He squeezed her hand. "We need to see what Steve and Dan Seabert think. Dan is an ex-SEAL, too, so I trust his judgment on this situation. We need to give them the time they need to parse it all and come up with a plan."

"I feel like I'm a death magnet to everyone in this valley."

"Don't talk like that, Sara. There's a *lot* of people who love you and want you to stay here."

Shaking her head, she said, "In the end, I'm going to have to leave."

"Well," he muttered, "if that happens, I'll be going with you." Looking deeply into her sad gaze, he rasped, "I love you, Sara. I meant it out there when I said it. Whatever happens? We're in this together for the long haul."

Rallying, she laid her fingers across his hand that rested on the bed. Closing her eyes, she whispered, "I think I have a way out of this for all of us. I don't want Logan, his family, or wranglers harmed, either." She lifted her head, holding his hand in hers. "My mother has been adamant that I should not relinquish what is rightfully mine as stated in her prenup and my father's will. We've had a lot of discussions and arguments about it. I don't care about the money, Wes. If I have a lawyer make up an amendment that disavows my rights to my father's fortune after he passes, and Manny is made his sole heir, he may stop trying to take my life. He'll be owner of my father's blood money."

He considered her idea. "But your mother is standing in the way of it? Why?"

Shrugging, Sara said wearily, "She's furious. She was lied to by my father, believed him, and then, after having me, she found out he was a Mafia don. It totaled her, Wes. Her rage is real, and in her mind, I deserve being in his will."

"And yet, she's painting a target on your back. It makes more sense to me now, Sara." He gave her a sympathetic look, lifting her hand, kissing it. "This is worth talking about to the FBI agent and DOJ prosecutor. We need to be sure they hear your side of the story. It could give them some other ideas on how to approach this situation, maybe."

Her skin tingled where his lips had brushed her flesh. Aching to simply lie beside him, her arms around him, pressed against his body, it was an impossible yearning that could not yet be fulfilled. Fighting her own selfish need for Wes, she understood better than anyone what was at stake and why. "It's worth a try," she admitted.

"Have you been in touch with your mother?"

"Yes. She knows everything that has happened." Lifting her chin, she said, "My mother is paying to have Rob and Chris become *our* bodyguards until this situation is resolved."

"Rob and Chris are solid," he agreed. "We were all on the same SEAL team together and they're good friends of mine. Steve was the head of our team. I worry about staying on Logan's ranch, too. I think it puts everyone at risk by doing it that way."

"Steve said Logan insisted on it, so he relented. Everything is up in the air, Wes. I don't know what to do or think right now."

"Hey," he whispered roughly, sliding his hand across her temple. "You've been shot at, chased, and nearly killed. You're still in shock, Sara. Don't be hard on yourself. We'll take this a day at a time. There's so much we don't know right now."

There was a soft knock at the door. Rob stuck his head around the door and gave them a grin. "Just want to let you know I'm out here, in case you need anything, Wes."

"Thanks, we're glad you're there, Brother. We're fine for now."

"You're only staying overnight. Steve wants me to drive you two down to the Wild Goose Ranch tomorrow after Dr. Ribas releases you. Chris will relieve me at 2000 hours and then I'll pick up this detail at 0800 tomorrow morning."

"Glad you're both here," Wes said, meaning it. "Have you heard anything else, Rob?"

He shook his head. "Nada. I think"—he looked at the watch on his thick wrist—"that Steve, the sheriff's people, the prosecutor, and FBI agent are meeting right now. We should know something after that. I hope." He waved to them and quietly shut the door so they could have their privacy.

"Chris was the one who kept the Ferret down after I hit him with a tree branch." She saw his eyes widen.

"What? You did what?"

"Didn't anyone tell you what happened? I assumed Rob or Chris told you."

"No, Sara. What *did* happen?"

She felt buffeted by his sudden emotional reaction. She told him in as few words as possible. Adding, "I didn't know that Rob and Chris were out looking for me. Steve was with you and he sent Rob and Chris to hunt the Ferret down." Her mouth curved downward. "I knew none of this. I was alone, Wes. And scared out of my mind. I was trying to climb that last, steep hill that leads to the mine to find out if you were alive or not. I was so tired, I could barely put one foot in front of the other. When I saw the Ferret, and he was coming in my direction, I knew I either had to stand my ground or he'd shoot me if I ran away."

Rubbing his face, Wes stared at her. "You knocked the Ferret out?"

"Yes, and Rob was coming my direction about the same time I did it. He zip tied the Ferret afterward, and I can't tell you how relieved I felt." She held up her hands. "I got some deep cuts on my palms because I hit him so hard with that pine branch that the splinters cut into them. I never felt pain from it."

Shaking his head, he gave her a look of pure admiration. "That's incredible, Sara. I was wondering why your hands were bandaged up."

"Stitches in one," she said. "I was so scared, Wes. I didn't think I'd live. I was so afraid he'd walk too far from the tree, and I'd have to come out from behind it to hit him and he'd hear me coming, turn around and shoot me . . ." She released his hand and stood up, pouring herself a glass of water, gulping it down.

"You're in shock," he murmured, holding his hand out to her. "Sit next to me."

"But . . . your ankle. I could hurt it—"

Wes reached out, gently captured her hand, tugging her toward the edge of his bed. "It will be all right," he soothed, guiding her so that she sat with her hip against his good leg, facing him. "Come here." He opened his arms, placing her head against his shoulder, her brow against his neck. Nothing had ever felt so damned good to him as in this moment with Sara leaning against him, her moist breath against his neck and upper chest, her arms timidly going around his torso as much as they could. Gruffly, he said against her brow, "I love you. I love you with every cell in my body, Sara. Let me hold you. You're the one who needs to be held, not me." He kissed her brow, her hair, releasing her hand and sliding his fingers gently through her clean, combed black hair. She smelled of pine and fresh air compared to the hospital odors, which he detested. Hearing her choke out his name, he moved his hand across her slumped shoulder, down her back and around her hip, holding her as tightly as he could under the circumstances.

His heart ached as he held her and she finally began to cry. Simply sliding his hand slowly up and down her back allowed her to release and heal. Mind spinning with the fact that she'd bravely defended herself, told him of her warrior core. Sara would not go down without a fight, even though the Ferret would have murdered her on sight. Her whole body shook from the terrible sobs clawing up and out of her. She had pressed her hand against her mouth to stop the sounds, and he'd gently laid his hand on her hair, whispering her name, whispering his love for her. What a brave, brave person she was when it came down to it.

Tears leaked from beneath his tightly shut eyes, as well. He cried for her, for the fear he knew that must have serrated her in every possible way. Somehow, although Wes didn't know how, they'd get through this. How he ached for a time when they could be healed enough to lie together, love together, and let the amassing dark clouds of her father's life of crime, go for just an hour or two. They needed that healing time, through their love for one another, to help them remain strong and alert.

June 17

Wes sat with Dan in his office at the sheriff's department at ten a.m. the next morning. Sara was pale and she'd slept poorly last night in that lounge chair, restless and rerunning her escape from the Ferret. He'd slept deeply, exhausted from the operation and sedative given to him, and he'd spiraled into a deep, healing slumber. She'd barely eaten any breakfast even though he'd cajoled her to eat more, not less. People in shock always lost their appetite, he knew.

"Sara, FBI Agent Harkins and the DOJ prosecutor, Brenda Carson, may want to speak with you later, after they get some more info. You're an important piece of this puzzle we're working through, and both of them wanted to ask a lot of questions so they could get a fuller picture on this situation."

Nodding, she said, "I'd be happy to, Dan."

"Good. Thank you. And Wes? They've indicated they want you to sit with them, as well, when the time comes. I'm sure that Chris and Rob will also be interviewed, but that's somewhere in the future."

"Anything to get this over with," he said. He'd been given a pair of crutches before leaving the hospital. They lay against Dan's desk. The wheelchair, which he would have to use to get around at times, was out in the back of the black Chevy Suburban. Rob was waiting out in the vehicle for them.

Dan frowned and said, "We're at a stalemate. The fifth guy brought in is lying. Says his name is Tony, but won't give us his last name. We're taking fingerprints and a blood sample for DNA to see if we can't find out his real name."

Sara asked, "What about the Ferret?"

Dan grinned a little. "He's a loyal Mafia soldier and refused to say anything. Took the Fifth."

"I wonder if Manny has gotten word that his latest attempt to kill me failed?"

Dan scratched his head. "I point blank asked the FBI agent and he was cagey and so was the DOJ prosecutor. My gut tells me something much bigger is in the works, but they aren't willing to talk about it. Yet. My bet is they have a RICO, Racketeer Influenced and Corrupt Organizations Act, investigation going on with the father and son and that's why they're closemouthed about it all."

"A RICO investigation underway?" Wes growled. "Sara said her father was into money laundering for the family business here in the USA, so that makes sense."

"That would certainly fall into a RICO crime," Dan agreed.

"Years ago, my mother said that she hoped that the FBI would undertake a RICO investigation against my father, and that includes Manny, as well. She's said that for years, but no one seemed interested. She went to the FBI office in Dallas a number of times, even telling them she would aid the investigation with what she knew. But no one ever got back to her about it."

"Could be that they were already investigating him by that time, Sara. These cases take years, sometimes a decade, to put together. I can't verify that they are," Dan said, "but I think there's a strong possibility they already have a RICO investigation well underway. It felt like a stand-off in my office when they tried to find out the Ferret's real name. Although"—Dan smiled—"I like 'the Ferret' nickname because he sure as hell looks like one. I also believe they already know this dude's name, but they aren't supplying it to us because of an ongoing investigation against your father's Mafia empire."

Rubbing her upper arms, Sara muttered, "The Ferret is a cold-blooded killer."

"Yes, a loyal soldier to the don," the sheriff agreed.

"So? Now what, Dan?" she urged.

"I think you know I've kept Rob and Chris deputized?"

"Yes," Sara said. "What does that do for us, Dan?"

"They were deputized on the way out to your call for help yesterday morning," Dan explained. "Anyone deputized is covered by the laws that all law enforcement operate under here in the USA."

Wes turned to Sara. "In plain language? Were Rob or Chris to find themselves in a situation where it was kill or be killed, they could legally defend themselves with a weapon. No one could sue them or take them to court so long as they operate under regulations set by law enforcement."

"Right," Dan said. "Rob and Chris are going to be living in the vicinity of the safe house that Logan Anderson has loaned out for you two. When there's a RICO investigation going on? Communication devices, cell phones, and all electronic surveillance is subpoenaed and a judge gives her or his permission for the FBI to listen in. I wouldn't be surprised if not only Manny has been taped and tapped, but his father in prison, as well."

"He's not in the general population," Sara said. "My mother said he's been given all kinds of perks no one else gets, a special cell, and he has a laptop, and the use of a phone."

"Well, according to the DOJ attorney, she said he's been put in solitary confinement as of yesterday, and every kind of perk he had before, has been removed from him."

Surprised, Sara sat up. "Really?"

"Yes. Why?" Dan asked.

"He can't run his Mafia organization without communication of some kind." She could barely contain her joy over this unexpected development.

Wes raised a brow. "Sounds like your father just got a huge demotion in his own family operation."

"Bingo," Dan agreed. "The prosecutor wouldn't say anything, but the expression in her eyes was a 'gotcha' kind of look that I think tells me that they're close to the end of this RICO investigation."

Sara frowned. "Well . . . if my father is in solitary? Who is running the organization, then?"

"Right now," Dan said, "your half brother is, from what the FBI agent told me."

Wes shook his head. "When the leader is decapitated, it's not a little change of power. It would be my bet that there's some huge undercover operation going on."

Dan said, "You're right, Wes." He turned to Sara. "Your father has been in a power struggle with the Russian Mafia don, Ivan Bobrov, for a decade. There's been bloodletting on both sides. I'm just wondering if Bobrov hasn't made a big chess move upon hearing your father has been removed from power. That would explain why your father's cushy cell with all kinds of electronic devices was downgraded for a gray single, solitary cell with nothing in it except the minimal things needed by any prisoner. He has no access to any form of communication except one phone call on a landline and it is recorded by the prison."

She gave the sheriff a quizzical look. "I've never known what's going on with them, Dan. I deliberately stay out of it. I know my mother has people inside the organization who give her tidbits of info about him and Manny. That's why she knew they were going after me."

"The woman prosecutor and the FBI agent are taking a plane out of here later this morning after they question each of you. They have made an appointment to speak further with your mother when they land in Dallas."

Shaking her head, Sara whispered, "I just want out of this nightmare, Dan."

"I understand. Do you have any questions?"

They shook their heads.

"Rob will drive you to the Wild Goose Ranch. Logan has had a camera and high tech alarm system installed throughout your house. The console for it will be in your bedroom, and Rob and Chris will have a second console in the mother-in-law house they will be staying in."

"Sounds good," Wes said.

"Does it ever," Sara seconded, giving Dan a warm look of thanks.

"I'll let the agent and prosecutor know you're ready to speak to them," Dan said, rising and giving them a slight smile. "If my people or me pick up on something? We'll be calling you to keep you in the loop."

Wes got up and put one crutch beneath his armpit, holding out his right hand across the desk. "Thanks, Dan."

Shaking his hand, the sheriff said, "SEALs stick together."

Logan Anderson met them at their new safe house shortly after noon. It was large, well-kept. The white picket fence around it, the mowed green lawn and flowers here and there, made it feel to Sara as if she were in a real home. Two wranglers came with Logan and they took all luggage and boxes inside the house for them. He gave Sara the key, as well as showing her the massive dead bolt for the front door. She walked around with Logan while Wes begged off, saying his energy was about gone and he needed to rest. Rob found the master bedroom off the main living room and made him comfortable in there before leaving for the mother-in-law house.

"I think I've told you everything," Logan said, walking with Sara to the front door. "That's pretty much it."

She nodded, giving him a grateful look. Rob and Chris had also been provided a blueprint of where all the security devices had been installed, most of them unseen. She would study the papers later. Right now, she was feeling very tired. "Thanks, Logan."

"We've stocked your refrigerator, the pantry, and the large freezer out in the attached garage," he noted. "If you need anything"—he pulled out a business card with a number written on the back of it—"just call me. This is my private cell number and I take this to bed and it sits on the bedstand. You can get me twenty-four seven."

Sara nodded. "I don't know about you, but I'm so tired I could fall over, and it's only noon."

He patted her shoulder gently. "It's called shock. When you two feel up to it? We'd love to have you over for dinner some night that suits you. Or maybe lunch. It's up to you."

"I'm sure we'll take you up on it, Logan. Thank you, for everything . . ."

He smiled a little and settled his Stetson on his head. "Okay, boys, let's roll." His two wranglers tipped their hats to Sara and then opened the door, exiting out into the bright, warm sunlight.

It was quiet. Hungrily, Sara absorbed the silence because it felt comforting and warm. The house was beautiful, adorned with nineteenth-century furniture that she was sure may have come down through Logan's family. A heaviness descended upon her and she felt drugged, her feet weighted, and barely able to keep her eyes open. Turning, she knew the master bedroom was off the living room, and trudged across the shining cedar floor. Halfway down the hall on the left, was a door that was half open. Pushing it open, she saw that Wes had lain down on the king-size bed, having wrapped up in a white cotton duvet. It was a bit chilly in the house, the air-conditioning on. Longing to be with Wes, but not wanting to disturb his sleep, she saw that he had put a pillow beneath his cast, lying on his left side.

Pushing off her simple and practical shoes, she climbed up on the bed, being careful not to wake him. Half of the duvet lay on her side of the bed and she snuggled under it after getting within range of Wes's form. Every cell in her body needed him. Being careful, she lay down next to him on another pillow. Needing touch with him, she curved herself around his back and legs, being careful not to bother his injured ankle. The duvet was warm, taking off the slight chill. She inhaled his male scent and it dissolved all her anxiety over the last two days.

Safe . . . she was safe. With Wes. Nestling her head into the down pillow, her breasts barely grazed his back. She could feel the heat of his body and drew in a long, deep breath, inhaling his presence into herself. Even though she wanted to wind her arm across his waist and plaster herself against him, Sara resisted. Above all, she knew Wes was dealing with a major operation and that was another form of shock to his body that he had to assimilate. There was no way she wanted to awaken him.

Just getting to lie in the same bed with him, the firm mattress supporting them, the warmth of the pristine white duvet filled with cotton, felt like an unequaled luxury compared to her sleeping in his arms in the midst of those logs that were scattered about on that hill. She'd slept for the most part because she'd been in his arms, her ear against his heart, the pulsing sound like wonderful music to her exhausted, emotionally strewn self. Instead of smelling the fresh scent of pine, it was the fresh scent of sheets and blankets that had been out in sunlight and fresh air as they dried. That was a fragrance that she loved because her grandmother always had her washing hung out on a clothesline, the sun and air blessing them.

Sara could feel the slow in and out of Wes's breath, each time barely grazing her body. He was sleeping deeply and as she closed her eyes, she wanted to do the same thing: just fall off that cliff and dive into a wonderful healing slumber. With him being next to her, she knew as her mind began to shut down, that they were safe. At least for now. The added blanket of protection was Rob and Chris, who would also protect them. The only worry that niggled at her was someone coming onto the ranch and finding them; or the innocent people who lived here being killed instead.

Frowning, she scrunched her eyes shut because she wanted to ignore that possibility. Right now, in this moment, she was warm, safe, and the man she loved more than life was right next to her.

Chapter Thirteen

June 18

Wes awoke, groggy and barely coherent. The dark burgundy curtains had been open before. Now they were closed, the room dark. He was warm. The bed was soft compared to the hardness of the ground that he'd slept upon for years out on SEAL missions. Wiping his face, he allowed his awakening consciousness to check out his ankle. There was no pain and for that, he was grateful. The pillow beneath it had given it a tilt so that circulation was good through the surgical area, and that reduced swelling. Pushing the top of the duvet away to his waist, he pulled it off his legs.

What time was it? Disoriented, he looked at his watch. It was eight p.m.! He remembered going into the bedroom, getting situated on the bed and adding the pillow beneath his ankle before he dropped off a chasm into darkness; that was how exhausted he was. He'd slept for eight hours?

Sighing, he sat up, looking around. Where was Sara? The second thing that caught his attention was the smell of garlic. Spaghetti? The door was shut and it was a heavy one, so there was no sound coming through it.

Grappling with his crutches, he slid off the bed and hobbled to the door, opening it. The fragrance of spaghetti hit him fully, and he looked down the hall. It was a straight shot through the living room and into the kitchen. He saw Sara at the gas stove, cooking. His heart swelled with love for her. He worried about her, knowing she'd been equally traumatized by the events of the other day.

Swinging down the hall, he stopped at the bathroom and then worked his way across the shining gold-and-crimson cedar living room floor. It was covered with several large handwoven Navajo rugs. Sara had changed clothes, now in a pair of gray sweatpants, a soft pink top, and her tennis shoes. Her black hair was in one long, thick dark braid down the center of her back. Around her waist, she wore a bright red-and-white-checked apron as she worked over the stove.

For a moment, a lump formed in Wes's throat as he took in the scene. He'd never entertained meeting someone like Sara, or even less, expected to fall in love with her so completely. She was perfect for him. But was he perfect for her? He glanced down at his ankle, which had a waterproof wrapping around it, the leg of his jeans pushed up above it. On his foot was a thick white hospital sock to keep his foot warm. He wasn't whole by a long shot. Badly wounded in his lung and now his ankle, and still struggling. No, he was far from perfect, unlike Sara.

She turned, meeting his gaze. "Wes! How do you feel? Are you hungry?"

He grinned a little and moved into the kitchen, pulling out a chair from the table and sitting down. "I'm feeling better. And yes, I'm hungry."

"You slept a good eight hours. Rob just dropped by after

I'd taken a shower and changed clothes. He was telling me that from his experience as a SEAL, men who got wounded or injured often slept a lot right after their surgery."

"Glad he told you that."

"I gave him a big bowl of spaghetti and six slices of garlic toast to go with it. He was a happy man." She laughed, turning to remove the pot of spaghetti from the stove.

He sat there, absorbing her, her husky laughter filtering through him like sunlight on a darkened day. "I'm sure Rob appreciated your kindness," he said.

She glanced over at him after delivering the steaming pasta to a colander and running it under cold water so the strands wouldn't stick together. "He did. I told him that I could cook for all of us. It's easy enough to make a meal for whoever has night duty."

"I'll bet he jumped at that offer." Wes chuckled, again touched deeply by her generosity toward others.

"Well," Sara said, placing the pasta into an awaiting blue and white ceramic bowl, "many men can't cook at all. That should change, but I'm not going to punish Rob. The man is a hero like you and Chris. You all put your lives on the line for our country. To me? That counts. If I can make one of them a nightly dinner? It's my way of thanking him for his bravery and courage under fire."

"I like how you see the world, Sara." His voice was a bit choked-up sounding, and he tried to hide the rush of emotions that came with it.

She grinned elfishly, bringing over the pasta and then a bowl of marinara sauce that contained sliced black olives, diced tomatoes, and was fragrant with herbs. "How many slices of garlic toast would you like?"

"How many do you have?" he teased, waiting for her to return before he put anything on his plate.

Opening the stove door after turning off the heat, she laughed. "Enough, believe me. You're a growing boy, Wes."

Inwardly, he preened from the way she saw him. In moments she had set a woven willow basket between them, containing a dozen thick slices of bread. Removing the apron, she hung it over the back of her chair, sitting down at his right elbow.

"Let's eat," she urged, handing him a small cut-glass bowl containing fresh parmesan cheese.

"You first," he said, handing her the bowl of pasta.

"Thanks," she whispered. "Are you feeling more rested?"

He picked up the bowl of sauce. "Better every minute. I dived so hard, and when I woke up at first, I wasn't sure where I was."

She traded bowls with him. "I have a confession to make."

"Oh?" He cocked his head, interest in his eyes.

"When Logan and his wranglers left, you were already asleep in the master bedroom."

He spooned the marinara sauce over the large amount of spaghetti on his plate. "One moment I was okay, the next, I was so tired, Sara, I could barely think, much less swing along on those crutches."

"Rob explained to me that it's normal after surgery to have hills and valleys of energy and then no energy."

"He ought to know," Wes said, some sympathy in his tone, "because he's been through surgery for a gunshot wound."

She frowned. "I'm glad you're not a SEAL anymore. That's such a dangerous occupation."

"Like what we're doing right now isn't?" he teased, setting the sauce bowl aside. "Just going out to forage for herbs and get RPGs thrown at us?"

"You have a point."

"I had a dream," he said, glancing over at her as he sprinkled a lot of parmesan over his meal. "Usually I get PTSD flashbacks, but this time it was different."

"Tell me about it?" She slowly twirled the spaghetti between her spoon and fork.

"Well," he hesitated, "I dreamed you were lying against me and it felt so damned good." He saw her cheeks flush red.

"That wasn't a dream, Wes. Later on, I came into the bedroom, very tired all of a sudden, and I quietly came and lay close to you under the duvet. I think I slept for about three hours, and then got up, took a hot bath, washed my hair and changed my clothes. I didn't want to disturb you and I don't think I did, but somehow, you knew I was nearby."

"It was a very real dream," he offered, picking up the warm garlic toast. "I liked it."

"Truth be told? I wanted to scoot right up against your backside and put my arm across your waist, but I was afraid I'd wake you, and I knew how badly you needed to sleep in order to heal."

"The dream was real," he said, in thought. He became serious. "I guess Logan thinks we're sleeping together."

"I gathered that, too. How do you feel about it?"

"What's not to like, Sara? I'm more interested in what you want to do. I don't want to push you one way or another. We've been through a lot the last couple of days and it's not easy to sort out your life when it's in that kind of chaos."

She gave him a thoughtful look. "We've admitted we are falling in love with one another. Living together is the next logical step to me."

"Separate bedrooms?"

"No."

He gave her a crooked grin. "I feel the same way." He wiped his mouth with a paper napkin. "I need to know the rules of engagement between us."

"Just let whatever we have, Wes, continue to unfold naturally."

He frowned. "Look, you're in charge, Sara. Neither of us are mind readers. I don't want to do something stupid or blow the trust I've built with you."

She nodded. "Let's put it this way from my perspective, Wes: If you hadn't just come out of surgery and your ankle wasn't bolted together with screws? I would have let you know that I wanted to love you and have you love me in return."

He sat up a little straighter, surprise in his expression.

She smiled a little. "In a matriarchal culture, two people who want to be together can be. The only rules they have are the ones they make between one another."

"I like learning about matriarchy." He teased her a little, seeing the gleam of humor in her eyes.

"It's fair. And it's equal. As much as I'd like to love you, I know how badly hurt your ankle is, so we'll have to wait a bit."

"Doc said in eight weeks I should be able to get out of this removable cast, and start my physical therapy on week five or six."

Her lips flattened. "I don't want to wait *that long*. Do you?"

Chuckling, he admitted, "No, I don't either." He saw her smile grow, his heart swelling once more with such fierce love for her.

"I think we should give ourselves a week. Let's see how you feel, Wes. I don't want to interfere with your healing."

"Well," he said dryly, looking down at his ankle, "it's an issue, but it's really out of the way . . ."

Laughing, she muttered, "We'll figure this out as we go, okay?"

"Okay, but you're in charge, Sara. You need to tell me where you're at."

"So far, I've been really clear and up front with you. Haven't I, Wes?"

"Yes," he admitted slowly, "you have."

"Then? If two people want to love one another, I'm sure if there's a will, there's a way."

"You should have been a SEAL," he told her, his smile increasing. "SEALs are really good at jury rigging things in order to make something work. Real MacGyvers."

She laughed. "Okay, how about we MacGyver our way through this issue moving forward?"

"Can I steal a kiss every now and then? Hold you against me?"

"Oh," she murmured, giving him a wicked look, "you can do a lot more than that. I'll leave that to your imagination. Somehow, I don't think there are any virgin SEALs around here."

"No, you're right about that," he agreed, pleased with her honesty.

"Logan left some information that I think you need to study, Wes."

"Maps?"

"Blueprints. Locations of the newly installed security, the hidden cameras and stuff," she said. "He also gave me a map of the layout of his ranch, which is huge."

"We need to look at the exit-entrance points to the ranch. They are weak points where someone could get in. Here in the house, as well."

"Okay. Logan also loaned us one of his company trucks. It's sitting inside the garage, with the fob on the dashboard."

"That's nice of him to do that. I need to call my insurance company. My truck was totaled. They'll give me a rental in the meantime."

"It's been a little hectic to try and do things like that."

"Think we'll get a day where things are quiet?"

"What's quiet mean?"

He chuckled and said, "Our lives are in chaos, no doubt."

By eleven p.m., Sara could barely keep her eyelids open. They had gone over the ranch map, the entrance-exit points to it, all of the security blueprints within and around the house where they were staying. Earlier in the evening, Wes had taken a hot shower, his ankle protected by the waterproof cast. He looked better, but she saw how tired he was, as well.

"I'm going to get the bed ready for you," she told him, rising from the kitchen table.

"I just need a pillow for under my calf to keep that ankle up."

She came around and leaned over, encircling his shoulders, resting her head against his after kissing his temple. "Do you know how nice it is just to be able to do this?"

He slid his hand over her clasped ones resting in the center of his chest. "I like this a lot, Sara."

"Then let's go to bed, Wes . . . All I want is to kiss you and hold you close tonight . . ."

The wobble in her tone tore at him. "I want the same thing, sweetheart . . ."

The soft cotton material of Sara's pale lavender nightgown fell to her knees. Wes wore a pair of pajama bottoms, but that was all. Earlier, she had placed a firm pillow beneath his broken ankle and gotten him situated near the center of the bed. Turning out the lights, Wes waited for Sara to brush her thick, black hair, a shining cape across her shoulders. There was something incredible as far as he was concerned, to watch her sit at the dresser, in front of the nineteenth-century mirror, brushing through the strands. The silence in the room was calming to him. He ached to make love with her, but knew under the circumstances, that just wasn't going to happen. He'd just come out of surgery and she was still in shock over everything that had happened to them. He might want to, but he was sure she didn't.

He'd learned a long time ago that sex was sex. That love, real love, while it incorporated sex, was so much more; wider and deeper. The drive to make Sara his was there, of course, but right this moment, it wasn't his goal. They both needed to be held. There was something soothing, healing, and steadying about holding her. And as soon as she finished brushing her hair, she came to their bed, snuggled up against him on his good side, away from his broken ankle, pulling the covers up over them. There was fatigue in Sara's eyes and he felt it in his bones, as well. As she settled against him, her head resting on his shoulder, her brow against his jaw, her arm sliding across his naked waist, she pressed her body against his, and he sighed.

"You feel so good," he murmured, turning his head and kissing her temple. Sara had taken a shower earlier and the scent of lily of the valley teased him along with the sweet fragrance that was only her.

"You do, too," she whispered, brushing her hand across his darkly haired chest.

Her fingers moved slowly, like a hot iron, and he felt himself growing hard over her innocent touch. With his arm around her shoulders, he kept her against him, their bodies melded warmly against one another. "This is heaven," he rasped, closing his eyes. "You are my heaven, Sara . . ."

With a soft, muffled sound, she kissed his chest. "I'm too tired to argue, but you are my heaven, too."

He managed a lopsided smile. "Go to sleep, Sara. We'll finish this when we're not so tired. Okay?" He felt her relaxing against him, realizing she had already dozed off, her arm limp across his waist. Contentment flowed through him. "I love you, sweetheart. Dream good dreams . . ."

June 19

The pale pink of dawn eased silently around the thick, dark drapes of their bedroom. Sara luxuriated in the strength and warmth of Wes's arm around her shoulders, still holding her close to him. The wonderful scent of him filled her flaring nostrils, a fragrance that awakened her further. He was still asleep, she realized, hearing the crow of the rooster somewhere outside their room. It was a sound that gave her comfort, because her grandmother had a huge bunch of hens, selling the eggs to those who dropped by to pick them up.

Nuzzling into his shoulder, she felt him stir, as if he had gone from a deep sleep to sudden wakefulness. Maybe this was an old SEAL habit? *Probably.* Lifting her hand, she followed the dark line of silky hair from his waist up to his chest. Wherever she moved her fingertips, his flesh tightened, enjoying her caresses.

She felt him shift slightly, his lips against her temple, kissing her, a sweet hello for their first morning together. Just the intimacy of the small act, filled her with longing for him. Barely lifting her lashes, she drowned in the stormy gray color of his barely opened eyes. Easing away, she shifted, lifting her chin, meeting and melding with his mouth that was so strong and worshipful as it slid across her lips. Closing her eyes, she hummed her pleasure so that he knew how much she enjoyed the kiss, her whole body lighting on fire.

Mind shorting out, she knew they were both wounded, her hands and his ankle. The way he took her mouth, tasting her, enjoying their melding, made her question how to love him without hurting his ankle. Somehow, they would find a way. There had always been a bond of trust between them, and it had never been stronger than right now.

Both her palms were bandaged, but her fingertips ranged across his shoulder, and following the solid, powerful line of his well-muscled back, she gloried in the way he reacted to her light exploration, his flesh tightening. How wonderful! Their breath was becoming shallower, faster. As he splayed his fingers across her upper back, the distinct impression Sara received was that Wes was deliberately, slowly, discovering the beauty of her body. The sense that he held her as if she were sacred as well as loved, opened her heart more fully. This was a man not interested in trapping or taking something from her as a woman; rather, he was glorying in every second his fingers moved across her upper back, and then sinuously, tenderly, down the long curve of her spine, committing her to his heart's memory. This was love, not sex. Love entwined with sex, yes. She'd never experienced what was building between herself and another man like this before. What little was left of her thinking mind dissolved in the heat as his mouth left hers, dropping small, purposeful kisses down the side of her neck, moving the nightgown aside to open it and follow the curve of her collarbone. His hand cupped her breast beneath the material, and she moaned in anticipation.

A sigh broke from her, and she pressed her hips against his, more than a little aware of his hardness and length against her belly. It sent a sheet of hot liquid down through her, moistening her inner thighs, the need of him inside her like a tsunami flowing through her lower body.

Urgency replaced the slow mapping of one another. His hand pulled her crumpled, wrinkled gown upward from her knees, to her hips. Moving away from him, she smiled down into his narrowed eyes that made her feel so deeply wanted, and pulled the gown over her head, dropping it away from where they lay on the bed. Just the feral look of his heated gaze moving from her upper shoulders, down across her breasts, the nipples tightening automatically beneath his gaze, made her lower body tighten with hunger for him alone.

Moving slowly, she placed her hands on the waistband of his trousers, gently pulling them downward. He lifted his hips and she worked the material off his good leg and then carefully, because the other trouser leg had been slit to allow it over the ankle cast, she removed the article of clothing. A slight smile pulled at her lips as she moved on hands and knees like a sinuous cat hunting for him.

"Lie very still," she whispered, placing her leg across his hips, and then slowly settling down upon his hardness that sent a fiery thrill through her. Groaning, he gripped her hips, and he arched, throwing his head back as her wetness slid across him. It was a male growl of satisfaction mixed with desire, his fingers digging into her hips, guiding her, asking for entry into her. She allowed him to navigate her so that he penetrated her very slowly and thoroughly, hot, sweet fluids gliding around them.

Flowing into one another, she made a low, guttural sound like that of a female jaguar in the midst of mindless heat, connecting with her male counterpart. He teased her, undulating his hips, drawing himself deeper and deeper into her hot, wet depths. And then, he was slowly moving her back and forth upon himself, growling, thrusting into the building fiery heights, both on a collision course with one another. She became enwrapped in a silky cocoon of red-hot pleasure, the scent of sex an aphrodisiac spurring them on, faster and harder.

The unexpected explosions, both coming simultaneously, made them cry out, but it was a shout of triumph, of love over nearly dying. It was a shriek of ongoing volcanic fluid rejoicing in release from her, bathing him lavishly with the tightness of her surrounding body. Nothing existed in that moment that seemed to her to go on and on forever, as he milked every last drop of her sacred woman's river of life that bathed his hardness. Light-headed, she lost her grip of her hands against his chest, her whole world, the universe becoming a wild celebration of mating with the man she loved beyond all reason. Growing faint afterward, she fell across his body, her head coming to rest against his shoulder and neck, breathing hard, raspy, moaning with such unexpected pleasure that tremored like earthquakes through her lower body. His hands trembled and moved up from her hips, following the line of her long back, fingers tangling in her hair, luxuriating in its silkiness, his mouth finding hers, kissing her, sharing their roughened breaths with one another.

Nothing existed except Wes. How could she tell him how wonderful a lover he was? He'd barely touched her, yet her body had opened with utter trust. Dazed, closing her eyes, sinking into his worshipping mouth, she felt dizzied, thrown out into a new, explosive, colorful universe that still was firing off inside her sated body, and wanting even more from him.

And, as if telepathically connected with her every feeling and thought, he began to move within her again, urging her to sit up, to allow him to bring her to another orgasm, one after another. Time ceased to exist, caught in the ongoing pleasure, the explosions convulsing through her, each time giving her golden moments of exquisite gratification as she'd never experienced before. Truly, Wes understood a woman's body like few men ever would. A man might ejaculate once, but a woman? Well, she could have untold orgasms, one after another. He cajoled, pushed, and stroked her inwardly, bringing her to that mindless, floating state and connected only by the raw, continuous gift of pleasure he was giving her.

She truly lost her mind, sinking into the pleasurable gratification that only he could give her. And what gifts he'd given her! At some point, weak and content, he lifted her off him, bringing her alongside him, their bodies sweaty and melded to one another. Sara lay in his arms, his body bordering her own, their breathing ragged, their senses overflowing and completely fulfilled. Opening her eyes, she looked up at him. "How's your ankle?" Her voice was husky.

He gave her a boyish smile and raised his head, looking down at it. "What ankle?"

She laughed with him.

"Okay, it's okay. No worse for wear," he admitted.

Relieved, she said, "Thank goodness."

"How are *you* feeling?" he asked, sliding his hand over her damp back.

"Mmmm, I have no words to describe how wonderful I feel right now, Wes." She gave him a warm look. "You are an incredible lover. Do you know that?" Instantly, she saw his cheeks redden. This man, who loved her, protected her, had grown shy and unsure of himself. How could he? Sara reminded herself of the wound of being thrown away by his parents. That wound, unfortunately, would never fully heal. His questions would never be answered. Her instincts told her that shyness over her compliment came from that time in his life. When someone wasn't wanted, why would they *ever* think they would be good at anything else? She made a silent promise to Wes that over time, she would carefully and gently delve into that so very private, wounded part of himself. Only in lancing an abscess could one release the toxins from it, and in her experience, getting a man to talk about his feelings would be difficult. Most men avoided discussions about their inner thoughts like the plague. But to heal, he would have to come clean with her and be honest about the wounds of the past. Love would be the final healer, relieving him of so many burdens he carried, that were never his fault.

"What made me feel good," he rasped, kissing her brow, "was how much you enjoyed it. That made me feel like flying."

"Oh, I flew all right," she assured him with a smile. "Never better. You're a keeper, Wes." Again, she saw pinkness come to his cheeks. She thought about rewording what she'd said, but maybe he needed to hear this from a woman who *did* want him in her life.

"I think we both know what euphoria means now?" He teased her a little.

"Euphoria? I was in full-blown ecstasy. I've never had six orgasms in a row, Wes. Ever! You brought out everything from within me."

He became serious, nodding. "Maybe because from the time we met, there has been a solid bond of trust between us?"

She thought about it, sliding her fingers across his brow, removing the perspiration. "Yes . . . yes, I feel you're right. When I first saw you, I felt this immediate trust in you and I had no reason to feel that way." She leaned over, brushing her lips against his. "You inspire me because I trust you, literally, with my life."

"We've saved one another's lives," he agreed, moving his fingers through her silky ebony hair.

"Literally and figuratively speaking," Sara agreed, emotion in her tone as she caught his hand, entwining her fingers with his. "I love you, Wes. I will never not love you . . ."

His fingers curved gently around hers. "It feels so damned good to be loved, but it also feels even better to love you . . ."

Laying her head on his shoulder, she murmured, "That's what real love is about: loving the other. It's a high to do it, to see it, to feel it . . ."

"And to be a part of it . . ."

"Oh . . . yes," she whispered tremulously, holding his heavy-lidded gaze. "I like that we loved one another at dawn this morning. Dawn is a new day—and it is, for us, even though our future is muddied and unsure."

"But we have one another, sweetheart. That isn't muddied."

She nodded, feeling satiated. "Always. I wish we could dream of a future that was clear and unobstructed."

"That will come with time, Sara. There's a lot going on right now. We're caught in the middle of it. What we do know"—he kissed her fingers entwined with his—"is that we love one another, that we have dreams that are on hold, but at some point, the water will clear for us and we'll see a path forward."

"I miss our Victorian home so much, Wes. It was us. I love the old mixing with the new. I love the building that has become my herb store, my clinic, and I loved having you there at my side. You learned everything so quickly and it felt like you were really enjoying what you were doing."

"I do enjoy it," he assured her, laying her hand out on his damp chest, putting his over it. "You're a wonderful teacher, people love you because you bring the sunshine and hope of healing with you, to them. You helped me, too, whether you knew it or not."

"Oh?" Her brows moved up and she held his gaze. "How did I do that?"

"I was lost. Before I drove up here to take this assignment to become your bodyguard, I was standing outside, looking up at the stars, replaying my life, thinking about the good and bad of it. I felt lost, and I couldn't explain why. Tom and his family gave me love, real love, and inclusion, like I really belonged somewhere, finally. But after I got the assignment and had to leave Tom and his family, I felt torn from the only loving mooring I'd ever had." He gave her a strained look. "When you aren't lovable, Sara, and someone comes along and tells you that you *are* worth loving, that changes your whole world. At least, it did for me. And then, when Steve gave me the file on you, and I saw your photo, my heart opened up like it was going to bloom. It was the strangest, weirdest feeling I've *ever* had. I didn't know what to think of it." He smiled softly up at her. "My heart's eyes saw you, knew you and fell in love with you on the spot. Only I didn't realize it at the time."

"How touching," she whispered, her eyes luminous with unshed tears. "When did you know that you love me?"

He laughed a little. "You probably won't believe me, but from the moment I saw you, I knew. I instantly rejected that thought, of course. No one could look at another person for the first time and know that they loved them fiercely. Forever."

She moved up on one elbow, her hair barely grazing his chest as she studied him in the gathering silence. "But you did love me even though you might have thought it crazy and impossible?"

Nodding, he sifted his fingers through her hair, growing thoughtful. "I began to accept that it was you, who you are, without preamble, accepting yourself for who you are and never apologizing for it. When I realized that, I began to accept that I did love you."

"But you never told me any of this. I mean, you never showed it to me, except sometimes, I'd glance over and you were looking at me. It wasn't an invasive kind of look, either. I felt like you couldn't believe you were here doing this. I thought maybe you were interested in what I did with herbology or perhaps just learning something new. Not me, personally."

Shaking his head he said, "Oh, no . . . it was me realizing I love you, heart and soul, and then I asked myself how I could *ever* hope to have someone like you love someone like me in return? A non-person. I didn't know my parents. I had no history, no . . . nothing . . ."

"And yet," she murmured, kissing the top of his ear, "I fell in love with you without knowing that history. You don't fall in love with a person's parentage, where they came from, or what they've accomplished, Wes. At least, not in my world, not how I see things. I saw *you*. A man with honor, integrity, who knew right from wrong, had unquestioned morals, was kind, and seemed to know that his male strength was something that could hurt or harm others. I always was aware that you had this ability to become what the baby, child, or adult needed from you, and you became it for them. I was blown away by that skill you have. It's breathtaking. I don't know who taught you that, but it's a gift. And that was the part of you that I fell so deeply in love with. You have this wondrous ability to sense another, and then somehow be able to gear yourself to their level of need so that real communication could be shared between you. I just stand in awe of you because of that."

Shrugging, he said, "Got me, Sara. Until you just defined it? I didn't know I had that ability."

"Well," she said, leaning over, kissing him swift and hard, "you are a one-of-a-kind man, and I'm so happy that you love me."

Chapter Fourteen

June 28

"Where are you taking me?" Wes asked as Sara drove them up a dirt road near the back of Logan's ranch. His ankle was healing well, and yesterday he'd had a special boot put on it, replacing the waterproof cast. Being able to walk around without crutches was freeing to him.

Sara gave him a flirtatious look. "Someplace special. Lea told me about it when I had tea with the girls over at their home yesterday. I want to see it in person and I want to share it with you."

"What do you want to see?" he asked, looking around. Although they were on what was considered safe property, he never eased his guard.

Rob was down with the flu and Chris was in the dentist's office with a root canal, and Wes had convinced everyone that he didn't need anyone to ride shotgun for them as a bodyguard while on ranch property. They'd been on the forty-thousand-acre ranch long enough to get a good feel for it. The employees, the wranglers, both men and women, were tasked with keeping their eye on anyone who looked out of place. Most of the wranglers were military veterans. Logan's ranch hummed with small businesses, with people coming and going. Luckily, it was not open to the public, the goods sold in town at Mama's Store. It was a closed loop as far as Wes was concerned. But that did not ease his alertness. The safest place could become dangerous under certain circumstances.

"Well," Sara teased, "Lea has taken us around to a number of tree groves that Logan's family had planted. And because she's a wood sculptor, she was always out in these different groves finding just the right piece of wood for her next project." She pointed to a grove that crowned a small hill. "In earlier generations, these groves supplied lumber for the valley and also for the silver mines in the mountains. They were true stewards of the land, not just taking what the land gifted them, but replanting and caring for each of these groves for the next generation."

"I'd heard from Rob, who has been reconnoitering these different groves on the property, that he's seen old, mature, and young trees in each section. Now I know why."

"Logan's family was the first one here in the valley. He's got quite a tradition going on."

"Yes, he does." The windows in the truck were open and he rested his elbow out the passenger side. It was ten a.m., the sky filled with puffy white clouds, a slight breeze, and the temperature in the mid-seventies. It was a perfect day.

"And you're taking me to this particular grove for a particular reason?"

Sara grinned. "You don't give up, do you?" Her body glowed from their recent lovemaking earlier that morning. She pined for her clinic, and to get back to her world of herbs and helping people, but so far, the sheriff wanted them to remain on the Wild Goose Ranch. She saw Wes slant a teasing look in her direction.

"Never."

She slowed as the road that led up to the grove became more rutted. Driving in under the trees, she parked the truck and said, "Climb out. We have a little ways to walk."

Meeting him at the front of the truck, she gripped his hand, pulling him along. "Come on . . . you have to see this!"

Wes followed, her tugging on his hand good-naturedly. No matter where they went on the ranch, he was always armed and he carried a radio on him.

"Look straight ahead," Sara said, excitement in her voice, pointing at a huge tree in the middle of the grove.

He saw one tree, probably the oldest in the grove because it was so tall, wide and had such a huge trunk. And it was decorated. "Ribbons?" he asked, giving her a glance of surprise.

Sara halted in front of it. "Lea brought me here," she confided, sliding her arm around his waist as his arm wrapped around her shoulders, drawing her against him. "She calls it the 'Wishing Tree.' In the United Kingdom, many people have a strong belief in fairy folk, gnomes and the little people. There are special places where the veil between our world and the fairy world is very thin. And there's always a tree there to tell people about the veil. People know these sacred places and they put ribbons on the branches, they write requests on pieces of paper and hang them on a branch of the tree. They ask the tree spirit to honor their request, and to coax the fairy folk to help them. Sometimes they leave money, but usually it's something far more special. It could be that a mother who has a sick child will cut off a curl of the child's hair, wrap it up and put a bright, colorful ribbon around it and tie it to the tree with the request. Or, they will leave a photo and hang it on the tree, asking for help for the person in the photo. Some will even leave a necklace or piece of jewelry that means everything to them, something they value, and give it to the tree, asking for help of some kind for a child, a parent, or for themselves."

Wes studied the tree in silence, seeing that all the lower limbs, each one at least ten feet in length, were covered with those gaily decorated and colorful ribbons. Some had a request taped to it; others a small envelope containing a message. He did see a few photos, and the morning sunlight lancing through the land would pick up a glint of a necklace or some type of jewelry. "I've never seen anything like this before," he said, a little bit of awe in his tone.

"Wishing trees, or a sacred wishing well, or a sacred ancient site, such as a stone circle, or a special standing stone, are seen as helpers to those who believe that they are closely aligned with the fairy folk. All across the world, people believe in the power of the sacred. And by giving a gift of food, grain, or fruit with their request, they hope the fairy people will grant their wish." She sighed and gave him a warm look. "Among my grandmother's people? They have a similar gifting. They bring cornmeal, a prayer, and sometimes a gift, too. It's done all over the world, Wes. I think it's beautiful. Nature is alive. And I do believe in fairies. Do you?"

He gave her a stressed look. "Well . . . no . . . I mean, I don't disbelieve. I just never knew about fairies in general."

"That makes sense," she said, giving him a gentle squeeze. "You went through so many foster families and probably none of the parents ever read books about myths, fairies, or anything else."

"No, I didn't have anyone read to me," he said, frowning. Pointing to the nearest bough, he said, "Do these people who give the gifts to the tree get their requests answered?"

"Many times, yes. If you come here with a humble heart, with humility, and your request is coming out of love for another, the fairy folks are far more willing to grant the request."

"You mean I couldn't ask to win the mega-million lottery?" he teased.

She laughed. "No . . . fairies don't like humans who are greedy or selfish or self-centered."

"Ah, I see."

"You're beginning to," she said, smiling. She stepped away from him and pulled a quart-size ziplock bag from her pocket, holding it up to him. "I wanted to come to this beautiful old tree and ask her and the fairy folk for help." She opened it up; the ribbons were gold and silver. Attached to them was a small note. "I know you probably think this is silly—"

"No," he said, giving her a concerned look, "I don't, Sara. What's important to you is important to me. I learn from you. Have you written a request of some kind in there?"

She tucked the ziplock bag away, the gift in her other hand. "Yes. And that's why I wanted you to come out here and share that moment with me . . . well . . . because it's important to me."

He walked over to her, placing his hands on her shoulders. "You're the most important person in my world. I feel honored to be here, to know about it. I'm not very up on Native American ways, and know nothing about the fairy people, but that doesn't mean I don't want to learn or be stretched or educated about something like this." He squeezed her shoulders and looked over at the wishing tree. "I mean . . . there must be at least a thousand gifts tied to this tree . . ."

"Lea was telling me this tree was planted by Logan's great-great-grandfather, who came here and established the ranch. So, it's pretty old."

He saw the unsureness in her green eyes, as if he would laugh at her. He understood the importance of the gift to the tree. Moving his hand through her hair that cloaked her shoulder, he rasped, "I love you just the way you are, Sara. What is the request you're asking for? Can you share it with me?"

Shyly, she whispered unsteadily, "I'm asking this beautiful old tree spirit if she and the fairy folk can help us so that we can live our lives without fear of being killed by Manny or my father." She held it up to him. "I miss my herbs, I miss the people I was helping, Wes. I want to stop running, stop hiding. With my father and half brother after me? We can't have the life together that we'd like to have."

His heart broke for Sara. Gathering her into his arms, wincing because he saw tears coming to her eyes as she held the ribboned gift, he choked out, "I know how hard this is on you. And everyone is hoping for some kind of break in this case."

"I shouldn't be so impatient," she managed. "Logan and Lea have been so kind and caring of us. Steve has provided Rob and Chris to guard us. I know I sound like I'm not grateful, but I am—"

"Let's put that gift on the tree together," he said, holding her watery gaze. "What you're asking for is reasonable, not unreasonable. I want you happy, Sara." He slid his arm around her shoulders, leading her to the tree. "Now, is there a special branch that calls out to you?"

She wiped her eyes and looked around. "This one," she whispered, and walked over and tied the gift to the tree. For a long moment, she cupped her hands around it after attaching it, closing her eyes.

Wes stood at her side, sensing she was praying to the tree spirit or perhaps to the fairy people. He'd give anything to see her request answered, but he knew how monumental, how impossible it really was, but he didn't want to say that to Sara.

When she released the gift, she dug in her other pocket and drew out a small leather pouch. Opening it, she walked to the massive trunk of the tree and sprinkled some golden cornmeal upon it, whispering something to it in Cherokee that he couldn't translate. Sara reached out, reverently touching the trunk and then she lifted her hand away.

"There, it's done," she said, tucking the pouch into her pocket. "Thank you for being here . . . for not laughing at me."

"I would never laugh at you, Sara," he rasped, taking her into his arms, feeling her slide her arms around his waist. Holding her tightly, he kissed her hair and kept her against his chest. "I love you. I know how much your life has changed, how much has been taken away from you." He kissed her temple and eased her away from him, seeing the anguish in her eyes. "Don't ever be afraid to share what's bothering you. Okay? I want to know what's important to you. I want to be a part of those times with you."

Nodding jerkily, she whispered, "In some ways, my request seems so inconsequential compared to your life. You don't know who your mother or father are. You have lost so much. All I've lost is my freedom to do certain things—"

"But they are no less significant. You can't compare

my situation to yours. What's important to you is equally important to me."

She gave him a weak smile and brushed the tears from her eyes. "In my dreams? I dream of us getting married and one day, starting a family, but I don't know how you feel about that, either."

An unusual sound caught his attention. He lifted his head, orienting toward it.

"What?" Sara asked, looking in the same direction, toward the road below that he was intently studying. "What is it, Wes? What do you hear?"

He frowned. "I don't know . . . it's a different sound . . . not the type we hear around the ranch." Gently releasing her, he moved her to the trunk of the wishing tree and moved a few feet away from it.

Wes got on his radio, calling Logan.

"Hey," he said, "there's an unusual sound coming our way out in the grove with the wishing tree. Do you have something going on with the fence and gate that's nearby?"

"No," Logan said.

Wes didn't like the sudden concern in the rancher's tone. He looked in the opposite direction. There was another sound. Very high above them and coming their way. With the grove trees creating a canopy, he couldn't see anything. "Now, I have a second sound, Logan. It sounds like a drone, or drones. Do you have some up and doing work in this area?"

"No. You're at the far end of the ranch, near one of the exit-entrance points. I don't have any crews in that area. And our drones are all on the ground."

The high, whirring sounds drew closer. Wes had an ugly feeling of danger. "Call Dan. Something's going on and I don't know what it is. Can you get some of your people

out here? I know it's a long ways from where you're at."
In fact, it would take forty minutes for Logan to get some
wranglers and pickups out to their location. His skin
crawled. The sound on the ground was getting louder.

"Wes!" Sara called out urgently. "They sound like
ATVs!!"

"Do you have ATVs out here, Logan?" Wes demanded,
drawing his pistol.

"No. I'll alert Dan. There's a highway about three miles
away and a road he can turn in on to get to our back gate
area where you're located."

Grimly, he said, "Get SWAT. I don't trust this situation.
I'm going to get Sara and make our way out of the grove
and to the truck. Once we get to it, we'll drive toward your
headquarters area."

"Roger that," Logan said. "I'm all over this. Stay safe."

Sara came up to him, worried.

Clicking off the radio, he wished to hell he could see
down the hill, but it was covered with trees of all sizes
and heights. He felt Sara's hand wrap around his upper
arm. "Come on, let's get out of here. I don't like what's
going on . . ."

He took one step forward and there was a *CRAAAKKKK!*
Instantly, Wes flattened on the earth, taking Sara with him.
She gasped, hitting the ground. A bullet whistled overhead.

Getting his first glance below the hill, he saw at least
four ATVs roaring their way. The men on them were in
camo gear. And they were all carrying rifles! Gritting his
teeth, he turned to Sara. "Crawl to the trunk of the wishing
tree. Stay there. Keep your head covered and flatten on the
ground!"

Eyes huge, Sara lifted her head. "Oh, no, Wes! That's
Manny and his group! I recognize the racing colors he

uses when he races. Oh, no!" She got to her hands and knees, moving swiftly to the trunk that would afford her protection.

Wes got on the radio, connecting with Logan, telling him what Sara said. Logan had already called the sheriff, and the SWAT team were getting ready to leave and head their way. The ATVs, four of them, were snaking up the long, rutted dirt road they'd come up on. He had a pistol, and the men who rode on the ATVs were all firing their weapons in their direction. There was no way he could hold them off. Terror drenched him inwardly as he moved to the tree where Sara was huddled at the trunk. She jerked a look in his direction.

"How did they find us?"

"I don't know," he growled, placing himself between her and the trunk.

"He'll kill us, Wes!"

Nodding, he took a deep breath, all of his old SEAL training coming back to him. "Help is on the way," he told her, but seeing the fear in her eyes, he was sure she was sensing what he was: that they were in a terrible situation and the chances of surviving weren't good. His heart squeezed with such grief that for a second, he wanted to cry. That quickly passed as he heard something overhead. Jerking a look up, he blinked. There were ten drones! And to his surprise, they were carrying weapons! *What the hell!*

The camouflaged drones, large ones, military types, passed overhead and then dove downward, following the arc of the hill's slope. They were heading for the group of ATVs growling up the road toward them.

More bullets flew into their position. Ducking, Wes pressed himself against the thick trunk of the tree, hands around the pistol. His mind spun. Who the hell owned those drones? They were military! And they were carrying weapons. Even more confusing, they flew overhead, aiming for the ATVs now climbing the road toward the grove. Whose were they? Where did they come from?

Wes saw several of the drones dropping what looked like grenades or something akin to them right on the ATVs below them.

Explosions rocked the area.

Wes dropped to his knees. "Open your mouth, Sara! Keep it open!" he yelled above the fray. The shock waves struck them. The power of the explosions stunned him. Below, he saw two ATVs suddenly thrown up in the air, bodies flying, and more gunfire, but the thick, black smoke rolling around prevented him from seeing everything. He heard Sara cry out. Jerking a look at her, she had covered her head with her arms, mouth open, pressed to the tree for protection.

Another group of drones dropped more bombs.

The fireball effect made Wes wince and he kept his body in front of Sara's. The next group of pressure waves slammed through the grove. Flame, black smoke, and carnage met his gaze as he watched as the other two ATVs were hit directly by the drones above. Holy shit! He had no idea who was behind this, but they were saving their lives, no question. Stunned by the attack, it was over as fast as it had begun.

Slowly, Wes stood, pistol in hand, looking at the carnage below them. There was no one left alive, that was for damned sure. Looking up, he saw the fleet of drones going higher and higher, moving back in the direction that they had come from. He didn't know if they were coming after them next, or not. But in a minute, the drone squadron disappeared from where they had originally come from.

Wes knew that they were near the corner of the ranch's property line, and this grove had grown in an L-shape within the boundary. He had so many questions and no answers.

Leaning down, he holstered his pistol, placing his hand on Sara's shoulder. "It's all right. We're not being attacked. Are you okay?"

She eased up into a sitting position, looking around, and then her gaze pinned below where the wrecks of four ATVs could be seen off and on between the fire and the roiling black clouds of smoke. "What just happened?" Her voice wobbled, fear in her tone.

Wes helped her stand, keeping her against the tree, him in front of her, his hand on her upper arm. "Damned if I know . . ."

A man in camo gear, bald headed, walked toward them, his hands up. Wes went for his pistol.

"Relax," the man called. "I am a friend." He kept his hands up and halted.

Wes eyed him warily. Whoever this guy was? His English was thickly accented and not his first language. He recognized the uniform of the Russian Spetsnaz, and grew even more confused. And where had he come from? Were those drones and that attack on the ATVs due to his presence?

"I'm Lev," he called. "I am a friend."

"Halt," Wes said. The soldier was at least six-foot-three-inches tall, heavy boned, his eyes dark brown, and he carried a pistol on his hip, a Kevlar vest across his upper body.

Lev halted. He looked at the ATVs, a pleased expression

coming to his broad face. "I come in peace. I am on your side."

"You own those drones?" Wes demanded, keeping his pistol on him.

"Yes. I know this is confusing, but we had intel that Manny Romano was coming to kill his half sister." Lev pointed to Sara, who had just gotten to her feet and walked to where Wes stood. "You see, we are part of a Russian group who has been at war with Leo Romano and his Mafia."

Scowling, Wes growled, "Russian Mafia by any chance? Because they don't let Spetsnaz soldiers like yourself onto US soil."

Lev gave a slight shrug and held out his large hands. "Well, you are right, my friend, but we bear you and Sara Romano no ill will. In fact, we got word that her half brother was coming here to kill her. And as soon as they accomplished that? They were returning to Dallas to kill her mother."

Sara gasped, her hands against her lips, staring in disbelief at the Russian. "But," she cried out, "is my mother all right?"

"She is fine," Lev soothed. "She knows nothing of what has just happened. She is working at her company. We have people in place to protect her, although she's not aware of what is going down."

"But," Sara cried, "why was Manny coming here to kill me?"

Lev gave her a feral smile. "Because your half brother just poisoned his father . . . your father . . . in prison and he is now in a coma at the prison hospital. He will die, we feel. And Manny was making a move to take over his father's empire, and you and your mother were on his list to remove."

Wes shook his head. "If you're Russian Mafia? Why the hell are you here?"

Lev took his impatience in stride. "My friend, what you and Sara do not know is that your half brother was planning a takeover of his father's empire. He wanted to keep tabs on your movements, so he had hackers infiltrate your mother's company and once he found where you were, he had henchmen put a tracking device in a backpack." He made a motion toward a small silver necklace she wore around her neck. "There is a very small bug in it. Someone had it embedded when you left it at a jeweler to fix the chain. I won't say who did it."

"What?" she whispered, stunned by the information. Automatically, she touched the necklace and then took it off, turning it over. She saw a very tiny device, nearly unseeable, on the back of the pendant. She held it up to show Wes, and then lifted it toward Lev. "Is that it?"

"Yes. Have it removed. Your half brother liked power. He didn't want your father telling him what to do. We keep watch on him. We have an insider close to him who passed on this intelligence to us." He shrugged. "We had to do something after Manny came here to kill you. He wanted no one left, so he could own the empire himself."

Scowling, Wes said, "But you're the group who's been fighting Romano's empire."

"Yes," Lev said, nodding and looking around. "In time, we will take over Romano's empire." He looked at Sara. "We wish you and your mother no harm, but we also want to know that since your father will die shortly, and Manny is now dead, you are legally the owners of his business.

We know you are not into the drug and money laundering business he has. Allow us to peacefully take over this territory for such purposes. We don't wish to go to war with you."

Sara gave Wes a look. And then she croaked out, "My father is going to die?"

"Yes. Manny put the poison in some chocolates he brought his father in prison. Your father had no idea what he did. The poison he gave him acts slowly, over many weeks, and now, your father is in the prison hospital, in a coma. It won't be long before he expires."

Manny's cold-bloodedness didn't surprise Wes. "Where does that leave things, then?" he demanded of Lev.

Lev smiled a little. Not really a smile, but as close as one would get to it. "We want a verbal agreement from Sara that she is more than welcome to the software company that is very successful, and she may continue to run it. What she must agree to is not utilize it as a front for her father's other illegal business."

"I walked away from my father and his illegal activities," she said. "My mother and I want nothing to do with it."

This time, Lev smiled. It was like an alligator smiling. "That is all I need to hear from you, then. We will go our way, and you will go yours. We will not interfere in your lives again. We will remove the people who worked in the two offices." He looked to his right and then back at them. "It's time to go. You will never see me again, but it was important you understand what was happening, and why. I am sorry for your losses. Now you are free to have the life you wanted. You will never be hunted again, Sara. You are free to return to Dallas to be with your mother."

"I'm going to tell my mother what happened."

Lev nodded. "Of course. We understand that. The FBI, who has been monitoring your father's illegal concerns, will want to speak to you."

Wes holstered his pistol, remaining on guard. "This is a standoff, then?"

"Yes," Lev concurred. "You leave us alone? We leave you alone. We each go our own ways. Are we in agreement, Sara?"

Shocked, she nodded her head.

Lev lifted a hand. "It's time for me to go. I hear that in about twenty minutes, the sheriff's SWAT team will arrive . . ."

Wes watched the soldier turn, take off at a loping run down the other side of the hill. In no time, he disappeared. Turning, he said, "I'm calling Logan."

Sara stood there, listening to the conversation, shock still rolling through her. Looking at the destroyed ATVs, what little was left of them, she could feel no loss of Manny, who had hunted her. She pushed the necklace into her pocket, lips tight. Brushing the debris from her trousers, touching the tree trunk that had taken several rounds into its thick bark, she stood there, trying to deal with everything that had just happened. Her feelings were mixed toward her father. It would take a lot of time to sort them all out.

Wes got off the radio, and he continued to look around the area. It was quiet now except for the crackle of fire and flames consuming what was left of the ATVs a quarter of a mile away from them.

"Let's go to the truck," he urged, holding out his hand to her. "I want to get you away from this . . ."

Giving a jerky nod, she gripped his hand, beginning a slow trot toward where their truck was parked.

"This is . . . crazy," she said, giving him a confused look.

"We'll get it sorted out. Right now? Once we get in the truck, I'm driving it down to the gate to wait for Dan and his SWAT team. Logan will be here in about fifteen minutes, too."

They both looked in the same direction, hearing what sounded like helicopters in the distance. Looking at one another, Wes said, "That's how the Russians got here. And that's how they're leaving." The grove was so thick that they couldn't see the birds, but they heard them lift off. In no time, the noise faded into the distance and disappeared.

"This is surreal," she muttered, keeping up with his stride, the truck closer.

"Seriously," he agreed. "But look at it this way? Lev and his Mafia stopped Manny from killing us, and then your mother. Even bad guys can sometimes do good deeds."

She shook her head, slowing as they approached the truck. "Why did they do it, Wes? What was in it for them?"

"My take is that the Russian Mafia wants to quietly take over your father's empire and doesn't want to have to fight you or your mother. It's a leveraging on their part. They're giving you your lives in trade for not getting into the Mafia business."

"I would *never* do that," she spat, anger surfacing. "It's wrong. It's all wrong."

Wes opened the door for her to climb into the truck. "I think Lev and his boss were counting on that."

Sara sat in the cab, rubbing her face, her whole life suddenly upended once more. The fear of dying, and then being rescued, and then suddenly being given back the life she so desperately wanted, was simply too much for her to absorb. As Wes climbed in, she gripped his hand. He leaned over, kissing her brow.

"I know it's a lot to deal with," he said roughly, starting the truck. "Let's get with Dan. We'll be meeting them at the gate." Squeezing her hand, he added, "We're alive, Sara, and so is your mother. That's what really counts . . ."

Chapter Fifteen

June 29

"Well, this is a helluva twist," Dan told Wes and Sara the next afternoon after they met him at his office. He laid out several reports on his desk, giving her a sad look. "First, Sara, I think your mother called you last night to tell you that your father died?"

"Yes," she said in a low tone, "she did."

"You have my sympathy."

"Thank you, Dan."

"And that our medical examiner here in Silver Creek identified the remains of your half brother, Manny Romano?"

Nodding, she clutched a tissue between her hands. "I never had any love for him. He was always so cruel to me, always wanting to hurt me. I hated having to spend a week-end once a month at my father's home after my mother's divorce from him, and he just waited to attack me when no one was looking. I can't say I'm sorry he's gone. That probably sounds awful, but it's the truth."

"Being a SEAL at one time," Dan offered, "you get to see the underbelly of the worst of men and what they're capable of. In a way, I understand how you feel. There are evil people in the world, no question. And they aren't salvageable, nor do they want to be changed from who and what they are."

"My father? He was also evil. I've got so many mixed feelings about him . . . it's going to take me a long time to deal with it, to come to terms with him. Myself . . . I'll be flying down to Dallas to attend his and Manny's funerals in two days."

"I'll be going with her," Wes told Dan, and he reached out, closing his larger hand over her two smaller ones.

"The FBI office in Dallas knows you're making plans to attend the two funerals," Dan said. "They want to set up a time to talk to you and Wes about this Russian named Lev. The one who brought his army of weaponized drones onto Logan's ranch to kill Manny."

"Before Manny killed us," she said, shaking her head sadly.

"Yes, Lev saved your lives, no doubt," Dan agreed quietly. "Interesting twist of one bad guy saving your lives and the other bad guy wanting to take them."

"What did you find out about this Russian?" Wes wanted to know.

"He's a lieutenant in the Russian Mafia that is in the Dallas–Fort Worth area. He works for Ivan Bobrov, the ringleader. The FBI knows about them and has tabs on them as well as the Romano group. What you may not know is that your father and Bobrov were archenemies and there has been plenty of bloodletting between them. About two years ago, Bobrov started infringing on your father's turf, and there's been pitched battles off and on since then. Your father was losing a lot of turf to Bobrov. The Russians are almost always ex-Spetsnaz or black ops soldiers, whereas your father's people were a mix of Sicilians and Americans who swore allegiance to his business. There were some military types among them, but most were civilians."

"The ones we ran into on the mountain, with the exception of the Ferret, were not military trained," Wes added.

"Correct," Dan said. "Bobrov was a general in Spetsnaz before he retired. He's a superior tactician and strategist. In the long run? I'm not surprised he was taking Romano's territory right out from under him."

"You said the Ferret was black ops," Sara said.

Wes nodded. "Yes, he was. Most likely, but the men he had under his command were not, as you just said."

"This Lev fellow?" Dan said, handing them a color photo of the Russian, across the desk. "He's black ops for sure. The CIA and FBI have a thick folder on him. Bobrov has assigned him to most of the battles they fight to gain new territory."

Sara studied the photo. It showed Lev in a camouflage uniform and he looked deadly. "The day we saw Lev? He seemed . . . well . . . almost nice . . . compared to how lethal he looks in this photograph."

Wes snorted. "An act. He's a cold-blooded killer. The reason he behaved in that way toward us was because he wanted something from you, Sara. They weren't interested in taking your life. And he wasn't wanting to start another war on your father's turf, with you. He wanted assurances from you and your mother that you were not going to pick up the reins of your father and half brother's illegal activities and continue the war with Bobrov. Since you agreed to stand down, he was nice toward you, Sara."

"Right," Dan said. "They wanted a verbal agreement from you and Tsula that you wouldn't step into and start to run your father's Mafia empire. They wanted to come in and take over, instead. They'll push out the men who are left and chase them off or kill them if they resist."

"My life spared so they could take over my father's Mafia empire," Sara said, shaking her head, thinking about the karma of it all.

"It's the FBI's job to uproot any group who is doing something illegal and they're working on taking Bobrov down," Dan assured them, sitting back in his chair. "They've got their job cut out for them. You don't mess around with Spetsnaz-trained soldiers. I can tell you that Wes, Rob, Chris, and the rest of that SEAL team run by Steve Carter, have had head-on clashes with them in Afghanistan. I can't say much more than that, but the Russians have a take-no-prisoners mindset. They don't maim or wound. They shoot to kill. And they're very good at what they do."

"But we're better," Wes said.

Dan nodded. "We're not cruel, though, unlike Spetsnaz."

"We have rules and regulations regarding combat engagement. They don't."

"How did Lev get to the grove where we were?" Sara demanded. "We heard what we thought were helicopters."

"They arrived by two helicopters. My deputies found the landing area and we identified the type of helos they arrived and left in. My guess," Dan said, "was that Lev and his people were closely monitoring Manny at all times. I wouldn't be surprised if they had a mole in his office and had bugs planted everywhere to listen in on his plans and conversations. They obviously knew Manny was coming to Logan's ranch to catch you alone so they could kill you. It was in Bobrov's best interests to send his hired gun, Lev, to protect you and take out Manny and his men."

"Only," Wes murmured, "the half brother didn't know that Bobrov or Lev had this intel, also."

"Which is why the FBI feels there was a mole planted in Manny's software office who placed the bugs so they could get this kind of intel."

"I feel so hunted," she whispered. "It's an awful feeling."

"The hackers and the bug placed in your backpack was how Manny knew you were here," Wes said. "And he sent the Ferret and his men after you that day we went up in the meadow. They had the ability to know your whereabouts at all times."

"But not always," Sara said, "because you helped us escape and evade them, Wes."

"It's possible," Dan told them, "that due to where you were, in high altitude mountains, that your location interfered with their GPS instruments, and it could have given them wrong data or it could have stopped working, which meant they were blind and couldn't find you, Sara."

"That answers my question about it," Wes said. "I was wondering how the Ferret suddenly showed up and located Sara after I'd broken my ankle."

"Weren't you at a lower altitude at that time?" Dan asked.

"Yes," Sara said, "we had gone down two thousand feet."

"And his locator may have worked at that elevation," Dan said, "which explains why he knew the general vicinity of where you were, Sara. Our forensic's lab took that other tracker, which is very highly sophisticated and nothing like the one Manny put on your backpack. The Russians put that in the pendant of your necklace at some point, but no one knows when it happened. It could be that it was done when you lived in Dallas. That is how they always knew where you were."

Dan handed her back her necklace, leaning across the desk, dropping it into her awaiting hand. "It's clean now," he said. "Just a necklace now, no longer a monitoring device."

She stared down at it. "I'm so stunned by the level of stealth . . ."

"Russian Mafia doesn't mess around," Dan said, nodding gravely. "And along that line? The FBI is looking at anything your mother normally wears on a daily basis and sending it back to their main lab in Washington, D.C. to be carefully searched."

"Unbelieveable," Sara whispered, "and to think two tracking devices from two different groups was watching my every move . . ."

"Black ops," Dan said, giving Wes a dark look. "I'm just glad that the tracker Manny had put on you was a cheap one. It had a lot of limitations and could only, at best, get within a quarter mile of where you might be located."

"Thank goodness Rob and Chris were there on the mountain with us," she said, suddenly emotional.

Wes gave her a proud look. "You're the one who saved yourself, Sara. You hit the Ferret over the head with that tree branch and knocked him out. All they had to do was find you and put the zip ties on him."

"Not something I ever want to live through again," she muttered. "I've had enough stealth to last a lifetime."

"I think," Dan said, "after you fly back from the funerals in Dallas, and come home to Silver Creek Valley, that your life is going to be pretty stable and quiet."

"Yes." She sighed, perking up a bit. "We'll get to move

back into our beautiful old Victorian home. I'll be reopening my herb business, helping my clients and making up prescriptions for the doctor in my laboratory. You have no idea how good it feels to not be hunted."

"You've had a rough time," Dan agreed, sympathetic. "But now, this sordid chapter of your life is almost over."

June 30

Wes stayed out of the way, more a listener and observer than anything else, as Tsula took the helm at her corporate office in Dallas to deal with her ex-husband's software company, the legal part of his activities. There were two FBI agents, her attorneys, Department of Justice attorneys, and an IRS agent at the table, as well.

Sara sat at her mother's right elbow. There were ten other people at the long, oval maple-wood table who worked on the nitty-gritty details of dismantling the Romano empire. Wes sat next to Sara and noticed the darkness beneath her eyes. The last two days, the burials of her father and Manny had weighed heavily upon her.

"The first item on the agenda is the Romano software company," Tsula said. "My daughter and I are going to sell it to another US global corporation, who will absorb it. The money that comes from that buyout will be divided between me and my daughter, Sara."

There were nods of agreement from everyone.

"Next on the agenda is the Romano family home," Tsula said, giving her daughter a softened look. She turned to a Realtor across the table from her. "We want to sell it outright. We have no interest in keeping it."

Wes thought he saw some relief in Sara's eyes. That house had been an ongoing nightmare memory for her.

She had cried off and on the last two days over everything that had happened, and he was grateful to be with her, to hold her, to allow her that grief-stricken release. Earlier, in another meeting, a host of estate lawyers and other legal eagles covered Leo Romano's will, and papers were signed by Tsula and Sara, giving them the ability to decide the fate of not only the software company, but the family estate, as well. Manny's mother, Victoria, would be given a lifelong stipend and she could buy another house of her choice and live wherever she wanted. Neither of them wanted to leave her destitute. She wasn't Mafia and really had no idea that the underbelly of the family was illegal. Like Tsula, Victoria had been lied to and thought Leo owned a very rich, vibrant software company and that was all. Wes liked the generosity extended to the woman, who was grieving deeply for the loss of her only son and her husband. She had no idea Manny was up to his hocks in illegal activity until the FBI sat down and told her. To say she was devastated, was mild.

Tsula looked at her daughter and then focused on the attorneys who were present. "My daughter and I will sell this house and the proceeds split evenly between us." She added, "We will give half of it to the IRS, because as far as we're concerned, it is blood money, and Leo never paid taxes and was involved in money-laundering fraud. Money stolen from others, as far as we are concerned. And I understand that this agreement has already been approved."

The two women IRS agents, and the DOJ attorneys, nodded.

One of the attorneys slid a document to each of them. "Yes, the paperwork has been completed," he told them. "And here are your copies of the signed agreement between yourselves and the United States federal government agencies involved."

Tsula studied the document thoroughly and then said, "My daughter and I will take the other half of the money and we'll be donating the proceeds to local organizations and charities where we live." Her voice hardened. "We do *not* want one cent from the sale of this house. Life is hard enough without living with the blood of others on one's spirit."

Wes saw the two male attorneys were nonplussed by Tsula's steely comment, her gaze drilling into them. Knowing Sara, her mother's Native American heritage played strongly into her wise decision, and he silently applauded her decisions. In Silver Creek Valley, Sara was going to create a charity to build more tiny homes for the homeless, including homeless vets. There already were tiny homes, but not near enough. The other part of the money would go to the battered women's shelter, with small homes being built for them and their children, where they could live rent-free until they could educate and support themselves once more. Wes applauded her choices. This was a valley that always took care of its own, where neighbor always helped neighbor.

"Also, the software company, which is in the process of being bought, has agreed to a half-million-dollar stipend that will go annually to Mrs. Victoria Romano. She should not be punished for what Leo and Manny did," Tsula said.

Again, more nods of agreement.

Wes liked that they had agreed to help Victoria, who bore no blame for anything that had happened. The generosity of Tsula and Sara made him proud of them. How many people would have done this? Probably not many.

"I will maintain my corporation here in Dallas," Tsula told the gathering. "My daughter will be making her own business in Silver Creek, Wyoming. This chapter in our lives is over and closed. This meeting is adjourned."

July 4

Sara moved to the front porch of their Victorian home. There was a large porch swing and she walked toward it. Wes was there, waiting for her. The darkness was almost complete. The fairgrounds would soon have fireworks to celebrate Independence Day. She came and sat down next to him. He placed his arm around her shoulders. The evening was balmy, in the seventies, a soft breeze every now and then.

"Did you get a nap?" he asked, kissing her temple.

"I did. Two hours. When am I going to start living like a normal person?" She looked up at him.

"Shock is the culprit," he confided, squeezing her gently.

"When will it leave?"

"Depends upon how you got it, the intensity of it, and how long it dragged on. The best thing you can do to help it dissolve is get sleep when you're tired. I know you don't like taking naps, but they're healing."

"Humph."

Grinning, he said, "At least tomorrow you open up the store and clinic. That's something positive."

"Oh," she muttered, "there's a lot that's positive, Wes. I guess I'm really stunned by how much shock can change a person's life"—she snapped her fingers—"just like that."

"Don't need to tell a SEAL about that," he teased. He became serious. "You know? I don't normally see things in terms of symbols, but today is more than a holiday." He looked down into her eyes. "It's you and your mother's independence day, too. You are now free of your past in every way except, of course, emotionally. But now? You can live your life without fear and you no longer have to run and hide. And your mother no longer has to worry about you, either. No more bodyguard."

She sighed, leaning upward, kissing him softly. "I've been thinking a lot about the symbolism of it, too, Wes. There's been so many twists and turns, so much evil at work to stop my mother and me from living our lives."

"But evil didn't win. Light did."

The rocking motion soothed her. "Yes, it did. In ways we could never have expected. I believe in the Light. I believe that love, as the most powerful human emotion that's positive, will triumph. I've always believed Light would conquer the darkness, the evil."

"It has, in you and your mother's case," Wes agreed quietly, rocking the swing gently with his toe. "It's nice to see good people who have good hearts, emerge from something like this."

"But that's not always the case." She sighed, sadness tingeing her tone. "Good people with good intentions here on Mother Earth are being murdered by that evil, by that darkness, all the time. Look how many wars around the globe we have presently . . . it's awful . . ."

"Hey," he said, kissing her temple, "don't go there. Tonight? Let's celebrate the good that came out of your mother's and your own situation. It's a win for the Light."

As if to double-check what he said, the first fireworks from the fairgrounds, bright green and red, exploded across the night sky in front of them.

Sighing, she whispered, "You're right, Wes, this is a

good holiday to celebrate my mother and myself being fully freed from my father's past. It feels good."

He squeezed her shoulders. "And we have a lot to talk about regarding us, when the time comes," he said.

Nodding, Sara watched white and golden light explode across the night sky, the boom of it echoing past them. "I can hardly wait . . ."

July 7

Wes was cleaning up in the lab at quitting time. He wore his canvas apron and protective gloves, as usual. Hearing the front door of the shop close, he knew Sara was finished with her twice-weekly clinic with her clients. After cleaning the flow hood, he pulled off his gloves and untied the apron, placing it in another container that was for items to be washed in their heavy-duty washing machine.

"Hey," Sara called, coming around the corner, "finished a little early today. Would you like to take a ride with me?"

Grinning, he nodded. "You bet." Where were they going? She had an impish smile but didn't say anything more.

Once in the truck, the evening sky still bright with sunshine, they drove a few blocks, parked and went into the no-kill shelter. Wes knew that Sara loved animals and had felt alone without a dog or cat around the house. She'd grown up with all kinds of animals around her, and had wanted to choose one of each for their home. His heart mushroomed with love for her because she always used the word "us" and "we." Little by little, for him, reality was settling in that they had something very rare: real love. Yes, loving one another was terrific, too, but it was her touch, the partnership that was cementing between them, that meant the most to him. Maybe it was because he'd never had a stable, fixed home. Sara was ushering in just that for him, and somehow he wanted to be able to share how important it was to him, also.

Meeting the volunteers who ran the no-kill shelter, they sat down with a gray-haired woman, Ann Jamison, in the office.

"So, Sara and Wes, have you decided how many of each you want?" Ann teased them.

They took the chairs in front of the desk and smiled.

"My mother has a beautiful golden retriever," Sara said. "I was so hoping there might be one here to adopt? I know most people never give up their goldens."

"Well," Ann said, raising her silver brows, "you are in luck! One of our longtime residents, Julia Mangrove, just passed away at ninety-five, and in her will, she asked that her golden retriever, Candy, be given a home where there's children. Julia ran a day care center here in Silver Creek for forty years. Candy is ten years old. The children loved her and she is so good with them."

"Well," Sara said, giving Wes a glance, "we don't have any children yet, Ann . . ."

"But we will," Wes said, giving her a softened look.

"Ah! Well, that's good. Would Candy fit into your daily life?"

Sara smiled. "I told Wes that I want a gentle, quiet dog, someone who loves people, and no breed is better at babysitting human beings than golden retrievers. My mother has one, and she has the run of the corporate office, she visits every cubical where her employees work, and is greatly loved. I want a dog not only for our home but also, my herb store and clinic. People just naturally calm down and become more relaxed if there's a loving, gentle dog around."

Brightening, Ann said, "Why, this is perfect! Now, we've had Candy for two weeks and the poor thing, she's so lost and still grieving for her mistress. She's very depressed."

"I think, coming home with us," Wes said, "that it will help her through this time of grief. Don't you, Ann?"

"Absolutely! Come on, let me show her to you. Let's see how you get along!"

Wes stood back when Ann opened the clean cage's door. There was a doggy bed for Candy, clean water, and her favorite toy, a green dinosaur, which Ann said she treated like a puppy she might have had. The golden had a white muzzle, showing her age, and white eyebrows, was about seventy-five pounds, a deep gold color, and kind gold-brown eyes. She immediately got up and wagged her tail as Sara stood in the doorway and knelt down on one knee, extending her hand toward the dog.

He choked back a lump in his throat, watching the dog instantly go to Sara, eagerly licking her hand in a hello. Sara simply wrapped her arms around Candy, who then sat, her head resting against her chest, eyes closed. It brought tears to his eyes, which he swallowed a couple of times, touched beyond words. Dogs always knew. He'd wanted one so badly while growing up, but none of the families he was in had one. And no cats, either.

"I think she's fallen in love with you," Ann chirped, smiling broadly, thrilled.

"She's so gentle," Sara whispered, sliding her hand across her golden fur. "So gentle . . ."

"She loves babies and children. And I know from the gossip that's gone around about your clinic—all good, by the way—that you take care of a lot of pregnant moms-to-be and their babies, after they are born. I think Candy would love to just be in the general area."

Sara nodded, smiling down into Candy's adoring brown eyes. The golden couldn't get close enough to her, absorbing her arms around her, holding her against her body. "How is she with kids crawling all over her? You know how the little tykes love to explore."

"Oh, heavens," Ann gushed, "she is so patient with them. Candy has *never* barked, growled, or bitten anyone. She is such a mother herself."

"Did she ever have puppies?" Wes wondered.

"Yes, two litters, but that was many years ago. Julia and I were dear friends, so I know a lot about Candy. The resulting puppies were given away to people who wanted them here in the valley. She was spayed after the second litter. And I think that was best, because Candy loved her 'job' of babysitting all the youngsters in the day care center. Why, she would even go lie between them at nap time in the afternoon. The children would snuggle around her, and it was just precious. She is such a sweet, loving animal."

Sara looked up at Wes. "Come and see how she reacts to you?"

Wes didn't want to break the spell of happiness, so he hesitated. Sara released Candy and stood up. As soon as she had, Candy was out the door of the cage and headed straight for Wes, wagging her tail, looking up at him with the same adoring expression. How could he not kneel down and pet this heart-centered dog? As soon as he had, she wriggled in between his thighs and laid her head on his chest as soon as she sat down. Grinning up at Sara, who was beaming, he said, "Well, I guess she's okay with me?"

Both women nodded.

"Oh," Sara said, "I think so. She loves you, too, Wes."

"Now," Ann said, "Candy doesn't necessarily like all

men. She knows good ones from bad ones. She'd never do that to a baby or child, but with men, she's wary. And I'm thrilled to see that she immediately came to you, Wes. You *must* be a very good man!"

He felt heat rush to his cheeks as he gently petted Candy's head and shoulders. She had thick, silky golden fur and she invited him to keep petting her. "That's good to know," he joked, smiling up at the women who were trading knowing glances and big smiles.

"In about a month," Sara told Ann, "we'd love to come back here and get a calico cat."

"Oh, my goodness! You won't have to wait a month! Just last week a woman found a starving calico female and brought her in to us. We have no idea how young or old she is, but she's beautiful and she's just the sweetest, most loving thing!"

"While Wes stays with Candy, can I see her?" Sara asked, hope in her voice.

"Absolutely! Come with me. We have a special section that is just for the kittens and cats."

Sara said, "Stay with Candy? I just want to look."

Wes grinned and stood. Candy immediately sidled along his right leg and sat down. It was obvious she had been trained. "Sure, go ahead."

They disappeared behind another door.

Candy looked up at Wes.

Wes looked down at her. "Well, it's just you and me, girl." And he absorbed the dog's expression, feeling as if she was truly happy to be with them. "I hope you get along with cats . . ."

It didn't take long for Sara to come back carrying a cat cage, with Ann bringing up the rear, glowing and happy.

"She's beautiful," Sara said, lifting the plastic cage. "Look at her . . ."

Wes peered into it and heard a big meow and a black, white, and caramel-colored short-haired cat with big yellow eyes studying him. "Looks good," he said.

"Ann said Candy gets along fine with kittens and cats, too. So, I think both of them could come home with us today. What do you think?"

Giving her a crooked grin, his hand resting on Candy's head, he said, "We've just started a family . . ." He saw Sara's expression grow soft, her eyes glistening as she held the cat cage in her arms.

"I love the sound of it, Wes. I truly do."

In a matter of half an hour, all the paperwork filled out, a new leash and collar for Candy, flea collars for both, they were almost ready to go. Sitting in the small room, the cat cage on Wes's lap, Candy sitting between them, Sara drew out her checkbook. "How much do we owe you, Ann?"

"Well, this is donation only. Some people can afford more than others. This place is able to remain no-kill because a number of the ranchers here in the valley give us a yearly donation to keep it going, and we're very grateful."

"If you had the money, is there anything you would change or fix here?" Sara wondered.

"Oh, my, yes! Our air conditioner is very, very old and I keep praying in church every Sunday, for Him to keep it going! And it's a huge one, a very expensive one, and I lose sleep over it all the time. The animals absolutely need air-conditioning in July, August, and September around here."

"How about Wes and I give you a twice-a-year donation? That might help with things that need to be replaced or repaired around here?"

"That would be wonderful!" Ann said.

Sara wrote out a check for thirty thousand dollars and handed it to the woman.

"Oh, my goodness, Sara!" She stared at the check. "Did you write this correctly? I mean . . . thirty thousand dollars?"

Sara smiled. "I've been left some money," was all she said, "and I want it to go to good people doing good works for all our relations." She smiled over at Candy, who thumped her tail, and then at Wes, who gave a bare nod, pride in his eyes for her generosity.

Patting the area of her heart, Ann said, "My goodness gracious! The Lord has answered my prayer! This will allow us to not only replace the air-conditioning unit, but make the duct work even better throughout the shelter. Oh! Thank you!" She came around the desk and threw her arms around Sara as she stood, hugging her to bits, weeping for joy.

Chapter Sixteen

August 1

"Did you mean it, Wes?"

He lay with Sara in his arms, the clock on the dresser opposite the bed reading 11:18 p.m. It was dark and warm in their bedroom, both of them naked, lying against the other.

"About what?" he asked, trailing his fingers through her silky hair.

"When we chose Candy? When I told Ann that we don't have any children yet. And you said, 'But we will.'" Sara looked up from his shoulder, holding his gaze. "Did you mean it or was it just a figure of speech for Ann's sake?"

His hand came to rest on her rounded shoulder and he felt the quiet strength within it. "No, I meant it. Why? Did it bother you?"

She sat up, her hip against his, facing him, her hand resting on his chest, over his heart. "No, it didn't bother me, Wes. I guess . . ." She looked away for a moment and then down at him. "We've never talked about this before. I assumed you might not want children."

Hearing the uncertainty in her husky tone, he frowned. Lifting his hand, he stroked her arm and rested his hand against hers. "Because I'm an orphan?"

"Partly," she admitted. "That you'd had so many different foster homes and each one was worse than the last one." Shaking her head, an ache in her low tone, she said, "And I could never blame you for not wanting them, just because of your awful experiences."

He took a long, deep breath, feeling her pain because he had always known she was a woman who would want children. "I used to feel like that," he admitted.

"What changed your mind? Now that you're older and more mature?"

He gave her a careless smile. "None of the above." He poked the back of her hand with his finger. "It was you. From the moment I met you, I couldn't get it out of my brain that you were a natural mother. And my being around the children you treated, watching how you loved them and set them at ease, or comforted them when they needed just to be held, told me that." He smoothed the skin across her hand. "Was I wrong, Sara?"

Shaking her head, she said, "No, not wrong. My experiences with men haven't been very positive. In fact, they've been rocky, given my father and half brother."

"I thought that might be part of it," he murmured. Lifting his hand, he enjoyed the curtain of her straight, dark hair, the moonlight seeping silently between the drawn curtains and the window sill, highlighting the strands here and there. That luminescent light worshipped her features that he loved so much. "Being a part of Tom's family showed me what was possible, Sara. And, thanks to him and his wife, Frannie, I finally got the love I was seeking even though it wasn't a concrete thought in my head. Just living part-time with them, sharing so many family activities, made me happy. I remember watching how they worked with their kids; they never yelled at them or hit them. Instead, they had incredible patience with them, a kind of show-and-tell they shared with them. I really liked the way they were like banks on the river of their children's lives, guiding and teaching them."

Sighing, Sara whispered, leaning over, barely touching his mouth with hers, "That is a lovely analogy . . . I like that so much . . ."

Moving his hand up her arm, curving it around her slender neck, he deepened their kiss. Wanting her, but understanding this was a very serious discussion between them, he reluctantly eased away, seeing the glint of interest banked in her eyes as she straightened.

"Did I tell you Grandmother Adsila called me earlier today?"

"No. I'm surprised. She doesn't like using a phone, much less a computer."

Laughing, Sara nodded. "When it's important? Grandmother picks up the phone." She moved her fingers across the soft, silky hair across his chest, luxuriating in the scent of him as a male.

"What was the call about?"

"Two things. You know, she never stands on being PC."

"I don't think any of you do," he chuckled, allowing the small ripples of pleasure as her fingertips explored him.

Again, a dark chuckle. "My mother had called her yesterday to tell her that everything having to do with my father, his estate, his software company, was finalized. That she and I were finally free. She asked me when she could meet you and what my intentions toward you were."

"Ah, the grandmother who stirs the pot."

Her teeth shown as she grinned. "My grandmother is the supreme matchmaker. She's well-known on the res. Everyone comes to her with the man or woman they are thinking about marrying. They want her seal of approval, and her blessing. So many on the res have come to my grandmother over the decades for herbal help, and they know, love, and revere her, and trust her judgment. So, yes, she's very important to our people in that way."

"Are you taking me to the res to meet her?" he teased, smiling up at her.

"I'd like to if you're okay with it, Wes."

"Sure. To me? The Cherokee Nation is like a large family."

"Very much so. Because I stayed my summers with Grandma when growing up, I saw what real family was like; not the way my father or later, Manny, treated me."

"I'd like to meet Adsila. When do you think we can make that happen?"

August 15

Wes wasn't prepared for fierce, black-eyed, gray-haired Adsila. They had flown into Asheville, North Carolina, earlier in the morning and rented a car. The Eastern Cherokee reservation was beautiful. Tucked away in the Great Smoky Mountains, the long, green valleys, hills, and then the towering loaf-like forested ones above it all made him feel nostalgic.

Sara drove the Ford truck off the main highway and chose a dirt road she knew well. The morning air was turning humid, the temperature in the low eighties already. Sara had warned him that summers were hot and humid in this part of the country.

She wore her hair in two thick, black braids, with red yarn around each of the ends. He could see the excitement in her green eyes. For her, this was her *real* family. Wes had had several other long discussions with her about the Native American way of looking at the world in general. Tsula had sent a family photo album to them earlier, and that helped him understand the lineage, the nieces, nephews, the aunts and uncles.

They drove about two miles into the valley, driving slowly into a deep grove of trees. In the center of it was a log cabin, well over a hundred years old. There was a porch wrapped around half of it, several rocking chairs on it. He liked that there was a big, black dog of unknown breeding, who lay out on the porch, warming himself in the slants of sunlight.

"That's Chester," Sara said, pointing toward the dog as she parked in the gravel driveway. "He's got three legs. Adsila loved Chester from *Gunsmoke*, the cowboy TV series, because he had a limp. When the dog, Chester, came to her door one day, at least ten years ago, he'd had a broken leg. Probably hit by a car was our guess. She took him to the vet on the res and she removed that leg. He gets around on three just fine."

"That's a happy ending for Chester. I'm glad that our housekeeper is staying with Candy and Callie," he said.

"Me, too," she said, unstrapping the seat belt. "They won't be lonely and we'll be back home by Sunday evening."

Climbing out, Wes spotted a small, thin woman in a red and yellow calico dress, come out of the door. That had to be Adsila. Her gray hair was in two braids, and he liked the liveliness in her dark eyes as her mouth stretched into a big, welcoming smile.

"Sara!" she called, climbing off the porch gingerly, throwing her arms open to her approaching granddaughter.

Giving a squeal of delight, Sara ran up to her, throwing her arms around the smaller woman, hugging her and kissing her cheeks.

Wes stood back, smiling, enjoying the love shared between them. They were surrounded by shade and trees. There was a hill behind the cabin, and a flat meadow beyond the grove.

"So," Adsila said, releasing her, "you bring your beau to me, eh?"

Laughing, holding her hand, Sara said, "Of course I did! I want you to meet the man I love very much . . ."

Wes saw the flinty look Adsila gave him from head to toe as she approached him. Her dark brown face was wrinkled with age, narrow but alert. He was being assessed and he stood still, holding her unflinching gaze as she measured him in so many silent ways. He hoped she would approve of him, but didn't know what to expect.

"Grandmother, meet Wes Paxton. He is the man who holds my heart."

"Nice to meet you, Ms. Adsila," he said, holding out his hand toward her. Did one shake hands? Sara never told him how Native Americans greeted one another. Adsila looked at his proffered hand. Silently, she studied him. Giving a loud sigh, she looked over at Sara.

"He is without a tribe."

"Yes, that is true, Grandmother."

Her gaze swung back to Wes. "You are a warrior."

"Yes, ma'am, I am," he answered deferentially.

"You are welcome to our tribe," she said.

He saw Sara glow with joy, but she said nothing. "Thank you, ma'am, it would be an honor."

"My granddaughter is a warrior with a heart." She poked her finger into his chest, the top of her head just at that height. "Your heart is wounded. I feel by being with us, that will heal over time."

He gave her a slight nod. "I need all the help I can get, ma'am."

Snorting, she scolded, "Do not call me ma'am! That is a white man's term. Call me *Elisi*, Grandmother, or I will box your ears, young wolf!"

Taken aback, he heard Sara laugh and cover her mouth with her hands, giving her grandmother a shocked look.

"I don't want boxed ears, Elisi. I'll remember to always call you that."

Crossing her arms, Adsila stared up at him. "You have no name, no family."

Wes looked over at Sara, who lost her smile.

"She doesn't know," Sara told him.

Mildly shocked that the old woman knew, he agreed, "I have no family."

"You need a name," Adsila said adamantly. "My granddaughter cannot marry a man without a name or a tribe. I will, from now on, call you *Waya*, Wolf."

The word sounded like "washa," and he brightened. "I like that name, Elisi. Thank you."

"Humph! Follow me! We have much to rock and talk about on the porch!"

August 25

"Well, now you have a family, you've been inducted into the Paint Clan of our people, and a name," Sara said as they walked Candy on a leash in the evening just after the sun was setting. There was a lovely park on the other side of Main Street where they took her because every dog needed sniffing time and being outdoors. Candy was outdoors whenever she wanted, however, since Wes had created a wonderful fenced paddock for her near the sidewalk that led to Sara's clinic and store.

Wes walked on the other side of Candy. "I like my name. Wolf isn't a bad one."

"No, and did you know we have a Wolf Clan? That is where most of our chiefs and leaders come from." She smiled over at him. "I think she sees that you are a warrior leader."

"She's scary," he muttered. While visiting Adsila, they had been given a small second bedroom in the cabin. The old woman insisted on cooking for them, and he got introduced to food of the Cherokee and he found it delicious. Since Sara saw he really liked Adsila's home cooking, she promised to do more of the same when they returned home.

"The Paint Clan," Sara said, "and they produce the healers and those who can see. Adsila is very psychic, but I think you know that by now." She smiled over at him.

"Shocked me. I thought for sure that you or Tsula might have told her I had been orphaned."

Shaking her head, Sara leaned over and petted Candy's head. The golden retriever dearly loved these walks every evening with her favorite humans. "She saw *you*."

"You see me, too."

"But I don't have the sight that Adsila does."

"But you're a healer, that's for sure."

"My grandmother taught me for fifteen years about herbs, every summer. And I loved it. I do to this day."

They turned into the park. A few people were walking their dogs there, too. The lawn was mowed, there were lots of squirrels that interested Candy, running up and down the many trees. Stopping at an oak bench, they sat down. Candy happily plopped down next to Wes, panting and looking around. Wes placed his arm around Sara's shoulders and she leaned against him. "Life's pretty good now," he said, pressing a kiss to her brow.

"Very." She slid her hand down his thigh. "I can't tell you how relieved I feel. It's hard for me to get out of my stealth mode and looking at everything and everyone as a possible threat."

"That's PTSD reaction," he assured her.

"Do you do that, too? After all those years in the SEALs, I would imagine you have that kind of knee-jerk response?"

"Probably always will," he agreed, petting Candy's head and neck. "You'll have it for a while, Sara, but I don't think you'll carry that reaction too long. It will probably go away the more you get into your daily routine."

"I hope so. We both seemed to be having less nightmares, too. Have you noticed that?"

"Yes." Then he gave her a heated look. "Good loving helps you sleep, too."

Sara snorted just like her grandmother. "Don't *even* go there! I'm not your sleeping pill, Paxton."

He laughed and spread his long legs out beside Candy. "I do sleep better afterward. No nightmares. Honest."

She gave him an evil look. "I'm glad, but sex is not a panacea, and you know that."

"True," he said, chuckling. "You look beautiful when you're fired up about something."

She rolled her eyes. "You want something. What is it?"

"Well," he murmured, "I think you're more like Adsila

than you thought," he said, producing a black velvet box from the pocket of his dark blue shirt. "Here. See what you think?"

Nonplussed, Sara sat up and took the box. "What is this?" she demanded warily, eyeing it and then Wes.

"Something good. Go ahead, take a peek. It won't bite you."

Her lips twitched and she opened it. Gasping, she whispered, "Oh . . . Wes!"

"Do you like it? The color of your eyes?" And he held his breath because it was a wedding ring set in gold with a rich green faceted tourmaline engagement ring that nearly matched the color of her eyes.

Touching the set, she shook her head. "I think you're more coyote than wolf. What a trick!"

"No trick," he said, holding up his hands. "I just didn't know how to give them to you, and was too scared to ask you to marry me. I thought you might turn me down, so I felt giving you the set might sway you to say yes."

She laughed and shook her head. "You're crazy!"

"Like a fox, maybe?"

She pulled the engagement ring from the box. "Put it on my hand?" She held it up to him to do just that.

He removed his arm from around her shoulders and sat up.

Candy sat up, too, very alert, eyes on the prize he held in his fingers.

"No," Wes told her, "this isn't something to eat, Candy." She was a foodie.

Laughing, Sara placed her hand so he could easily slide the ring on her finger. He did so and she whispered his name, threw her arms around his shoulders, and kissed him senseless.

Coming up for air, he grinned and absorbed her joy, her eyes dancing with happiness. "Can I get a yes, you'll marry me, out of you?" he teased her mercilessly.

Giggling, she whispered, "Yes. Yes, I will marry you!"

Relief flowed intensely through him. Candy was thumping her tail joyously between them, her gold-brown eyes shining with happiness, too, as if she understood what was happening between them.

"Good," he said, and leaned over, capturing Sara's mouth, kissing her long and sweetly. Candy was still trapped between them, but didn't seem to mind at all, panting and happily continuing to thump her long plume of a tail.

Slowly, their mouths parted, their eyes barely open, fastened upon one another.

"I love you, Sara," Wes rasped against her wet lips. "With my life."

She closed her eyes, sinking into the heat of his exploring mouth engaging hers. Humming, she finally needed air and broke their molding, fiery kiss. "And I love you so much," she whispered, eyes brimming with tears of joy.

Wes brought out his linen handkerchief and handed it to her. "Tears are always good," he said, hoarse with so many emotions flowing through him.

Candy barked.

Both of them jumped, looked at her and then laughed.

Sara hugged the dog. "Yes! We are getting married, Candy!"

"She was just putting her two cents worth in," Wes said, giving her a boyish smile.

Sara sat up. In the evening light, she could still see the glimmer of forest-green fire in the gemstone. "It's so beautiful, Wes. Thank you . . ."

"No, thank *you*. You said yes." He teased her with another grin.

"We need to get back before dark," she said, standing, smoothing her slacks.

Wes rose and Candy came to his left leg, waiting for him to move forward.

He took Sara beneath his arm, holding her close, feeling her arm around his waist, squeezing him with all her woman's strength. "Today is the best day of my life," he told her, becoming serious as they walked out of the park and down the sidewalk.

"I feel the same way," she confided softly, giving him a loving look. It was the best day of her life, too.

"I never thought I'd get married," Wes confided much later that night as Sara slipped into their bed after her shower. He inhaled that light scent of lily of the valley that he loved so much.

"Me either," she confided, sitting next to him, moving her hand across his chest. "When I tell Mom and Adsila about this"—she held up her left hand—"they are going to pounce and want a date for our wedding."

"Hmmm," Wes said, capturing her hand against his heart. "I'm open. Is there a time you'd like?"

"I'd love a winter wedding. The reason is, that is the slowest part of my herbal season. All the herbs are either in oil for salves or ointments, or dried. In the winter, I get to rest a little, and that would be a good time. What do you think?"

"Where do you want the wedding?"

"I was thinking in Dallas. I'd like Tom to give me away. I know he would. Unless you have someone else in mind?"

"Tom will do that for us."

"Mom would fly Adsila out and we could all stay at her home, which is very large and has five bedrooms."

"I'll call Tom tomorrow, and ask him. Before or after Christmas?"

"Adsila will be happy if we marry on the winter solstice, the twenty-first, just before Christmas. That's a very special time for us."

"I like that. Then we can spend Christmas with everyone. A big, crazy-quilt family coming together."

She smiled softly. "Sounds wonderful. You call Tom and then I'll call Mom and Adsila tomorrow. They'll be walking on air."

He guided her down to lay her head on his upper arm, on her back. "This seems like a dream to me," he confided, kissing the line of her hair, inhaling her scent. "We went from being on the run, to this. Feels on some days like whiplash to me. I keep expecting the past to pop up and we're on the run again."

Sighing, Sara smoothed a few damp strands of hair from his temple. "Me, too. It's August. Maybe by December we'll be out of that reactive mode."

Nodding, Wes said, "There's one really important thing we haven't discussed."

"Oh?"

"When do you think we should think about starting a

family?" He saw her eyes widen beautifully, a glistening look in them.

"Whenever you want."

"I think I'm ready for that, Sara. It's more important that you choose a time or season."

Her lips curved softly. "Well, if I am lucky enough to get pregnant, we might have a baby next September or October."

"That's when most of the demands on your time to be foraging and drying herbs is pretty much done."

Nodding, she said, "Well, since you're going to go from bodyguard to being a mission planner, that means you stay home, with me. You won't be gallivanting around the country or world, which makes me really happy." She curved her hand along his naked shoulder. "I want you home, with me. Every night."

"I got that," he assured her. "Steve is fine with me working in the planning section. I have the background and depth to do that. My specialty is Central and South America, so I'll be in that section. He utilizes people's experiences and strengths, and I like that about him."

"We'll have to invite him to our wedding," she said, thinking ahead.

"He'd come to Dallas, for sure. He's that kind of guy."

"SEALs stick together, no question. I'd love to have Rob and Chris invited, too. They helped save our lives."

"Well," he hedged, "Chris's already on a long-term assignment down in Peru, so he won't make it. He's a security contractor with Helping Hands, an American charity down there."

"Maybe Rob can come, then?" she asked hopefully.

"I'll check in with him and ask."

Satisfied, she raised her arm, bringing him over her

body. "I love you, Wes Paxton, with all my heart." She hummed her satisfaction as he eased over her, keeping most of his weight off her.

With a low growl, he captured her smiling lips as she twined her legs around his, capturing him, her hips moving teasingly against his. Sara was more sinuous cat than human as she seemed to ripple across his body, hardening him in an instant, that purring sound deep in her throat as she rubbed against him. Her lips were slick and heated against his own and he gripped her hips, guiding himself into her slick confines, which welcomed him. A groan of satisfaction reverberated through him as she tightened around him, his mind dissolving into the rhythmic fire that exploded to life between them. Leaving her mouth, he maneuvered her onto her back and surged into her, feeling her limbs hold him captive in the best of ways.

Leaning down, he teased her hardened nipples, suckling each of them in turn, and she became like moldable flesh and heat in his hands as he stroked in and out of her, feeling her tense, knowing she was going to orgasm.

Sliding one hand beneath her hips, he brought her up to an angle and it triggered that beautiful, spilling moment that made her cry out, her fingers digging into his shoulders, pelvis frozen against his, as he continued to milk that sweet spot within her until she suddenly collapsed from the intense pleasure he'd given her.

Smiling down into her shadowed features, his heart swelled with joy and pride. There was such a flowing naturalness that had always been there between them from the first. Tonight was no different and in fact, seemed even more intense and pleasurable for both of them as never before.

"My turn," she whispered, nipping at his earlobe, and

she rolled, pushing him on his back, straddling him and pressing her hands down upon his chest, holding his heavy-lidded eyes. Sliding his hand around her hips, she had him positioned inside her, and as she moved, his lids shuttered closed, his lips drawing away from his gritted teeth, trying not to come, but also inviting her to orgasm once more as he withheld his own release. His love for Sara rippled through him as he felt her suddenly stiffen, her fingers digging convulsively into his flesh. Riding that wave of her second, explosive orgasm, he finally allowed himself to release almost simultaneously. He felt flung into some far-off place where colors and light danced around him, where only heat mixed with light and gripping, deep pleasure, lived.

Slowly, very slowly, he became aware of Sara lying against him, their bodies damp, their breathing ragged and uneven. Weakly, he raised his hands, splaying them out across her upper shoulders, moving them down the long, graceful curve of her spine. Hearing her groan of satisfaction combined with his own deep growl as his release completed.

In moments, she moved to his side, nuzzling her face against his neck, her arms curving around him, holding him close. Not wanting to open his eyes, Wes knew he held heaven in his arms. Their hearts were beating in staccato rhythm, like drums being played, their bodies damp, their breathing becoming synchronous over the minutes afterward. Moving his hand slowly up and down her back, he luxuriated in her heated form molded to his. In that moment, a memory, that flash of the night when he'd stood outside beneath the black sky and glittering stars above, wondering where he was, who he was, feeling lost and aimless.

Wes barely opened his eyes, a trickle of sweat down his temple, looking up into the semidarkness of their bedroom. No longer was he lost. No longer was he unsure of where he stood in his life of thirty years. Now, he knew without question, his life was something precious, new, and filled with so much promise compared to that night. Had it been less than a year? Closing his eyes, feeling Sara's lips brushing his cheek, he felt a new peace, a sense of coming home, really home, for the first time in his life. As he caressed her shoulder, he silently promised he would love her for the rest of his life. Forever.

Chapter One

May 15

Did she have the courage to move to Wyoming?

Leanna Ryan ran her dusty fingers down the column of a piece of driftwood sculpture she had just finished creating for a client. She lived in Brookings, a small seacoast town in Oregon, and collecting driftwood during a meditative morning walk along the nearby beach was something Lea looked forward to, with her mug of coffee in hand. It was how she started her day: calm, quiet, and contemplative.

The velvety smoothness of the wood soothed her fractious inner state. Wood was alive, warm to the touch of her cold fingertips. She slid them with knowing experience as she followed the curve of the sperm whale she had fashioned. The wood soothed her, as it always had. It was another form of escape, Lea admitted to herself, but it was her passion: woodworking in all its various forms, and it was the world she chose to live within. Her father, Paddy, an Irishman from the Galway Bay area, was a master carpenter, known for his handmade, one-of-a-kind furniture.

He charged high prices and his clientele was more than eager to give him what he deserved.

He was seacoast Irish; his father—her grandfather, Connor—made his living as a trawler fisherman along the Oregon coast. Boutique grocery stores along the West Coast eagerly paid handsomely for his fresh catch. Paddy didn't want to be a fisherman, furniture was his passion, just as it was hers. Only, Lea had decided after that traumatic afternoon as a thirteen-year-old, to devote her life to woodworking. She didn't want to be a trawler fisherman, either. Paddy had often teased her that she had his woodworking genes, not the fishing ones. Her mother, Valerie, who was well known in North America for her art quilt creations, said Lea had not inherited any sewing genes, either, and they always laughed about that. Fabric didn't draw her. But wood always had.

Her red brows dipped, her hand smoothing the long flank of the whale she'd created, its golden-brown sides gleaming in the midmorning sunlight as it poured through the wood shop window. Sunlight was rare in Brookings. It was a tiny seacoast village that was usually hidden beneath the gray, scudding clouds over the Pacific Ocean. There was always lots of rain, too. Lea loved the rain and the moodiness of the Pacific Ocean here along the coast. It suited her own emotional nature.

Was she really ready to leave the only safety she'd ever known? Go east to Wyoming? Every time she thought about it, her stomach clenched in fear. She was twenty-nine years old. What woman stayed with her parents until that age? Single. Not interested in romance. Focused solely on her career and enhancing her master carpenter skills and wood sculpture skills.

She was such a coward. Oh, no one accused her of being

that, but inwardly, Lea knew that she was. And it shamed her in ways she couldn't give words to. Any man who flirted with her, or asked her out, she said no to. Luckily, she had plenty of women friends and she was more than grateful for them being a part of the fabric of her life. Her friends were her lifeblood. Full stop.

"Well," Paddy said, entering the wood shop, "looks like this will be the last sculpture you create here, colleen."

Warming to her father's Irish brogue, she turned, wiping her hands on her canvas apron she wore while working. Her goggles to protect her eyes were hanging around her neck. Lea smiled as her father wandered over to the table, his blue eyes twinkling as he halted opposite her. She saw him admiring her work and he looked very pleased with her efforts. "Looks like," she agreed.

"This is already sold," he said. "I'll box it up for you and make sure it's crated properly."

"Thanks," she murmured, loving the whale that she had created, rising in a breach, the tail in the water. Looking around, she whispered, "I'm really going to miss you and Mom . . . this place," and she gestured around the large, clean shop that had many windows to allow in plenty of light.

"Well," Paddy said gently, "it's time, Lea. I'm glad you're leaving to fulfill *your* dream."

She nodded. "Who knew when I was thirteen years old, that I'd read *My Friend Flicka* and *Green Grass of Wyoming* by Mary O'Hara, and want to live where she wrote those books."

"As children, we dream without inhibition," Paddy said, sitting down on a nearby stool, clasping his sixty-five-year-old gnarled hands. "And you've always wanted to go to Wyoming. It's a good thing to bring a lifelong dream to reality," he assured her.

Lea took another cloth, a clean, dry one, and began to wipe down her whale one last time. "Isn't it funny, Dad? How after I was beaten up by those boys as a girl, that I found Mary O'Hara's books? They were like an anchor to me, a homing beacon to overcome my shock and trauma, and focus on something good, beautiful. That was the beginning of my dream to go live in Wyoming."

"Your mother found them for you at the library," Paddy agreed, frowning.

Laughing softly, Lea continued to wipe the four-foot-high whale until the molten gold color of the driftwood gleamed. "I guess I didn't realize at that time how traumatized I was by that one incident."

"Hmph, it was more than an incident, Lea. Those boys broke your nose and fractured your left cheek. They meant to hurt you bad." He looked away, swallowing hard, then raised his chin and held her gaze. "It changed your life, colleen. Before? You'd been a loving, outgoing, carefree wild child. Afterward? And no one can blame you, you crawled deep inside yourself. Those boys couldn't take that you were blossoming into a young woman who was wild, carefree, and so full of life and hope."

"Some days, Dad? It seems like it was yesterday." Gently moving the cloth across the head of the whale, she added, "And other days? The incident doesn't bother me at all."

"Unless you run into strange men at the grocery store or any other public place," Paddy said, sadness in his tone. "And then it all comes back and you react."

"I can't help my reaction, Dad. I wish I could. And two

or more strange men nearby will send me into a panic that I can't control, either."

"Your brain sees these situations as a danger because of what happened to you," he agreed sadly.

Lea put the cloth down on the table. "I have to get on with my life. You and Mom have taken care of me long enough. Time for this baby bird to leave the nest."

"We'll miss you, but it's good that you're going," he agreed. "That letter from that rancher in Wyoming, Mr. Logan Anderson, wanting to hire you to come and do woodwork for him in the kitchen and living room, was your ticket to the life you've been dreaming about, Lea. It's a new door opening up for you. I'm glad you took the challenge and agreed to meet with him and look at the year-long project he has laid out for you."

Nodding, Lea pulled up a second wooden stool and sat down across from her father. "He'd wanted you, Dad. But you handed over the assignment to me. When I saw it was Wyoming, I wanted to go despite my issues with feeling unsafe out in the world. I'm glad you gave it to me. It's time for me to get on with my life and stop hiding from it."

"And when you talked to the rancher, you seemed settled."

"I asked him a lot of questions," she said, smiling a little. "He was patient. He seemed . . . well, nice . . ."

"But not a threat to you?" Paddy asked, prying.

"No." Lea shrugged. "For whatever reason, he didn't scare me like most male strangers do. I can't explain why not."

"Maybe the lure of Wyoming has dissolved some of this fear within you?" he asked her.

"I'm not sure, Dad. All I know is that while I'm battling

a fear of leaving the place I've lived my whole life, the yearning to go to Wyoming just got stronger because we talked to one another."

"Your mother and I think you should give Wyoming a try. It's a long-term project and it sounds like he's got the money to support your efforts. He's seen your work on our website, and he likes it. The unfamiliar is always scary for all of us." He gave her a soft smile, holding her unsure gaze.

"If he hires me, that will be the best, but if not, I can always get another job. Time to go," she agreed. "As I get older, I'm not as afraid as I used to be, and that's a good sign that the past isn't controlling me."

"You've made a lot of progress, Lea. Always pat yourself on the back for that. It takes courage to live, not just survive and breathe."

Grimacing, she folded the canvas apron, putting it away beneath the large, long table. "There's so much more to do." She straightened. "If you'd told me that *one* incident could wreck a person's life, I wouldn't have believed you. But"—her voice grew hoarse—"I do now."

Paddy stood and came around the table, giving his only daughter a strong, loving hug. "A day at a time, colleen, a day at a time." He released her, clasping her upper arms. "Just think, you're going to Wyoming, the place you've dreamed about. *That* has to excite you and make you happy. Everything is packed and we've put it in the back of your truck with a waterproof tarp over all of it. Your carpenter tools are in there, as well. Your sculpting tools are in your black nylon bag sitting on the front seat. You're ready to go."

Lea forced a smile for her dad's benefit. She hated being

a wet blanket to her parents and often masked her reaction for their benefit. "You're right. Off on a new and glorious adventure." So why didn't she sound more enthusiastic?

May 24

Dread was replaced with excitement as Lea drove her Ford three-quarter blue and white truck closer to Silver Creek, Wyoming. The valley sat south of Thermopolis, below the archeological and dinosaur area of Wyoming. She'd just driven through Bighorn Canyon National Recreation Area and it was spectacular! There were plenty of mountains around the huge canyon area, but right now, the highway leveled out, descended several thousand feet to a huge plain below. Silver Creek Valley was filled with lush grass, ranches, and rolling hills dotted with stands of pine and deciduous trees here and there.

Her gaze was always on the types of trees in the area, most of them pines of the species she'd identified so far. The mountains were still clothed at the very top with white, gleaming snow.

It snowed often in May, she was told by a waitress when she'd stopped at a restaurant several hours ago. She'd seen several bighorn sheep, males and females, which had been thrilling. Lea had stopped and photographed them when-ever she could safely pull over and take the shots. She'd never seen bighorns before!

With every mile, her heart lifted with a carefully shielded and closeted joy. The southern half of Wyoming was plains, desert, and some gorgeous sedimentary buttes that looked like torte cakes created by soil, in white, red, and cream layers. She'd taken photos of them, too. Then, she'd rolled into central Wyoming where the Wind River mountains

and Indian reservation inspired her. Her hometown of
Brookings was surrounded with thick, green, old-growth
forest; that part of Wyoming reminded her deeply of it,
soothing some of her homesickness. She could see huge
natural gas rigs dotting the area the farther north she drove.
If she didn't miss her guess, they were fracking, which she
disliked and didn't believe in. That bothered her because
she was environmentally oriented. Each rig, and she lost
count of how many dotted the landscape, reminded her that
it was an oversized hypodermic needle slammed through
the skin of the Earth, sucking life blood out of her, harming
her. She knew not everyone looked at it like that. Natural
gas was a cleaner fuel than oil or coal, no argument. But she'd
heard about the many earthquakes created by fracking,
breaking through the layers of sedimentary rock beneath
the surface in Oklahoma, and the damage it was doing
above and below ground to get to this natural resource.
Oklahoma had more earthquake tremors than nearly anywhere else in the U.S.

As she approached the town of Silver Creek, the plain
flattened out and she left the mountains behind. Now the
hills were softly rounded, clothed in dark, thick, green
grass, ranches to her right and left off the highway. This
was a lush, verdant valley. To her artist's eye, it reminded
her of a dark green emerald, faceted into the earth, full of
life, vigor, and vitality. She saw many herds of Herefords
in different pastures along the way, all heartily eating the
nutritious fare. There were some patches of snow here and
there, but the green grass had the say and Lea was sure the
cows were very, very happy with their lives at the moment.

Traffic increased as she drove past the SILVER CREEK
sign at the right side of the two-lane asphalt highway. It
said: POPULATION 10,000. Below it, the sign said that the

town was incorporated in 1905. She'd seen photos of this magical place that reminded her of a gypsy-like, Bohemian hideaway. But photos she'd seen online couldn't match what she saw in person as she slowed to twenty-five miles per hour in midmorning traffic. There were bright wooden crests on nearly every business, looking like a colorful hat for each one. Some had silver or gold outlining the color of the wooden building's headdress. She saw a light blue hardware store, the crest darker blue and outlined in silver. There were narrow alleys in between these 1900s-era buildings. The donut shop was painted a fuchsia color with a pink crest outlined in gold, flashing in the morning sunlight across the clear blue sky. On the other side was a bright red Dairy Queen, with a white crest outlined in red, the company colors, with a flash of gold.

She didn't see many major corporate businesses along the half mile of buildings packed on either side of the four-lane highway. Most looked owned by individuals, not megacorporations, the main street of the town looking like a fabulous collection of Easter eggs bracketing the street. Huge pots of brightly colored flowers were hanging on antique brass lamps on both sides of the street for a good half mile or more. May was still a snow month, so Lea figured they would be filled with cold-loving colorful blooms until June first.

In the center of town, there were three major traffic lights. Most of the vehicles were either pickup trucks, ranch flatbed trucks, or muddy SUVs. She saw few other types of cars, but they all had out-of-state license plates and most likely were tourists just like herself. At ten a.m., the town was waking up. To her delight, she saw a large bookstore, The Unicorn, to her left, and it was painted a pale lavender color with a dark purple crest outlined in shiny silver paint. Below it was painted, in silver lettering: 1905, the year it was built. Next to it was a large restaurant that took up half a block, Olive Oyl's. It was a two-story brick building; the crest painted a bright yellow, orange highlights with gold trim. She saw a sign that said: LUNCH AND DINNER. There were lots of pickups parked in front of The Unicorn bookstore. That was a good sign! She saw a sheriff's black-and-white Tahoe cruiser parked in the mix, as well. Hungry, Lea decided to stop at The Unicorn bookstore because it had a large sign out front that said: COFFEE, PASTRIES and BREAKFAST/LUNCH. She never ate breakfast, per se, but coffee was her saving grace.

Parking in a space in front of the bookstore, she took the large black nylon bag holding her carving tools off the passenger seat and placed them out of sight, down on the floor of the cab. Climbing out, the chill of the thirty-degrees-Fahrenheit temperature made her glad she'd pulled on her trusty purple goose-down nylon jacket that fell to her hips. Taking a purple, white, and pink knit hat her mother had made for her last Christmas, she pulled it over her cap of short red hair and looped the muffler of the same colors, around her neck. Picking up her small back-pack, Lea hitched it across her left shoulder and locked the pickup. Patrons were coming and going, with large cups of coffee and sacks of pastries in their hands, wearing big smiles.

Lea stopped and peered through the large plate glass window. It showed aisle after aisle of books that were arranged nicely so that people passing by might be tempted to come in and check them out. Lacy white curtains were arranged around the top and sides of the window, giving it a decidedly feminine look.

Walking into the bookstore it smelled welcoming, and

automatically, Lea inhaled the scent of thousands of old leather-bound books. It was a dizzying fragrance to her and she stepped aside so other patrons could come and go, just looking around, admiring the two-story building. This place reminded her of the ancient library of Alexandria, Egypt, thousands of books crowded perilously on very old, stout, wooden shelves that had to be made of a hardwood or they would have bent and bowed under the weight a long time ago.

Laughter and chatting filled the air and it was satisfying to hear sounds of happiness, ratcheting down the tension within her. She smelled the coffee, lifting her nose, inhaling the scent deeply and with appreciation. There was a full service restaurant on the right side of the huge area, a cash register and L-shaped counter on her left. She could smell bacon frying, the scent of vanilla pancakes, and her mouth watered. The door was polished gold brass with a window from top to bottom. No one was at the cash register. She looked and saw that the coffee bar was down on the right. There was an entrance to the busy restaurant for those who wanted a sit-down meal. The aisles opposite that area were filled with books, all neatly labeled: astrology, astronomy, environment, numerology, tarot, and on and on, in alphabetical order.

Lea loved the old, highly polished oak wooden floor. It pleasantly creaked beneath her boots, the sound telling her the wood was not only well cared for, but also, in very good shape despite its age. More than likely this floor had been placed in 1905. The golden color of it brought light into the aisles. There were plenty of antique lights above her as well, probably from the 1900s, all brass, all carefully polished, with the latest bright lightbulbs, which threw a lot of light. A person could spend hours in this place, Lea decided. She saw lots of short wooden stools, all oak, in every aisle, so patrons might sit down on one and open up a book to check it out. There were also some porch swings that had been recreated to become like sofas with soft, colorful cushions upon them, where readers could sit in one of the many alcoves to enjoy the book they'd chosen to peruse and while away a few minutes or an hour.

She was in love with this place.

Arriving at the coffee bar, a tiger-maple counter, twenty-five feet long, caught Lea's knowing gaze. It was beautiful, with golden horizontal bars against a reddish darker wood, well cared for, too. Behind it, she saw a woman in her late twenties, blond hair, flashing green eyes, her lips in a smile as she served her customers, who waited patiently in line for their coffee orders. They were farmers, ranchers, and white collar types, a mix of women and men. Two girls in their late teens, the baristas, were making up the coffee orders as fast as possible for their eager clients.

Lea stood back and studied the overhead menu. She could see three waitresses delivering breakfast to the patrons in the restaurant. The glass bakery case up front had cinnamon-laced rolls drizzled with white frosting, and so many other yummy pastries. She leaned down, her stomach growling. There was an orange and pineapple pound cake, by the slice, for sale. Deciding on her order, Lea walked to the back of the line, glad that there was time to just absorb this wonderful old place with all its eccentricities. She spotted a man in his late twenties or early thirties in the restaurant and he looked like the manager in charge of running it.

Four customers ahead of her, Lea noticed the sheriff in a dark green khaki uniform, his black Stetson on his head, broad shoulders. He wasn't that old, maybe in his early thirties, dark brown military-short hair and green eyes. She wasn't immune to good-looking men and from an artist's perspective, this law enforcement officer was very handsome in an interesting way. When he picked up his coffee and ambled down past the line, she read SEABERT, D. on his gold brass name plate across the left pocket of his jacket. He had green eyes like her, but they were a darker jade color, and he gave her a quick perusal. Not feeling threatened, she was sure the county sheriff made it his business to know who was new in his town and jurisdiction. Lea knew she posed no threat to him and he nodded, smiled a little, as he ambled past her, heading for the door. Dressed in a pair of worn blue jeans, her light tan hiking boots and a violet-colored jacket, Lea thought he might be wondering if she was a New Ager like this bookstore was.

Hiding her smile, she focused on the rest of the people in line, curious about who lived in this Bohemian dream that was clearly out of Queen Victoria's nineteenth-century rule. This bookstore and its owner just never caught on to the twenty-first century, and Lea found it delightful.

Turning her attention to who she thought might be the owner of The Unicorn, it didn't take a detective to spot her among the other hardworking employees. The woman was dressed in gypsy-like clothes: bright red, orange, and yellow flowers on her ankle-length skirt, a white blouse, and a colorful blue scarf around her shoulders. Her blond hair was held up with an orange scarf, and she wore long, dangling gold earrings and at least ten or fifteen multi-colored bangles on each arm. The rings she wore on her small, slender hands were many and flashed with green, blue, and pink gems in each of them. The bright Kelly-green sash she wore around her waist had tiny gold bells stitched onto one edge of it, and every time she moved, they tinkled pleasantly.

Lea loved this woman's audacity to be herself. She looked like the wild child Lea used to be, and sadness moved through her. From the time she'd started school as a six-year-old, she'd worn colorful skirts, blouses, and scarves, just like this woman. Her choice of clothing had drawn a lot of attention, but as a young girl, she didn't care. It was her artist's eye, her appreciation of all colors, that had decided what she wanted to wear. And her mother, who was a wonderful seamstress as well, would take the fabric they'd pick out at a quilting store in Brookings, and make her the big, swirling skirts she loved so much. Those were happy days for Lea and she left it at that, enjoying watching the owner chat warmly and sincerely with each customer as they came up to the counter to order. Many of them also bought egg and ham sandwiches along with some baked goods. Just about every man in front of her left with a sack of food, bakery items, and the largest cup of coffee they could order, in hand.

"Hi!" she said, greeting Lea. "I'm Poppy. What can I get you this morning?"

Smiling, Lea said, "One of everything?"

Laughing, Poppy said, "You're new to town, aren't you? I haven't seen you in here before."

"I am new. My name's Lea Ryan. Could I have a large mocha latte? And I'd love a slice of your orange and pineapple pound cake."

"Sure," she said, calling out the coffee order to her busy baristas. Grabbing a bakery tissue, she hurried over to the bakery case and placed the slice into a paper sack. Coming back, she took Lea's money and ran the order through her cash register.

"I see you have tarot readings here?" Lea asked.

"Yes, I'm the tarot reader." Poppy's eyes gleamed. "Are you in need of a reading?"

"I'd like one, yes. Could I get an appointment?"

Poppy saw her line of waiting customers was slowing. "Why don't you go over there." She pointed across the way toward an open door. "That's my office. Go sit down on the couch and have your coffee and pound cake. I'll be done here in another fifteen minutes. We're about finished with the morning rush." She gestured toward the line.

"How much do you charge?" Lea asked, taking the coffee brought up by one of the employees.

"On the house," Poppy said. "You're new. I'll bet you're looking for answers and information."

Lea grinned and stepped aside for the next customer. "You got that right. Thanks, Poppy." She turned and headed for the open doorway that was about six aisles away.

Poppy closed the door to her office and sat down at her messy desk, clearing a space for the tarot reading. "My husband, Brad, will take over for me now. Have you ever had a reading before, Lea?" She quickly shuffled the over-sized cards.

"I have a friend in Brookings, Oregon, who is a tarot reader," she explained. "I never got a reading from her."

"Oh?" Poppy smiled and tilted her head. "And why not?"

Shrugging, Lea said, "I liked my life the way it was. I didn't want to know about any changes that were ahead."

Laughing, Poppy said, "There is nothing *but* change in our lives, Lea. That's the only thing we can honestly count on."

"Well, mine's been pretty quiet until just recently."

"What are you doing in Wyoming? That's a long ways from Brookings, Oregon."

A grin edged her lips. "Touché. I'm meeting a potential employer about a job later on this morning."

"Great!" She held up the deck. "I'm going to do a three-card reading. The first card will represent your recent past. The second, the present. And the third, your future." She held out the deck across the desk to Lea. "You can shuffle them as you like. Mentally, as you shuffle the cards, ask them: What are the energies surrounding me presently?"

Lea had finished her pound cake, which had been delicious, and half her coffee was already gone. She wiped her fingers on the sides of her jeans and took the deck. "Okay," she murmured.

Poppy sat back, remaining silent while Lea did as she instructed.

"There," Lea said, laying the cards on the desk.

"Well done." She separated the cards into three different piles and then picked them up in no particular order.

Lea watched, fascinated. What would her future hold?

Poppy picked up the first card, stared at it, and then turned it around and flipped it over. "This is the four of Pentacles," she said. "It shows a woman standing in her beautiful garden, dressed regally, and she's holding the pentacle, which is the symbol for money. This is your recent past. This represents who you are: a woman who loves being alone, with her garden and making good money at whatever career she's chosen. You are happy and content. Life is good." She tapped the Rider-Waite tarot card with her fingertip. "This is a card that says you have everything you want."

Lea nodded. "Wow, this is accurate! I live in a small

seacoast town and I'm a master carpenter and wood sculpture artist. I make a very good living and I'm working at getting established."

"Well, you certainly had a wonderful world in your past. Why would you want to leave it? Or, perhaps you're wanting to set up your own business here in Silver Creek? We have an artist's colony here, you know? But no one who is a wood artist. You'd fit right in!"

Holding up her hands, Lea said, "I'm here to see if I get a one-year job that involves a lot of carpentry, along with some sculpture."

"Oh?" Poppy queried, her gaze thoughtful looking. "Which ranch?"

Lea smiled a little. "Are you psychic, too?"

"Oh, just a little," she admitted with a smile. "The main economy here in the valley is based on farming and ranching, although that's changing, and Silver Creek has become a highly popular tourist destination. It's the ranchers who have the kind of money it would take to hire your kind of specialized services, not the farmers. Not really psychic, just logical."

"I like your style," Lea said. "Yes, it's for a ranch owner."

"Hmmmm, there's only one rancher in the valley who I think has probably hired you. That would be Logan Anderson, owner of the Wild Goose Ranch."

Shocked, Lea sat back, staring at Poppy. "And you know this how?"

Tittering, Poppy shook her head. "Logic, again. Logan usually comes in here a couple mornings a week for his large Americano and a sit-down breakfast. In fact, he was in here yesterday and was talking about hiring a master carpenter to do work for his kitchen." Her eyes gleamed. "That *has* to be you, Lea. Am I right?" She gave a giggle.

Laughing, Lea said, "Yes, it is me. I haven't taken the job yet. We've talked on the phone, but I wanted to see his home in person and do an assessment, to see if it's something I really want to do or not."

"Ohhhhh," Poppy purred, giving her a sly look, picking up a second card. "I have a feeling this is a done deal. You just don't know it yet." She flipped it over. "My goodness," Poppy said, frowning, "that's the Tower."

Lea stared over at the card. The illustration on it was a huge tower and the triangular top of the castle was being struck by a bolt of lightning, people falling out of the windows. Even she knew it didn't bode well. *Great.* "What's it mean?"

Sitting up, Poppy said, "Expect the unexpected. Things to occur to you out of the blue. You don't see them coming. Look, this isn't always a bad thing. You can have a nice surprise that you didn't expect, also."

"Then why are you frowning like that?"

Grinning, Poppy said, "Your parents didn't raise a dumb kid, did they?"

"No, they didn't." Lea pushed the card with her finger. "So, my present, being here, is like a bolt out of the blue?"

"Yes. But understand that even bad things or unexpected things that happen can turn out to have a silver lining; something you never saw coming. But it does mean stressful moments when you least expect it, at a minimum. I hope you're adaptable and flexible?"

"I've lived with stress most of my life. I'm pretty used to it."

"If you're a flexible, adaptable person," Poppy said, "you will have a far better chance of negotiating these situations than people who are stuck and unbendable by nature. Are you really adaptable?"

"Yes, I'm pretty flexible," Lea agreed.

"Good! Then no problem. You'll have ups and downs by being here, but hey, that's Life 101. Your future card will tell us how it's all going to turn out." She flipped the card up from the deck. "Ah," she murmured wryly, "the Fool."

Lea stared at the young man with a staff, standing on the edge of a mountain cliff with his dog, off on some kind of journey. It looked like he was taking a step into thin air off the cliff, not worried at all about it. Was this good or bad? She gave Poppy a questioning look.

"The Fool is about taking a new journey, Lea. You're off on a brand-new track, a new lane or a chapter in your life you've never had before. This is a good card, one that means you are free of any worries, stresses, or demands from your earlier life. It's a risk-taking card. But not all risks are bad," she counseled. "We all go through times when our lives are steady and calm and the same, day in and day out. But then, life has cycles, and so the Fool is the person who entrusts herself or himself, to a new road that they are challenged to take."

"But 'fool' means just that," Lea muttered, worried. "Someone who does something without thinking or caring what the consequences of their decisions might be." She pointed at the card. "This guy is standing on the edge of a cliff and he looks like he's going to step right off it and into thin air. Who in their right mind would do that?"

Poppy smiled. "Risks come in many forms. And the beauty of the Fool card is about trusting our spirit, our faith in ourselves and others, our heart, and following our passion, no matter where it might lead us. The Fool has faith in whatever develops through the synchronicities life reveals, finding everyday magic, doors opening without struggle, and moving forward toward a new life, regardless. He has the faith that as he steps off the cliff into thin air, he will not drop and fall to the ground below. That sounds pretty good to me."

Frowning, Lea said, "You really hit the nail on the head when you said my life has been very quiet, very same, day in and day out. It's the way I needed it to be."

Gently, Poppy laid her hand on the cards. "I guess the tarot has decided you're ready for your next adventure, Lea. It's nothing to be afraid of. It can mean another chapter has begun to open up in your life, is all."

"I liked the last chapter I was in," she hesitantly admitted.

Giving her a long, studied look, Poppy wrote down the three cards in a nearby notebook along with Lea's name. "Tell you what? After you get done with your interview with Logan Anderson, come back and see me. Let me know what happened. We can always do a full tarot spread for you and it will give me a lot more information that may be of help to you."

"A new chapter. Okay, I can try to adjust. I can't go back to my home because I've more than worn out my welcome with my very tolerant, loving parents. It's past time I flew the nest and started standing on my own two feet."

"There you go," Poppy encouraged, smiling warmly. "You have what it takes, Lea. Logan is well respected around here. He started a wonderful midsummer festival for the town, and now it's so popular we get tourists coming from overseas for it. He's a really nice guy. No one speaks ill of him here in Silver Creek. He and his family have been on this land for four generations. I'd be hard-pressed to hear you say you didn't like him."

Lea stood up. "Well, I'm about to find out."

"Just take the road north, out of town. Logan's ranch, the Wild Goose, is four miles out of town and on the left. You can't miss it. His great-great-grandfather, Cyrus Anderson, was a metal worker and sculptor. He settled into the valley, trying to make a living at it, but he couldn't. So, he turned to cattle ranching, which he became very successful at. The Wild Goose is forty thousand acres of wonderful, lush grassland, woodlands, and it's the biggest spread in the valley."

"Which explains why he's willing to ask someone like me to do some one-of-a-kind woodworking for his home."

"Oh, that!" Poppy stood up and smoothed down her skirt. "The Andersons have a long history here in the valley. It was cattle ranching and selling lumber to the silver mines in the mountains west of us. When Logan was born, things started to change. He wanted to transform the Wild Goose into something other than just a cattle ranch. He'll tell you himself about the changes he's already made, and I'm sure he'll share some of his dreams for the future of his family's ranch. He's very innovative. I think you'll like him."

Lea hoped so. "Thanks for the free reading, Poppy. I will let you know how the interview went."

Connect with Us

Visit us online at
KensingtonBooks.com
to read more from your favorite authors, see books
by series, view reading group guides, and more.

for sneak peeks, chances to win books and prize packs,
and to share your thoughts with other readers.

facebook.com/kensingtonpublishing
twitter.com/kensingtonbooks

Tell us what you think!

To share your thoughts, submit a review,
or sign up for our eNewsletters, please visit:
KensingtonBooks.com/TellUs.